North of Beautiful

Justina Chen Headley

LITTLE, BROWN AND COMPANY

New York   Boston

Little, Brown and Company

Hachette Book Group
237 Park Avenue, New York, NY 10017
Visit our website at www.lb-teens.com

Little, Brown and Company is a division of Hachette Book Group, Inc.
The Little, Brown name and logo are trademarks of Hachette Book Group, Inc.

First Paperback Edition: February 2010
First published in hardcover in February 2009 by Little, Brown and Company

The characters and events portrayed in this book are fictitious. Any similarity to real persons, living or dead, is coincidental and not intended by the author.

Library of Congress Cataloging-in-Publication Data
Headley, Justina Chen, 1968–
    North of beautiful / by Justina Chen Headley. –1st ed.
        p.cm.
    Summary: Terra, a sensitive, artistic high school senior born with a facial port-wine stain, struggles with issues of inner and outer beauty with the help of her Goth classmate Jacob.
    ISBN 978-0-316-02506-5
    [1. Beauty, Personal–Fiction.   2. Birthmarks–Fiction.]   I. Title.
    PZ7.H3424Nm 2009
    [Fic]–dc22

                                                                                        2008009260

10 9 8 7 6 5 4 3 2 1

RRD-C

Printed in the United States of America

For Mama,
who is everything **true** and **beautiful**

A map says to you,

"Read me carefully, follow me closely, doubt me not . . .

I am the earth in the palm of your hand."

— *Beryl Markham*

PART ONE

Terra *Nullis*

chapter one

Fate Maps

NOT TO BRAG OR ANYTHING, but if you saw me from behind, you'd probably think I was perfect. I'm tall, but not too tall, with a ballerina's long legs and longish neck. My hair is naturally platinum blond, the kind that curls when I want it to and cascades behind my back in one sleek line when I don't. While my face couldn't launch a thousand ships, it has the power to make any stranger whip around for a second look. Trust me, this mixture of curiosity and revulsion is nothing Helen of Troy would ever have encountered.

Please don't get me wrong; I've got all the requisite parts — and in all the right numbers, too: one nose, two eyes, and twenty-four teeth that add up to not a bad smile. But who notices pearly whites when a red-stained birthmark stretches across the broad plain of my right cheek? That's exactly why I never went anywhere without my usual geologic strata of moisturizer, sunblock, medical concealer, foundation, and powder.

So what was with the crocodilian gaze, hungry and appraising, I was getting from the guest speaker in my Advanced Biology class? Without thinking, I cupped my cheek in my hand. No matter how cleverly I masked myself, sometimes I still felt as conspicuous as one of my town's oddities, say, Mac's two-legged dog who walked on his hind paws. Or the doe with the cantaloupe-sized tumor on her belly who defied death, hunting season after hunting season.

I half expected the speaker to say something. People always did. I'd heard all the comments, too, ranging from the chummy ("My next-door neighbor thirty years ago had a birthmark on her face") to the urbane ("You know, I saw Gorbachev once and his birthmark really looked like it did in pictures"). Good-intentioned or not, every remark made me bristle. If you don't rush up to the grossly overweight with a "Hey, I know someone who weighs three hundred pounds, too," then why was it acceptable to remark about my face?

The researcher finished printing her name on the board, Dr. Noelle Holladay. Why do parents do that to their kids: make our names prime targets for teasing? The one advantage of mine — Terra Rose Cooper — was that the mapping terms that made up my name could almost pass for normal, unlike my poor older brothers, Mercatur and Claudius, who were named for some of history's most important mapmakers. Thank you, Mr. Cartography, our father. Anyhow, not one of the seniors in my class (me being the only junior) could appreciate the forced holiday cheeriness of the researcher's name, slumped as they were in various stages of post-lunch catatonia.

To dodge Dr. Holladay's probing gaze, I bent my head down and busied myself with finishing the compass rose I had started drawing on my jeans earlier that day. It was the old-fashioned kind that figured prominently in all the antique maps around my home and in my doodles for the last six months. As if by drawing and redrawing arrows and the cardinal directions, I might find True North. What most people don't realize is that our world actually has two norths: True North that stays in one fixed place in the North Pole. And Magnetic North that moves some forty kilometers northwest every year, following the ever-shifting gyrations of the molten iron within Earth's inner core.

Whether my compass was pointing to True North or Magnetic North would remain a mystery, because just when my compass was filling in quite nicely, the classroom dimmed. Dr. Holladay said, "I'm going to show you . . . show you . . . fate maps."

Despite myself, I was mesmerized by these huge pictures of fertilized eggs, so zoomed in, I could practically see the DNA strands waving like Tibetan prayer flags in the wind. Only these weren't imprinted with prayers, but with prophecies. What would mine say? She'll be great at snowshoeing. Shy in front of crowds. Obsessed with maps, yet perpetually lost. Stricken with wanderlust, but never allowed to go anywhere. (My parents considered Seattle, five hours away, an exotic locale.)

"Weird, isn't it? Someone's destiny, right here?" Karin murmured to me. She craned forward in her chair, studying the photo, magnified some fifty thousand times larger than life, as if she wanted her fate to be mapped out that neatly. No one needed a fate map, road map, or atlas to know all the points of interest that Karin had planned for her life — first stop: high school podcaster; final destination: her own daytime show à la Oprah.

Me, I just wanted to get away from here. That's why I've had my fate map platted out since junior high: finish high school in three years. Escape to a college far, far away. Graduate in record time, and land a lucrative job where I'd make so much money no one could tell me what to do, where I could go. So it may not have been my True North, but it was close enough. It was the destiny I chose, dictated by me, not my dad.

Just as I've done since I popped my early admissions application to Williams College in the mail, I ignored the sour backwash of guilt. I still hadn't told my boyfriend, Erik, about my fast-track plan. That our fate maps were diverging as soon as the school year ended. I couldn't let anything, not even a miracle boyfriend, tether me here.

"... the genome mapping project will unlock DNA," said Dr. Holladay, her face glowing with the promise of scientific discovery. "One day, we'll be able to ... able to ... ascertain the genetic markers ... for every disease."

But all maps lie, I wanted to tell Karin and the rest of the class and especially this stop-and-go geneticist. Even the best maps distort the truth. Something's got to give when you take our three-dimensional world and flatten it down to a two-dimensional piece of paper: Greenland balloons; Africa stretches.

"You're the last person who needs a fate map," I whispered to Karin.

Apparently, Dr. Holladay boasted genetically superior hearing in addition to sticky eyes, because she asked, "Do you have something to add, Terra?"

"No, nothing," I said hastily. Karin raised a questioning eyebrow at me, and I lifted my shoulder in a half-shrug response. How the hell did the geneticist know my name?

In case Dr. Holladay believed in the Socratic method of teaching and was planning to interrogate me, I broke eye contact and kept coloring in my compass. I wasn't being facetious or a kiss-up with Karin; it was the plain and honest truth. Fate couldn't have been kinder to any girl, even if Karin swore her nose was wider than the base of Mount Rainier. Those were times when I wanted to shake her. Who cared about oversized nostrils when everything else about her was exquisite?

I, for one, was introduced to my flaws when I was four.

Mom tells me there's no way I can possibly remember something that happened twelve years ago with any kind of clarity. For the record:

it's hard to forget the first time someone calls you ugly, especially if it's the prima ballerina of your tiny tot ballet class.

The second I walked into the ballet studio, Alicia — said diva-in-training — had complained, "But Miss Elizabeth, Terra is too ugly to be a princess." She tapped one foot impatiently, her pink ballet shoes scuffed on the toes like she was used to kicking girls who were already down.

Everyone, Miss Elizabeth included, turned to stare at me. So while Prokofiev's *Cinderella* swelled inside the studio, I felt like my cheek was swelling into a hot air balloon. If I couldn't be carried away to the far-off yonder, then I wanted to disappear beneath the cloying makeup I'd worn even as a newborn freshly released from the hospital. But that winter day, Mom was out of town, and my brothers had no clue, my father no interest in camouflaging me for dance. Rescue came in the form of Karin — the other new girl who was fresh from Los Angeles. She told Alicia flat-out: "You're uglier than the ugly stepsisters." To this day, Karin denies that what she actually said was "You're uglier than Terra." And she could be right that my memory might be colored (so to speak) because I'm hypersensitive about my cheek. But it doesn't matter whether she said it or not. We've been best friends since.

The lights flicked on, and without the cover of darkness, Dr. Holladay returned to pacing nervously in front of the classroom. Two dark patches of sweat stained the purple blouse under her spindly arms, the telltale sign of nerves. I felt sorry for her, almost ran up and threw my jacket around her. But her sweat would dry and disappear. In an hour or two, she'd be just another tourist visiting the Methow Valley for our two hundred kilometers of groomed cross-country skiing trails.

"So if I were you, I'd put your family's medical history on paper. Go back as far as you can," Dr. Holladay cautioned us softly.

Karin scribbled down this piece of advice dutifully. I drew the black ballpoint pen back and forth, harder and harder, until the nib bit through the thick material of my jeans. I didn't care if it hurt. I worked on my compass until it bloomed with thirty-two petal-like arms, each pointing in a different direction. There was no end to the places I wanted to visit. Kashgar or California, it didn't matter so long as it took me someplace other than here.

chapter two

X Marks My Spot

YOU MIGHT WONDER WHAT WOULD make a world-famous cartographer transplant himself and his family to the Middle of Nowheresville, USA. I wondered, too — all the time and mostly in class where other kids didn't realize Kennedy High was just a pit stop in purgatory. (But then again, you might be wondering how a mapmaker could be a celebrity at all. Let me tell you that the least likely, most geeky person could be world-famous in the right circles — comic book creators, undercover bloggers, my dad and his mapping algorithms.)

Purgatory wasn't an ugly, godforsaken place. Hardcore sports enthusiasts actually consider the Methow Valley a destination hot spot: mountain biking in the spring and summer, ice climbing and skate skiing in the winter. *Sunset* magazine named it the best place to buy a second home. Even the *New York Times* did a full-blown article on my halcyon hometown, which had the ironic effect of driving everybody but the business community crazy with the influx of tourists and vacation-home seekers. Now, we actually have traffic jams on Main Street.

So here we've been since I was four instead of Seattle, Dad's hometown, or San Francisco, where Mom grew up. And all because of a map.

See, according to my brother Claudius, the only one who ever tells me anything, Dad had staked his considerable reputation on the theory that America had been first discovered by the Chinese — Zheng He, to be exact. That explorer led expeditions all through the Indian and Pacific Oceans, and apparently to America if you believed the bronze plate map that had been "found" fourteen years ago. My father, Dr. Grant Cooper, did. He himself had endorsed the China map —incontrovertible proof that the Chinese had landed on U.S. soil, predating Christopher Columbus by a good sixty years. His name, his research, his doctorate — Dad had gambled it all. So confident of its provenance, he even commissioned an expensive etching of Zheng He's recovered map.

It took two years, but like the Vinland map before it — that calf hide map that supposedly proved that the Vikings had set foot on American soil in 1440 — the China map was also proven a fake. A clever fake. But a fraud nonetheless. I hadn't seen Dad's copy of the map since we moved. No one had.

Luckily, one day and seven classes were all that stood between me and Thanksgiving break. In thirty minutes, I'd ask Erik to drive me to the post office, where, with any luck, my early decision letter from Williams would be waiting.

When the bell rang, I wasn't surprised at how fast everyone else jumped up, mouths hastily wiped of nap drool, notebooks slammed closed, sneakers pounding toward the classroom door. What surprised me was how reluctantly *I* got up to leave. After a full hour of feeling like some researcher's private peep show, you would have thought I'd be elbowing my way out. *Excuse me, pardon me, move it!* But the idea of facing yet another empty post office box when I knew acceptance letters had been mailed last week made my heart work overtime even as every other muscle went flaccid, already on break.

Karin pointed to the compass on my jeans and said, "Cool. Can you do that to mine?"

I looked down at Karin, feeling gangly next to her scant five-foot-one. Not that she'd ever want to, but Karin could still shop in the kids' department, she was that tiny and bird-boned.

"Sure." I slung my backpack over one shoulder and grabbed my notebook while I ignored the panicked voice that demanded, *And where the hell are you going to find a spare second, Terra?* I couldn't even keep up with my own doubled-up school load, not to mention I had already promised Erik I'd redesign the logo for his wrestling team sweatshirt over Thanksgiving break.

"Today?" she asked.

"Oh, I can't. I'm working tonight, remember?"

"Oh, right. So this weekend?"

"Sure." I sighed as I followed Karin to the door. The problem was, I had already committed virtually every working hour, Friday to Sunday, to the Nest & Egg Gallery. Not only was there a new exhibit to set up, but I still needed to update our Web site.

"You know," Karin said thoughtfully, "you could make a killing doing art on people's jeans."

"This isn't art."

She frowned. "I think it is."

It used to bother me how effortless Karin's self-assurance was when my confidence was of the hothouse variety, carefully cultivated under highly regulated conditions. One wrong look, one mean comment, and my façade would wither. Nothing fazed Karin though — not a presentation in front of the entire school, not even podcasting when she didn't have a clue how to do it.

I was so close to the door and the post office and my future when Dr. Holladay called, "Terra, one second."

What now? I'd seen that well-meaning expression on Dr. Holladay's face before, which always prefaced the did-you-know-there's-something-wrong-with-your-face conversation. *Why, no, I never noticed I wore a quarter-inch-thick layer of makeup on my face; thank you so much for pointing it out to me.*

A self-preservation instinct — no doubt a gene some geneticist would isolate and identify one day — took over. I yanked the door open and hissed, "Come on," to Karin, before shooting over my shoulder, "I'm sorry. I've got to get to work."

"This is important," she insisted.

And then, Mrs. Frankel — traitor, our biology teacher who had been completely silent during the entire class — miraculously recovered her voice. She now chimed, "Remember what I talked to you about last week?"

God. Last week, Mrs. Frankel actually had the gall to tell me privately, "You know, you'd stop breaking out if you didn't suffocate your skin under all that makeup." Being holier-than-thou about skincare is an easy position for the wrinkle-free to take. After all, Mrs. Frankel might be approaching fifty, but you'd never know it. Even her lips were naturally plump as a young woman's, though they were now pursed into an earnest line.

The last person I wanted to witness an intervention for my face was Erik, but Karin qualified as a close second. So I muttered to her, "I'll call you later." Thankfully, she nodded and left.

Without preamble, Dr. Holladay said, "My sister has a port-wine stain." Her fingers brushed a delicate path from her temple to her inner eye and then, finally, a clean sweep of her entire cheek. "A V2 distribution, like yours."

I gritted my teeth. Did she actually think that telling me this made her open-minded? That throwing around a dermatological term to describe my condition made us instant friends? Or that we, God forbid, shared a karmic bond?

"That's nice," I mumbled.

"No, it's not!"

I stepped back, blinked hard at Dr. Holladay's ferocity. Then I lobbed an accusing glare over at Mrs. Frankel. With a wry smile and hands folded neatly on her desk, Mrs. Frankel explained so carefully she could have been testifying in court, "Noelle's sister was one of my best friends growing up."

"So you told her about me?" I asked, my voice going squeaky and high, a mouse caught in a trap. God. And Karin and Erik both wondered why I was in such a rush to get out of our small town? I might as well string a welcome sign around my neck with an arrow pointing north: TOURIST TRAP AHEAD.

"Look, I didn't mean to upset you. My sister had laser surgery a few months ago." Dr. Holladay approached me cautiously, the way you would a toddler on the verge of a tantrum. One wrong word and it would be forty-five minutes of soothing and backpedaling. "You can't even see her birthmark anymore."

"Uh-huh."

"The surgeon is right in Seattle. . . ." Her voice drifted off, expectantly.

I just smiled politely back at her.

Dr. Holladay's eyebrows furrowed, unable to comprehend why I wasn't beyond excited. "You're not interested?"

"Not really."

She cast a bewildered look over at Mrs. Frankel. "I thought you said she'd want to know."

I shook my head. Sorry, no.

Mrs. Frankel stood up behind her desk. "You wouldn't have to hide anymore, Terra."

"I'm not hiding." The sharp corner of my notebook cut into my chest, so tightly was I holding it, this flimsy shield of paper. Quickly, I lowered it to my side.

Dr. Holladay asked, "Do you realize what this could mean? Your entire life could change. You're really not interested?"

"I'm really not," I told her truthfully. There was a time when Mom and I obsessed over every last technological advance — the newest laser, the latest techniques. That was before I went to a convention about port-wine stains in downtown Seattle almost four years ago, when I was twelve. For months after Mom had heard about the conference, she planned our trip, a military assault orchestrated down to every last minute. She compiled hit lists of specific surgeons for us to hunt down. Sessions we would divide and conquer to maximize our time: Hemangiomas and malformations (me). Laser therapy (Mom). Smart Cover Cosmetics makeup clinics (both of us).

"Look, I appreciate your concern, but nothing has worked," I told them.

"But this is a new procedure." Dr. Holladay crossed her arms, disapproving now.

"They all are."

"Don't you know what's going to happen?"

"Yes." That single word was whip-sharp, the way Dad sounded on a bad day, but I didn't care. As if I could forget how some of the conference attendees had looked wistfully at my smooth face while their birthmarks were hardened and purpled and cobblestoned? How they'd comment offhandedly that sometimes their birthmarks bled spontaneously, stigmata without any hope for redemption. How I knew that looking at them, I might as well be staring at my own reflection as I grew older. I gripped my notebook to my chest again to stop from shuddering.

"Then why?" Dr. Holladay's smooth forehead wrinkled with dismay. Like all judgmental people, she thought she knew best, and that I was simply wallowing in my small-town ignorance.

I wondered briefly what she would say if I told her the truth, played out the scenario: Okay, let's say I wanted the surgery. Let's say I told my mom about it. Oh, and let's remember that a gossip columnist is better at keeping secrets than my mom. So, of course, Dad finds out. Did Dr. Holladay have any idea — even the tiniest inkling what could happen if my father — Mr. I'm Not Wasting Another Penny on Your Face — found out? I think not. But I didn't say a word, because in my family's unwritten code of conduct, what goes on at home, stays at home.

"I've got to go," I told them.

Dr. Holladay shrugged in what I wrote off as defeat, but she had one last volley in her: "This totally changed my sister's life. You can't tell me you wouldn't want yours changed. No matter how beautiful we thought she was, she always felt like an impostor."

The truth of Dr. Holladay's words stuck to me like thick glaze, unpleasant and hard to shake off. Flustered, I couldn't move, not even an inch off the square grid of linoleum where I stood. For all adults go on and on about beauty being skin deep, let's be honest here. When your dermis is filled with rogue blood vessels that have been herded under the thin skin of your face, you get mighty suspicious whenever anyone mentions anything that sounds remotely like Inner Beauty.

Dr. Holladay went to her laptop computer then, and I thought she was just powering it off, packing up to leave, her job here done. Instead, she dug inside her briefcase and brought a brochure to me in five efficient steps. "At least take this. The dermatologist's information. In case you change your mind."

"I won't," I told her even as I reached for the brochure, ever the sucker for lotions that infomercials vowed would make blemishes disappear. Ever the collector of treasure maps that promised the world but led nowhere.

chapter three

Reference Points

BY THE TIME I MADE it outside, Erik was in his truck, one of the last ones in the parking lot. As usual, the thumping bass emanating from his pickup was so loud, I could have been approaching the town pub on karaoke night. Erik didn't notice me, too busy playing the drums on his steering wheel, until I opened the passenger door.

"Sorry I'm late." I practically had to shout to be heard over the music. I shoved my backpack, bulging with my usual library of books and binders, onto the floorboard.

"What took you so long?"

"A guest speaker wanted to talk to me after class." While I turned the volume down, I waited for Erik to ask me for more information, but he just nodded and threw the truck into reverse.

"I got a new idea how to drop three extra pounds before the season starts," he said.

"How?"

"I'm gonna wear a plastic bag over my parka. See if I can sweat off my weight that way."

"Good luck with that. Hey, could we drop by the post office first?"

"Sure." He was so easy, my Erik. I felt like an idiot and an ingrate for being annoyed because all he could talk about was wrestling, making weight, and building lean muscle mass. I knew better than anyone it was a minor miracle he chose to be with me.

My palms, clammy when Erik drove up to the post office *(please be an acceptance letter)* were corpse cold when we pulled away. How was it that every bill collector and catalog company had found a way to contact us, but not Williams College? I stuffed the junk mail into my backpack, so disappointed I couldn't muster the energy to think of a single thing to say to Erik.

As the truck trembled in neutral in front of the Nest & Egg Gallery, I looked over at him, wanting him to say something to me. To assure me that a letter would arrive tomorrow. That my dad would be so proud he'd send me to Williams, no problem. But that was as much wishful thinking as Erik actually asking me why I've been compulsively checking the mailbox for six days in a row. He was singing to the radio under his breath, off-tune and always a word behind.

I grabbed my backpack with one hand, the door handle with the other, my body executing an escape plan I hadn't realized I wanted. As I slid out of the truck, though, Erik called, "Hey, Terra."

Hopeful now, I turned and waited. *Tell me, Erik, say the right thing.* "Yeah?"

"You forgot something." He scooted over to the warm spot I had just vacated, meeting me more than halfway, and kissed me.

The first five seconds of that kiss did everything I'd hoped his words would: anchored me in the here and now. Stress vanishing, I breathed in Erik's scent, knowing I'd always associate fresh-cut wood and worn leather with him. I wrapped my arms around him, toying with the short hair on the nape of his neck, softer there than anywhere else on his body. His hand snaked under my jacket, grazing the side of my breast in a way that made me want to slip into the narrow backseat with him, but his hand continued its one-way path down my back to slide inside my jeans. I don't know why it irritated me now when from the first time we hooked up, his hands had been Lewis and Clark, exploring north and south of my waistline, all expansion ho! Not that I ever did anything to stop him.

Only today, I pulled away. A slight, confused frown creased Erik's forehead.

"I'm late for work," I said with a chagrined smile.

"You're always so busy, working, studying."

"I'll make it up to you later."

His chagrin turned into a full grin. "I'll hold you to that," he said, reaching for me again. I kicked myself for letting him grope me, because he slid the brochure from Dr. Holladay out of my back pocket. "What's this?"

"Nothing." I reached for the brochure, but Erik blocked me with his shoulder while he glanced through it, flipping it from one side to the other before handing it back to me.

"So," he asked, "you going to do it?"

"No."

"Why not?"

"Why not what?"

"Why not fix your face?"

That question yanked out every memory of my being called ugly, each episode a different reference point that made up my map of reality. Like the time when my brother Claudius was studying French in high school and hit upon a term he didn't understand — *jolie laide.* Dad had translated, "Pretty ugly," and then continued, laughing, "like our Terra." He might have chuckled, and that laugh may have blunted his words, but it only sharpened his message. As mapmakers and adventurers alike know, all you need to figure out where you stand is a single reference point on a map.

I sucked in sharply now. Like all those times at home or after my laser treatments when I couldn't wear my usual makeup, I didn't show my surprise, couldn't show my hurt. How could I if I was going to be impervious to Dad? If I wanted to continue to be the ballsy, unflappable girl Erik thought I was, the one who snagged him on Halloween night over a year ago?

Karin's dad lived for one day all year, and that day was October 31. To say Mr. Mannion decorated for Halloween would be like saying that Colville is small. Two years ago, the utilities company actually issued a warning for the sheer wattage his 60,000 orange lights consumed. So last year, Mr. Mannion had restrained himself by constructing a mock cemetery lit by old-fashioned lanterns for Karin's annual Halloween party — Ghouls Gone Wild.

By the time I arrived the morning of that party, Karin's bedroom had transformed from podcasting studio to Museum of World Fashion, beginning with Cleopatra's robe, complete with asp, hanging from her door. On her bed lay an exhibit of colonial America as interpreted by Hollywood — a Native American dress (very short, beaded, and made of faux deerskin) and its Puritan counterpart (very long, white collared, and made with yards o' faux cotton).

Karin pointed to them. "We could go as Thanksgiving."

And guess who would be wearing the Mayflower muumuu, all guts, no glory? "God, I might as well dress as a turkey."

"That could be cute." She looked thoughtful.

"I was kidding."

"You know, Dad's got a brown bodysuit from the time he went as Dirt, and Mom and I went as paparazzi, remember?"

"How could I forget?"

"I'd bet anything Mom has some feathers somewhere."

Between Mr. Mannion's vast costume collection and Mrs. Mannion's crafts supplies for the preschool she ran in their home, I started to get scared, very scared. More firmly, I said, "No."

"It would be sexy."

"Peacocks are sexy. Turkeys get eaten," I answered, and decided it was time to take my costumed fate in my own hands. "What's this?" I held up the black gown draped on her desk chair, slinky as snakeskin.

"Oh, that's too small." Karin had moved on to the mermaid hanging on one of her bookshelves. "I could be the S&M Starbucks mermaid, carry a whip and a tray of Kahlua shots? What do you think?"

"Podcast-worthy."

So while she ran downstairs to snag a serving tray from her mom and the Zorro whip her dad had scored off a costume designer in Hollywood, I slipped into the gown. Even if the dress covered me from neck to toe, I might as well have worn nothing at all, it was that sheer and that body hugging. Just as I fixed the hip-length black wig over my head, Karin returned. Embarrassed, I started removing the wig until I noticed, for once, Karin was eyeing me enviously.

"Oh my God," she said, inching slowly toward me as though I were a mirage, half-visible and on the verge of disappearing. "You look like Angelina Jolie in her Billy Bob gothic era."

"I do?"

"I'll bet you a hundred bucks no one's going to recognize you."

Secure in my white Goth makeup, I let myself dance that night the way I do in my bedroom alone, arms in the air, hips swirling. I felt someone watching me. Which wasn't exactly a new feeling. What *was* new was the appreciative look on Erik's face, his lips quirked into a sexy smile, shaking his head every once in a while like he couldn't believe what he saw. And this, from a guy who hadn't said more than "hey" to me since he started school here four years ago.

Discomfited, I made my way toward the back door. But Erik was at my side like a lost adventurer chasing the North Star.

"Who are you?" he asked, peering hard at me.

"Someone you should know," I said, not recognizing the sassy girl who used my mouth to answer him.

"Really, who are you?" And then, surprised: "Terra?"

I nodded, ready to run.

Instead, his eyes ran down my figure. "So that's what you've been hiding."

"C'mon, that's Terra," said one of his friends, Derek, a beefhead who had lost more than a few brain cells in football scrimmages. His chest puffed up like he was leading a rescue mission of national importance, and he nudged Erik hard. "Dude, you got beer goggles on."

My preference for guys ran to the lean types, guys who were cross-country runners, skate skiers. Guys who kayaked and played soccer. Not barrel-shaped boys who considered the gym their vacation home. But suddenly I saw the allure of a bulky build, because without warning, Erik threw a punch at Derek, adding just enough muscle so his friend — his friend! — reeled back into the wall. The body that made Erik perfect for wrestling, football, and mountain biking — his bulky arms, solid chest, and thick legs — also made him perfect for standing up for me.

You could say I didn't fall for Erik or even his assumption that I was hiding my body, not my face. But that I fell for the comfort of his muscles and the confidence of his power. If Dad's verbal pushes ever came to physical shoves, I'd be ready. With a rush of gratitude, I closed the gap between us and kissed him until my head reeled and the shy girl I usually was floated away.

"You've got a lot of balls for a girl," Erik said against my lips.

"That's not what I have."

"You sure?"

"You can check for yourself," I said, and led him toward one of the gravestones. I glanced back just once and caught my reflection receding in the glass door, a figure in a tight black dress that left nothing to the imagination.

chapter four

God's Wings

WHAT WAS MY PROBLEM? I thought as Erik pulled away before I had a chance to wave a last goodbye. Vaguely irritated because he was always leaving first, I sloshed through the thick frosting of snow and ice on the boardwalk in front of the Nest & Egg Gallery. As Karin pointed out last night when we were studying DNA, I was lucky. I repeated that now: I was lucky. Erik was a great guy — pretty cute, way athletic, and best of all, into me. So how come it sounded like I was convincing myself?

The fairy lights I had strung around the gallery windows winked cheerily in the gray afternoon. Nest & Egg was the only modern building on Main Street — that is, the only one that looked built for this century with its exposed wood beams and pitched roof. Every other building was saddled with our town's faux circa-nineteenth-century Wild West motif and country-cowboy façades, right down to their regulation storefront signs: names carved in wood, the letters painted in faded hues chosen from a pre-approved color palette.

I skidded on the treacherous boardwalk, swearing under my breath for forgetting how prone these historically accurate walkways were to becoming ice rinks in the winter. One more tourist to fall and bruise his tailbone, and there would be mutiny on the city council's hands, led by the co-founders of the gallery, better known as the Twisted Sisters for their commando knitting group. No one in town knew how these unassuming-looking older ladies had strong-armed their way (or sweet-talked, depending on your opinion of their building) past all the town ordinances. But I did. My girls didn't take kindly to losing any battle — whether it was their building design, the art they curated for our various shows, or the college I would attend.

"Hello!" I called as I opened the door and simultaneously stamped the snow off my feet. The industrial carpet lining the entry was starting to smell musty from getting wet and drying, a cycle that repeated itself at least ten times in a day, more if we were having a good tourist day. Note to self: steam-clean this place early next week. Otherwise, on first whiff, all the tourists would whip around and visit the upstart glass-blowing studio across the street.

"So . . . ? Any news?" called Lydia, the oldest of the Nest & Egg co-founders, from the lofted studios. She had probably cranked her hearing aid, listening for my arrival.

As she started toward the staircase, I muttered under my breath, "Oh God," and hustled past the handmade note cards and small crafts up front in our gift shop, bypassing the café and espresso cart on my left. With my eyes on her, I called, "Just stay there, Lydia."

But did she listen? Do flat maps depict the Earth accurately?

In a town where everyday dress was backcountry camping — the tourists in SPF clothing and high-tech hiking boots, the locals in beat-up T-shirts and water sandals — Lydia took it upon herself to personify local color. She was an *artiste,* damn it. So in a flurry of torrid purple and teal batik (her designs, naturally), Lydia picked her stubborn way across the catwalk in her ridiculously dainty shoes.

I rushed across the open gallery space now. "Lydia, stop!" At the bottom of the steps, I added more loudly this time, "I'm heading up."

The fewer trips Lydia made on the staircase, the better. Whether she admitted it or not, her footing had gotten less sure in the last year. Just six months ago, she stumbled in the parking lot out back and broke her wrist. Then two months ago, she missed the curb altogether and tripped. Luckily, she hadn't broken anything else then. No matter how much the other Twisted Sisters and I nagged her, Lydia refused to move to one of the ground floor studios or to wear orthopedic shoes despite being eighty-nine.

"Did you hear something?" she asked at the top of the stairs, her faded green eyes gleaming expectantly behind her purple glasses.

I shook my head and took the stairs two at a time while holding onto the steel railing fashioned into sinuous vines.

"You'll hear soon enough," she said. "It just takes longer for mail to reach us here. But, really, you should be going to —"

"Rhode Island, I know."

"My grandsons attended RISD," Lydia announced as though this were news to me. The way Lydia spoke, her syllables overly articulated, the Rhode Island School of Design was the only place in the world worth attending for anyone with artistic talent. "You still have time to put in your application." And then with a condescending sniff: "I suppose if distance is an issue, there's always Cornish in Seattle."

Distance was the deciding factor for choosing Williams — the farther from home the better. Until three months ago, when Mrs. Frankel handed me the application to Williams, I'd never even heard of the college. But then I read the materials, learned about its reputation for being a small, highly respected school, one that had more art majors than any other, one where you could study art history as well as have studio time, one that graduated titans of business. One that was 2,800 miles from home. Williams College was tailor-made for me. I couldn't let anything derail my escape out of Terra Nullis, the empty wasteland of my home. Not even Lydia.

"I can do art without art school," I said lightly as I hugged Lydia. "You did."

"But —"

"Oh!" I pulled back from her, pretending I had just remembered something incredibly important. "I need to finish the poster."

"What poster?"

"The one for next year's shows, right?" I ambled down the catwalk, deliberately slowing my normal race-walk pace so that Lydia wouldn't have to work to keep up. While she detailed the information that had to be included on the poster, I slid the door to my studio space open, dropping my backpack on the floor. It landed with a *thunk* next to my foot.

The artist spaces at Nest & Egg weren't large or lavish but resembled the Japanese sleeping pods I read about in one of my travel magazines: tiny compartments I couldn't wait to rent someday like other businesspeople. I'd catch some Z's for a couple of hours before attending a meeting or hopping onto another flight. Two people could barely fit in my treasure box of a studio, but Lydia followed me inside. Lack of space was only one of the reasons I cast a worried look at Lydia. Mostly, I didn't want her to see the collages I was working on, not until they were done. Maybe not even then.

How were the Twisted Sisters — Lydia, Beth, and Mandy — going to take it that I had created collages of their lives, stolen from stories they shared with each other over the last three years with me listening in? As soon as the gallery opened, I started hanging out, uninvited and probably unwanted. I mean, really, a twelve-year-old lurking around a gallery doesn't do much for art sales.

Anyway, on a day when they were all twittering and flustered about a new graphic design program (Lydia even smacked the monitor as if that would change the font), I shooed them away. One newly designed invitation for an artist's reception later, I became the first Nest & Egg "intern," paid in free art materials and studio space. As soon as I was of age, they promoted me to Goddess of All Things Technical, the official title on my business card, and a bona fide paid position.

I was too slow to hide the canvas on my table. Lydia immediately spotted my work-in-progress, scrutinizing it intensely just the way Dr. Holladay had studied me earlier today. Worse than feeling vulnerable, I felt like a traitor, because it was Mom's life I had on display, naked and exposed when she wanted nothing more than to gloss over her life with an impermeable all-American sheen.

The collage was papered with packages of baking soda and cream of tartar from the 1950s that I had bought off eBay. At the center was a magazine ad of a housewife, vacuuming in heels, pearls, and a dress so ironed, it could have been armor. I had replaced the woman's face with Mom's rodeo queen portrait, taken long before she ballooned. All of this was set atop a photocopy of the architectural drawings for our kitchen. Over the collage I had draped a rusted section of barbed wire, uncertain how to attach it.

"You're almost done with this, aren't you?" Lydia asked me now without lifting her eyes off Mom's collage.

"Almost," I said.

"You need to ask Magnus how to work with this wire."

"I'm afraid to!" It was a safe admission; we were all a little intimidated by Magnus's temperamental bluster. Prima donna or not, he was one of our most popular artists, metal being his medium. Not only had a part-timer in the Valley collected seven of Magnus's pieces, but a software tycoon had recently commissioned an enormous work the size of a small car.

"Well, yes, there's that," murmured Lydia.

I was relieved. She understood. But then Lydia leaned over my worktable and with her bent fingers, she gingerly touched the wire. Her eyes lifted, asking me for permission. I nodded. She drew the wire down a few inches, transforming it into a crown of barbed thorns around Mom's head.

Envy and wistfulness shot through me at how Lydia could so swiftly deepen merely decorative to thought provoking, changing Mother in Domicile to Madonna of Domestic Prison. "How did you do that?"

"It was always there. Sometimes, you just need to play with your art."

Uncomfortable with Lydia's probing look, I straightened the tools of my trade on my worktable — razor blades, extra sharp paper-only scissors, gloppy medium — and almost had to laugh, because that was exactly it. What I did was craft, a trade. I made collages; I designed wrestling team logos, for God's sake.

"This isn't art," I told Lydia.

"How can you say that?" She crossed her arms and jutted out her jaw, her battle stance.

Luckily, the bell chimed, cutting Lydia off. From downstairs, we heard the unmistakable clumping of cross-country ski boots on the floor. Lydia and I grinned at each other, even if the tourist-slash-potential-customer was nicking our floor with every thoughtless step. The gallery needed money badly. Smack in the middle of prime summer tourist season, forest fires burned through thousands of acres for a solid three weeks in August. No one but emergency crews came to the

Methow then, and the firefighters didn't exactly have time to peruse or support the local art scene.

I was about to head downstairs, but Lydia held my arm. "Finish this," she ordered, her knuckle-swollen finger pointing at my canvas. Those arthritic hands could no longer make the art that her mind still saw.

"But —"

She left me then. I followed her out to the catwalk, but stopped at her fierce words: "I'll do my work; you do yours."

Still, I held my breath until Lydia made it safely down to the gallery floor and greeted the tourist with a cheery "hello," as though there were no place she'd rather be than at the cash register.

Back alone in my studio, I picked up a blank canvas from a stack in the corner that I had bought in bulk a few weeks ago. Instead of finishing Mom's, tackling the impossible of turning good to great, I could start something new. Something for me.

How did the old mapmakers handle all that expectant blankness, waiting to be filled with destinations when they had never ventured farther than their town walls? They relied on explorers to discover new lands, pathfinders to whack out new trails, and patrons to fund their work. I was none of those.

I toyed with a couple of old skeleton keys, all rusted shanks and heart-shaped heads that I had discovered at a garage sale in Omak. They were the last things I expected to see, trapped like fossilized dragonflies in a glass jar.

How much easier would life be if I just had a key to my fate map?

I leaned back in my chair and stared at the wind deities at each corner of the reproduction maps that surrounded me on the walls: Zephyrus in the west, Notus in the south, Euroas in the east, and the nastiest wind of all, the one that shot icy blasts, Boreas, who commanded the north. The front two legs of my chair crashed to the floor. Mrs. Frankel, Lydia, Dad, and Erik — they were my own wind deities, buffeting me with their competing wishes. Mrs. Frankel, who wanted me to go to Williams; Lydia, who lobbied for art school; my dad, who'd only pay for state school; and Erik, who wondered why I'd want to leave for school at all. God's wings, the cartographers called them. Maybe. I dragged my gaze off the old map of Europe now, but still felt their wishes beating on wings so strong, I'd be blown off-course if I didn't stay focused.

So I ignored the blank canvas, set aside Mom's nearly completed one, and powered on my laptop to start the poster for next year's exhibitions. I had to earn this week's paycheck, heralding real artists and their real artwork.

chapter five

T-O Maps

MOST MORNINGS, I SPRANG OUT of bed at five sharp — and not because I was a natural early bird. Hardly. While my face might have been far from ideal, I made sure my body came as close as humanly possible. You would be surprised what two hours of daily exercise and five hundred stomach crunches can do for you.

This morning, though, I lingered in bed for a few extra warmth-filled minutes, tired from studying math until late and then from suffering insomnia until later. Thank you, Dr. Holladay. The presence of her brochure in my bedroom was as palpable as her voice: *Take it.* And Erik's: *Why not fix your face?* Finally, I just had to bury the dermatologist's information under my bed.

That didn't stop me from wondering whether this surgery actually might do the trick. But wondering is just a breath away from hoping, and I couldn't stand dealing with the disappointment if yet another surgery failed. So I hauled myself outside now to let the frigid winter air shock some sense into me.

See, after twelve years of intensive laser therapy — once a quarter starting when I was four months old and tapering off to a yearly visit when I turned ten — Dad deemed my face a lost cause. All those laser blasts may have lightened my birthmark a smidge, but that was like measuring the difference in darkness between two and two fifteen in the morning, the "improvement" so imperceptible.

The air outside smelled so strongly of evergreen and juniper, I could taste Christmas in my mouth. A scant half inch of new snow had whitened the ground overnight, covering yesterday's mud-stained old snow, recasting it fresh, beautiful. Frozen, it made a satisfying crunch with my every step. Bundled up like an Arctic explorer, I was glad no one saw me with the headlamp around my forehead — or my face au naturel. The risk of anyone witnessing either was pretty low this early. Not even Karin knew about my pre-dawn exercise routine, and I never dissuaded her from her assumption that lucky genes endowed me with a naturally lean and toned body.

I switched on my headlamp, and with a deep breath of lung-freezing air, I started out. For five months a year, I looped around and around our property, stamping out my own T-O map — the medieval circular map that used a T to divide the world into three parts. By the time I reached the first bend on the trail, my legs had warmed up, my muscles loose and free.

Running in snowshoes takes a certain rhythm. The trick is to slide them forward but land firmly so that the metal claws underneath dig into snow. That way, you don't slip and fall. After four circuits, my leg muscles ached. I plodded on, brooding about Dr. Holladay's brochure. After that port-wine stain conference a couple years ago, I had promised myself never to imagine my life without my birthmark. Years of fruitless treatments had something to do with that. But mostly, it was the girl who had been trotted out at the conference as the poster child of a new laser therapy, proof that stubborn port-wine stains could be completely erased.

"So," said the proud scientist on the stage, Henry Higgins to her Eliza Doolittle, "tell everyone how you feel now."

I don't think he expected her response. I know I didn't.

"Well, yeah, I feel different," she said in a high, halting voice, "but everybody made such a big deal about my face afterward, it was, like, God, was I really that ugly before?"

I didn't know how to process that — no one in the audience did. The awkward silence in the ballroom made me hyper-aware of my two hangnails and the dandruff dusting the shoulders of the man sitting in front of me. But now I thought I knew what that girl meant. It's not like I'd come to love my birthmark — not by any means — but I'd grown used to it the way I'd accepted that Dad's my dad. Both are permanently inked on my fate map. Why tempt disappointment?

I was on the homestretch of my seventh loop when I tripped on a sagebrush, half hidden by the heavy snow. With any luck, by April, high school would be bordering on distant memory, and the snow would melt enough for a proper run. Freezing in the cold now, I thought wistfully of my spring running route, even that one last hill my brothers nicknamed Agony for its pure, brutal incline. But all my workout routes — spring running or winter snowshoeing — circled me right back to my real Agony: home. From the trail, the kitchen lights gleamed against the dark. I wasn't ready for Dad yet. So I stayed on this well-trod path for a couple more loops.

An hour and a half after I'd set off, I opened the mudroom door to hear Dad already snipping at Mom: "Are you sure you need to use all that butter?"

It wasn't even six thirty, which meant that Dad was getting an early start on his daily harangue. Instead of being a cartographer, he wished he had been a professor. But what he really should have been was a director, the way he lived to tell everyone what to do, when to do it, and most of all, how to do it better. Knowing nothing about the subject matter never stopped him from giving stage directions. Like this critique of Mom's cooking. As if he'd ever held a spatula in his life.

"I doubt your doctor would be fine with you eating even one one-hundredth of that. All you have to do, Lois, is make smart substitutions." Like a rattlesnake, there were warning signs that Dad was ready to strike. And when he did, his words were swift, precise, deadly. Like now. "You wouldn't be so fat if you'd just use your brains. Cooking right is a matter of being intelligent and resourceful."

I strained, but didn't hear Mom's response to his needling. I never did.

As tempting as it was to head back outside or upstairs for a shower, I gripped the doorknob on the mudroom door and then eased it closed soundlessly. Sweat dripped down my back while I stood there in the mudroom, the sports bra damp under my breasts. I shed my polar fleece jacket, holding it to my chest.

"Isn't Beth your age? Now there's a woman who doesn't eat bacon." Dad's insinuation was as pungent as the bacon sizzling in the kitchen.

God. Today had to be the day I got the acceptance to Williams.

Dad continued, "You know, you could use the sharpest cheese available, and then halve the recipe amount. It's really very simple."

Never engage Dad when he is in one of his moods. Just fade into the background. That was my brothers' modus operandi. They've faded so far into the background, you'd forget they were even part of the picture. Take Claudius. He was a senior at Western Washington, a scant three hours' drive away, but did he ever come home for the weekend? And Merc? He worked as far from here as possible, first San Francisco, then Boston, now Shanghai.

But I couldn't recede away, couldn't stay out of it, not when Mom's hands were probably trembling as she waited for Dad's next attack — a snide comment here, a pointed remark there. Reaching back, I opened the mudroom door and slammed it to announce my arrival, then deliberately clomped loudly down the hall.

"Hey, Mom, Dad," I said, greeting another unhappy morning in the Cooper household. I grabbed a glass out of a cupboard and filled it with water from the fridge, all the while casting Mom surreptitious looks to check how she was doing. Around three years ago, Mom's stomach went from a shy dip over her waistband to an all-out nosedive. Now, standing at the counter, her stomach rested on her thighs, her breasts on her stomach. Her body had become a worn-out totem pole, settling on itself. It hurt to see her giving up, giving out.

"How far did you run today?" asked Dad, spoon en route to his mouth, where each bite would be chewed fifteen times exactly, no more, no less. I didn't have to look at the contents of his spoon to know what he was eating. Mondays and Wednesdays it was oat bran. Every other day, cholesterol-lowering oatmeal dampened with non-fat milk, no brown sugar, no raisins, nothing to sweeten its plainness.

"About five miles," I said.

"Good. I'll log in seven and a half today. The last thing we want to be is flabby, right?" *Chuckle, chuckle.*

I kept my face impassive so I wouldn't become an accidental party to this put-down moment, whose focus could veer from me to Mom in the span of a second. My hand clenched my cup, and I drank deeply, drowning the "shut up, you asshole" that I longed to say. After all these years, you'd think Mom would have built up some immunity to him. But, freshly insulted, her shoulders slumped, as she kneaded the dough for scones, a precursor to the Thanksgiving feast she had been planning for the last three weeks. My brothers were boycotting; what else was new?

"Is there more green tea?" Dad asked. Without looking up from his magazine, he nudged his teacup closer to the edge of the table.

Translation: Pour me more. Now.

No, Dad could never be accused of ordering Mom outright, he was so careful how he phrased anything. His comments may have sounded innocuous to the untrained ear, but make no mistake about it. They were poison-tipped darts. Just once, I'd have loved to see Mom snap back, "You've got two feet. Use them."

Apparently, Mom was taking too long. Dad lifted the teacup and wiggled it in the air, no word. Just a sidelong look at Mom and a shake of his head.

Translation: God, could you be more inept?

Say something, I thought, clenching my own glass so tightly I was surprised it didn't shatter. With a soft, suffocated sigh, Mom scraped the dough clotted on her fingers so that she wouldn't dirty the teapot. That resignation broke something in me.

"Dad," I said, recklessly pointing to the kettle no more than four feet away from him on the kitchen island, "the tea's right there."

I might as well have called him an idiot, Mom's intake of breath was that sharp. Warning bells clanged in my head, but it was too late. Dad lowered the academic journal he was reading ("Look at me, am I not the picture of cerebral?"). His face had settled into a smug expression, the right side of his mouth lifting, his eyelids half lowered — a look of complacency that meant he had been waiting for the right moment to pounce.

He slid a thick envelope across the table in my direction. Williams College, my name on the front, envelope already ripped open.

chapter six

Trap Streets

"SO," DAD SAID, TONE LIGHT, "when were you going to tell me you were applying here?"

I shook my head. "I didn't think I'd get in."

"You did."

I couldn't quell the quick smile of pleasure as I reached for the envelope. "I did? Mom, did you hear?"

"So, Lois, you knew?" Dad asked quietly.

"No!" Mom and I said at the same time. I raced ahead with "I applied on my own."

The envelope was in my hand for a mere second before Dad announced, "You're not going." A pause. Then he leaned back in his hardback chair, flattened his magazine on the table, breaking its spine. "Remember what I told you. I'm only paying for Western Washington."

"But —"

"No buts." He slapped his hand on the journal so hard his empty teacup rattled. "If that was good enough for me and good enough for your brothers, it's good enough for you."

I swallowed. That college was good, the campus pretty. But it was also huge. The entire population of my town is a whopping 349 people. Western Washington University boasts 13,000 students. That makes six times more students at Western Washington than at Williams College. While I wanted to get lost in the world, I didn't want be lost at school. I wanted to meet people who would understand how the sight of a tree's jasper green needles against a cloudless sky could make my heart go *POW*! People who wouldn't think I was weird because my body remained with them, but my mind had already escaped to the studio, figuring out how to replicate the colors on canvas — which scraps of paper would work and which I needed to find.

That was why I succumbed to Mrs. Frankel's sales pitch, hopeless against her promise: *Williams is big enough you'll meet lots of great kids, but small enough you'll actually get to know your professors. These are the soul mates who'll be your friends for life.*

"I'm not paying for some overpriced private school filled with spoiled brats who grew up in country clubs." Dad picked up his teacup, pointed it at me. When he realized it was still empty, he jiggled it in the air again, signaling Mom. She hustled over with the teapot. "Not when you'll just end up working for someone who graduated from a state college."

"Williams is one of the best small colleges in the country," I parroted Mrs. Frankel, and wished that once, just once, Mom would say something to support me. But she only hurried back to her scones, scoring the perfect circle of dough with a knife — deep enough to pull the pieces apart once they were baked, not deep enough to separate them raw.

"Yes, and it has a great art program," Dad said.

How did he know that? As hard as it was, I stopped from opening the envelope to read the acceptance letter and steeled myself for what I knew would come. It was the same thing that happened to Mom when she once admitted she'd love to open a bakery ("Do you know anything about profit-and-loss statements, Lois? That's a lot of croissants you'd need to sell to break even") and Merc when he announced he wanted to major in Asian studies ("And be hired to do what, exactly?").

Dad's mouth curved into a smile more mocking than wry. "But your collages . . ."

My mouth dried. How the hell had he known about those? I kept them all — my completed collages, my works-in-progress — at my studio.

"The ones you made for your brothers last Christmas? Well" — *chuckle, chuckle* — "they aren't exactly what you'd call art, now would you?"

The sting of his disregard hurt me more than I thought it would. I blinked back both my tears and response: *I'm going to Williams because a ton of their alumni run major corporations, like I will.* But I didn't want to hear that esteem-scraping *chuckle, chuckle* again. Claudius always told me, "Just cry, okay? Dad will stop picking on you if you just cried in front of him." It wasn't that I couldn't cry. I wouldn't, not in front of Dad. Every tear was bitter surrender.

So I made my face go as expressionless as a blank canvas and told myself this was just a trap street — one of those fictitious roads cartographers hid in maps to catch plagiarizers. Or in Dad's case, to catch one of his own attempting to break out of his rigidly drawn grid lines.

For a brief moment, we watched each other before I dropped my eyes the way I did whenever I ran past unfamiliar dogs and didn't want my presence to challenge them. To be honest, one of the best things Williams had going for it other than its academics and arts program was being a five-hour airplane flight away from home. Western Washington, a mere three hours' car ride away, might have been enough of a buffer for Merc and Claudius. But me, the last in the line to escape? Mom couldn't even bear to have me mention college, always changing the subject so fast I felt guilty for even bringing it up. That three-hour car ride was near enough for four years of unplanned drop-in visits — and where Mom went, Dad was sure to hover. I'd remain cooped inside Dad's boundary lines.

Dad returned to his magazine, ignoring me when I left the kitchen. The last thing I saw was Mom, sliding the batch of cheddar cheese and bacon scones into the oven that no one but her would eat.

However much I wanted to slam my bedroom door, that would have accomplished nothing except Dad taking it out somehow, some way, on Mom. So I contented myself with kicking my backpack into a corner. I was about to flop onto my bed with my admissions letter, but really, what was the point? I tossed it, unread, on my desk and picked up my phone where I had left it charging.

Impulsively, I punched in Erik's number, knowing that he was still in bed, fighting off another morning.

"Hey," he said groggily. "God, what time is it?"

"Early." I could picture him rolling over to his side, squinting at the alarm clock since he hadn't thought to look at the cell phone for the time before he answered the call.

"So . . . what's up?"

I blurted, "I got into college . . . Williams . . . and my dad won't pay for it. He opened my envelope, can you believe it?"

"Where's Williams?"

"Massachusetts."

"Well, why'd you want to go all the way there?"

In a way, Erik was no different from Dad, both not wanting me to escape Colville, even if the reasons were different. I knew it was a mistake to have called him, but before I could make my excuses, Erik made his: "Hey, I gotta hop in the shower. See you at school." And then without waiting for me to say goodbye, he hung up.

Feeling stupid for even calling, I lowered myself to the floor to begin my first set of sit-ups, vigilant for any fighting downstairs. I didn't dare turn on any music. I crunched up in the silence, lifting both my chest and butt.

Going to a private liberal arts college far from home had only been a dream — even from the start when Mrs. Frankel pushed the Williams application packet into my hands. I mean, just where was I going to get a quarter of a million dollars to pay for four years of tuition? Dad made too much money for me to qualify for financial aid. (I had checked before I wrote a single word of the essay, and I still applied.) After the last couple of years at Nest & Egg, I'd pulled in a grand total of ten thousand dollars. That wouldn't pay for a single quarter at Williams. My abs protested. Not another sit-up.

Breathing in deeply, I forced myself to continue. The trick is to tell yourself that you'll do just one more. One crunch up. An achingly slow release back to the floor. Now, just one more. Each sit-up brought me eye level with Merc's old maps. This bedroom used to be his. The few times Merc had been home since moving out ten years ago, he always asked me when I was going to take his maps down, put up my own artwork. But I couldn't. I might as well go without makeup in public. That's how exposed I'd feel having my collages displayed in my own bedroom.

I finished my first set of a hundred sit-ups, paused, drumming my fingers on my taut stomach. The one modern map on the wall — twelve years out of date now according to the copyright — still looked like the punk rock porcupine I saw forming as a little girl when Merc pushed in its colorful quills, one pin for each place he planned to visit. Unlike his cartographic namesake, Gerardus Mercatur, Merc wasn't just laying down lines for lands that had already been discovered, transferring a globe into a flat map. He was seeing the world. It couldn't have been an accident that he moved to the one part of the planet Dad never wanted to discuss, never wanted to visit, never wanted to acknowledge existed: China.

On my second set of sit-ups, focusing on my lats for that ultimate, well-balanced abdomen, I heard a faint murmur downstairs, barely audible. Mom. I stopped and hugged my knees to my chest hard, listened even harder. Nothing more came from her.

Dad and his storm cloud of doubt? That, on the other hand, was loud and clear: "No. She's not going. And how would you know anything about the right choice for college?"

Silence.

Then Dad: "Oh, that's right. You didn't go to college."

In rebuke, without fear of consequences, Dad slammed the door, his special way of telling Mom she didn't deserve his respect. Mom's hurt silence echoed all the way over to my bedroom.

A better daughter would have run down the hall without hesitation, without thought, to soothe her mother, but I knew how important alone time was after a Dad-thrashing. In history last year, we watched a grainy video of Jackie O, half a moment after JFK had been shot. Her first instinct was to pick him up, press him together, make him whole. That's how I bet Mom felt now, except that it was her own shattered pieces she was trying to press back together, to make whole.

Then, like a broken movie reel — sound effects delayed after the action has long since rolled — came Mom: pot clanking against the iron of the gas stovetop. I had no doubt that Mom was crying while she cooked, salting domesticity with anguish, the recipe of her life.

Outside, Dad's truck revved. He usually sent his flunky (that would be me, since Mom never drove in the snow) to do his errands. I couldn't imagine what took him out this early in the morning, and I didn't care. He was gone.

Another crash from the kitchen. I gave up on stomach crunches; my stomach ached enough as it was. I flipped over and started on push-ups. God, how many times had I begged Mom to divorce him already?

"I don't want you to have a broken family" was Mom's standard response.

"Mom, it's already broken."

"I've never worked" was her other favorite excuse, and she'd flush with embarrassment while she scoured or baked or continued whatever chore she was doing.

"You could get a job," I'd tell her.

"Doing what, exactly?"

Now, I headed to the shower, let the water cascade over me, washing me clean. Over my arms, down my back, on my face. Then it was time to start the laborious task of covering my cheek. My vanity table — a present from my parents for Christmas when I was eight — could have doubled as a chemistry lab, filled with so many vials in a spectrum of beiges to cover my birthmark year-round: darker shades to match my tan in the summer, lighter for my winter paleness. I picked up a cotton ball, spritzed it with toner, and dabbed across my forehead, down my nose, my good cheek, then my bad.

That was the only thing Mom lived for these days: my face.

My face.

Hastily, I scooted my chair out from behind the vanity table and scrabbled under my bed, my cheek to the floor, stretching until my fingertips skimmed the rough cardboard edges of a box. For a good two months, I hadn't looked at this box. Weird how twice in twelve hours, I was pulling it out, my Beauty Box.

In the morning light, I could see the smudges that my fingerprints left in the dust last night. I wiped the lid clean with my sleeve, revealing the plain brown of the box. At first, I kept meaning to decoupage it, lay down strips of beautiful, handmade papers from India, Japan, and China in glowing reds and fiery oranges, but I never got around to it. First, I couldn't find the exact papers I could envision so vividly in my head. Then primping the box didn't seem worth the bother, since I'd stopped believing in the articles I clipped out of magazines: the fairy tales of girls my age who dropped fifty pounds, whittling themselves from size huge to size nada. The promised land of skin peels where women lost a decade from their faces. The magic wand of a laser beam: now you see the spot, now you don't.

On top of all those articles lay the brochure from Dr. Holladay where I had slid it in last night. As I removed the dermatologist's information from the box, I could hear Erik's "Why wouldn't you fix your face?"

Good question. Why the hell not?

Sitting back on my heels, I almost smiled at the look I could picture on Dad's face when he finally saw mine, unmarked, blemish-free. How he'd be forced to realize that no matter how hard he tried to control me and Mom, he couldn't. If I had to use every last penny I had saved on the surgery, so be it. It wasn't like I had a snowball's chance to fund my own college pick anyway.

"Hey, Mom!" I called as I ran to the door and down the hall. My hair was still wet from the shower, dampening my shirt. I ignored the cloth clinging coldly to my back. "Mom!"

Before I spotted Mom at the kitchen island, I saw the lone defiant cube of butter in front of her, stripped of its wax paper, teeth marks gouging out a corner.

"Are you hungry?" Mom asked as though everything were normal, even as she dabbed her greasy mouth with a dish towel.

I felt like throwing up, thinking about what Mom was doing to herself in this kitchen. "No, not really."

"How about eggs? I can make you scrambled eggs."

"I'll get myself some cereal later. Mom —"

"Peanut-butter toast? Doesn't that sound good?" She was already bending down to the lowest cupboard where the food processor was stored, her sweater stretching tight across her back so that it clung to her dimpled rolls.

"The jarred stuff is fine." I headed for the refrigerator to retrieve it.

"I'll make it fresh."

"Mom . . ."

"It's no trouble. I want some, too." Only then did Mom look at me, daring me to object to her high-fat comfort breakfast.

I sighed and nodded. "Sounds great. What can I do?"

"Nothing." Then as an afterthought: "Just keep me company." From the pantry, Mom collected a bag of honey-roasted peanuts (I tried not to think about the fat grams) and dumped a good cup, cup and a half, into the food processor. Loud grinding displaced our silence until the nuts were reduced to a thick paste. Then she sliced the bread she had baked yesterday, toasted it while I watched.

Once the bread was slathered with peanut butter and plated, the scones taken out of the oven and buttered, and Mom and me at the table sitting across from each other, she looked lost again, her job done. She took a bite of the toast, then without chewing, took another.

"A guest scientist visited our school yesterday," I told her, and placed the brochure on the table that last held my admissions letter. I slid my sacrificial offering to Mom. "She gave me this."

Her eyebrows lowered quizzically while she read the headline, her lips moving as she formed the words: "New Port-Wine Stain Breakthrough." Her mouth fell open, face brightening. In that moment, Mom shed more than ten years. She shed my father. Like a before-marriage and after-marriage makeover, a vestige of the local beauty queen she had once been could have been sitting before me. But then Miss Northwest Apple Blossom Rodeo Queen 1960 disappeared, consumed inside Mom's body again.

She breathed my name, "Terra," each syllable gilded with hope. "I'll try to make the appointment for the day before Christmas break. You won't miss anything on the last day of school, right? And that way you can recuperate without anyone seeing you."

This was worth it, I assured myself. Don't we all need something to hold on to, something that tells us it's going to be fine — whether it was an explorer in the New World, armed with only a map whose edges faded into the Unknown? Or Mom with a brochure, rich with promises that my face would finally look normal?

"Great idea, Mom!"

She nodded again and grabbed not another piece of peanut butter toast but my hand. She squeezed. "You're going to be so beautiful."

I couldn't tell which one of us was lying — me with my fake enthusiasm or Mom with her eyes set on the shimmering mirage of my beauty. The timer on the oven buzzed, and we both jerked back in our seats, surprised. Both of us giggled nervously as if we had been caught doing something illicit, something forbidden, simply by hoping.

Every map tells two stories: its contents — the physical, social, or political landscape. And its creation — how the cartographer came to make the map. I told other people's stories. Not mine. But that night, while Mom and Dad slept, I couldn't help it; I had to create my own collage map, chart the terrain of my thoughts. The urge was insistent, undeniable.

So in the privacy and security of my locked room, I assembled my materials. My best tools were in my studio, but I had the basics here: a matboard I kept meaning to bring to Nest & Egg, now dented from tossing shoes carelessly on top of it in my closet. An ancient bottle of gluey medium that I inverted now so that the substance would drain to the top. An old makeup brush losing its bristles. And the hundreds of images from my Beauty Box.

Sitting on the ground, I dumped everything out of the box and pawed through the ads, the articles, the marketing brochures. I almost laughed. Brochures, maps — they were both as much fantasy as they were fact. What mapmakers didn't know, they just made up. Uncharted territory? Heck, toss in a man-eating monster. Unexplored ocean? Throw in a sea serpent. An abundance of imagination and guesswork defined unknown lands.

I winced at the sudden sharp pain pricking my cheek. The memory of laser treatments, like beauty, was skin deep. I cupped my cheek, comforting it. So what if the surgery was just a Band-Aid? Or the promises in the brochure as trustworthy as fabricated landmarks on an antique map?

I selected a magazine ad for colored contact lenses — the model's eyes an unnatural violet, the shade Karin declared perfect for me. That, I centered on my blank board. I layered other images around that focal point of Beauty, spiraling out into a large circle. Models with thin, muscled thighs. Models whose foreheads could never fashion a frown. Plumped-up lips. All with smooth, smooth skin as unblemished as new canvas.

I stood up, looked down at my collage of a map. Here, then, was the Land of Beautiful that I would try to breach.

chapter seven

The Topography of Guilt

YOU WOULD HAVE THOUGHT THAT after years of laser therapy, nothing about the treatment would have fazed me. And in fact, for a while, nothing did. Not the pre-surgery preparations. Paperwork, check. I had filled out all the forms — insurance, medical history, HIPAA — in my studio, where Dad wouldn't discover them. Emla cream, check. Right on schedule, an hour before heading for Children's Hospital, I rubbed on the numbing lotion outside of Costco. Soon after, our mammoth load of groceries chilled in the trunk, my cheek chilled in the driver's seat.

It was the operating table that unnerved me. Still, I put on the hospital gown. I sat on the operating table. I lay down. Clearly, my four-year hiatus from treatment had softened me so I forgot what it was like to recline supine on the table, control stripped from me as effectively as if I had been strapped down. But as soon as the back of my head rested on that table, I remembered. My earliest memory of Dad was of him pinning my arms so I wouldn't flail when the laser beam worked on my three-year-old's face. I didn't realize that a tear leaked from my eye now until the nurse touched my shoulder gently and asked, "You doing okay?"

"Yes," I lied, and disguised my furtive wiping away of the tear by brushing my hair back.

"You need me to get you anything?" Mom asked from where she hovered in the periphery, sending me pained looks every now and then as if she were the one laid out on the table.

"No." Yes, another face. Another father. How's that for a start?

"Are you sure, honey? Some water? Ice chips? I can run and get you a Popsicle for after?"

Forget the laser; Mom's worry was doing the job just fine. "Mom, it's my face, not my throat they're lasering."

The nurse handed me heavy glasses to protect my eyes from the laser beam, but it didn't stop me from seeing Mom retreat in hurt silence. I wanted to knock the glasses out of the nurse's gloved hands. I wanted out. Hope may have brought me to the hospital, but guilt kept me on the table.

"Okay, then. Is your cheek numb?" The nurse was the nonplussed teacherly sort, the magical kind with twinkly eyes who could calm a group of hyper kindergarteners just as well as she could one snarky junior-who-was-technically-a-senior. I swear, her calmness was hypnotic, because instead of bounding off the operating table, instead of sassing back — "Could you please anesthetize my mom?" — I nodded. I actually nodded, submissive as a dumb, sedated lamb.

"Good," she said, and grabbed crushed ice in a piece of gauze from a large pink bin. "We'll just numb your cheek up even more so the laser can penetrate deeper."

The doctor walked in, a permanent resident of the Promised Land with her corkscrew curls and dewy skin. "So," Dr. Joseph said brightly, her white teeth gleaming with predatory eagerness, "ready to do this?"

From the corner of the room, Mom whimpered. I lifted my head just as the nurse and the doctor turned around. But Mom had returned to her silent fussing with the curtain in the corner of the room.

"Perhaps it would be better if you waited in the lobby, Mrs. Cooper," said Dr. Joseph, swiftly assessing Mom's nerves. Mine were just as unsettled, but unlike Mom's, they were well-hidden, trained to bunker deep under my bravado so Dad would never know how his potshots riddled me with doubt. I kept my eyes off the harmless-looking laser the doctor picked up, the exact shape of Mom's glue gun for her crafting projects.

"Is that what you want, Terra?" Mom asked, her voice soft like a piece of bruised fruit. I could hear her real unspoken question — *do you want me to leave?* — fermenting around us.

What do I want? The question bounced in my head, a question I didn't want to delve into too deeply. I was scared of the answer.

"Let's just do this," I said firmly, staring at the paneled ceiling.

The laser whistled, short and sharp. Unprepared, I jolted as though waking from a nightmare.

The nurse laid her hand on my arm. "We're just calibrating it, remember?"

"Yeah, right." I laughed nervously and then took a long, deep calming breath, pretending I was embarking on an epic five-hour snowshoe. I had to envision finishing. I had to envision returning in one piece.

"Here comes the puff," cautioned Dr. Joseph as a cold blast of air darted at my cheek.

And then the laser — powerful enough to facet a diamond — began, zapping me over and over within the boundary line of my birthmark from temple to cheek, the inside edge of my nose to my jaw. And then the circuit began again. Experts describe the procedure as feeling like a rubber band snapping against skin, which makes it sound deceptively pain-free. But it's more like getting spattered with a drop of hot oil, sudden and sizzling. Try a hundred — or two hundred and fifty — laser blasts in a single session, and one word comes to mind: deep-fried.

With each blast, the light from the laser passed through my skin and into the gnarled blood vessels of my port-wine stain, boiling the red blood cells until each of the vessel walls erupted.

I closed my eyes.

This is what I wanted, I reminded myself. *This is the price of normal.*

Two weeks ago, on one of our teacher-in-service days, a teaser for Christmas break, Karin and I had made plans to catch a matinee at the nearest theater in Wenatchee, a whole hour's drive away. The guys had decided to sneak in some skiing at Loup Loup against the wrestling coach's orders, but flinging myself down a mountain on nothing but two thin pieces of wood had never appealed to me. So I told Erik I'd meet up with him afterward.

As planned, I drove to Karin's house right at ten in the morning. You would think by now I would know to be fifteen minutes late, because usually I have to wait for her to finish getting ready — the extra swipe of pink lip gloss in front of her hallway mirror, the running around to locate the perfect coordinating necklace she only just remembered, the last brush of her hair. But today, as I approached her front door, I heard her loud "Thank God!" as if I were the one who was perpetually late, and she yanked the door open, face averted. Then with a dramatic fling of her hair, she unveiled her face, fluttering her hands under her jaw line, and announced, "It's a disaster."

Above her upper lip was an unmistakable pimple.

What? That little thing? I almost scoffed, but tears were welling up in her big blue eyes.

"The photographer's coming in half an hour!" she wailed.

"What photographer?"

"Remember? I told you that the *Methow Times* is doing a story about my podcast with Kennedy's famous alum."

"You did?"

She shrugged — it didn't matter — and turned back to glare at her reflection in the mirror. "I can't have my picture taken looking like this! I look so ugly."

"Wait a second," I said, and returned to my car to retrieve my backpack with its usual stash of emergency makeup. The light was bad in the hall, so I steered Karin in front of the windows in her living room, where I inspected her makeup job. She had made the number one mistake in camouflage: she gooped on the wrong shade of foundation, one that matched her skin too perfectly. The key to masking yourself is to use two shades of makeup, one lighter and the other darker than your natural skin color.

"Go wash your face," I told her briskly, glancing at the clock.

She held still for me while I patted on the lighter foundation with my middle finger, her anxious breaths blowing warm anxiety on my cheek. Makeup tip number two: personally, I use a finger, not a makeup brush, for more control. Anyway, after her fifth question about whether her pimple was disappearing, I had to break the truth to her, "Karin, there's only so much makeup can do. Plus, we're not exactly the same color." I moved her face gently to one side, then the other, peering at my makeup job. The pimple was entirely covered. As I bent down to select a bottle of slightly darker foundation, holding it to the light, I confessed, "So . . . I'm going to do some more laser surgery."

"What? Why?" she demanded. "Doesn't it hurt?"

I shrugged. "There's some new laser." With my finger, I pressed the darker makeup on top of the base layer, taking care not to rub. All that would do is wipe off my carefully applied camouflage.

"You shouldn't do it," she said.

At last, the tiny part of me wound tight since I declared my intention to Mom loosened. *Talk me out of it, Karin.* I stepped back, nodded at my work, and then slipped my pocket mirror from my backpack. "Have a look."

"Okay." She took a deep breath like she was about to dive out of an airplane, and then checked the mirror I held out to her. "Wow, I almost look normal," she said, surprised. Staring at herself in the mirror, Karin continued, "I still don't know why you'd have more surgery when you're so good at covering yourself up." Her eyes widened and she finally lowered the mirror. "You should be a makeup artist."

"I don't think so."

"Oh my God," she said, nodding over my protest. "You could do all the stars. Then you could have your own makeup line: Terra Rose. Or Terra Cooper. Maybe just Terra. Yeah," she said, beaming. "Terra."

I packed my foundations while Karin's brainstorming spooled out from her brain to her mouth, apparently bypassing her ears. She didn't hear my unspoken "no comment" or "I'm really not interested" and certainly not my "Hello? I want to be an artist, not a makeup artist. What are you thinking?" Finally, Karin paused in her monologue about my future megabillion cosmetics company that would take on Revlon and Estée Lauder. "You'll stay, right?" she asked uncertainly. "In case I need a touch-up?"

The photographer wasn't from the *New York Times.* Or even the *Seattle Times.* This was our Valley's little paper with a total readership of not many.

"Please?"

How could I say no when I knew the fear of having my own mask slip? I nodded even though I could have been skiing with Erik. Well, maybe not that. But I could have been in my studio, working.

Fifteen minutes later, the photographer arrived complete with her huge pack of equipment. I had never been to a professional photo shoot before, and despite my misgivings, it was fascinating how she set up the shot, posing Karin in front of her. She didn't take the picture so much as make one.

"Why don't you get in this one?" the photographer asked, gesturing me to sit next to Karin. "We could show people how Karin conducts her interviews."

I recoiled. But before I could decline, Karin did it for me: "Terra never has her picture taken if she can help it."

I bristled, wanting to tell Karin to stop assuming things about me, but it was no random assumption. She was right. I hated having my picture taken, loathing every single shot I was in. If I could get rid of my pictures in the yearbook, I would.

The photographer glanced sharply at me to confirm. But Karin smiled, well-meaning, understanding, an I'm-in-this-with-you-Terra smile, the same as in ballet class when we weren't even three feet tall and she stood up to my bully.

"That's right," I said, nodding benignly at the photographer.

So I stepped far back from the action and watched as the photographer repositioned Karin yet again to create my best friend's first fifteen minutes of fame.

An hour later, my cheek throbbed to a dull drumbeat of pain. That's what I got for trying to show Dad. What would the researcher, Dr. Holladay, say now if I told her: See, I wanted to take control of my face, but — *out, out damned spot* — my birthmark yet again bested the latest and greatest that new pulse-dye laser technology had to offer. I quickly checked my cheek in the rearview mirror. There it was, my port-wine stain in all its blazing glory, eggplant purple now from two hundred and fifty shots of the laser and swelling turgid like a newly pumped soccer ball. My cheek looked even worse than any other treatment that I could remember. So now I kept my eyes firmly off the rearview mirror, off my face, and on the road ahead.

"Terra, you look great," Mom chirped, filling in my silence as I looked both ways down a street I didn't recognize. With a few turns here and there, we somehow went from the Children's Hospital parking lot to one of Seattle's hilly streets, and now I was lost. Mom continued, "Just great. I really think this doctor knows what she's doing."

My face, slick with antibiotic ointment, pulsated in disagreement. How the hell was I going to drive the five-hour trip home when I just wanted to curl up in the backseat, pop another two Tylenol, and sleep until I didn't feel anything? I clenched the steering wheel and made a mental note to tell my brother Claudius that the mnemonic he taught me to remember Seattle's street order — "Jesus Christ Made Seattle Under Protest" — only worked if you knew where you were. I didn't. Were Mom and I heading toward James or Madison — or had we already overshot and were well past Seneca, University, and Pike? Face it, I was the blind driving the blind, and had been ever since I got my driver's license and Mom staked her claim to the passenger seat.

"So which way should we go?" I asked, more rhetorical than anything since I knew Mom would shake her head.

"This street isn't on the directions." She helplessly rifled through the pages I had printed last night.

I know, I know. I should have taken a closer look at the map before putting the car in gear. But all I could think about was making a fast getaway from the new doctor and her useless laser, and how irritated I was with Dr. Holladay. And irritated at myself for lashing out at Dad with my face. And my mom for dragging me here, with her "Oh, Terra, you're going to look so beautiful" pep talk.

On cue, Mom hoisted around to look at me. "You really, really look wonderful."

More cars surrounded us than on the busiest summer day in our one-street town. I needed to pay attention, focus on the traffic. Still, I brushed my hair over my right shoulder so that Mom couldn't miss — couldn't deny — what everyone else saw so clearly. I demanded, "How can you say that? It looks the same as every other laser treatment."

"Baby steps," she said stoutly. "It'll be three months before we see the full effect of the procedure."

"That's what they all said."

"You know, at your next appointment, we'll be able to hit all the spring sales." From the corner of my eyes, I could tell Mom was ogling all the boutiques we passed, filled with clothes that she wanted so badly to buy for me, as if I could actually wear that edgy shirt, that clingy skirt in my high school where girls go hunting with their dads.

"Mom."

"We'll need to get you all new makeup, too, once your birthmark's gone. Won't that be fun?" My mother's hope is two parts determination, one part delusion. Even through my annoyance, I envied that. She continued, "I bet you'll be able to pull off purple eye shadow now. Maybe for the prom —"

"Mom," I interrupted, unable to listen to any more of my mom's fairy tales about my ugly duckling face. "Look, after six doctors and eight different types of treatments, my cheek isn't going to get any better. I'm part of the ten percent who can't be fixed."

"Terra, you just need to have some faith."

I let out a small sigh, her hope smothering me like mulch too thickly applied, and stretched my fingers from their death grip on the steering wheel. "Do you have any idea which way we should be going?"

"If we keep driving, we're bound to bump into the highway, don't you think?"

"Mom, you lived in Seattle for ten years!" I heard the accusation in my tone. So did Mom.

A tiny furrow of hurt puckered her forehead, and Mom fussed with the seat belt, loosening it for more breathing room before she admitted, "But your dad did most of the driving."

And now I did most of the driving for Mom. She'd never been a comfortable driver, but after her sister, my Aunt Susannah, died in a bus crash, Mom practically had panic attacks whenever she got behind the wheel. Still, there it was, another opening, like the ones I'd been seizing since my admissions letter came from Williams. Maybe Massachusetts wasn't part of my plan, but *some* college was, even if it was in Bellingham. Straightening in my seat, I said, "You know, you're going to have to drive again next year."

That uncorked her firmly stoppered denial, and Mom's breath released, sharp and explosive. Getting admitted into college was easy compared to getting her to admit that I'd be leaving next year.

I eased off the gas and coasted to a stop at the red light. More gently, I added, "We'll practice in the spring when the snow melts, okay? It'll be fun."

Mom fidgeted nervously with the directions in her lap, not believing me any more than I did her beauty pep talk. "Why do you have to rush through high school?" she demanded. "You're going to miss your own senior prom."

"Technically I am a senior."

"It's not the same."

"Mom, I'll probably be going with Erik to his senior prom."

"It's not the same."

I took a deep breath and slowly exhaled. Unbidden, my hot, swollen cheek throbbed uncomfortably, the way I'd imagine guilt would, laid open. I should have taken the doctor's advice, been knocked out for this treatment, but then who would have driven us home? Not Erik. The way things were going between him and me, even being his date to the senior prom was hardly a given. Yesterday, when I was supposed to get together with Erik for a quote-unquote study session in his pickup truck, I had outright lied: "Sorry, I'm starting to come down with something."

"With what?" he asked.

I didn't answer right away. I just didn't want to get into the whole fixing-my-face conversation again, which only made me uncomfortably suspicious that Erik would never be with me if I hadn't mastered the Art of the Makeup Mask.

"Look, I gotta run," he said abruptly, and hung up before I could make amends.

Two hours after navigating our way out of Seattle, we drove into the pseudo-Bavarian town of Leavenworth, marking the halfway point home. Mom pointed to King Wilhelm, one of those awful touristy joints that served a healthy portion of oompah-pah accordion music with their sauerkraut. "There," she said, "just what I need."

As surreptitious as any look that had been leveled at me, I glanced at Mom's hands locked together in a permanent state of worry. Her fingers were so bloated she didn't wear jewelry anymore — not her wedding band, not a bracelet, not even a watch.

"Maybe we should just go home," I said. I couldn't bear hearing one more of Dad's comments about her weight.

The traffic light shifted from red to green, and suddenly Mom said, "You'd be able to come home for the weekends if you went to Western Washington."

"But I don't want to come home!" There it was: the truth leaping off the edge of my thoughts where it had been balancing precariously since forever. I didn't know if Mom recoiled or if I jerked away, but we both scooted to the edges of our seats.

Mom's hurt swelled in the car, her feelings banged up by my one unguarded comment. Softly, she sniffled. "It's just that it feels like yesterday when you were born. You know, I always wanted a girl."

The topography of guilt must be made up of hidden crevasses and needle-sharp spires, because I felt sliced up as I bumbled my way to common ground. I knew that she had pushed for another try at a girl when Dad was completely done with having kids. Even as I stared resolutely out the window — *I can't back down now, I have to go, I have to get away from Dad* — I knew Mom was blinking back tears. God, why did I say these things to her, of all people?

It was freezing outside, and the heater was pumping but not warming up this old Nissan. Still, I cracked my window open and breathed. My first whiff of rain-wet air was mixed with exhaust.

"Once your birthmark is gone, everything is going to be better," Mom promised. "Everything. See, we really do need to celebrate."

"What?"

"Progress! Your face!"

Stick to the agenda; don't stop until she acknowledges college, I commanded myself. But I couldn't. Her insistence about my beautification rubbed me raw in a way that my father's comments about my ugliness did not.

The traffic light turned green, and I hit the gas, wanting nothing more than to go go go. And we were still only halfway home.

"Pull over there." Mom pointed to an empty spot behind a so-shiny-it-looked-new Range Rover. A boy my age dressed head to toe in black was pulling something out of its back. "I need coffee."

Coffee meant scone, which meant needless calories.

"Are you sure?" I asked.

"I really could use some. But if it's too much trouble . . ."

Which was Mom's way of saying "yes, now." So I slowed down, turned toward the empty spot just as we hit black ice, hidden under this innocuous, innocent snow. The car wheels spun out of control.

"Terra!" Mom cried.

I whipped around to make sure she was okay — knowing full well she was — when the one I should have been concerned about was standing bull's-eye in our trajectory. Mom was gripping her seat, bracing herself. I pumped the brakes the way Dad had taught me.

The last thing I should have done was close my eyes. But that was what I did, unable to watch as our car slid into the truck and killed that boy.

chapter eight

Longitude

NO SOONER DID WE SLAM into the Range Rover than Mom's dirge of oh-my-God, oh-my-God started. I lifted my head off the steering wheel. It wasn't Mom whimpering. It was me. I bit my lower lip to stop from making another sound too out-of-control for comfort and then forced out a question: "Are you okay?"

Mom's panicked little breaths hung in the cold air inside our car, frozen in fear. That damned broken heater. This damned broken car. I gripped the steering wheel even tighter, hoping it'd stop my trembling. It didn't. I turned to Mom, asked her so loudly, I could have been yelling across a long divide, "Mom, are you okay?"

She barely nodded in response, her wide eyes on my forehead, confirming what I knew but was too afraid to check in the rearview mirror. The skin above my eyebrow stung. Only then did I feel a slow trickle making its way down the side of my face. Since Mom wasn't grabbing a Kleenex to stanch the flow from my forehead, the cut couldn't be that bad. And then I remembered the boy.

God, the boy.

"Oh, no!" I yanked on my door handle and ran to the front of the car, catching a flash of crimson jumping out of the black Range Rover at the same time.

A woman's worried voice cried through the still, cold air, "Jacob!"

I swallowed hard, took a deep breath as though preparing to plunge into a fast-running river. And then I crouched and peered beneath my car.

No boy, no blood, no guts.

"Thank God," I muttered, leaning my head against the truck in relief.

"You know," said a deep voice from behind me, "there are easier ways to meet a guy than to run him over."

I swiveled around to see a guy near my age, very much wearing black, very much alive. Outside of Halloween and my infrequent trips to Seattle, I'd rarely seen anyone quite like him: an Asian Goth in a black trench coat, black jeans, black rock concert shirt. Apparently, neither had the good people of Leavenworth who were gathering on the sidewalk on the other side of my mangled car. They watched him vigilantly as if being a Goth guy was vaguely dangerous, like those homeless men shambling about downtown Seattle, muttering to themselves in a whiskey haze.

"Jacob, are you okay?" came the woman's voice from behind us now, strident with insistence. Even distraught, she was still the portrait of wealth, hair colored preternaturally blond, a red overcoat cinched tightly around her waist, and perched in high black boots. You could almost smell eau de Republican wafting from her as she threw her arms around Jacob.

"I'm fine," he said.

"God, I thought you were behind the truck." She shook her head, reeling at the miracle of his survival. And then her eyes settled on me and I witnessed a second miracle as she transformed from distressed woman to avenging warrior. She threw back her long hair and straightened to her full height, a few inches shorter than me and Jacob, but it was her laser-sharp tone that made her deadly: "Do you know what you almost did? You could have killed him."

"Mom, chill," said Jacob. "You skidded, too, remember?"

Mom? I looked from Jacob to his mother, two disparate maps connected in a seam I couldn't see. The only adopted Asian kids I'd ever seen were Chinese girls, all under ten, who visited Colville with their families. I knew this because I used to make a study of them, wishing I was so obviously adopted no one could mistake me for being biologically related to Dad.

"I wasn't driving recklessly," she said, eyes accusing reckless driver me.

If I was going to be yelled at, I wouldn't take it crouching down. But Jacob blanched when I stood up shakily, almost at eye level with him.

"God," he said, "your face."

God, my face, indeed.

I flinched away as though Jacob had slapped me and quickly averted my raw hamburger cheek. Lovely. I focused on the I VOTED FOR KERRY sticker on Jacob's back window, which covered the older I VOTED FOR CLINTON and I VOTED FOR MONDALE ones. Let's face it: his mom didn't look like the type to litter her vehicle with bumper stickers. So I was guessing this was his Range Rover and chalked him up as a rich Seattleite taking in the kitschy Christmas festivities here in town. What would he have thought of my town's Western hoedowns, fiddling festivals, and big bug contests?

"You okay?" He touched my arm gently. Whether he was reassuring me or trying to get my attention, I didn't know. I just didn't want anyone to look at me, least of all him, this too-cool-to-be-true Goth guy. "You're bleeding."

Despite myself, I glanced up at him and touched my fingers to my forehead, almost surprised that they came away wet with blood, but more surprised that he wasn't staring at my birthmark.

"Of course she's not okay. She must have hit the steering wheel," announced his mom, as though her discovery made it a fact.

"Here," he said, salvaging a Starbucks napkin from his pocket. That, he folded in half and held out to me. Even his fingernails were painted graveyard black.

"Don't use that," Jacob's mom ordered, snatching the napkin out of his hand and wadding it up. As if I was actually going to hold that sketchy wad of germs against my open wound. Who knew where that napkin had been? "I've got a first-aid kit here somewhere." And then she strode around the Range Rover to the passenger's side.

Jacob patted his pocket and pulled out another napkin. "Take it," he urged. "It'll be next century before she finds the first-aid kit." He smiled at me crookedly. A faint scar stretched from his left nostril to the top-side of his upper lip, tugging his mouth higher on one side than the other. It looked like someone had sketched his face fast, the edge of their drawing hand smudging his upper lip. His own eyes dropped to my mouth, completely aware of my stare. I grimaced, forgot I was supposed to be hiding my face, and then embarrassed, I pinched the napkin between my fingers and asked, "Is this clean?"

"God, you're one of those."

"One of what?"

"Those germaphobe control freaks." Then he laughed. "You are, aren't you?"

A child's muffled wail, bewildered and overwhelmed, cut through my own bewildered denial.

"It's okay, honey," I could hear Jacob's mom soothing loudly to be heard over the caterwauling. "Just a little accident."

If anything, the kid's howling strengthened, a baby Pavarotti: "I want Jaaaa-key!"

Jacob sighed, "Great," and ambled to his mom's side, his ankle-length black coat fluttering behind him like an explorer eager for adventure. This was my chance to check on my mom, call the police, find a tow truck. Instead, after a quick glance at Mom — she was still mounded in her seat — I watched Jacob.

Another earsplitting screech from the Range Rover and Jacob nudged his mom aside with a "Mom, I got him," before disappearing into the truck so that only the bottom of his coat showed. "Hey, Trevor, what's going on, little man?"

I should have kept an eye on his mom. As soon as Jacob got the wailing to ratchet down decibel by decibel to blessed silence, she frowned over her hurt expression and then spun around to march to Mom. Oh God, now what?

I hurried around the back of our car just as she introduced herself crisply, "I'm Norah Fremont. We need to trade insurance information." When Mom didn't respond or retrieve our insurance card, Mrs. Fremont prompted her, "Your insurance information is probably in your glove compartment."

I blurted out, "Do we have to?"

"Have to what?" Mrs. Fremont turned to me, her thin eyebrows arched.

"Have to tell insurance."

"Your car . . ." She waved helplessly at the lump of metal that used to be our car, the front crumpled like a shar-pei's face.

"— is pretty much totaled," finished Jacob. I had been so focused on his mom and mine, I hadn't seen him come over, carrying a little boy, three or four, with blond hair and dewy green eyes, their mother in miniature. "You're better off having it hauled to the junkyard."

"Are you kidding?" I crumpled his napkin still in my hand, swallowing my instinct to throw it in his face. Crushed or not, that car was my freedom. "I'm not abandoning my car."

"You won't have to. Insurance will take care of it," Mrs. Fremont said confidently.

That was it. Sure, we could report the accident and insurance could pay for the repairs, but then our premiums would go up and we'd hear about it endlessly from Dad. That was about as appealing as living with Dad for the rest of my life. A breeze dragged a strand of hair across my cheek. It felt like the lash of a whip. I bunched my hair into one hand, cheek exposed, but there was nothing I could do about it.

As if the ramification of the accident only now occurred to Mom, she said, "Oh, Terra." She looked so vulnerable sitting there, pleating and unpleating her sweater, my heart contracted hard.

I crouched so Mom could look directly at me. With a hand on her soft upper arm, tense but no longer taut with muscle, I assured her, "It's going to be fine, Mom. I'll take care of everything. Dad won't even know."

From behind me, I could sense Jacob and Mrs. Fremont eavesdropping. Sure enough, when I stood, they were watching me with a canny understanding I didn't like. Not one bit. It felt too close to pity. Mrs. Fremont, who I expected to shoot one last zinger at Mom, instead held her hand out, saying, "There's no sense staying out in the cold. Let's get a cup of coffee, warm you up."

Those were the magic words. Mom levered her way out of the passenger seat, one hand on the doorframe, the other on the seat, huffing. I bit my lips, trying not to be embarrassed. Still, my eyes sidled to Jacob to see if he was watching Mom's struggle, but he was already leading the way to the coffee shop, holding Trevor on his hip. Soon, Mom was trailing the Fremonts through the shop door.

The police needed to be called. Auto body shops consulted. A tow truck scheduled. I was almost done architecting my plan for this crisis when Jacob backtracked out of the coffee shop to me, Trevor now riding astride his shoulders.

"Aren't you coming?" Jacob asked.

Behind him, a man walked out with a commuter cup, steaming appealingly and making me acutely aware of the arctic temperature out here. My feet were so cold, even my toenails felt frozen. And that didn't cover my shivering that had nothing to do with the temperature. God, I had almost killed him!

Jacob's gray eye shadow created a smoky effect, better than anything I could ever have achieved. The result: his black eyes gleamed darker than obsidian under his tangerine-tipped spiked hair as he waited for my answer.

I shook my head. "I got to make a couple of calls."

"You might as well make them where it's warm."

A sign that said CELL-PHONE FREE ZONE hung in the window. I nodded toward it now. "You're not supposed to make calls inside."

"Do you always follow the rules?"

I narrowed my eyes at him. First, there was the control freak bit. Excuse me, the *germaphobe* control freak bit. And now this accusation of me being a blind rule follower. I didn't like the picture he was painting of me. Anyway, I had to admit, "Warm sounds good."

"Come on, then."

As I stepped away from the mangled mess of my car, I spotted a small, compacted piece of metal lying on top of the curbside snow, a relic of my car. Even though Jacob was watching me curiously, I couldn't help snagging the remains of my freedom, twisted into an ugly lump.

"Coming," I said, flushing as I shoved the metal into my pocket.

"What are you doing?" asked Trevor now, his high voice piping like an out-of-tune flute.

I straightened, flushed, blinked at Jacob's brother.

"What's wrong with your face?" he asked before Jacob chastised him, "Hey, rude."

I said, "It's okay." Frankly, as much as I hated point-blank questions, I didn't mind them from little kids. Unlike adults who stared, wondered behind my back, or made lame comments, kids simply accepted my answer and moved on.

So I told Trevor how I had surgery to get rid of my birthmark, which was like a big freckle. That satisfied Trevor. And I noticed that Jacob still didn't stare. If he wondered about my birthmark, he did it silently. Then he turned for the coffee shop, nothing more important to him than the little kid riding astride his shoulders. A couple of women walking down the sidewalk drew imperceptibly closer to each other, sheep in a wolf's presence, when Jacob passed. If he noticed or cared, he didn't let on. He sailed to his own longitudinal line, straight through the gawkers with a pleasant nod. Once clear of the onlookers, Jacob glanced over his shoulder at me, checking to make sure I was with him. I hurried, smiling to myself, to catch up.

chapter nine

Orientation

"HONESTLY, HOW LONG DOES IT take for the police to come around here?" I asked Jacob where he had parked himself in front of the window. For the last couple of minutes while he was ordering his coffee, I was on the phone and then in the bathroom, washing up. For as much as I bled, I had seen worse with my brother Claudius, who always managed to mangle himself. Now I peered up and down the street for any sign of uniformed help. "I mean, it's not as if there's a whole lot of crime being committed."

"It's Bavaria," he said. "They run on slower time here."

"This isn't Bavaria. It's Disney." I pointed across the street to Ye Olde Christmas Shoppe and the Nutcracker Museum above it. "See all those Santa decorations? It's December twenty-fifth every day of the year here."

He laughed, fingered a sugar packet, and started tapping it against the table in time to the accordion music playing over the speakers. "So, made all your calls?"

"Just about." There was one call I wasn't planning on returning (Erik's — if I hadn't told him about the laser surgery earlier, I wasn't planning on telling him now). And another call I wasn't planning on making (Dad — the less he knew, the better). Roughly three hours and two hundred miles separated us, but I could hear my father all too clearly in my head.

The thought of Dad cued my concern for Mom. Automatically, I glanced over my shoulder to where she was sitting with Norah on mismatched threadbare chairs, one a soft fern green and the other what used to be orange but was well on its way to becoming coffee-spill brown. At their feet, Trevor was happily motoring around some grungy trucks he had fished out of the coffee shop's battered toy box. Meanwhile, Mom and Norah were cackling like old chums with no troubles in the world when an impending fight was waiting for us at home.

"I've never seen Mom this relaxed with someone she's just met," I said without taking my eyes off them.

"My mom could make even the most hardened gangbanger spill his guts. All my old girlfriends stay friends with her."

Old girlfriends? I sidled a glance at Jacob, wondering if he was dating anyone now and then looked back out the window hastily. As if I had a chance with a guy like him. Geez, what was I doing here with him anyway? He was the kind of guy who'd shun me when he was with a group of his über-cool Goth friends, pretend he didn't know who I was. I dug out the piece of metal I'd scavenged and placed it on the table, a boundary line separating our two totally different worlds.

"So," Jacob drawled, holding the O for three long beats.

"Yeah?"

"So I figure, you must be in my debt."

That got my full attention. I turned completely to face Jacob, not even bothering to hide my cheek since it was a little late for that. Besides, he didn't seem to mind it.

"And how do you figure that?"

"Another second" — he touched the piece of the bumper on the table — "and I would have been a double amputee. That is, if I didn't bleed out first."

I grimaced. "God, could you not talk about it?"

He shrugged, silent. And then he smirked. "Who would have known?"

"What?"

"I bet you can't watch horror."

"Or read it." I made a point of looking him up and down. "I take it you do."

"Actually, no."

"Really? I thought that was one of the prerequisites of being a Goth and all." I waved in his general direction.

"You poor, misinformed soul," he said, shaking his head, checking over his shoulder, and then he tossed down the packet of sugar. "Just a sec." He strolled to the counter where not one, but two cups were waiting. I started to get up, but he shook his head and brought the drinks over to me.

"You didn't have to do this. I should be buying *you* a drink. I'm the one who almost killed you, remember?" I protested.

"Or amputated —"

"Ack," I said, holding up my hands, "forget I said anything."

"It's hot," he warned me as he set the white coffee mugs on the table, and then continued relentlessly as he dropped onto his barstool, "But I kind of like having you in my debt."

"You wish." I grinned at him, my first official smile of the day. "So you guys here to celebrate with Father Christmas?"

"Nah, we're on our way to Colville."

"Really? That's where I live."

"No kidding. That'll be the best part of spending Christmas break there then." He smiled at me easily, picked up his coffee cup, breathed in, and set it down without sipping. "Technically, we're there for an easy holiday. No cooking or decorating."

"But . . ."

"But officially?" He glanced at his mom and then faced the window, his shoulders hunching. "News that Dad left her for the barista in his office cafeteria broke before Mom could contain it. Heaven forbid anyone know."

Trevor's truck impressions roared impressively over the coffee shop hubbub. "He left you guys for a barista?"

"She's five years older than me. God, what a pathetic cliché."

The door to the coffee shop opened, a cold wind blowing in. An even colder blast of open revulsion from the curly-haired woman who followed reminded me of my cheek. Suddenly, I was aware of it throbbing, no longer frozen from the cold. I swear, the way she continued to stare at me, I wouldn't have been surprised if she shrieked out loud the way people did back in the medieval times when port-wine stains were thought to be the mark of the devil. Without thinking, I angled my body away from the door, the woman, and Jacob. How could I have forgotten to position myself so that my bad cheek faced the wall? Dumb, dumb, dumb.

"Hey," Jacob said softly.

I shook my head. He placed a gentle hand on mine. Through my haired veil, I glanced at him, unprepared for his look that held so much concern.

"Don't let her bother you," he said.

"It's hard not to," I answered him quietly, my hands tight in my lap, "when your face is the first thing people notice."

He didn't disagree the way Mom would have with her constant denial of anything remotely disagreeable. Say, the second-grade girls who pointed at me when I had to go back to school after a laser treatment, calling me "Grape face." Mom had said then, "Oh, they're just jealous of your gorgeous blue eyes." Yeah, right.

Instead, what Jacob said was this: "Let her stare."

"What?"

"Yeah, most of the starers are just curious. Smile back. That's what I used to do."

If he wasn't going to play dumb, I wouldn't either. I knew he was talking about the whitish scar stitching his lip together. "So people stared at you?"

"Cleft lip, tough to ignore." Absently, he rubbed his scar with his finger. "Stares pass, though."

It made no sense that I was actually considering his advice when I'd dismissed the very same thing from so many well-meaning people before. The difference, I suppose, was that he actually knew what it was like to be so obviously marked. "So smile, huh?"

"Doesn't hurt." And then he pushed my drink closer to me. "Tell me if I guessed right."

"What is it?" I asked, lifting the cup to my lips, edging my body back toward him in degrees like a flower tracking the sun.

"Wait!"

"What?" I lowered my cup hastily, wondering if maybe there was a stray hair, or worse, a newly boiled bug inside the cup.

"You got to smell it first. It's the proper way to cup coffee."

"Cup coffee?"

"Taste it."

"What? Are you the coffee police or something?"

"Come on, don't you ever stop and smell the coffee?"

I followed his gaze to the list I had jotted down of everything I had done to contain the situation: call the police. Find a tow truck. Check in on insurance. Everything crossed off . . . and written down after the fact. Compulsive, I know.

So what could I do? I inhaled: rich and sweet and . . . "Caramel macchiato?" I guessed, and took another more appreciative sniff of the hot drink, a decadence I'd always coveted but never splurged on.

"*Upside-down* caramel macchiato," he corrected me.

"I've never heard of that."

"You put the caramel in first, then add the shot of espresso. The flavor is better this way since the caramel swirls all around."

"Cool." I inhaled again. "When can I drink it?"

"Now. But technically, you're supposed to slurp and spit."

I arched an eyebrow at him. "I don't think so."

He laughed but watched me as I took my first slow sip so I wouldn't burn my tongue. I closed my eyes. It was nectar for the caffeine-addicted.

"So you like it?"

"Love it." I allowed myself another slow sip before asking, "So why'd you pick this?"

"You seem like the kind of girl who only takes her coffee black. Am I right?"

"I heard a 'but' in there," I said. "But what?"

"But you're too much of a control freak to risk tasting the fattest thing on the menu in case you like it too much to say no the next time."

"I'm not a control freak."

He just lifted his eyebrows and drank his coffee. Controlling how much I exercised and what I ate and drank had everything to do with maintaining an ideal body to distract people from my less-than-ideal face. It had nothing to do with my being a control freak. But that didn't explain why I refused to be put under for my laser treatment, opting to slap on Emla, the anesthetic cream, so I could stay awake during all two hundred and fifty zaps from the laser.

"My studio's messy," I said, more defensively than I cared to admit.

"You're an artist?"

"Not really," I said, wishing I hadn't said anything. "I dabble."

"Well, for a dabbler, you get things done. You called the tow truck. The police."

"So?" I squashed the flare of guilt at Erik's unanswered text messages, his voicemails I was ignoring. As much as I didn't want to talk to him, I wanted to keep talking to Jacob.

"So you didn't freak out after the accident," Jacob said like he was impressed, like composure was something to be proud of.

What came out of my mouth was more truth than I'd ever revealed to anyone: "I'm always freaking out inside."

His expression didn't change, betraying no surprise or denial or even curiosity. "Aren't we all?" he answered. He looked like he was going to say more, but this conversation itself was caramel macchiato for me, a dangerous indulgence in intimacy that I couldn't afford — especially since Jacob was headed to Colville for two weeks. Much more than my face felt exposed, and it scared me.

So when he set his cup down, I made a big deal of the straight black coffee inside: "Oh, and what's that you're drinking? Is that black? Not a single grain of sugar? And who's calling who a control freak? I mean, there's got to be at least one study that links black coffee to control freakedness."

His lips twitched into that crooked smile, which meant I was back on safer, more superficial ground. "My mom's a coffee bean buyer."

"She is? That's so cool," I said, casting another glance over at Norah, who had her cell phone out, checking her messages with an experienced glance. My mom still got confused by any function more complex than answering and making a call. Norah was exactly who I wanted to be — put-together, successful, and financially independent.

"Hmmm . . . ," said Jacob noncommittally. "*That*" — he pointed to my syrup-laden, milk-drowned coffee cup on its way back up to my lips — "is the enemy to purists."

"Yum." But then, of course, I had to know, "Is this really the fattest thing on the menu?"

"I called it," he crowed triumphantly. "Just enjoy it, Control Freak. It's not like you're going to order it every day."

Without much more than an unhelpful "you're better off hauling the car to the junkyard," the police took down the accident report and left, all within seven minutes. I timed. The tow truck driver wasn't much more encouraging. After a couple of deep, face-creasing frowns and heavy sighs, he told Mom, "You're lucky just the car was damaged."

Right. I almost lost it then. Just the car.

In no way would Dad ever consider the mangled piece of metal the tow truck hauled away just a car. This was a two-fer opportunity: browbeat Mom and strip something from me. He already took Williams College. What more could he take? Anxiety nibbled at my composure, especially now that there were no more excuses to linger in the safety of Leavenworth's Perpetual Christmas.

We were already an hour late getting home. I could imagine Dad's irritation building into that latent volcanic pitch of his, eternally steaming but never erupting into a full-blown yell. God forbid he actually had to heat up leftovers for dinner. But I didn't check my cell phone and knew Mom had forgotten to charge hers. Like me, Trevor dreaded the drive. He was straining to break out of his mother's grip beside the passenger door.

Jangling her huge set of keys in her other hand, Norah asked Mom, "Ready?"

"Are you sure you can drive us?" Mom asked for the fiftieth time on the sidewalk. She clutched the crumpled bag of her second muffin, long since eaten, as if it had magical regenerative properties. "You really don't need to do this."

"It's on the way to the River Rock Lodge. You said so yourself." Norah threw open the passenger's door for Mom. "Besides, we've already placed your entire Costco haul into the back. So hop in."

Mom flushed, chastened like a little girl, and walked obediently to the passenger door as if she was used to being ordered around. There was a time when Mom was the one who took charge. Like when I was eight and had catapulted over my bike's handlebars, turning too sharply when I tried to follow Claudius's lead. He dropped his mountain bike, ran to the house, hollering for help. It was Mom who had sprinted out of the house. Mom who had followed the siren of my shrieks down our long driveway to where I sat on the road, clutching my bleeding, rock-gouged knee. Mom who carried me to the car effortlessly. I remember thinking that she was so strong, my mom. How I would always be safe in her arms. We headed straight to the Country Clinic, where Mom stationed herself next to me, watching over the doctor's every stitch on my knee until he told her he hadn't been under such scrutiny since he was an intern. Where was that woman now?

A flash of anger shot through me, making me hot even though the temperature outside had dipped another five degrees since the accident. I didn't know if I was madder at Norah for managing us or Mom for not managing a thing since the crash. I tossed back my hair, ready to assert our independence. Which didn't make sense, because who could I have called to drive us home? Erik? He was the last person I wanted to see right now. And Karin's family was spending Christmas in

76

Los Angeles since her dad had found a special effects master who was clearing out his studio.

"No!" Trevor shrieked, twisting out of Norah's grasp. "I'm not getting in."

Suddenly, the accomplished coffee buyer who could negotiate complex deals in Colombia, Indonesia, and Ethiopia was trumped by this little boy. Norah looked helplessly on at the impending tantrum. "Come on," she wheedled.

After another angry NO!, Mom crouched down and asked Trevor, "Were you playing with a backhoe?"

Every bit of his nascent testosterone was utterly offended. Trevor corrected her, I swear, with a sniff: "A front loader."

"Well, you better tell me what the difference is because I always get them so confused," Mom said. "And what exactly can a front loader do that a backhoe can't?"

Before we knew it, a docile Trevor was scrambling into his car seat.

"Come on," Jacob said to me while he slid in, sitting in the middle between Trevor and me. "I won't even make you sit next to the punk."

"Hey!" said Trevor, but he didn't even complain when Mom buckled him in.

It didn't take more than five, ten minutes for me to give thanks that someone else was driving, leaving my hands free. So while Mom twisted around from the passenger seat to chat with Trevor and some mindless kids' tunes played, I scrounged in my backpack for an ibuprofen and the latex glove I had refilled with ice at the coffee shop. Now, I placed the glove gingerly on my face, grateful it numbed my cheek, wishing it could numb my brain. The thought of Dad waiting at home scared me.

"You okay?" asked Jacob.

I nodded, suddenly exhausted. I couldn't swallow my yawn the way I hoped to.

"You should rest," he said.

"Yeah."

In front of us, the moms started chatting; I wasn't paying attention to anything except for my cheek as I waited for the ibuprofen to work its magic, until Jacob sighed, "Here we go."

"What?" I whispered.

"Yes, he's adopted," muttered Jacob with an ironic smile.

Then, from up front, Norah echoed, "Yes, of course, he's adopted."

"I don't mean to sound totally ignorant," said Mom, "but I didn't realize that Chinese boys were given up for adoption. I thought it was just girls."

"Cleft lip," Jacob mumbled.

I couldn't help but glance at the faint scar that left his top lip askew. I wanted to trace his scar tenderly, first with my finger and then my lips. I cleared my throat.

His mom continued matter-of-factly: "Of course, some Chinese boys are given up for adoption. A lot of them have cleft palates, cleft lips. . . ."

Thankfully, Mom didn't jump in to share the travails of having a daughter with a port-wine stain. Their intimate conversation soon died back to safer topics, like favorite movies and holiday plans. Half an hour later, I was still awake, thoughts of Dad polluting any hope of napping. In front of me, Mom's head lolled back. If I was careful, I could rest the crown of my head against the window, but every large bump made me bang against the glass.

I don't remember leaning against Jacob, my good cheek on his shoulder, or even closing my eyes. But I do remember the soft, soft stroke of his hand against my hair, lulling me to sleep.

chapter ten

Dead Reckoning

THE EFFECT DAD WANTED WHEN he built our house ten years ago was ocean schooner, ironic considering he never went beyond a twenty-mile radius of the mountain-locked Methow Valley if he could help it. Still, it was a beautiful home, all wood and natural stone on the inside, small but without a square inch of wasted space. It was nothing like Karin's house, sprawling all over their riverfront property.

Our landscape would have been the same austere desert as everywhere else in the Valley, all spiny sagebrush, dirt, and stones, if it weren't for Mom. Honestly, the joke around here is that even the blackest thumb can grow rocks; you can't stick a shovel anywhere without digging up rocks, rocks, and more rocks. But every spring, Mom tamed the arid land into a proper garden like the ones on the coast, transforming sandy soil into lush green lawn. Even a few flamboyant flowers will take root and sprout under her attentive watch. Those, she trapped behind wire fences to prevent deer from considering the garden their all-day, all-night free buffet.

Tonight, our dark house gave the appearance of a beached ship, marooned on our hill. With all the lights out, save for the ones in Dad's office on top of the house, you'd think it had been abandoned.

I didn't blame Norah for asking Mom, "Are you sure your husband's home?"

"Oh, he's waiting up for us," murmured Mom.

The truck chugged up the unplowed driveway, clotted with new snow. The truck's gears ground, our progress slow. The porch lights flicked on. Behind the door, I knew Dad was donning his good old boy face, the one that charmed strangers, acquaintances, and friends alike. The front door opened, and out he stepped, waving as though he always greeted us with good cheer and glad smiles.

Framed in the porch light, Dad hardly cut an imposing figure, not much taller than me or Mom. His hair used to be thick and blond, but had thinned out and darkened to a limp brown. Anyone who's been under someone's thumb can tell you that power, true power, is never about size or looks.

I sighed when Norah parked the truck. It lurched and then stopped like it didn't want to be here any more than I did. I tossed the glove, gushy with melted ice, into my backpack.

"Hey," said Jacob in a low voice while I unbuckled myself, "I'll come with you."

"That's okay," I said, all confidence, not so much to convince Jacob as it was to gear myself up. It was one thing for Mom to tell Dad that we had to go shopping in Seattle for Christmas since — miracles! — the boys were coming home for the holidays. And another when he saw me wearing my early Christmas present from Mom. Where she had gotten the money for the surgery, she wouldn't say, only that she had the cash and I wasn't to touch my savings. I hadn't let myself think ahead to this part of the day, and from the way Mom wasn't making any moves to get out of the truck, I was pretty sure she hadn't either.

"Okay, Mom, let's go," I said finally.

Jacob followed me out of the truck. "I'll help you unload your stuff."

I kept Jacob's introduction to Dad brief, especially when I saw the curl of distaste on Dad's lips when Jacob set the box of groceries on the ground to shake his hand. If I weren't so worried that Dad might get a good look at me, I would have laughed at the battle on his face, torn between keeping up his chivalrous good-guy act and his disgust at Jacob's black lipstick! Eye shadow! Painted nails! Public performance won out over moral outrage, and Dad shook Jacob's hand.

"Honey," Mom explained to Dad, "we had a little car trouble." As though she were timing her entrance perfectly, Mrs. Fremont chose that moment to slip out of her Range Rover and pick her way across the snow-covered gravel to us. Very quickly, Mom introduced her to Dad, including the fact that Norah was an executive vice president of coffee buying. "Wasn't it nice of Norah to drive us home? They're spending Christmas up at River Rock Lodge."

With Norah before him, Dad had no option but to agree. "Very nice. Thank you, Norah."

"My pleasure, Grant," said Norah, shaking his hand in a firm grip. "Well, with any luck, you'll have the car back in no time. Let me know if I can help out in any way."

Dad bristled. "No, that won't be necessary." The cold night air grew colder, but I wasn't sure if anyone else noticed the drop in temperature. And then Dad caught himself, softening his words with a self-deprecating laugh. "You've done more than enough bailing out my girls."

My girls? That muffled sound would be me, gagging.

"By the way, where *is* our car?" Dad asked mildly.

"In a —," Mom began.

A wail erupted from Norah's truck. Let me just say that I'd never been so happy to hear a kid howling in my life, because with Dad, information was power. The less everyone said about the accident, the better. I made a mental note to bring some of Mom's homemade pastries to Trevor tomorrow. Staying in the shadows, I said, "I think Jacob's little brother needs to go to bed."

I could feel Jacob watching me curiously, but honestly, what he thought of me and my screwed-up family didn't concern me at all, not when I had a whole night with Dad to contend with. Exhaustion sloughed off me. Contain the situation. That's all that mattered now.

Jacob hefted the box easily in his arms and asked, "So where to?"

I could have kissed him for ending this land mine–filled conversation. I could have kissed him period. Flushing, I headed for the door. "Follow me," I said.

Had Norah, Mom, and Dad helped, most everything could have been unloaded from the truck and placed in the kitchen in one trip. But Norah was waylaid by the enormous wreath on the front door. "You made this? You actually made this?" I could hear her say in astonishment.

So Jacob and I hauled the groceries in by ourselves. In the living room, Dad had stationed himself on his leather chair, ostensibly to flip through his usual academic journal. I knew better. He was in a prime location for data gathering, midway between me and Mom.

"Thanks for your help," I told Jacob softly on the way to the kitchen so Dad couldn't overhear. When Jacob didn't answer, I found him standing, transfixed, before the antique maps that lined the hallway, Dad's prized collection. All good collectors try to say something with their collections, make a statement, express a certain point of view. I could almost hear Dad's pedantic patter: "The fundamental question all mapmakers have tried to answer — since the Cro-Magnons scratched hunting maps out on cave walls and animal skins — is this: just how big is the world? And how much do I own?" Dad's viewpoint was clear: move a boundary, and what was yours yesterday is mine today.

Jacob readjusted the ten-pound bags of potatoes and yams in his arms, shifted his weight, and slowly walked the length of the hallway almost sideways so he could study the maps. He set the sacks onto the kitchen counter and said, "There's one missing."

"What?"

"You've got every continent up there except for Asia."

"Shhh," I whispered, and shook my head. I couldn't help my reaction. No one ever breathed a word about the missing China map, the debunked one that was to blame for our exile here. I glanced nervously through the doorway to see if Dad had overheard. So far, there was no telltale angry rattling of the journal in his hands, no warning narrowing of his eyes. I turned back to Jacob, who was watching me, his face carefully blank.

In a louder voice, one meant to be heard, he said, "Okay, if that's it, I better roll."

I nodded.

He lowered his voice to tell me, "So I'll be here until New Year's."

"Great." I meant it. I remembered what he said about spending Christmas here — no friends, his parents just splitting. Before I knew what I was saying, the offer slipped out of my mouth like a fish from a bear's jaw, inadvertently released: "If you want someone to show you around — not that there's much to see, I'd be happy to."

No answer.

God, what had I just done? Of course, he wouldn't want to tour around town with me looking like this. I flushed and picked up the potato sack to store it in the pantry. To my surprise, Jacob took the bag from me, trading it for another napkin. He smirked. "It's clean."

"What?" Then I saw that he had written his number on the napkin.

I laughed out loud before I thought better of it and before I could tell Jacob that I had a boyfriend. All of my intentions disappeared when Jacob grinned back at me, his eyes bright with amusement. Reluctantly, I followed him outside, telling myself how stupid I was being. He just needed a way to kill time while he was stuck in the Valley.

Too soon, the Fremonts drove away, but not before Norah made plans with Mom for a crash course in Wreath-Making 101. I yearned to call them back. But Mom and I were stuck on the wrong side of our own Mason-Dixon Line, the free world vanishing along with Norah's rearview lights.

Silently, Mom turned to face the closed front door. With a sigh, she told me, "Go do your homework."

"Are you kidding?" What if this was the time when Dad lost his control and actually hit Mom? The possibility of that was never far from my mind. "I'm not leaving you, Mom."

"Would you please listen to me for once?" Without thinking, Mom reached out to cup my face with both hands the way she did when I was little, but she stopped short just as I stepped out of her reach. Still, it stung where she would have touched my cheek, phantom pain same as a missing limb. I knew what she was saying: Dad would have a bigger fit about my face than the car. It'd be best for both of us if I just disappeared.

"Okay," I said reluctantly.

Mom nodded, fussed with her sweater, yanking it down over her stomach, and walked into the house. I headed for the stairs, but still caught Dad's grim expression as I hurried past the great room.

"What happened to the car?" he asked Mom.

At the staircase, I couldn't make myself move the way Mom wanted me to, out of danger's way. I sat on the bottom step, a cowardly watchdog who knew her duty but was too scared to perform it. On the last night Claudius spent at home before he left for college, he came into my bedroom and told me, "Look out for Mom," probably the same way Merc had told him five years before that.

"We had to leave the car in Leavenworth," Mom said so softly I could barely make out her words.

"Why would you do that?"

"We got in an accident. The important thing is we're okay."

"So it was Terra's fault."

"There was a lot of ice —"

"God, can't she do one thing right? Either of you?" demanded Dad. "I told you there was no reason to go all the way to Seattle. You could have gone to Wal-Mart in Chelan. But no . . ."

"At least it was just the car."

"Just the car? Just the car, Lois?"

That was Mom's tactical error; it always was. Saying too much when she should have stayed quiet, apologizing one time too many, which only magnified the problem. Teachers wondered why I didn't speak up more in class. Why would I when I knew how precarious words could be, how betraying they were, how vulnerable they made you?

"I didn't realize we had so much money that we could dismiss the cost of repair so easily. But you wouldn't know about that, would you, Lois? You get to stay home, eat all day, and do what, exactly, aside from getting fatter? Just the car," Dad repeated. We had had to economize since Dad quit his last job and was now doing freelance work for a few mapping companies. And now, at last, he called for me, "Terra!"

I shivered as I stood up. Once, when I tried to tell Karin about how scared I was of Dad, she had frowned, asking me: "But he never hits you, right?"

I shook my head. And her face cleared: "So he just yells at you? I know, it freaks me out when my dad yells."

"Well, he doesn't actually yell either," I tried to clarify.

"Then what's so scary about him?" From her dubious tone alone, I could see how Karin had no idea how terrifying words spoken quietly could be. How words chosen precisely to wreak the maximum damage ticked like a bomb in your head, but exploded in your heart hours later, leaving you scarred and changed.

My stomach churned so badly I felt like throwing up. But I forced myself to round the corner, forced myself to look at Dad. He was still too busy picking at the last fragments of Mom to pay attention to me, but then he turned, his mouth half open like he couldn't get his barbs out fast enough. Dad flinched when he saw my face, my dark purple face twinned with his quietly enraged one.

He backed into his chair, a rich distressed leather that I remembered Mom agonizing over, it was so ridiculously expensive. But he was "worth it" — Mom's words.

I waited for Dad to say something, but he didn't. Silence, too, can be torture.

And finally, he asked, "Did I or did I not expressly forbid any more money to be wasted on your face? Did I or did I not say that nothing would ever change your face? Funny, but I thought I had made myself very clear." A pause and then very quietly: "Who paid for that?"

There was no way I was about to tell Dad that Mom had found the funds for my surgery somewhere.

"I asked, who paid for that?"

I glanced over at Mom, willing her for once not to say anything. Mistake. Dad intercepted my look.

"Please, God, tell me that you didn't waste my hard-earned money on that," Dad said, rolling his magazine and slapping it in his open hand. "Please, God, tell me that I haven't been scrimping" — *thwack!* — "and saving" — *thwack!* — "to put all you kids through college and you flush my money down the drain on" — he waved at my face with his police baton of a magazine — "that." His face was reddening with every word. "When are you going to accept that nothing you do will make you look normal?"

I sucked in my breath, kept my face immobile. *Don't listen, don't listen.*

"It wasn't your money," Mom said finally.

No, Mom. Don't.

Dad misinterpreted Mom's statement and glowered accusingly at me. "I see." A pause, long enough for me to wipe the sweat off my forehead before it trickled onto my sore cheek. "Clearly, you're stupider" — *thwack! thwack!* — "than I thought you were to waste your money. Clearly" — *thwack!* — "you have too much discretionary income. You can pay for the car."

I swallowed hard, seeing my college nest egg disappearing and Williams College spinning even farther out of my reach.

A long pause lulled me into thinking that the discussion was over, but I was wrong. As though the thought were only now occurring to him, Dad languidly spread out the magazine, its pages curling up now.

"You know," he mused, "I've seen run-over deer look better than you."

Even in my sleep that night, I heard Dad, ranting on and on about the car, about how stupid I was for not being able to control it on the road in any condition. Every word, every accusation chipped away at me until I was nothing at all. When my alarm clock rang, I slammed my hand on the buzzer to shut it up, completely unable to motivate myself out of bed. None of my regular tricks worked, not even the reminder that Erik expected me to have a killer body hiding under my clothes.

What I wanted to do was eat. No, not eat. Gorge. I would inhale waffles slathered with maple syrup. Bacon fried so crispy it broke with a satisfying crunch. Scrambled eggs with blue cheese. Thick slices of bread covered in warm, freshly ground peanut butter.

No wonder Mom found solace in food. I would, too.

But as I headed out of my bedroom, I saw my computer. I didn't need food, just someone to talk to, and it was too early to call Karin, who slept in every morning that wasn't a school day. At least I could write to her. She beat me to it though; there was already an e-mail waiting from her.

> Hey, Terra,
>
> Guess what? I got into USC!!!!!!!!!!!!!!
>
> I know I was complaining that xmas without snow wasn't xmas at all, but guess what? One of Dad's weirdo costume contacts told me Entertainment Tonight has summer internships (!!). So guess who's going to apply?
>
> And this is Karin Mannion, signing out in sunny California . . .

I caught a glimpse of myself in the mirror across the room as I got up slowly from my desk, wild-haired, red-faced. And green with envy.

Jacob was wrong; I wasn't a control freak. Just a jealous freak.

Karin, who didn't need to escape in the first place, had found more than a way out of here, but the fast track I needed. I jerked away from my reflection, flopping back down on my bed. Without thinking, I threw the sheet over my face and winced. Even the weight of soft flannel felt like granules of glass rubbing against my cheek.

I ripped the sheet off and stared up at the ceiling.

Lost sailors studied the stars to pinpoint where they were in the wide blue sea. Dead reckoning, it was their best guesstimate.

Stars or no stars, I knew exactly where I was. Stuck under Dad's thumb, where I would be forever unless I found a new escape map — and fast. One thing was for certain: I couldn't stay beholden to Dad's pursestrings that he wielded as both whip and chain.

chapter eleven

Mother Map

EVEN FREAKS AND CONTROL FREAKS have to eat at some point. So I threw on my clothes and waited until seven in the morning before venturing downstairs, when I was sure Dad would be holed up in his office, working on his routing algorithm to move people from one place to another with the utmost efficiency. The person he most wanted to define and contain wasn't in the kitchen, where I've always assumed I could find Mom. More troubling, there was no telltale lingering scent of her cooking and baking, as though she had never been here.

"Mom?" I called softly.

I looked in the master bedroom. The bed was neatly made, duvet fluffed, throw pillows tilted at the exact angle Dad liked them. I checked the den, the living room, even the pantry. Back upstairs, I stuck my head in my old alcove-sized bedroom next to the attic. No Mom. Worried now that maybe Dad had done something to her while I slept, I raced down the stairs, flung open Claudius's bedroom. Still no Mom.

How did I ever think I could go across country to college and leave Mom alone here? I couldn't. It would never be okay while she stayed with Dad. Who would listen for her when Dad went off on her? Who would make sure his barbs never became physical blows? Who would take care of her when he was done?

There was a thud outside the mudroom. I ran over to throw open the door, found Mom surrounded by freshly cut boughs, mounded high. Her face was flushed pink, and she was panting from exertion.

"Good morning, Terra," Mom said brightly, wiping the sweat off her cheek. "I was wondering when you'd finally get up." Her smile dimmed as she scrutinized my face. "Are you feeling okay?" Without waiting for my answer, she was already heading back inside the house, brushing her hands on her pants. "I'll get you an ice pack."

"I'm fine, Mom." I reached out a hand to stop her. "What are you doing with all this?"

"Getting everything ready to make wreaths with Norah."

Right, I had forgotten. Mom muttered now to herself, counting off on her fingers. Then she shook her head impatiently. "Floral wire! How could I forget that?" She bustled through the mudroom while I gazed at all the greenery, enough for at least four wreaths, maybe five. Mom had already brought out two bags of ornaments, all bought at countless end-of-season close-out sales online. Next to those was a bag of festive holiday ribbons and a cardboard box with wire forms that would be used as the wreaths' bases — a few square shapes amid a bunch of circles and wire hangers.

"Ready?" Mom asked, tossing a spool of green wire into the box. "They're expecting us at eight."

"Mom, it's only seven."

"It'll take at least twenty minutes to load everything in your father's truck, and then it's a twenty-minute drive to their hotel."

"But if we leave now, we're going to be way too early."

Her shoulders slumped in disappointment. "Okay."

I hated Mom's easy acquiescence, hated how guilty I felt at deflating her that easily. So without a word, I grabbed a heap of pungent evergreens into my arms and trudged to the garage. Some of the needles scratched my chin. Hastily, I lowered my load so they wouldn't brush my tender cheek.

Mom, for once, held the car keys, and as she opened the trunk for me, she chattered: "You know, Norah with all her traveling here and there for her job just didn't have time to learn how to make basic crafts. Can you imagine not knowing how to make a simple wreath?"

I could.

What would it be like to fly around the world, be at ease in countries where the customs were as foreign as the languages themselves? Make enough money I could escape to the most expensive resort in town for a week and a half and not worry about the cost? I couldn't wait to find out. With a grunt, I shoved in the mound of evergreens, made a note to vacuum the trunk later so Dad wouldn't gripe, and wished I had the foresight to lay a sheet inside to corral most of the pine needles.

As soon as everything was packed, Mom handed me the car keys. "Okay, we should go now."

My protest died at the apprehensive look she cast over her shoulder as if she expected Dad to thunder out of the mudroom, cut off our escape. That's what this was. Escape. Now, I couldn't have been more aware of the empty spot in the garage where our other car should have been parked. But that was at the shop in Leavenworth, more fodder for Dad.

I clambered hurriedly into the driver's side, adjusted the seat to fit me, and then as I swiveled around to look over my shoulder before I backed out of the garage, I caught sight of my face in the rearview mirror. And winced. I had made it a point not to look at myself when I got up, and for good reason. Overnight, my cheek had swollen to the size of a grapefruit, my bruised face now a battered purple. As far as grooming went, I hadn't done more than drag a brush through my hair and yank it into a ponytail. Thankfully, I had brushed my teeth, and my sweatshirt, while not newly washed, didn't smell. Still, God, did I really have to see Jacob looking like this? The problem was, going back inside to change was only courting Dad's wrath.

The gravel crunched noisily beneath the truck's wheels. Neither Mom nor I spoke until we were well down the road to town. Even then, Mom clenched her hands in her lap as she stared stoutly out the window.

"You doing okay?" I asked Mom.

"Of course!" she answered brightly.

Our town was deserted this early in the morning. Even the coffee shop had only one car in front of it, instead of the usual five or six crowding every parking space.

"That way," Mom directed, as though I didn't know to head over the bridge that spanned the Methow River.

I swallowed my sigh. "So when was the last time you went to River Rock Lodge?" I asked Mom.

"Oh." She thought hard, her forehead wrinkling with the effort. "Too long to remember."

"Me, too." I had been inside the massive lodge only twice, and then only to pick Karin up during her brief stint hostessing in its five-star restaurant. Apparently, Karin wasn't cut out for the service industry. I didn't blame her. It was a seven-figure world up there on that mountain, where summers meant lavish weddings and falls saw hour-long cowboy cookouts that cost more to attend than I made in a day at Nest & Egg.

As we drew closer to the mountaintop, I couldn't help but grip the steering wheel tighter. What the hell was I doing up here? I felt like a country bumpkin, smelling of pine and wearing needles where the boughs had shed on me. I picked one off my chest. When I checked the rearview mirror, the bags jammed with dollar decorations in the backseat could have been mistaken for trash. I breathed out heavily. Norah was probably just being polite about making wreaths with Mom, the way I was when I asked Erik about some new wrestling hold he was mastering, not intending for him to go on. And on.

The main lodge rose before us at the apex of the mountain, a mega-sized Lincoln Log toy structure. Miraculously, Mom knew where the Fremonts were staying: the private cabins. So I continued past the main lodge and its expanse of wide open snow field. A man in a green parka and jeans waved to us from his small tractor while he groomed the field, laying down fresh cross-country ski tracks for the guests. Beyond the field was a small, but steep, sledding hill.

Even driving as slowly as I could up the mountain, it still wasn't eight when I parked next to Norah's sleek Range Rover.

"Maybe we should get some coffee," I suggested, killing the engine. And then, evil me, I added, "And scones. There's got to be some kind of café inside. . . ."

For a second, Mom took my bait. She nodded. But as we both got out of the car, a familiar screech, muffled yet distinct, came from the cabin. Trevor was up and that was all the invitation Mom needed. She was at their door, knocking, before I could stop her.

"Mom," I said.

Too late. The door opened and there was Jacob, hair tousled from sleep, wearing a T-shirt and baggy flannel pants, barefaced as me. Stripped of his Goth accoutrements — all his makeup except for his black nail polish — he couldn't have been more intimately revealed to me other than being naked. Even clothed as he was, I swallowed hard at the sight of him.

"Hey," he said, smiling almost as though he had been waiting for me.

Good thing Norah called from the bedroom — "Jacob, you're letting out all the warm air" — otherwise, I would have kept standing there, my mouth wide open. She padded to the entry in a cute sweatsuit, her hair twisted into a loose knot, somehow managing to appear both comfortable and sophisticated.

"Lois, you're right on time." Norah lifted her coffee cup. "Can I interest you in some? It's my personal blend. I only roast it for a few people at my company."

"Why?" I asked.

After a thoughtful sip of her coffee she answered me with a question of her own: "Why don't I pour you a cup, too, and you tell me? Have a seat."

"Mom," Jacob groaned. "Don't test them."

"You can bring in everything from their car," she answered sweetly, and then checked to confirm with Mom. "Right?"

I lost track of their interchange when Jacob yawned, stretched. His T-shirt lifted a good couple of inches to reveal nicely muscled abs, not the rock hard, super-defined six-pack that Erik sported. But smooth and hairless and begging for me to run my hands over them. Forget caffeine, I was wide awake now. Jacob caught me gawking. I felt the blush start at my chest, willed it to stay there. His lips quirked into a grin I recognized, black lipstick or not, before he stopped in front of me.

Oh God, now what?

"Keys?" he prompted innocently.

"Oh, right." I fished them out of the pockets of my jeans, handed them to him. Again, the knowing smile.

"What do you smell?" Norah was asking Mom. She gestured more emphatically at me to join them at the round table in the large living room. "Sniff. And tell me. Use any words to describe it. Sound, colors, anything."

Coffee, that's what I smell, I wanted to say, but didn't dare. Not with Norah watching us so expectantly, her eyes glittering like she had given us a gift. Mom looked perplexed as she sniffed her mug, too.

When neither of us answered, Jacob stopped slipping his feet into his Vans by the front door. "Caramel, nuts, earth, monkey poop . . ."

That made Trevor chortle from where he was sitting atop one of the beds, miniature trucks surrounding his construction site of pillows. He cackled, "Monkey poop!"

"I'm not kidding," said Jacob, eyeing me mischievously. "Monkeys eat the coffee beans —"

I wanted to gag, pushed my coffee cup away from me. "Too much info, thanks."

Norah rolled her eyes. "Kopi Luwak beans aren't in this blend." She pointed to the door meaningfully as she looked at Jacob.

"I'm going, I'm going," Jacob said good-naturedly. Of course, he ambled out of the cabin without putting on a jacket. Yes, I noticed. What was it with him and braving the elements without the proper gear?

Mom took a hesitant sip of the coffee. "It's . . . bright."

"Yes!" Norah beamed like a teacher with a precocious student. "Exactly. Part of this blend comes from Guatemala, my favorite Central American. The beans there are so complex."

"Guatemala . . . ," echoed Mom faintly, and I knew what she was thinking about: Aunt Susannah and how she had died in that country.

"You should see the coffee plantations there." Norah looked into her dark brew dreamily, missing Mom's consternation. "Each tribe has their own pattern of woven clothes. Seeing them scattered among the dark green coffee trees is one of the most evocative sights I've ever encountered. Ever. For someone who loves interior design, Lois, you would just fall in love with the country, all those colors."

"Really?" Mom asked, cautiously curious.

"I really need to get back there sometime soon. You should come with me." Norah sipped her coffee with a meditative expression.

"Oh, I don't —"

Norah's lips had pursed, as she concentrated on her coffee and she interrupted Mom's protests now. "Definitely bright. And something more." She rubbed the fingers in one hand together as if trying to filter the taste itself.

I took an obedient sip and tasted . . . coffee.

"Coconut," Mom said, looking surprised. She set the cup down on the table, excited. "In the back of my throat."

"Yes! And a little floral, right?" Norah asked, nodding as if willing Mom to taste it. She leaned toward her now, her eyes probing, as Mom sampled the coffee again.

Mom's lips puckered; she nodded.

Norah sat back, satisfied. "The best Kenyans are the pinnacle of the coffee world. This is definitely my favorite East African bean."

"Guatemala, Kenya . . . do you really visit all those places?" I asked and sipped again.

"Oh my God, yes. And I take the boys whenever I can."

"But aren't you scared?" Mom asked. I was glad she did. It's what I was wondering, too. That, and how she could discern all the different beans and their flavors that went into crafting this coffee. I took another sip; coffee.

"My first trip to Ivory Coast, I was still a baby. I was so scared, and I remember sitting on the Tarmac thinking, the Ivory Coast is so far from home." Norah cradled her mug in both hands and shrugged as if traveling afar was a normal, everyday occurrence. It probably was, for her. "I just never let fear stop me from having an experience."

The door opened and Jacob blew in with the wind. He carried a massive armload of the fresh greenery while also managing two of the paper sacks. "I'll help you," I said as I stood up. "I have defective taste buds."

"That's because you haven't been trained to pay attention," Norah said, shaking her head adamantly.

"Here we go," Jacob mumbled to me as he strolled past me to the table. "Where should I dump this?"

Norah waved to the floor before continuing, "Show me anyone with average sensory abilities but with a real passion for coffee, and with practice and coaching and paying attention, they can heighten their skills in tasting." She considered the pile of branches at our feet warily. "And that's what I hope it's going to be like making wreaths." Without any hesitation, Norah cleared the newspaper off the table, tossing every section on the floor.

Mom nearly choked at that. And Dad? He would have had a major conniption at such blatant slovenliness.

Norah raised her eyebrows at Mom. "Whenever I tidied the tasting room, my mentor would always ask me, 'Are you going to keep house or taste coffee?'"

Mom blinked as she processed that. It took me a second, too, to understand that maybe not everyone was as compulsively neat as Dad — or us. And then slowly, Mom smiled. "We're going to make wreaths."

I heard a muffled groan from a pained-looking Jacob, who was standing close to me.

"Yes?" said Norah, her eyebrows arching up.

Jacob nudged me. "Terra was going to show me around town, right?"

I was? And then I recalled my impulsive offer last night. I just never thought he'd actually take me up on it. Of course, it probably had more to do with the threat of floral tape and ribbons than hanging out with me. None of that, though, seemed to bother Trevor, who bounded over when Mom wiggled the largest wire form at him and told him she'd help him make the biggest wreath ever.

"So you're okay if we left for a little bit?" I asked Mom.

"Go on," she said without even looking at me; she was too busy pawing through the greenery to find the choicest boughs for Trevor.

"Your mom will be fine here," said Norah, who fingered her wire form suspiciously. As I turned to follow Jacob to the door, I caught her taking a fortifying draught of coffee.

Jacob waited for me, his dark eyes fathomless. What was I going to do with him? Talk about with him? He'd been to half of the world; my world was Colville, two blocks of downtown.

"Do you want to change?" I asked Jacob, not that I minded the clothes he wore as pajamas. Not at all.

"Nah," he said.

"So where to first?" I asked, holding my palm out for my car keys that he was still holding.

"You're the boss," he said, but he eyed my keys doubtfully before tossing them to me. He retrieved his own from the rack next to the door. "But I'll do the driving."

Once we were sitting in his Range Rover, waiting for it to warm up, Jacob didn't even pretend that he wasn't studying me intently. "You look like shit."

If this were Karin, she'd tell him to go to hell. Me, I couldn't help but duck my head and apologize, "I can't wear makeup for a week."

He spread his hands wide — So? "No," he said, touching me gently on my exposed wrist. "I meant, you didn't sleep. Your dad didn't take the car well, did he?"

I snorted. "Definitely not."

"So you forgot this." He reached into the backseat, pulled out my post-op care instructions that must have slipped out of my jacket pocket last night. If Jacob hadn't known all the details about my laser surgery last night, he certainly knew now. I took the paper as he said, "I was going to drive back with it last night, but . . ."

I knew he was referring to Dad, somehow knowing my father had spent a good chunk of the night grilling Mom, fact-checking her story, cross-referencing it with mine. More ashamed of my father than my face, I couldn't meet Jacob's eyes, relieved when he looked over his shoulder to back us out of the parking space. On the drive down the mountain, I might have been able to keep my gaze planted firmly on the vista outside, but I couldn't block out the musky scent of his creamy leather seats. Even our cars sprang from different worlds. Vehicles here in the valley came in one basic style: Subaru station wagons, purchased specifically for their ability to handle snow. So Jacob's entire lifestyle? I couldn't even begin to fathom it, this world where Guatamala and Kenya were part of his memory, not just push-pins on my map.

"What?" Jacob asked, his gaze penetrating.

"Nothing." My denial was rote, a knee-jerk reflex of my mouth.

We drove in silence for a while, more because I think Jacob wanted to give me space than not having anything to say.

"And this is Nest & Egg. We don't need to go in if you don't want to," I told Jacob when we approached my gallery near the end of Main Street. This had to have been the world's shortest and worst tour on record. Neither of us had dressed for the cold, him out of some warped fashion statement that precluded warm outer garments and me out of impatience to hurry Mom from home. I was lucky I had slipped on my boots. So basically every few yards, we had ducked into a store, even the ones that sold awful T-shirts imprinted with things like My Paw-Paw Loves Me, complete with bear prints.

Obviously, Jacob took his touring duties seriously, because the look he sent me was pure *are you kidding?* He grinned. "And miss out on the chance to see your messy studio?"

"Who says you're going to see my studio?" I asked, getting the distinct and unpleasant sense he was approaching the gallery as an anthropological study where he'd ferret out more clues about me.

Instead of heading straight inside to warmth like a sane person, he leaned in close to the poster I had created for all the exhibits lined up for the next year. That sign was now hanging in front of the gallery to entice town shoppers and winter sports enthusiasts to visit Nest & Egg again . . . and again. I shivered, hugged my arms tight around myself.

"Great font," said Jacob, straightening.

"Thanks, I found it," I told him, surprised he noticed. Most people don't see the difference between old world typefaces like my favorite Bembo, with its gorgeous delicate curves, from the supermodern ones, like plump Bodoni. For a full two days, I had congratulated myself for locating the perfect old-fashioned typeface — Windlass — a font that would have been at home on a fifteenth-century map, perfectly matching the mood for the new year's overall theme: Journeys Beyond. The Twisted Sisters' choice, not mine. I personally thought it sounded like a mortician's tagline, but I had been overruled.

The parchment-colored ribbon I had glue-gunned to the back of the sign was tied in a lopsided bow and listed drunkenly from the iron stand. Clearly, Lydia's work. She may have been the initial visionary behind the gallery, but she roved through life the way she had once painted: with huge, broad brushstrokes, leaving detail work to others like me.

Compulsive, true, but freezing or not, I couldn't let the bow stay crooked. I had to fix it, make the length of the ends match, the loops perfectly symmetrical.

"What are you doing?" Jacob asked as I slipped the sign off the metal hanger that one of Lydia's former lovers had welded as a good luck gift. I tried to ignore him when I set the poster on the ground and retied the bow, an impossible task when he started guffawing. There is no other way to describe the braying emanating out of that boy.

"What?" I snapped.

His lips barely moved but his words were clear: "Control freak."

"Excuse me?"

He blinked innocently and then said, "But you're pretty messy for a control freak."

At first, I thought he meant my poster design, which had more elements than my usual posters, namely a large compass rose like the one I had doodled on the jeans that I was wearing, faded now after a few washes. In January, we were featuring Journeys Beyond Time with a show full of timepieces, paintings, sculptures, and one enormous hand-carved grandfather clock. But then I choked when I saw my artwork under April's show, Journeys Beyond Place. When had the Twisted Sisters substituted the piece we had agreed to feature — a family tree created in encaustic, using an old wax-painting technique — with one of my collages? And when had I ever agreed to be in a show?

"Oh my God," I gasped.

My stress ratcheted up another level when I saw that it wasn't just any collage, but the one I had made for Mom — now displayed for all the world to see . . . including Dad.

"You didn't say anything about starring in a show," said Jacob. He looked at me curiously. "Your dad, too."

"What?"

Jacob tapped the poster again. Directly under my name was my father's: Dr. Grant A. Cooper, special guest speaker, The History of Cartography.

"This can't be happening," I breathed out.

"You didn't know your dad was coming, did you?" Jacob guessed softly.

"I didn't even know I was in a show."

But the implications of this poster, my name, Dad's presence sank in. A couple of days ago, I had broken the news to the Twisted Sisters that not only wasn't I applying to art school, I wasn't even going to Williams College. Hell hadn't broken loose; silence had, cold as a whiteout blizzard. Clearly, the Twisted Sisters — who else would have led this foolish charge? — decided to map the future they thought I ought to have.

The enormity of the show hadn't occurred to them. How could it? I kept such a strict church-and-state, never-the-twain-shall-meet separation between them and my parents, they had no idea of what Dad was truly like.

chapter twelve

Gerrymandering

"**WHAT ARE YOU GUYS THINKING?**" I demanded, shaking the sign, my writ of war.

Clearly, I shouldn't have called earlier to let Lydia know I might swing by this morning, but I had needed her to move my Beauty Map off my desk in the off-chance that Jacob would want to see my studio. The Twisted Sisters were more than prepared for me, just as they were anytime a new artist was invited to visit the gallery before their show. Lydia, Beth, and Mandy advanced upon me, a squadron of gray-haired cheerleaders wielding their blue and white pom-poms dangerously. I glanced at Jacob, had enough time to groan but not to warn him about the upcoming embarrassing spectacle.

The women now shook their pom-poms vigorously in the air. "Terra! Is! Here!"

It was a quirky gallery tradition, funny and somewhat heartwarming when the Twisted Sisters were welcoming new artists into their community. But embarrassing when that new artist happened to be me, and when a boy who I thought was cute looked on.

I couldn't have been happier to resemble a human eggplant than I was now, because the Twisted Sisters stopped shouting as soon as they got a good look at my purpled cheek, swollen alarmingly.

"Oh, Terra, are you sure you should be here?" asked Lydia, her brows puckered with worry, her pom-poms listless at her sides.

Beth, who worked in oil paints — hence, her perpetually ruined clothes — nudged her, meaningfully. "Remember?"

Remember what? Then I recalled how I had told the gallery co-owners (okay, lectured them) before the laser surgery that I'd come to work during the last half of Christmas break when my face returned to some semblance of normal so long as they didn't make a big deal about it. Lydia recovered quickly, going all grandma-cheerleader on me, now back to shaking her hips.

"God, just stop. You're going to hurt yourself," I told Lydia. Mandy, the youngest of the Twisted Sisters at sixty-six, crouched in preparation for her signature Herkie jump. I had no doubt that Lydia would copy her. "C'mon, Mandy, don't egg her on."

Beth flipped her hair, braided into one ropey strand, over her shoulder. "You know the tradition."

Lydia nodded her head so vigorously, her silver curls bobbed like a dog shaking off a dip in the ice-cold Methow River. She punctuated each word with her pom-pom : "What . . . are . . . you . . . afraid . . . of?"

"You guys," I said. "God."

Short of knocking Beth's arm out of my way, tripping Mandy, or yanking the pom-poms from Lydia's hands, I couldn't even set foot into the gallery space. Suspecting imminent success, they created an arch with their shimmering pom-poms that I was supposed to run under.

"Come on," encouraged Lydia.

That's when I noticed Jacob's smirk. Unlike Erik, who would have slunk out of the gallery at the first sight of all this gray hair, Jacob was leaning against a bookshelf, looking like he had nothing better to do than witness my imminent humiliation.

"There's a glass gallery across the street," I told him, ignoring the collective intake of offended breath from the Twisted Sisters because I referred him to our competition. "I'll meet you over there."

But Jacob looked entirely too amused to budge until the Terra Rose Cooper Show was over. I glared at him. His smirk widened into a grin.

It wasn't just that I didn't want Jacob to see me doing anything idiotic — he had already seen both me and my mom at our worst — but I didn't want him to see my artwork. And that, I knew, was hanging up. Otherwise, why the grandma-cheerleader antics? According to Nest & Egg tradition, every debuting artist was feted with this surprise pom-pom routine, technically having been invited to see a piece of their artwork on the wall. It was a visual nudge for the new artists to finish the ten pieces required for their show. More than a couple had gotten cold feet and never delivered. I wondered now whether the idea of an encore performance with the pom-poms had simply scared them away for good.

"So, we're waiting," chimed Jacob, gesturing at the expectant arch of pom-poms.

I swear, Magellan didn't have it this hard circumnavigating the world. There was no way out of this.

"Fine, fine," I grumbled, trying to ignore Jacob snickering in the background. And then, like every other debuting artist before me, I ran under the arch of outstretched arms and shaking pom-poms, and stopped directly before my collages. Three of them were hanging on the center wall, the space of honor reserved for the headlining artist.

"What do you think?" asked Lydia softly, coming to my side. "Don't they look gorgeous?"

They did. Framed, my collages actually looked finished. Real. More than that, they looked like they belonged on a wall, rather than resting in hodgepodge stacks on the floor. I chanced a glance at the Twisted Sisters, wondering if they recognized their lives in these collages. But Lydia's green eyes glinted in the gallery lights, showing nothing but maternal pride.

Anyway, how could they possibly know that hidden among the fragmented maps and artifacts like buried treasures were their stories, collected the way I did scraps of paper, car parts, sugar packets: Beth and her world travels. Lydia and her crusading causes. Mom and her kitchen accoutrements.

"Tell me now that you aren't an artist," Lydia said. "Tell me now that you don't belong at art school." When I turned toward her, she quickly conceded, "Or Williams." Her voice turned into a muted, frustrated wail. "The school your parents want you to go to doesn't even have a fine arts program!"

For a moment, it was hard to disagree while the Twisted Sisters stared at me expectantly, these gift givers who only wanted to deliver unbridled delight.

"Oh, you guys" was all I could manage. It was odd how much easier it was to accept my dad's criticism than these women's opinion, as if there were something suspect about their high regard for me and my work. Embarrassed by all the attention, I studied the exhibit poster that had been forgotten in my hands. Even though the type size of Dad's name was the same as mine, it loomed on the page, his very presence casting a shadow on my sanctuary.

"Once your parents see this, how could they not insist you go to Williams at least?" asked Lydia.

No, if Dad saw this, how could he not ask, *Is this really art?*

Like a siren's song, his seemingly innocent rhetorical questions pulled down the unwary, drowning them in self-doubt. Dad might as well have been here, holding my head steady so that I could take a good hard unflinching look at my collages. What I saw now were inane efforts at making a statement: Mom's collage map wasn't even done. I had chickened out of calling Magnus tohelp me with the wire. The edges of the maps I had sliced with a dull razor blade were fuzzy, because I had been too lazy to change it for a new one. Now, I wished I could recut each one of those maps, create utterly clean border lines. But they were affixed as permanently to my canvases as Dad's dismissal was fixed inside my head.

I couldn't divulge any of that to the Twisted Sisters. The truth felt too close to betraying Mom. Too close to admitting that my family fell far short of their own happy households, their well-adjusted and successful children. I smiled weakly and then shook my head, more firmly.

"I can't be in the show," I said, redrawing the boundary line back to where it belonged before my gerrymandering mentors messed with it. They were artists; I was a studio manager for artists.

Now, it was Jacob's gaze I felt as acutely as yesterday's laser on my cheek. Without knowing how, only just that he did, Jacob saw through the protective layers of my denials, down to my core. I didn't like it. Not at all.

Lydia guessed, "All of us get queasy at the thought of other people looking at our art. But it's part of being an artist — showcasing your work. Sharing your visionary statement with others."

How could I answer with the truth? All roads leading to my insecurity shared the same starting point: Dad, the prime meridian.

"One," I said, and spun around, my back to the collages, "the framing is better than the artwork."

"You know that's not true," protested Mandy, who truly did excel in finding the right frame to best show off art.

"And two," I continued, ignoring how my heart pounded the way it did whenever I geared myself up for an encounter with Dad, my tension building until I could skitter right out of my skin. "We're going to witness three major temper tantrums from the other artists who aren't going to want to share their show with an amateur."

No one looked convinced, not the Twisted Sisters. Not Jacob.

Trapped, my face throbbed in time to my pulse. There it was, my way out of this too-intense scrutiny. So I deployed yesterday's surgery, a menstrual-cramp type of excuse that would end all argument. And I said flatly, "My face hurts. I don't want to talk about it anymore, okay?"

Just as I suspected, no one argued with that, not when I took the collages down, one by one, and left them there on the floor.

No sooner did I reach my studio than my cell phone vibrated in my back pocket, the tickling of a guilty conscience. It was Erik. Of course.

"God," I said, hitting my forehead. I had blown off Erik's voicemail yet again last night and then forgotten to call him this morning when I was chauffeuring Mom. I softened my voice, dousing it with the usual happy, carefree lilt that I added whenever I spoke to him: "Hey!"

"Hey, what's up, stranger?" he said.

"Not much," I answered in a low voice. *Liar,* I berated myself, even as I peeked downstairs to see the fallout of my diva-esque departure. From where I stood, stationed behind a wood column carved with twisting vines and leaves, I could safely eavesdrop on Jacob's conversation with the Twisted Sisters. He was crouched before my collages, inspecting them. Even up here, I felt more transparent and more exposed than going barefaced in public. Vaguely, I heard Erik on the phone, followed by an expectant pause. I asked, "What?"

"My cousin Max is here, remember?" he repeated patiently.

"Yeah. Are you having fun with him?"

"We were going to catch the late show. I can pick you up at eight."

"Oh," I said, my breath letting out in a deep sigh. It was a long hour's drive to the nearest movie theater. Even if it had been fifteen minutes away, I didn't want to go, didn't want to try to disguise my cheek. Absently, I rubbed my hands together and winced, noticing for the first time the thin line of blood welling on my thumb where one of the hanging wires must have scratched me. "I'm still not feeling so great." Technically, that was true. My face hurt, and I wished I could curl up into a deep Rip Van Winkle sleep. Wake me when college starts. Yet here I was in the gallery, wondering what another boy thought about my art.

And thought about me.

I couldn't help but peek over the railing when Beth's voice carried effortlessly to me: "And how do you two know each other?"

Then I smiled at the intimate, teasing tone in Jacob's voice, as though he knew I was eavesdropping: "Terra ran into me. Literally."

"What's wrong with you?" Erik asked.

I left the catwalk to sit heavily at my desk chair, brushing a sliver of origami paper off my otherwise pristine work surface and into the garbage can beneath my desk. On my desk was Erik's Christmas present, his collage, still an empty canvas, cotton duck, nothing more.

"I'll be better soon. I promise." But I had the feeling he wasn't inquiring about my health.

"No, I meant —"

"I have to go, okay?" It was ironic that Erik finally seemed ready for our first real conversation beyond his personal best time pinning his opponent, his weight loss, his pickup truck. This was the conversation I'd wanted to have all along — but now, I didn't have the heart to start.

Or the energy to finish us. Gently, I told Erik, "I'll call you later, okay?" And this time, I hung up first without waiting for his reply.

"So," said a voice from behind me, one I already recognized. Despite myself, a tiny flare of excitement brushed away the last of my lingering guilt.

I swiveled around in my chair, away from Erik's nonexistent collage. Jacob was leaning against my door frame, looking around my studio curiously, nodding as if what he saw only confirmed his deepest suspicions. I became acutely aware of my neat bins, the rows of matching tins, all of it labeled precisely. The labels themselves were tied with satin ribbon, orange on one side, green on the other.

"So this is messy," he said.

"I just cleaned up."

He eyed the trash bin with its one tiny sliver of paper. "Uh-huh."

"Suddenly, I'm having serious regrets for not maiming you yesterday."

"Bloodthirsty. Sure you're not a Goth in hiding?"

That's when I noticed he had already placed Mom's collage beside my desk, no fanfare, no expectation of anything.

"Thanks," I said softly.

He shrugged. "Is your work always this provocative?"

Provocative — I thought about that apt description, and how Erik would have described my collages: cool. Or neat. Or weird. If he noticed them at all. I now spied my Beauty Map, propped against the wall by my worktable. In my call with Erik, I had completely forgotten to check where Lydia had hidden it. With my foot, I nudged Mom's collage surreptitiously over to camouflage mine before Jacob could see my Beauty Map.

As I straightened, Jacob made a light, impatient sound. Had he seen?

"God, you're bleeding again," he said. I tried to hide my hand at my side, but he dug into his pocket and withdrew a napkin. "Don't worry, it's clean. I promise."

"I —"

He held my hand and pressed the napkin to my cut thumb gently. "Remind me to keep a bigger stash if I'm going to keep hanging out with you."

And what makes you think I'm going to hang out with you? That's what Karin would have responded, flirting by way of challenge. But with my cell phone in my pocket, still warm from my conversation with Erik, I took a step back and said flatly, "I don't need rescuing."

Perched on the edge of my desk now, his legs splayed wide, hands on either side, Jacob looked completely at ease while I felt fidgety, self-conscious, yet utterly conscious of his every movement. "No," he said, "it seems to me that you do your fair share of rescuing."

That reminded me of Mom. The clock on the wall read almost ten. Which meant we had two hours before Dad would need the car for his weekend extreme fitness regimen at the gym — ninety minutes of running, biking, or swimming, followed by an hour of weights and fifteen minutes in the steam room to leach out toxins. It was a matter of personal pride that he wasn't an ounce over his college weight.

"I forgot to let Mom know we have to be back by noon." I started to reach for my cell phone and asked, "What's your mom's number?"

Jacob simply pulled out his own phone and dialed. "Hey, Mom," he said into the phone, his eyes locked on mine. "You Martha Stewart yet?" He listened, toyed with three platters that nested one on top of the other, each carved with eggs, the largest with life-sized ostrich eggs and the smallest dotted with fingernail-sized hummingbird ones.

"You've already made two wreaths?" Another pause. "Trevor made one? So we'll be back around" — he looked at me — "eleven thirty."

"Eleven fifteen," I whispered. It'd take a good fifteen minutes just to tidy up his cabin and then another fifteen to load Mom's supplies into the truck. We couldn't afford to be late today, not after Dad was already angry about our car.

When he hung up, Jacob said, "All set."

"Thanks."

His attention shifted to the world map on the wall behind my desk. Leaning back, he traced his finger from Washington State over the Pacific Ocean to southern China, and then he shot me a self-conscious look, moved his finger to Africa. I almost felt his touch skimming along my face. I had to admit, it wasn't hard to imagine Jacob commanding a fleet of ships to chart an unknown land, Terra Nullis.

Chart me, instead.

God, where did that thought come from? It made no sense. Jacob wasn't even my type — my fantasies involved tall, lanky guys, the kind with blond hair and blue eyes. Guys who'd pay attention to me, proving to everyone that I was special, a girl to be cherished. My fantasy guy may not have been Erik, exactly, but it was definitely not a Goth who was lean, my height, and kept his fingernails well-manicured in black.

"Antarctica," Jacob said, his finger on the continent. "That's where I would go."

"Too cold for me. I'd go to Kashgar." I stopped talking when I noticed Jacob staring at the map the way I do after one of Dad's sotto voce tirades, wishing myself and Mom anywhere but here. Had I said too much? Did he think I was weird wanting to travel the Silk Road?

"Sometimes," he said slowly, "I think I was born in the wrong century. Everything's already been discovered."

"Not everything."

His head snapped to me as though he had just spotted uncharted territory. "You didn't tell the Twisted Sisters the truth."

"Which is . . . ?"

"You're afraid of what your dad will say."

"I'm not!"

He arched his eyebrow at me.

"I already know what he'll say," I amended quietly, expecting Jacob to ask me what that was.

But Jacob didn't probe, following up instead with a harder question, "Why does his opinion matter so much to you?"

That, I had never considered, and I flung back into my seat from the impact of his question. Why did all of us, my brothers included, run around in half-panic, trying to please Dad, especially when cajoling a single compliment out of him was harder than getting him to part with a dollar?

"For someone who's not afraid of your dad's opinion, you're treading pretty damn close to his footsteps," continued Jacob.

I frowned at him, offended. "God, why would you say that?"

"You're both mapmakers." Jacob waved his hand around my studio, at Mom's collage, at the others on the floor. All littered with pieces of world maps. Reproductions of antique maps. Cross-country ski maps. Except for one: my Beauty Map. For that, I only included the inhabitants, the beautiful people.

Dad's work was purely high-tech, coding the software for global positioning systems, first for the military back in the eighties and then spinning off to do consulting work for software mapping companies.

"I'm using maps, not making them," I corrected him.

"I don't know. Looks like you're creating your own atlas. Except you don't sign yours."

My instinct was denial, but I was drawn to Mom's collage again, the map of her life reduced to a floor plan of our kitchen, bounded by her four points of reference: the refrigerator, pantry, stovetop, oven. Hers, all the ones stacked on the floor, my Beauty Map — none of them were signed; none included a mapmaker's cartouche, that highly embellished mark that contains the cartographer's name, date, even the person who commissioned the piece.

Jacob cocked his head to the side. "The question is, where's your map?"

I opened my mouth, closed it without a word. The studio, tiny to start with, hemmed in on me now. I was embarrassed, didn't want him to see my map of beautiful hidden behind Mom's collage. In our silence, I swear, I heard this conversation — his questions — reverberate with the perfect pitch of a hard truth I had no desire to hear. I pushed away from the desk hard and stood up, trembling.

"You don't know what you're talking about," I said.

Jacob went silent, which surprised me. I figured him for a last word kind of guy. So I peered up at his unsmiling face. And then he did the unthinkable in my family: he apologized.

"Sorry," he said, shaking his head ruefully. "Mom says if I don't muzzle it, I'm going to be persona non grata with more than my school administration."

"Let me guess. You were a pain in their ass, too."

"Pretty much. They asked our multimedia teacher to censor our newspaper. So we started a blog and a manga column instead, which got shut down, too. And then I talked about censorship in my speech in competition."

"Competition?"

"Speech and Debate. I do oratory. And Lincoln-Douglas debate."

"Don't you get scared?"

"About what?"

"Talking in public." Being wrong. Exposing your beliefs. Pick your poison. Those were all mine.

"You get used to it. You'd be a great debater," he said.

I shook my head. "Are you kidding? That'd be my nightmare."

"Look at you."

"What?"

Jacob gestured at Mom's collage. "You're not afraid of making statements either."

But he was wrong. Making statements in the privacy of my studio was one thing; declaring them in public something else entirely.

chapter thirteen

Boreas

MOM'S WREATH-MAKING EXTRAVAGANZA WITH NORAH must have inspired her. Just four days later, our house had officially become an oversized Chia Pet, sprouting bushy garlands around every door, window, and staircase. It was Christmas Eve, and I wasn't sure where else Mom was planning to hang these new boughs now blocking the mudroom door. Perhaps around Claudius's and Merc's necks as Pacific Northwest leis. I nudged the greenery aside so I could push the door open, slightly annoyed, but I couldn't blame Mom; I was excited for my brothers to come home, too, for our first family Christmas since Merc moved to China two years ago.

Once inside, I stamped my feet on the rag rug on the mudroom floor to dry my boots before kicking them off. Nothing irritated Dad more than stepping into a puddle of melting snow in his socks. The thick scent of evergreen forest, freshly baked bread, and garlic, lots of garlic, practically assailed my nose. Before I had left this morning for Nest & Egg, I popped eight oiled heads of garlic, carefully wrapped in an aluminum foil cocoon, into the oven, worrying that that wouldn't be enough for all the dishes Mom had been planning. From its pungent scent, Mom had roasted more.

Even though my stomach was distended from my annual Christmas Eve breakfast with the Twisted Sisters at the gallery, I started anticipating Mom's brunch spread. Which was sick. I made a mental note to eke some time before dinner for a hard, fast snowshoe.

On my way to the kitchen, I nearly tripped, swearing under my breath until I spotted the culprits lying innocently on the floor: two battered hiking boots, each the size of a sleeping dog.

"Claudius!" I cried eagerly, sprinting down the hall, and collided head-on into what felt like a flannel-wrapped wall. Before I knew it, I was swept into my brother's long arms, but his hug morphed so fluidly into a choke hold, it barely qualified as affection.

"Hey, I can't breathe!" I protested, and batted his hands away, feeling the familiar ridgeline of scars from one accident or another. For someone who made a hobby of strangling, pummeling, or otherwise threatening me with death by mortification, Claudius was the biggest klutz on the planet. Masochistic, probably, but I missed his torture — and Merc's. Still, I wasn't their easy victim. With a deft move I had learned from watching countless wrestling matches, I almost elbowed Claudius in the gut, but he whirled me around at the last second. So all I got was air.

"Careful of her face," Mom cautioned softly from the stovetop.

Instantly, Claudius released me, and I could have been in elementary school again, him terrorizing me until Mom berated him with that single hated phrase: careful of her face.

I wasn't above taking advantage of our mom-made distraction and punched Claudius in the shoulder. My hand made contact with new muscle. "Ouch." I shook out my stinging hand. "Since when do you work out?"

Claudius curled his bicep so it bulged beneath his flannel shirt. "Squeeze," he said.

I wrinkled my nose. "No, thanks."

"Come on, squeeze."

"Really, no."

My brother — The Klutz, Dad called him ever since he broke his ankle on a stationary bike — now shrugged, a careless lift of his shoulders that would have shook his entire bony body the couple of times I saw him last summer. He claimed the brutal hours at his internship in Seattle made it impossible to drive home on the weekends. Right. I'd seen his pictures on MySpace, and let's just say, he wasn't filing papers all day, every day. Apparently, he wasn't just guzzling beer either. It was as if these last months away from Dad had breathed manhood into Claudius, filling him out in his sophomore year at college. Equal parts of envy and urgency flooded me: I had to get out of here, too.

"Yo, Raisinette —"

Can anyone blame me for aiming a punch at Claudius for using that nickname? Too bad he ducked my blow. When had he gotten so quick on his feet?

"I thought you were done with laser surgery?" he asked, frowning.

I turned to Mom, my getaway vehicle. "I'll plate the food, okay?"

"That'd be great, honey," she said.

Claudius followed me to the kitchen island, unrelenting: "You looked fine." For all his teasing, he was the only one in the family who questioned my treatments. In fact, once when he found me sitting cross-legged in front of the one full-length mirror at home, he had dropped to the floor next to me.

"I'd miss your face if you changed it," he had said, and probably added an insult in the next breath, though I can't remember what exactly.

Whether I was six or sixteen, I wished I could believe him. But just as his namesake, Claudius Ptolemy, had seriously underestimated the size of Earth in his landmark atlas, *Geographia,* my brother seriously underestimated the magnitude of the port-wine stain on my life. And Mom's.

"Hey, aren't you going to say hi to me?" asked Merc, materializing from his old bedroom, his hair standing up like he had just awoken from a nap. Where Claudius and I took after Dad with our height and bony features, Merc was all Mom — huge puppy dog eyes with brown curls, now shot with gray. When had he gotten so old?

Anyway, Merc wasn't supposed to get in until tomorrow, Christmas morning, and I had planned to move my clothes and makeup back to my old closet-sized room upstairs later today for his visit. I gasped, "What are *you* doing here?"

"Great to see you, too." Merc rolled his eyes, but I caught the smile in them. "We hopped on an earlier flight. Claudius picked us up on his way here."

"We?" I asked.

"What do you mean, on my way here? More like a three-hour detour." Claudius snorted while popping a mini-muffin in his mouth. Without warning, he broke into his trademark victory dance, an odd mixture of turkey-head bobbing and gangly arm movements, thankfully unwitnessed since his middle school days. He crowed, "Who's the favorite brother?"

"Please tell me you don't do that in college," I said. I couldn't resist mimicking him, jerking my body convulsively, too. Even Mom took a break from her stirring to laugh.

Naturally, that had to be the moment when the reason behind the "we" in Merc's usual "me" stepped out of the bedroom. The short woman tucked her pixie-cut hair behind one ear and blinked groggily for a better look at our antics.

"You must be Terra," she said.

Embarrassed, I dropped my arms, straightened my body. Not Claudius. He seizure-danced his way to her. I didn't mean to stare — I'm sure anyone would have — and this is saying something: it wasn't his "dancing" that had me gawking, openmouthed. It was the woman who was laughing — now hiding behind Merc to stay out of Claudius's reach. First off, she wasn't Merc's usual type, the extreme athlete who played varsity sports year-round. You know the girls: the ones with messy ponytails who always looked like they'd either just finished working out or were on their way to the gym, the soccer field, the ski slopes. The ones who actually considered a field hockey stick or tennis racquet their favorite accessory. The ones who enjoyed shopping for swimsuits.

This woman was soft. Round. She exuded style from her orange glasses to her brown suede boots. Her brown hair was *coiffed,* for God's sake. Her orangey minidress was decidedly edgy, one that would wear the wearer if she weren't confident. But she wore it easily, not minding that her stomach pooched out or that her thighs were a mite wide for such a short dress.

"Elisa, this clown is my kid sister," said Merc, and my brother, who I've never seen so much as brush shoulders with any of his girlfriends, actually held her hand. Uncomfortable because I felt like I was intruding on an intimate moment, I strode hastily over to Mom, where she was removing a pungent casserole from the oven.

From the corner of my eye, I saw Elisa push her glasses higher on her thin nose, assessing me as frankly as I had her. I couldn't help it. I wrenched around, headed for the refrigerator, wishing I was armored in full makeup. It had been a week since my laser surgery, and while my cheek had calmed down to a claret red instead of figgy purple, there was still only so much makeup could hide. And trust me, I had tried.

But then Elisa disarmed me: "The way Merc talks about you, I have to confess, I'm nervous."

"You have nothing to be nervous about," I said.

"You can say that again," muttered Claudius.

I would have punched him, but he darted well out of my range, now at the table, waiting for food like an oversized Great Dane.

"I hope everyone's hungry," Mom said, handing two plates to me, each heaped with a large wedge of spinach strata, weeping with melted blue cheese. As she waddled back to the stovetop, Mom said, "So Elisa is from Quebec. She's a lawyer, too."

"*Was* a lawyer," Elisa corrected.

"Who could swear at her clients fluently in English, French, and Mandarin," said Merc.

Elisa laughed, bumped her hip against Merc's. My normally reserved brother — ex-girlfriends' claimed corpses were less stiff than him — pulled her close, tucking her under his chin. I exchanged a look with Mom: what alien was inhabiting his body? She smiled back at me, obviously approving of the takeover. I did, too.

"I have my curriculum vitae, too," said Elisa, "if anyone needs to reference-check."

"Dad will," I said, and immediately wished I hadn't. Mom checked the clock nervously.

"Where is he, anyway?" asked Merc as he dropped Elisa's hand.

For Merc to have to ask, he obviously had been away from home too long. I wanted the luxury of forgetting, too.

"Working out," Mom, Claudius, and I answered at the same time, trained clockwatchers, all of us.

"On Christmas Eve?" Elisa grabbed the next set of plates from Mom. "That's dedication."

No, it was stubborn determination, nothing less. Same thing that got me out of bed every morning.

My cell phone rang loudly; I had forgotten I had turned it to full volume so I would hear it above the loud crunching of snow beneath my running snowshoes.

"Someone doesn't want to miss a call," said Claudius.

Actually, someone wanted to miss a call, even if I wanted the satisfaction of receiving it. I wasn't sure who I was avoiding more — Erik for not knowing me at all, or Jacob for knowing me too well. What he'd said, how he'd challenged me in my studio scared me. In either case, I hadn't answered their calls in the last couple of days. Gingerly, I pulled my phone out of the kangaroo pocket in front of my polar fleece pullover. Erik. I hastily set the phone on the table. But I had forgotten how fast Claudius could be; he snatched it from beside my plate before I even reached for it.

"Why are you still going out with that bonehead?" he asked, disapprovingly, eyeballing the caller ID.

"Which bonehead?" jumped in Merc. "You're dating someone?"

"And to think I actually thought I missed you guys," I grumbled, grabbing for my phone. Naturally, Claudius tossed it to Merc.

"Brothers can be so mean," murmured Elisa, but she smiled indulgently at Merc before plucking my cell phone out of his hand and setting it back in mine. "I have five."

"Five? God, you deserve some kind of lifetime achievement award."

"Are you kidding?" Merc nudged a plate closer to her. "She's their little princess. You can't go to her condo without stepping on one of them."

"That's not true," Elisa laughingly protested.

"Oh yeah? She's practically running a boutique hotel, they're always flying in for a visit."

Resentment pricked me like a fine sliver I hadn't noticed until I brushed against it. Why hadn't my brothers called to check on me? Merc had clocked out of our family long ago, but Claudius I could usually count on talking to at least once a week until he had mysteriously stopped returning my calls at the beginning of the school year. Didn't they want to see if I needed anything? To make sure I was surviving Dad?

The garage opened, creaking angrily as if channeling Dad's constant state of irritation. Mom and I exchanged a bewildered look: what was Dad doing home so early? He never broke from his weekend workout program.

No matter how long my brothers had been away, they both fell back into our routine, ingrained by habit and one too many unpleasant consequences. We could have been the inner gears of a delicate chronometer, our movements practiced and dependent on the others. I rushed to the kitchen island, brushing all the crumbs from the counter into my cupped palm while Claudius hauled to the mudroom to put away his boots. Merc inspected the kitchen to make sure nothing else was out of place — not a plate, a fork, or a newspaper. Meanwhile, Mom rewrapped the white cheddar cheese in Saran while she bustled to the refrigerator. I was about to fix Dad a plate when I spotted the butter cubes I had removed that morning to soften at room temperature for baking. Hastily, I handed them to Mom. Neither of us spared a sigh for the butter that had reached the perfect consistency and would just harden back to normal inside the cold confines of the fridge.

Not once had Claudius ever brought home a girlfriend. And for good reason. After all, it had taken a scant millisecond for Dad to dismiss my friend Karin. The reason? She had come over once when she was twelve, her fingernails painted bright red. Apparently, that was a sign of her inner slattern. This, after years of seeing Karin and her doll at our house in matching pigtails, dropping me off at hers with my stuffed bunny. Further proof of Claudius's wise decision was unfolding fast over hors d'oeuvres served in our great room. As usual, Dad was skipping Mom's crab-stuffed mushrooms ("You didn't think to use low-fat cheese?") and whetting his appetite instead with pointed questions that may have been directed at Elisa, but were really aimed at Merc.

"So what exactly do you do in China?" asked Dad where we were gathered around the fireplace, Mom bustling alone in the safety of the kitchen. I eyed Claudius enviously, where he sat apart from us nearest the stairs for a quick getaway, palming one of the glass orbs from a rattan basket Mom had displayed on a side table.

"That's a good question. I'm taking some time off from law. Unlike Merc, I don't thrive on reviewing documents for corporate financings." Elisa speared an olive, popped it into her mouth. "So I'm deciding my next step."

"Your next step," Dad repeated, his mouth downturned, magnetically drawn southward to hell. He shot me a meaningful look. "That's quite a law school bill you racked up to" — he made quote marks in the air — "decide your next step." *Chuckle, chuckle.*

"Better now than never." Elisa grinned, obviously expecting Dad to grin back.

Wrong answer. Dad leaned back in his chair, arms crossed, displeased.

I glowered at Merc, who sat stoically beside Elisa on the sofa like one of the terracotta warriors I had read about when he announced he was moving to China, standing guard for the dead but doing nothing for the living. Since Merc wasn't checking his cell phone or messaging compulsively on his BlackBerry, obviously, Elisa mattered to him. So what was with him not briefing her on what constituted an appropriate response to one of Dad's loaded questions?

Mom staggered into the living room under the weight of yet another tray, this one overflowing with freshly baked bread, warmed brie, and prosciutto-wrapped shrimp. Immediately Elisa made room on the coffee table, nudging aside the platter of mushrooms while I set the heavy basket filled with pinecones the size of loaves next to the fireplace. Claudius was staring at the floor, tossing a cobalt blue globe of glass from hand to hand.

"Sit down," Elisa urged Mom, holding her hand gently so she couldn't leave. "Relax awhile."

Relax? Who was relaxing? Mom glanced at Dad as though she was having the same reservations as I was. Despite his leisurely swirling of a glass of red wine — a four-ounce pour, no more, no less — not even Dad was relaxing. He was waiting.

"Oh," said Mom nervously, casting a look that bordered on wistful at the kitchen, "I still have a few things left to do."

I stood up. "I'll help, Mom."

"It can wait," said Elisa, smiling earnestly.

After a beat, Dad pointed his wine glass at the empty spot next to Merc. "You heard her. It can wait."

Reluctantly, Mom sat on the other side of Merc, so we were lined up, four prisoners on the execution block of the sofa. Elisa sliced herself a tiny wedge of baked brie, settled it on top of bread, and bit. Her eyes closed in food ecstasy.

"You really need to try this," she said, leaning back to give Merc a bite.

Mom scooted to the edge of her seat, reaching for the cheese herself.

No, Mom, don't.

Tonight she was wearing a holiday red sweater. The unfortunate effect of the too-tight sweater was that it accentuated her bulges, more fodder for Dad.

With a smile that was a smidge too smug to be courtly, Dad asked, "So, Elisa, how do you keep your girlish figure?"

Mom's lips pursed from the tart aftertaste of Dad's comment. God. I hated it when he did this, diminished Mom with compliments aimed at other women.

"Yoga," Elisa replied.

"Hmmm, you should try that, Lois," Dad said to Mom.

Either oblivious or determined to ignore the undercurrents, Elisa peered closely at the swag draped on the mantelpiece and coiled like an evergreen boa around the burning soy candles. She turned to Mom, waving around the room. "Merc said you made all of this?"

"Oh, it's nothing." Still, Mom smiled, pleased, and she set her morsel of brie onto a tiny plate. That, she perched on the precarious ledge of her lap that wasn't already claimed by her stomach. "Terra helped out so much."

"No, this is all you, Mom," I corrected her. Unfortunately, there was only one man Mom would ever be tempted to leave Dad for, and that man was a myth. I don't mean a mythic romantic hero, such as Mr. Darcy or even Orlando Bloom. But Santa Claus, the red-suited wonder. I bragged, "Give Mom a few accessories, and she could make any place feel homey."

"I can see that," said Elisa, glancing around appreciatively. "There's just one thing missing."

I frowned. "What?"

"Your art."

Swallowing hard, I set down the glass of sparkling cider I had just picked up. Not this, not now, not with Dad listening.

"Your mom told me about your show, Terra," explained Elisa. "You all must be so proud of Terra."

I almost choked on that thought. Proud? Dad had yet to look me in the face since my laser surgery.

"Your collages are going to look so wonderful up," Mom said, putting her arm around me, hugging me close to her soft body.

"Oh, not really," I demurred. She was completely unaware that her second cracker, piled with an even larger wedge of cheese, came dangerously close to scratching my exposed cheek. I could smell the cheese, the rich, slightly rank scent making my stomach churn.

"Terra's first show," Dad boomed for the listening benefit of Elisa. I tensed. I couldn't help it. The cut couldn't be long from now. He smiled, teeth showing, a human hyena — all *chuckle, chuckle* — while preparing for the kill. "Too bad she didn't think to do this a couple of weeks ago. She could have included it in her college applications."

I shot Elisa a sharp look: *Don't say anything.* But she murmured, "I'm sure Terra will get in wherever she applies."

That was a bragging opportunity any normal parent would seize: *Why, yes, she already got into her top choice, Williams.* Mine were silent, Mom nibbling on her cheese, Dad scanning the newspaper in his lap.

"So does anyone want anything?" I asked. Mom was the only one without a beverage. "Mom, something to drink?"

As soon as I uttered the words, I wanted to take them back. They were a beacon, directing Dad's attention to the half-eaten wedge of brie in Mom's hand.

"Should you be eating that? Your diabetes and all," he said, concerned husband.

"I don't have diabetes," Mom said softly.

"Your doctor warned you." *I'm warning you.* He looked over at Elisa with a helpless shrug, implying: Gosh, it's hard to be the responsible one, isn't it?

I couldn't stand it: Mom eating what she shouldn't. Dad pointing it out to her. All of us pretending we were a normal, healthy family. Every one of my repressed retorts to Dad's piercing comments felt ready to burst free, here in the living room.

"Still eating?" he asked Mom softly, the cobra ready to strike. He looked at me again, meaningfully: *Take the food away from Mom.*

Impulsively, I opened my mouth to tell Dad where he could stuff the cheese. I wasn't his personal garbage disposal.

But Elisa interjected, "Merc framed the piece of art you made for him last Christmas, Terra. It's the first thing you see when you walk into his apartment."

"Really?" I said. Merc had never even acknowledged he'd received the collage, much less thanked me for it. He was too busy, I had told myself. Now, he nodded briefly as if that admission had cost him, as if he knew what this conversation was going to cost me.

The smirk on Dad's face deepened like he was enjoying his own private joke. "I have one of Terra's kindergarten pieces up in my office." *Chuckle, chuckle.*

"I'm sure she was the best of her class then, too." Elisa leaned over to slice another wedge of brie cheese, placed it on a cracker, and offered it to Merc. He shook his head, no thanks. So she urged it on me. "I would love a Terra original. Do you have anything I could buy?"

Dad scoffed, "You mean, pay for her cutting and pasting?"

Only now did Elisa's smile waver, finally feeling Dad's verbal bullets hitting closer and closer to their mark. Finally understanding that hubris was never a threat in the Cooper household with him on the watch. It was like witnessing Joan of Arc prepping for a battle she hadn't consciously set out to lead, the role thrust on her. She first eyed Merc, then Mom, Claudius. Me. Cowards, we all found something else to focus on. Coming to each other's defense usually worsened things, like the time when Merc backed Claudius's decision to major in English, and Dad threatened to stop paying for Claudius's education, period. (Claudius was now majoring in chemical engineering.) So Elisa charged forward with a mild "A lot of experts consider collage one of the most important art forms to come out of the twentieth century."

Dad made an impatient motion with his hand. "They also call paint splotches art."

"Oh, you should come by Nest & Egg tomorrow and see some local art," I told Elisa, hoping to derail her and diffuse Dad's rising anger.

"Picasso, Man Ray, Miró, Motherwell — they all used collage," Elisa continued relentlessly. "Just like you, Terra."

There was a deadly pause. Never box Dad in, never make him look bad, or worse, ignorant. Now he leaned forward, hands clenched into fists. For a second there, I thought he was going to lunge for her, but he swiped the *Economist* magazine from the shelf beneath the coffee table.

"We should go," Merc said in a low voice, standing up.

"What?" Elisa cried, her eyebrows furrowed. She ignored Merc's outstretched hand. "We're just having a healthy discussion."

She looked over at Dad for confirmation; he ignored her just as she had Merc's lifeline of a hand. See, that was it; there was nothing healthy about a discussion at our house. There was only one opinion that counted: Dad's. He snapped the covers of the magazine open, busied himself with reading about this week's news. Tonight's was in the making, right here before our eyes.

"Come on, Elisa," Merc urged. I could hear the *please* in the weighted silence after his words.

She studied Merc, then nodded. This time, she took his hand and followed him out of the great room, cold now despite the wood blazing in the fireplace. I shivered. Boreas, the brutal North Wind, had made his icy presence known.

As soon as Merc's bedroom door closed, Dad's accusatory gaze roved the great room and stopped on Mom like a hawk spotting a hapless rabbit. I was surprised to see she had actually trailed Merc and Elisa to the edge of the hall, a stormchaser who had turned her back on the real storm advancing stealthily.

As Dad's mouth opened, Claudius stood, glass globe in his big hand. He said flatly, "You're crazy."

Dad's jaw worked as he leapt out of his leather chair to his feet. "What did you say? What the hell did you say?"

"I said, you're crazy."

That was the worst possible insult Claudius could have leveled at a man who prided himself on being, above all else, highly rational, always logical, supremely fair. And completely delusional, but none of us told him that. Dad quickly closed the distance between him and Claudius. A year ago — a summer ago — Claudius would have cowered. He would have teared up. He would have apologized. Today, they stood facing each other — no longer nose-to-nose. Dad was a complete inch shorter. When had he shrunk? When had Claudius grown?

"Claudius," said Mom softly, cowering, an apologetic expression already creasing her forehead, curving her lips.

But Dad stepped even closer to Claudius, who didn't rear back. Instead, my brother pulled back his fisted hand. It hovered there, Polaris the North Star in our living room.

For a long moment, Dad stared at that balled threat in disbelief. We all did.

"Claudius, just stop," Mom pled.

And then Dad snapped, "You want to hit me? You want to hit me?" He angled his face, exposing his cheek. "Hit me, then."

Still, Mom didn't make a move toward them, didn't separate them with her own body. Instead, she was breathing little pants of fear, a trapped animal. And then, there it was. Her look. Aimed straight at me, that look that willed me to act, to intervene, to sacrifice myself, if need be.

I forced myself to Claudius's side, and I said the words I never thought I would hear myself speak: "Claudius, you should go."

He turned to me, startled and betrayed, his hand lowering so that now he gripped the glass ornament between both palms.

"Just go," I whispered, nodding to his bedroom door.

His answer was a sound of shattering glass, accompanied by a sharp "shit!" I gasped. Blood dripped from Claudius's hand to the hardwood floor.

"God, what did you do now?" Dad asked. "What the hell did you do now?"

Honestly, it was obvious. The tension in our house had felt so taut I could have crushed it in my hands. Claudius had done just that. The glass orb he had been clenching had shattered, squeezed to the breaking point between his hands. And now, Claudius, shaking, tried to pull a jagged shard from his bleeding palm.

Dad turned on Mom, vicious as a starved dog. "God dammit, Lois, I told you it was completely idiotic to put glass on display."

"I'm sorry, I'm sorry," Mom said, flustered, trembling.

I wasn't even aware that I echoed her words — "I'm sorry, I'm sorry" — as I led Claudius away from Dad and to the kitchen, where I could flush out his wound in the sink.

"It's not *your* fault," Claudius told me, glaring at the great room, leaving no doubt whom he was blaming.

Neither of us dared another word when Dad stalked into the kitchen, clenching Claudius's coat, his own forgotten.

"We're going to the hospital," Dad barked. "Now."

Even as Dad marched out of the house, pushing Claudius ahead of him, Mom shuffling behind, I could hear the ghost of our collective "I'm sorry, I'm sorry," as everyone but Dad accepted the blame, apologizing to each other for much more than this latest accident.

chapter fourteen

Orienteering

MERC HADN'T BEEN HOME FOR more than eight hours, and here he was, packing to leave. From where I stood in the hall, I could hear Merc and Elisa arguing in their bedroom. The candles around the great room had burned low, flickering moodily as if dancing to their belligerent tone.

"Aren't you overreacting a little?" asked Elisa. "God, your brother is headed to the hospital."

"It was a mistake to come here." Merc was as implacable as Dad.

"Or do you mean, it was a mistake to bring me here?"

No answer.

I retreated to the kitchen, removed all the different dishes still warming in the oven, our Christmas Eve banquet.

"I'll leave," said Elisa. "You should stay."

Another grim pause and then Merc: "I don't have to take his bullshit anymore."

"But the bullshit wasn't about you. I'm a big girl. I can handle it."

"That's just it. I don't want you to have to handle it."

Quietly but firmly, Elisa said, "But you weren't either."

I swallowed hard, leaned my head against the cold steel of the refrigerator door. I could imagine how Mom and Dad started this way early in their marriage: one placating, the other fuming. When had the tenor of their arguments completely changed so it wasn't about calming, working things out, but blaming? What had happened so that all the power coalesced with Dad, vanished from Mom?

I couldn't stand the fighting anymore, and before I could think better of it, I crossed the kitchen to stand before Merc's bedroom. He was in the adjoining bathroom, hastily stuffing his toiletries back into his shaving kit with Elisa looking on. She was shaking her head, disapproving. Or disillusioned. I couldn't tell.

"You can't leave already. You just got here," I said. I waved in the direction of the kitchen. "Dinner's ready. . . ."

Merc flinched, glanced at me, and then looked away guiltily, busying himself with recapping his toothpaste.

I couldn't modulate my voice, which came out as a wail, an accusation, a plea: "I haven't seen you in two years."

"We've got to go," he said simply, and then brushed his hand impatiently through his thick hair, leaving his curls even more unruly.

Elisa closed in on Merc carefully as though she were caging a wild beast. "Maybe we can stay at a hotel or something."

"The River Rock Lodge," I offered. "I'll bet there's room. I'll call now."

"No," said Merc. He zipped the shaving kit, tucked it under his arm like a football. I half expected him to thrust his arm out, barrel past Elisa and me to the front door. But Merc stopped at the bed, wadded up the jeans that he had left on the floor, and wedged them into his luggage.

"You're not really leaving, are you?" I asked, dismayed. "Mom's been planning this for six months. You should have seen her these last couple of weeks. She made all your favorite food."

At first, I thought maybe I had broken through to Merc. He was closer to Mom than any of us, or at least he had been when he lived at home. He held his green T-shirt like he had forgotten he was folding it. But then he scrunched that, too, and stuffed it into his luggage. Without a word to me, he strolled to the door where I was still standing. Maybe now he'd tell me that, of course, he'd suck it up and stay at the local resort. Or maybe he'd relent and stay here and I'd pack my things and move back upstairs for the week the way it had been planned. Instead, he bent down to grab his briefcase. I stared dumbly at him as he threw the strap over his shoulder and then lifted his luggage and Elisa's off the bed. With one last regretful look at me, he was out the door.

"I'm so sorry," said Elisa, looking at me sadly. She wrapped her arms around me, hugging me hard so I got a whiff of green tea and peonies, like she was wearing China on her. And just as swiftly, she held me away from her and murmured, "I'll see if I can change his mind."

Merc was waiting at the front door, his BlackBerry already out as if this latest episode with Dad had shaken off the easygoing personality he had been trying on. The affectionate, carefree boyfriend was gone. Mr. Let's Make a Business Plan was back. Still, how could Merc focus on the bottom line now? A car outside honked, its headlights flooding our entry.

"Where are you staying?" I asked.

"At a friend's," said Merc. He shifted his briefcase uncomfortably in his hand, guilty at being so eager to leave again. "Call me about Claudius."

I nodded, not trusting myself to say anything. I didn't want to cry in front of them, not with Elisa looking at me so pityingly. So I waved hurriedly like I had a billion more important things to do, shut the door, and then watched them blearily through the window. When Merc had left for college, I was in first grade. Back then, I didn't realize my big brother was leaving for good. I did now. As soon as the rear lights vanished, I sequestered myself in the kitchen, putting away the rest of the dishes Mom had painstakingly prepared, starting a week ago. Then I wandered around the house, blowing out the candles one by one until I reached the great room. There, near the hearth, was the shattered glass globe, bits of our crumbled world mingled with Claudius's blood. I got the broom, swept away the evidence of our fractured family, and as I was about to throw the glass away, I scavenged the largest shard, placing it on the empty coffee table where I wouldn't forget it. Back in the kitchen, I filled the sink with hot water and a cup of vinegar, the way Mom disinfected our floors every Monday and Friday. With an old rag, I got to my knees and mopped up the blood.

Finished, I let my weariness became a shroud, wrapping around my limbs, my face. Even though it was just six — when Christmas Eve dinner was supposed to be served — I grabbed the piece of glass I had salvaged and shuffled to my bathroom. Bed, I yearned for my bed. But I halted before the mirror. My face was molting. Tears and nervous sweat had made a mess of my makeup, cutting runoff lines down my cheek. A couple of weeks ago, after Mrs. Frankel so helpfully pointed out my obvious acne to me, I broke down and bought a new cleanser. Now, I used it to wash my mottled mask off, gently patted my face dry. The mere act of sudsing my face usually freed me to breathe as though I had removed a punishing corset. But tonight, my lungs felt so tight, so squeezed, I could have been petrifying from my insides out. I slipped into one of Claudius's old oversized T-shirts and fell into bed.

About an hour later, the doorbell rang. Irrationally, I expected it to be Merc come back to spend a merry Christmas with us. So I bounded light as Santa's reindeer to the front door, sure it couldn't possibly be my parents. The nearest hospital was forty-five minutes away. Besides, they'd enter through the garage.

No sooner did I open the door than my grin faltered at the same time as Erik's. He couldn't quite mask the shock of seeing me au naturel any more than I could have feigned real excitement at seeing him, makeup or no makeup. As he continued to stare, I wanted to point to my cheek and remind him, *But you were the one who wanted this, remember? You're the one who asked — and I repeat — Why not fix your face?*

"You're Terra?" asked a guy I hadn't seen, hidden as he had been behind Erik. They had the same stocky build, the same pale coloring. This had to be his cousin Max.

Despite Erik's mumbled introduction, I discerned his meaning all too clearly: he was embarrassed to be associated with me. The girl he wanted to show off was the one in the pictures he tacked in his locker, displayed on his bedroom wall, the blonde with a killer body in a string bikini, wearing a ton of makeup and not much else. Instead, he had crashed onto a land he had known about but had never seen. Me, uncovered. Terra Incognita.

If I hadn't felt ugly enough standing there with his head ducked down, studying the piled snow off the porch, I was fully aware that I was wearing Claudius's graying T-shirt. All in all, not my best sartorial moment.

The awful thing was, I couldn't stop smiling at him and his cousin, my mouth embalmed in a fake grin. And that's when it hit me — where I'd seen Erik's expression before. Why it was so painfully familiar. It was the same expression Dad wore in public with Mom, sheepish and mortified rolled into one uncomfortable mass. Terra Humiliata.

The fact was, I was sick of it. Tired of hiding my face. Tired of apologizing for it. So I did what Jacob told me to do. Let them stare. I didn't even avert my face a single degree. I just told Max flatly, "I had laser surgery last week to lighten my birthmark," as if it was no big deal.

"Oh yeah?" he said. Unexpectedly, Max swiveled around, yanked his pants down.

"God," I said, holding my hand over my eyes. The last thing I thought I had wanted to see tonight was Merc walking out the door. I was wrong. It was this stranger's rear end. "Please don't tell me this is one of those stripping telegrams?"

Max laughed and said to Erik, "You didn't tell me she was so funny."

I heard Erik's answer in his silence: *I didn't know she was so funny.*

And then, as if I could miss the big, black block letters tattooed just under his waistline, Max tapped the girl's name on his hip: Eden. Apparently, Eden was a polluted paradise. "You think that laser could take this off?"

"I don't know," I said.

He looked crestfallen.

"But I could ask my surgeon the next time I see her," I offered.

"Yeah?"

I nodded.

"Very cool," said Max, grinning at me, and then, thankfully, jerking his pants up where they belonged.

"Yeah, but word of advice, no more girlfriend names. And if you insist on doing that again, avoid the butt. Being on a guy's ass isn't a compliment. Got it?"

"I hear you."

Erik looked relieved and bewildered at this exchange, more wordy than any conversation he and I shared. Then he handed me a present, so exquisitely wrapped with perfectly sharp creases and embellished with bells and ribbons, I knew it had to be his mother's work.

"You better open it alone," he said, a real smile now. I cringed inside. Why did it have to be such a suggestive leer?

"You didn't have to," I said. I tried to find something more to say to him, came up blank. And then, because the neurotic artist in me had to know: "So did you open my present?"

He nodded, relieved. His way out of our conversational black hole, too. "Yeah, it was cool."

"Cool?" I had an image then of Jacob standing in my studio, how he had somberly called my collages provocative. I recovered, smiled at Erik. "Okay, cool."

Later, after Erik and Max left to join their families for Christmas Eve dinner, it was a good thing I unwrapped his gift alone in my bedroom, door locked, blinds drawn. Inside the box was a slinky nightie, fuchsia, a color never before seen on my body — except, obviously, in Erik's fantasies. It rankled, that flimsy piece of polyester, especially since I was a cotton T-shirt–wearing kind of gal. I didn't even bother taking the lingerie out of the box. Whoever said it was the thought that counted was wrong, dead wrong. Did he really think I wanted this? That I would wear it for him? Like, when, exactly, was that going to happen? And worse, did his mom know what she had been wrapping? Or, oh God, I groaned, threw myself back onto the bed. She hadn't picked it out, had she?

But then again, for all I knew, Erik's reaction to my collage could have been the same as mine to his lingerie: bewilderment and not a little mortification that I knew him so little. It didn't matter that I had spent the better part of the week working on it, that ode to us. After discarding image after image, I had finally settled on a gothic cross for the focal point, a reminder of when we had gotten together over Halloween. But when I had affixed the photograph of the cross over the map of the Northwest, I couldn't help but think of a certain Goth guy. And how I suspected, as I propped the wrapped art on Erik's doorstep this morning, that I was giving it to the wrong boy.

chapter fifteen

Here Be Dragons

CHRISTMAS MORNING WAS SUPPOSED TO dawn clear and blue, according to the meteorologists. It was still black when I woke. My eyes were drawn to the out-of-date world map hanging over the foot of my bed. I couldn't see the lines or colors, the room too dark for that. But I could picture the world's borderlines in my head, long since inaccurate because the countries themselves had changed after the map was printed in 1990: Germany reunifying, the Soviet Union dissolving. Estonia declared independence. So had Namibia. And now almost two decades later, Merc had declared his, leaving abruptly last night. What did that signal if not that he didn't need or want us at all?

I rolled to my side and peered between the slats into the darkness, where, far off, the North Star twinkled. Downstairs, Mom was rustling in the kitchen, unable to sleep either. She was probably whipping up a batch of butter-laden shortbread. Or maybe double chocolate brownies, Claudius's favorite. If she couldn't soothe our family, she'd soothe our stomachs. Claudius's palm only needed a few stitches last night; luckily, the glass hadn't severed any important nerves. Unlike the news that Merc and Elisa had left. As soon as I broke that to Mom, she had started crying, great, heaving sobs the way she had when her sister died. Not caring that Dad was watching and listening, Mom had collapsed at the kitchen table. He had actually approached her, and I bristled, suspicious of his intentions. Dad saw my glare. He turned around and hastened to his office, head hanging low.

I had been so mad — mad at Dad for his belated remorse, mad at Merc for leaving, mad at myself for not being able to stop Merc. Without thinking, I sent my brother a scathing e-mail, telling him what I couldn't say in person. Even now, I could feel my accusations spitting acid words from my computer:

> You should hear Mom crying now. She's been waiting for 2 years to see you again. First, you don't call us, not even once in the last year. And then you forget her birthday. How hard is it to remember? Valentine's Day, Mom's birthday. And then you just bailed.

Well, you get the gist.

Apparently, Jacob was right; I'm good at making statements. It's the fallout that I can't handle. And if there was one thing I was certain about, it was that my brother, Mr. Married to My BlackBerry, had read my message. If he answered, it would be no different from his irregular missives: a handful of inadequate words, all lowercase because he couldn't waste a split second on holding down the shift key to capitalize anything.

Unable to stand another second communing with my inner critic, I threw off the heavy duvet, the flannel sheets. I padded to my closet, reached over to flick on the light. The glare of the bulb inside my closet reflected off Merc's framed diploma from Western Washington, one more relic he'd left behind in this room, a reminder of a past he no longer wanted. Or needed.

Over my huge T-shirt, I wrenched on a thick, shapeless sweater. Then I foraged for some thermal underwear as well as my polar fleece pants from the dirty laundry bin. I smelled them — not bad. Besides, what did it matter? I wouldn't see anyone this early.

My headlamp was still hanging around my bed knob where I had left it yesterday morning. Behind me, I shut the bedroom door softly and crept to the mudroom and broke out of this homegrown jail.

The wind nipped at my uncovered fingers, ghostly teeth hungry for flesh, as I strapped on my snowshoes outside the mudroom. Clumsily, I thrust my boot into the openings in the metal shoes, snapped the ankle strap, and then tugged my favorite mittens on. I wiggled my fingers beneath the pilled polar fleece, and when that didn't thaw them, I rubbed my hands together. My warm bed upstairs beckoned, but so did my insomnia. I had already wasted enough time beating myself up, especially considering Dad had done such a thorough job of that in my head. So I grabbed my poles and set off on the trail behind the house.

Once I rounded the bend, the lights in Dad's office switched on, a warden sensing an escapee. I couldn't help myself; I stopped, stared up at his Aerie perched atop the house. Which, as Claudius had snickered once, was what Hitler called his own retreat and hideout in Obersalzberg, the eagle's nest.

I imagined Dad up there, pounding away at his bank of computers, surrounded by the most precious of his antique map collection. Overhead on the ceiling was the mural he'd commissioned of the Mappa Mundi, the medieval map that divided the world into three unequal parts — not unlike our family. Dad commanded the bulk of our world,

Mom and me splitting the bottom half, side-by-side. Merc and Claudius? They were safely off the grid. In a bit, Dad would take a break, open a book of travel essays, and read about expeditions pitting man against the wild in some epic adventures he'd never take.

Like me.

Let's face it; the second I stepped a single degree outside my comfort zone, I regretted it the way I did my rash e-mail to Merc. The wind rattled the fat boughs of an evergreen tree, somehow spared a shearing by Mom. I trudged through the snow at a quick pace, now warming too fast. A trickle of sweat slid down my back. Go slower, I told myself. Stop rushing. A week post-op, I still wasn't supposed to sweat and irritate my broken capillaries. Besides, it wasn't like I was in any big rush to return home.

At the edge of our property, I switched off my headlamp. The stars cast enough light so I could pick out my trail, which I knew by heart. I had just turned my back on the view of the open valley when a furtive motion to my right startled me. Most likely, it was just a deer. Bears didn't venture out just yet, but you never knew. Two years ago, a cougar meandered down the mountains to a neighbor's house, forced out of its usual haunts in the protected national forest by hunger. I looked for a large branch, but didn't find one. If I couldn't outrun the animal, I'd blind it. I whirled to face the noise as I switched on my headlamp.

"Could you aim your light somewhere else . . . ," said the one voice I'd managed to dodge successfully for the last few days, ". . . unless you plan on blinding me, too?"

"God!" I jerked back, stumbled, and fell on my butt in the snow.

A dark figure appeared before me. Laconically, Jacob held out his hand. "If you wanted to see me, all you had to do was say so."

"I didn't want to see you!"

"That's what they all say."

They? Who, they? As in other girls?

"You're the one at my house at five in the morning," I pointed out.

Jacob laughed, pulling me to my feet. "For the record that makes twice you've practically run me over."

"Excuse me?"

For a second, I thought he was reaching for my face. Instead, he turned off my headlamp and held my hand while my eyes readjusted to the darkness. He may or may not have had a girlfriend, but I most definitely still had a boyfriend. So I pretended to cough, pulled away from him, and began babbling. Honestly, I have no recollection what I said, just that words spewed out of me.

"You okay?" he interrupted.

"I'm fine." I smiled brightly.

Jacob shook his head. "Don't."

"Don't what?"

"Don't fake it."

His honesty stung almost more than the blasts of laser on my cheek. I stepped back from him, spinning away from his gaze that stripped away the defenses that fooled everybody else. I faced the dark, hulking mountains.

"Hey," he said, and touched my arm. "What's up?"

I admitted, "Christmas sucks."

"Tell me about it."

I glanced at him and then really studied him, this boy who could disarm me with a few words. Jacob, as usual, was in the wrong getup for this weather — and for this town — in his head-to-toe Goth black. That thin trench coat. Those flimsy Vans. At least today he had on gloves and a polar fleece beanie. He shifted the shovel he was carrying over his shoulder.

"I hate to ask what you're planning to do with that," I said, and then added more curiously, "and what exactly are you doing here at this hour?"

"Geocaching for Kryptonite."

"Geocaching?"

"Yeah, it's like Easter egg hunting with a GPS." He lowered the shovel to the ground and pulled a cell phone–sized device from his trench coat pocket. "You know, global positioning software —"

"I know what GPS is. My dad does work for some GPS companies." I narrowed my eyes at him suspiciously. "Is this some kind of weird Seattle thing?"

"You kidding? Geocaching is a worldwide adventure game. People hide treasure caches everywhere, even in Antarctica. You just load in latitude and longitude coordinates to find them."

"And people actually go look for them?"

"Well, yeah."

"Why?" I demanded.

"Because it's fun."

"You're kidding."

He laughed at me then. I had the suspicion that he was enjoying my dubious reaction. "Yeah, it's fun to take something from the cache and then leave something."

"Like what?"

Shrugging, Jacob answered, "Toys, stickers, pins. Anything small. And then you write about your find in the logbook."

"This is very geeky."

He frowned in disbelief. "I can't believe you, daughter of a GPS designer, have never geocached."

I shook my head. "My dad thinks it's illegal to have fun."

"Well, you know what they say."

"What?"

"There's a first for everything." Jacob consulted the GPS device and faced north, where there was no path, just untouched snow. Untouched by human feet, at least. I could make out the slender holes punched in from deer hooves. Much too boisterously for five in the morning, he said, "Okay, this way. The Kryptonite is close."

"You've got to be kidding me, right? Kryptonite where I live?"

"Apparently. That's the name of the geocache, anyway." Jacob stepped off my path away from me.

I didn't follow.

He paused. "We won't know if it's here unless we look."

We. I flushed at that. Stop it, I told myself. He was not my type. But then again, was Erik, who had stood on my own doorstep and pretended not to know me in front of his cousin?

Jacob eyed my well-trodden path, the one I had stomped along every day this winter and the winter before that. I still hadn't budged off it. He followed the trail to the hill, where it disappeared. "So you always go the same way every day?"

"So?"

"So." Jacob returned to me, holding out his GPS device. "Lead the way."

For as long as Dad used to work on the software that ran these devices, I could count the number of times I had actually held one. Maybe twice. Definitely no more than three times. They freaked me out, that unerring ability to find someone's exact position. Frankly, I wouldn't have put it past Dad to implant some kind of tracking device inside me and Mom so he could pinpoint our location, every minute of every day. I shivered, wrapped my arms around myself. Despite the unrelenting cold, I dithered.

"You know," Jacob said conversationally, as if he had all the time in the world while he was getting frostbitten, too, "two days after Clinton ordered the Defense Department to turn off the jamming signal so civilians could use GPS, the first geocache was logged and hidden. A big, old five-gallon bucket of prizes."

"Really?" I couldn't help it. I was intrigued. "That's the last thing the military probably thought their tracking system would be used for: games."

"And five days after that, there was a cache logged all the way over in Australia."

I looked past him into the vast darkness. "And now there's a cache here."

"And now there's a cache over there somewhere." He jerked his head northward.

"Why would anyone put a cache here?"

He shrugged.

"My path ends up over that way, you know," I told him.

"We can make our own."

The stars were still gleaming in the dark morning sky. I gripped the GPS tightly in my hand, easily imagining the satellites circling up there, some 12,000 miles overhead, providing the directions we needed to locate this Kryptonite. I shot him a challenging look before I stepped deliberately off my trail. He grinned and slipped, his Vans providing zero traction in the snow.

I sighed, walked in front of him. "Just so you know," I said over my shoulder, "I'm only doing this to keep you from killing yourself." I set off, GPS in hand, my snowshoes forging a new wide path across the pristine snow with Jacob's soft laughter accompanying me.

"You know, those devices require user guidance," Jacob called up to me after we had been trudging for a few minutes.

"You don't say." I finally turned around, hands on my hips. "What happened to relaxing? Enjoying the ride? Stopping and smelling the coffee?"

"Are you quoting me?" He glowed — he actually went radioactive — with glee.

I spun around fast, or as fast as I could with snowshoes on my feet. His laughter splashed over me, rich and smooth, caramel macchiato. What I wanted to do was turn back, tackle him, taste that laughter on his lips. . . .

I cleared my throat, forced myself forward as I read the GPS for the coordinates and veered sharply so that we had to step over a boulder mounded with snow.

"You know, sometimes the most direct route isn't the right one," he said, almost losing his balance on the rock.

"Hey, I'm making this up as we go."

"And where are we going, exactly?"

"North . . . ish."

"North-ish." A pause, and then: "Is that Terra for I'm lost-ish?"

I couldn't help it. I laughed. "I'm directionally challenged, what can I say?"

"Give me that," he said, commandeering the GPS and after a brief consultation, quarter-turning. "This way."

"Which way would that be?"

"West . . . ish." His feet slipped on the snow.

"Honestly," I said, tramping up to his side, "you wouldn't last a day in the backcountry."

"And you would?"

"I'd survive . . . I'd just be lost."

"So we'd make a great team," he said, sliding again. This time, he grabbed me for balance, and we both tumbled.

"Ouch!" I said, my forehead knocking against his chin. "Shit! My face."

But I forgot all about my face, any pain, any potential scarring, because somewhere in our fall, his arms had slipped around me, taking the impact. He rolled me over to my back, looked down at me anxiously, and then breathed out, relieved. "You're okay."

His face was so close, it was tempting to pull his head, those lips, to me.

"God," he murmured, his breath on my cheek making me shiver. "I forgot you were the trouble magnet."

"Me?" I poked him in the chest. "You were the one who pulled me down with you."

Jacob merely grinned, swift, teasing, warm, and then he lay back on the snow, gazing up at the fading stars. I blinked at his profile, wanting nothing more than to lean over his chest, kiss him. But Erik. There was Erik. I jerked back, confused, and tugged my parka down so my bottom was on it instead of directly icing on the snow.

"You've been avoiding me," he said, still staring overhead. He actually sounded miffed. "You didn't return my calls."

"Christmas has been . . . stressful."

"Or was it because of what I said in your studio?"

I sat up, uncomfortable with this conversation, and would have set off except I didn't know which way to go. Slowly, Jacob faced me. His stare was so probing I could have been back on the operating table, the unrelenting overhead light glaring down on me.

"You really want to know why I don't want to be in that show?" I asked, hugging my knees as close as the unwieldy snowshoes would allow.

"Yeah."

"I'm afraid people will laugh. No." I shook my head, tired of my denials. "I mean, I'm afraid my dad will laugh."

The wind blew but didn't rumple his hair. It was too shellacked with gel to move. Jacob nodded. "I can see that."

For a second, I was taken aback, hurt that he thought my artwork was laughable. I mean, I didn't think my collages were exactly worthy of anyone's private collection, but they weren't all that bad, either. Were they?

"Everyone laughed at the Impressionists. Monet, he was a complete joke," Jacob said. The sun was peeking over the hill now so I could see the black stubble over his lip. "And the pointillists like Seurat. Are you kidding me? Oh, and Jackson Pollock. No one could stop laughing at his drips of paint."

As he listed one master after another, I went completely speechless.

"How do you know all this?" I demanded.

He hesitated. "My dad's an art history buff."

No way in a million years could I ever have imagined a content-rich conversation like this with Erik, much less at five fifteen in the morning, me without makeup, reeking in yesterday's workout clothes, and sporting a dopey headlight around my forehead.

"So, really," continued Jacob as if this were perfectly normal to expound on art in these circumstances, "when you think about it, the artists who make people stop and think, who push the form, who make you uncomfortable, who are laughable, well, they're the ones who get remembered." Idly, Jacob dug a hole in the snow with his shovel and then another one next to it. "So why wouldn't you want to join the ranks of the ridiculed?"

I had to laugh. Really, I did. My face burned, all those facial muscles needed to form a smile. But I didn't mind. When I stopped laughing, I didn't flinch under his steady gaze that peeled away all the hardened layers I'd decoupaged over myself — years of denials, Covermark, fake smiles.

"That's not what's really holding you back though," he guessed.

How did he do that? Excavate the truth armed only with his divining rod of persistent questions? Discomfited, I bent over to pick a lone pinecone lodged in the snow. I threw it as far as I could and admitted softly, a dirty secret, "I need money."

"And?"

"Artists aren't exactly rolling in dough."

"Point taken. But aren't you forgetting something?" A pause, then, "What if someone wants to buy your artwork?"

I thought about Elisa, who claimed she loved my artwork, who asked if I had anything to sell. Even if she had only said that to get in good with her boyfriend's kid sister, the very fact that she sounded like she meant it had made me feel good. Still made me feel good.

"So," I said, brushing my hair out of my face. I had to know. "Are you? Laughing at my art?"

He answered solemnly, "My stomach would rupture if I laughed any harder."

I smiled, relieved and pleased that he thought my art was decent. *Ridiculously* relieved and way too pleased. I should have been alarmed that what Jacob thought — a guy I met a scant week ago — meant so much to me. But I wasn't.

"Okay, then," I said, standing.

"Okay, then." He held his hand out, and I pulled, helping him to his feet. With my hand still nestled in his, he asked, "Forgiven?"

I flushed, grateful that it was too dark for him to see what his touch did to me — and this through a mitten. "There's nothing to forgive. You were just being honest."

"Then here's the deal. We'll be honest with each other." He took off his glove, held out his hand, waited for me to do the same. "No bullshit."

Skin to skin in the cold, we shook hands.

A wind rattled the sage bushes around us. Standing there, unmoving, I became distinctly aware of how frigid the air was, despite the rising sun.

"Let's go," I said, working my mitten back on.

Jacob nodded, checked the GPS, and then grinned at me. "So tell me, am I good? Or am I good? According to this" — he waved the yellow device — "we are exactly where we ought to be."

"We are?" I looked around at the small clearing, seeing nothing resembling treasure or Kryptonite. "So now what?"

"So now we look."

"For what?"

"A small box." After a few minutes of us tromping aimlessly around, forming crop circles in the snow, Jacob mentioned, "There *was* a clue."

My teeth chattered with cold. "Now you tell me?"

"Yeah." He pulled out a printed sheet with coordinates. "I'm a geocaching purist, but in times of extreme discomfort —"

"Like impending frostbite?"

"— then I give in." So he read the clue: "'Sit down and enjoy the view.'"

"That's the clue? Sit down and enjoy the view?"

"That's what it said on the geocaching site."

"What kind of clue is that?"

Jacob sniffled, his nose running. "Having fun?"

I shot him a dirty look. "Tell me again why we're doing this?"

He crouched down, brushed away some twigs beneath a snow-mounded sage bush. There was nothing but compacted dirt. A snowdrift fell onto his head when he released his hold on the bush. He shook the powder off and finally answered, "This is what I did with my dad growing up. We'd head all over the place while Mom was traveling. Dad would always say, no matter where Mom went, we at least knew exactly where we were. Geocaching was our thing." He stood up, shrugged nonchalantly, didn't say another word.

He didn't need to. I could feel his sadness as palpably as the frigid wind rattling the trees surrounding this clearing.

"Sit down, sit down," I mumbled, now determined to find the stupid cache. I scanned the deer-nibbled trees at the edge of the clearing, their branches picked clean of pine needles like ears of corn. Next to another mound of snowbound sage bushes, I spotted a humpbacked log that looked promising as a bench. I pointed to it. "Is that anything?"

"Yeah!" Jacob bounded heedlessly to the log, shoveling off the snow with his hands until he cleared away enough to find a hollow. He dropped to his knees, and using his shovel, scooped out snow until there was a small pile behind him. I kneeled next to him, peering at the small hole. He asked, "Can you shine the light in here?"

I switched on my headlamp.

He was such a city boy; he stuck his hand inside. I downgraded his survival rate in the wilderness. "You know," I told him, "that's not a good idea. . . ."

But he grinned at me, wicked triumph, and withdrew a package wrapped in a dark green garbage bag. "You were saying?"

Curiosity got the better of my need to retort. So instead, I asked, "What is it?"

He stripped off his gloves, tossing them on top of the snow pile, where they were bound to get wet. I sighed, picking them up. He noticed and held out the package: "Here, trade. Do the honors."

So I swapped the gloves for the package, shaking it gingerly. "What is this thing?"

"A treasure box."

"None of us buried anything here."

"Someone did. So open it already," he said impatiently like a little kid, practically bouncing on his toes in his sneakers.

Whoever it was wanted to make sure the box stayed dry through snow and squall. Swaddled within two other black garbage bags was a plastic tub. Inside that lay a smaller package, bundled in a clear gallon-sized Ziploc bag. And inside that was a tin box.

"This feels sacrilegious," I told him, my hand resting on the lid.

"So unwrap the mummy."

"When you put it that way . . ." As I pried the top off the box, I knew that Pandora had been lying. How could she not have known her world was going to change by lifting the lid? I peeked inside, slammed the lid down. "Oh God."

"What?" He stepped closer to me.

I whipped the top off and screamed. He jumped back.

"What? Don't tell me you're scared," I said, laughing. And then I showed him the contents piled in the box: a tiny plastic doll, the length of my finger. A dollar bill. A shoelace. A toy compass zipper pull. "So this is why we walked all over for the last hour?"

Jacob rummaged in his pockets, and for a half second I thought he was going to pull out one of his napkins. Instead, it was a key chain with a little globe of the world. That, he tossed into the box. "You take something and leave something. So what do you want?"

I held up the cheap compass. "You'd get more lost than anything with this."

"Getting lost is just another way of saying 'going exploring.'"

From the box, Jacob retrieved a stub of a pencil and a tiny pad of paper, scrawled with different handwriting, over fifty logs. I read the messages over his shoulder: *Great cache. Could it be harder to find though?* And my favorite: *Watch out for rattlesnakes.*

"Rattlesnakes?" he asked.

"I'm telling you, don't go putting your hands under rocks, inside logs. . . ."

He eyed the hunchbacked log suspiciously, but then shrugged. "Have you ever thought that might be a warning to keep away the muggles?"

"Harry Potter?"

"No, people who don't geocache. I mean, think about the Beware of Dog signs little old ladies hang when they just have a Chihuahua or some other kind of rat dog. It makes them feel safer, keeps away the bad guys."

"Here be dragons," I murmured.

"What?"

"Nothing," I started to say, so used to Erik not tracking with me. But this was Jacob, so I explained, "That's what the old cartographers used to do. Include sea monsters, dragons, dog-headed men in areas where the Church didn't want people to explore."

"That wouldn't have stopped me." Jacob gazed off into the horizon, where dawn was breaking orange behind the mountains. He could have been Zheng He, the Chinese explorer who sailed the Pacific and Indian Oceans, a full century before Columbus. Well, Zheng He, except for the eunuch bit.

"Would any place scare you?"

"Hell, yeah. Plenty of places. Angola. Afghanistan. Pakistan. But I'd still go if the conditions were right."

I swallowed. The difference between us couldn't have been more glaring. Jacob was the kind of well-traveled guy who'd wing it without a hotel reservation, much less an itinerary. I needed everything plotted, every contingency thought through and covered.

"Here be dragons." Jacob nodded, wrote the words down.

"No one will know what it means."

"We will." And then he signed the log: *MM.*

I guessed, "Mappa Mundi?"

"What?"

"Map of the world."

"No, try again."

"Come on, just tell me. What does it mean?"

"Look it up."

"You know, I hate it when teachers tell me that."

His face turned so solemn, I thought I had lost points with him, but he pointed up to the sky. "Have you ever seen that orange before?"

A brilliant sunrise was cresting over the mountains, the kind that made me want to burrow in my studio to recapture the colors. After a few minutes, Jacob placed the pencil and paper back inside the box. "So you need to choose something, your first geocaching trophy."

I swept aside a few random objects until Jacob said, "Stop." He lifted a scrap of paper from the bottom. There was no mistaking the yellowing paper inside the plastic envelope, the frayed edges, the thin boundary lines; it was a piece of a map. There were more fragments of the map in the bottom of the box. "'Travel bugs,'" he said, reading the typed note included in the bag. "You're supposed to take this and put it in another cache. I've just never seen one that was filled with so many of the same travel bugs." Jacob placed the map fragment into the palm of my hand. "So Merry Christmas, Trouble Magnet. It's perfect for your atlas."

"Yeah," I said. "It is." My hand closed around the paper carefully, not wanting to let this perfect Christmas present go.

chapter sixteen

Deaccessioning

CLAUDIUS WAS HIDING OUT IN his room, earphones on, lost in the murky, magical deep of his old fantasy novels strewn around him. The thick book was propped on his knees, his favorite, the one set in Noor. His hands were swaddled in bandages.

"Hey, Claudius," I said.

He didn't hear me, somehow, perfecting the art of having both music and story pump into his brain at the same time, a collage of senses. It was a gift I wished I had; my brain seemed to shut down with too much stimuli. Just as I had when I was a little girl, I marched over to his bed and gave him a good shove: pay attention to me. He jolted, an abrupt return to reality.

"Jesus! Talk about heart attack. I thought you were the Beast," he said, raking me with his glance. "You could be."

"Gee, thanks." I was about to sock him in the shoulder, but nice sister that I am, I didn't want to risk retaliation with his bandaged hands. "How're you feeling?"

"Oh, this? It's nothing."

"So, good Christmas, huh?"

"Yeah, merry Christmas and all that."

I lowered myself to the floor beside his bed, leaning my head against his mattress. I breathed in deeply, catching the ever-present aroma of roasted garlic mingling with today's turkey and candied yams.

I had missed this, hanging out with Claudius, even though most of the time when we had holed up together in this room, it was to get away from Dad and his sharp-shooting comments. My ears pricked up like a guide dog's now, trained to listen for that telltale edge in Dad's voice. Right now, it was a mere murmur, hardly louder than the stereo set on low volume as background noise. The critical tone was incessant, but not overly vindictive. I didn't need to intervene for Mom yet.

My stomach grumbled from missing breakfast, but I wasn't about to risk a run-in with Dad. "Do you have anything to eat?" I asked Claudius when my stomach gurgled for the second time.

He nodded to his backpack leaning against his chair. "Granola bars. Hand me one, too, would you?"

I stretched, dragged the backpack to me, and poked gingerly inside. You never knew what microscopic — and not so microscopic — beings lived inside boy bags. What I found was a box of granola bars (thankfully, each cryogenically wrapped in plastic) and an envelope inscribed to Claudius from a girl whose handwriting was a charming hodgepodge of upper- and lowercase letters.

"So . . . who's this from?" I asked, wiggling the card at him as I tossed him his granola bar.

"God, give me that!"

"Hmmm . . . touchy, aren't we?"

Claudius ignored the granola bar that bounced onto his bed and lunged for the envelope instead. My reflexes were better; I leaned away and switched the envelope to my outside hand, farther out of his reach.

"Watch your hands," I said. Sometimes — I have to admit it — there's nothing more satisfying than being a little sister, the brattier the better. I grinned at him. "So spill and I'll give it to you. Who is she?"

"No one."

"No one . . . or no one you're bringing home?"

Claudius shot me an answering smile before falling back onto his pillows. "No one I'm bringing home."

Victory. A confession. I flicked the envelope at him. "God, what was Merc thinking? That was relationship suicide bringing Elisa here."

"Maybe that's what he wanted. How much do you want to make a bet he's broken up with her already?"

"Pessimist."

"Twenty bucks."

I shook my head. "I liked Elisa."

"Yeah, me, too. But that's beside the point. Make that fifty bucks. They're not together anymore." He made a slashing gesture with his hand. "She's been deaccessioned."

That hurt, that reminder of how our family was so screwed up, we couldn't even share the people we loved with each other. And when we did, Dad removed them from our lives, like fake maps plucked out of a collection. The ambivalent way I was feeling about Erik, he might be on the deaccession path, too, about to be excised from my love life. I had never broken up with a guy before, but I was pretty sure I could find it in a how-to book. Or ask Karin. She was coming home tomorrow, and I couldn't wait to talk to her. I took the last bite of the granola bar. Claudius was back to his book. This — being incommunicative, feeling isolated even when we were in the same room — wasn't how I wanted my family to be.

"I'd like to meet your no one," I told him.

"For sure."

"No, I mean it, Claudius."

Nothing.

I kneeled so I could see his face, but he had just turned the page. I didn't want to let go of our conversation yet, especially when I had so much to say. Like, how come you stopped calling? Like, how come you never answered my calls? Asking those questions was too hard, because I was afraid of his answer.

"Hey, I wanted to show you something," I said instead. Carefully I removed the yellowing map fragment from my pocket. I hadn't had a chance to inspect it, and as I handed it to Claudius, I noticed what looked like a snake's body close to one of the stubbled edges.

Claudius set aside his book, handled the fragile piece delicately. His brow furrowed as he studied it. "Where did you find this?"

"In a geocache on our property."

"No shit."

"How do you know about geocaching?"

He shrugged, as if saying, how could you not know? I wondered that myself. Was I so focused on following Merc's college-to-career path that I never looked around, never saw what was right here?

"So what is it? Do you know?" I sat so close to Claudius I could smell his aftershave (aftershave!). I would have teased him about it, but in a single fluid motion, Claudius swung his legs around me, bounded off his bed to his desk, and plunked himself in front of his notebook computer. As I watched, he Googled an image of the China map, the one I had only heard about but had never thought to seek for myself. He scanned the document until, unerringly as if he knew that map by heart, he found the same coiled snake body in the middle of the ocean. "See? There?"

I did. My piece was part of the sea monster whose head emerged from the water, whiskered like a catfish, cute in an ugly kind of way.

"Ironic, isn't it?" Claudius said, holding up one of his bandaged hands. "I cut my hands on the glass back then, too, when Dad tore the map off the wall. That stopped Dad. He, Mom, and I went to the hospital."

Did Claudius even hear himself? I stared at his hands, thought about the scar on his right knee from falling off his skateboard when Dad started in on Mom for misplacing his screwdriver. The healed gash on his left arm from the time he fell down the stairs while Dad was grumping about Mom not washing his favorite running shirt before the Cutthroat Classic half marathon. All those cuts, bumps, bruises. Claudius wasn't clumsy, except on purpose when he had a father to distract. How come none of us had noticed that?

"God, Claudius." I leaned toward him, willing him to listen. "You don't need to protect Mom. I'm here."

"I know." He looked at me, a glance where guilt mingled with regret, and I knew what he was getting at. It was as close to an apology as I would receive for him pulling back this autumn, retreating from me, cutting us off from each other. But as I stared at those bandages wound around his hands, I didn't want Claudius to apologize for taking a break and looking out for himself for once.

"You needed time off," I said.

He shrugged, not admitting the motives behind his self-imposed silence. And then changed the subject fast. "I bet this is part of the China map. It's got to be."

"So what happened to the rest of the map? How'd this piece get into that geocache? On our property?" I asked.

"No idea. You could ask Dad."

"Yeah, right."

We both rolled our eyes. Neither of us mentioned Merc. He'd just blow off our question; any e-mail we sent would be lost in his overflowing dam of an inbox. And Mom? As usual, she'd be clueless.

"Well," said Claudius at last. "Good thing Dad doesn't know about the geocache. He'd hate knowing that people were trooping around the property."

"That might have been the point."

Just then, Mom called from the kitchen: "Terra, could you come here for a second?"

As I left Claudius's room, he said, "Cassie. Her name is Cassie."

I smiled at him. "Thank you."

Two days after Christmas, Mom and I were putting away all the decorations while Dad was working out at the club. Claudius had just left to go snowshoeing with some of his friends, his hands too sore to plant the poles for skate skiing. Mom had a specific order for removing and storing each ornament, and I was getting a headache trying to remember which nutcrackers went in which box. Packing had none of the joy and excitement of unpacking. It was pure chore, this sad epilogue to Christmas.

I was relieved when Mom sent me to the kitchen for more packing tape. While I was there, I decided to check my e-mail on the kitchen computer. And there, unexpectedly, was a response from Merc. I bit my bottom lip, forced myself to click on his message with mounting dread. I needn't have worried. There was no answering emotion, no betraying anger, just a succinct order, signed with his initials: bring mom. mc.

Bring Mom where? I was going to close the e-mail, but I scrolled down and found a confirmation letter from United Airlines for two electronic tickets to China, one for me and the other for Mom.

"Did you find the tape, honey?" Mom asked, coming right up behind me.

I turned to her. "Merc wants us to visit him."

"Visit him?"

"In China." I pointed to the e-ticket on the computer screen.

But Mom was already shaking her head. "Oh, I don't know."

Her doubt echoed mine. God, the thought of going to China was intimidating. First, I didn't know the language, not a single word of Chinese. I'd never been on an airplane farther than California, when we went to my Aunt Susannah's memorial service after her freak bus accident in Guatemala. No one was able to explain adequately what had happened, only that the bus she was traveling in had lost control in the winding mountain road and careened off the cliff. Every person inside had been killed. After that, travel became too precarious for us, uncontained danger lurking at every turn; and for Mom, driving itself transformed into a death wish.

Merc may have sent us those tickets to China, but the chances of his work intervening so he couldn't show us around were a given. Which meant I would be the one figuring out the routes, the restaurants, the stores, the sites, the train stations, the cabs, the buses. And what would happen if something went wrong? Like getting lost? That, too, was a given.

Unable to watch Mom shake her head and ashamed of my own relief at her automatic, emphatic no, I returned to the computer screen, to the e-tickets reserved for us. I had an inkling what those British P.O.W.s in Germany must have felt back in World War II when escape maps were smuggled to them, sandwiched inside playing cards. How they'd carefully soak the cards in water to get to the precious cargo, those maps made of silk. How they must have been thrilled and terrified, knowing they were holding freedom in their hands. And how daunting their escape into the unknown must have seemed after being cooped in their tiny prisons for so long.

chapter seventeen

Aphrodite Terra

THE BEST CHRISTMAS PRESENT I received arrived three days late and came wrapped in funereal black. Jacob unfurled out of the dark morning, a bat flying from its roost.

I barely contained my scream as he materialized before me, his footfalls pattering on our graveled driveway. "God, what are you doing here?" And then anticipating his answer, I held up a mittened hand. "Don't tell me I'm predictable and you knew I'd be out now."

"Then I won't, creature of habit."

"Creature of habit!" I breathed out, mock offended. "For your information, I was going . . ."

I stopped, embarrassed to tell him that I was going geocaching. As I had started out this morning, dissatisfaction wormed itself into me like a beetle attacking the hard heartwood of a tree. I was sick of staying on my normal path, following my regular routine. I was sick of seeing the same things. I yearned for something different. So I had backtracked quietly into the house, checked the geocaching Web site on our kitchen computer, and found more than forty caches in Colville alone. Who knew? Dad kept his battalion of GPS devices around the house, so I pocketed the one from the kitchen junk drawer.

Jacob grinned at me now, so knowingly that my erratic heartbeat had nothing to do with being surprised and everything to do with bubbling anticipation, a distinctly and uncomfortably girlfriend-y feeling that Erik's presence never elicited. Jacob had come here for me. He had waited for me. And I had him all to myself this morning.

Then I saw his hiking boots. Brown, sturdy, waterproof. And his Gore-Tex jacket. "What is this? Goth goes granola? You almost look . . ."

"Normal?" He batted his eyes, thickly made up.

"Thank God, no."

"Good, normal is so overrated."

I laughed, my first real laugh this Christmas season.

"Ready to shake up your routine?" He lowered his own headlamp, flicked it on.

I reached up, flicked it off. "I'm doing that just fine on my own."

"No one is fine by themselves, Control Freak." A pause. "So there's a geocache in town. . . ."

"I'm in."

The look he gave me . . . My stomach quivered in that exact same way when I watched *Before Sunset*, yearning for a guy to know me so deeply and truly, we were only really complete when we were together. That I could talk, go on wild tangents, make obtuse references, and he would divine my meaning before I knew what I was trying to say myself. Erik had fallen asleep next to me on the couch, complaining later that the movie was "just people talking." He had no idea that this movie could have been a love letter written for me.

With that, Jacob placed his hand on the small of my back and led me to his Range Rover. The pressure of his touch through my jacket and my sweater was more assurance than any promise ever made to me. It was a touch that said, *I have your back* and *I am here for you*. If a girl wasn't careful, she could fall in love with a touch like that.

"*Memento mori . . . ,*" I said as Jacob was poised to log our find onto the mouse-sized paper in the microcache we had just discovered, an old mint tin with a magnet that stuck to the underside of an old thresher. I could still picture the *MM* he had scrawled at our first find, dark and bold, almost an etching.

His head jerked up, so startled the pencil scarred the paper with a jagged line.

"So, remember that you must die, huh? Morbid." I sighed, feigning boredom. "A little clichéd, no? I mean, you being Goth and all."

"Hey, if it's a good philosophy, it works. Death is imminent. Live every day like it's your last."

"Well, yeah, the Romans should have taken that to heart, what with their lead poisoning and all. But did they have to sign all their sculptures with MM?"

"Alright, Control Freak," he said, "then we need a new name for our team."

Our team.

"So what do you want to call ourselves?" he asked.

"The reformed Goths?"

"Speak for yourself." He glanced heavenward, captivated by whatever he saw. He pointed overhead. "You know, Venus was out last night. Did you see it?"

I followed his gaze to the sky, now lightening to a vivid pink. "No. To tell you the truth, stars and planets look the same to me."

"You just have to look at them carefully." Then, that mischievous grin again. "Did you know that every landform except for one is named after women and goddesses on Venus?"

I thought for a second, guessed, "Everything except mountains?"

"Yeah."

"How very phallic."

Jacob laughed. "Yeah, and all the continents are named after goddesses. Aphrodite Terra. Ishtar Terra."

"Ishtar?"

"As in the Babylonian one who was celebrated for her sexuality. And Lada Terra."

"Which goddess is that?"

"The Slavic —"

"Sex goddess?" I guessed.

"Love goddess," he corrected.

"Men obviously named everything on Venus. Am I right or am I right?"

He smirked, not denying it. Then, either he noticed me shivering or he was trying to distract me, because he said, "Let's warm you up before this becomes your memento mori day."

If this had been Erik, I knew what he'd be talking about, warming up the two of us in the backseat of his truck. Or sneaking into his bedroom while his parents were at work.

But this was Jacob. And he asked, "Is anything open yet?"

I glanced down at the GPS, checked the time. Just before six thirty. The entire economic mecca that is Main Street consists of three realties, a half dozen restaurants (only one serves healthy food), a brewery, a bookstore owned by a man who loathes browsers, and a half-stocked grocery store where the chances of finding out-of-date batteries were greater than finding a decent apple — and this in a valley flush with orchards. So there was really only one option. "Snagtooth Coffee might be."

"They have coffee?"

I nodded.

"Is it decent?"

"It's drinkable."

"Good enough," he said. "Let's go."

As Jacob charged down the hill, me following, I had to admit, even the spiny sagebrush that my mom abhorred, the bane of her spring and summer gardening, looked beautiful snow-glazed.

"Come on!" he called.

I picked up my feet and flew down the rest of the hill until I almost caught up to Jacob. I leaned down, balled a handful of snow, and threw it at him. Laughing hard, I sprinted away, feeling the snow kicking up my back.

And then in case he was contemplating retaliation, I spun to face him, raised my hand in warning. "I've got two older brothers who taught me everything there is to know about snowball fights."

"Duly noted. But if you're planning on having coffee with me, you need to go this way." He pointed in the opposite direction where I belatedly made out his car on the street. "Last one there treats."

I veered to the left, cut my own path through the snow. It was a minor correction, but even with Jacob's head start, we reached his Range Rover at the same time.

"So, did your Christmas get any better?" I asked Jacob when we settled in for the short ride to Snagtooth Coffee. It was so cold I could see my breath, but the seat warmer was already doing its job. I leaned all the way back, blissfully warming in the passenger seat.

Jacob rolled his eyes and put the car smoothly into drive. There is something terribly sexy about a good male driver, especially a driver with impeccable navigational skills. It must be something about being in control, the guy knowing where he's going, that appealed to me.

"That good, huh?" I asked.

Jacob started to answer but as he leaned down to change the radio station, he grimaced and gazed in pain at me as if to ask, *Country music? For real?*

"We're lucky to even get this station," I told him, laughing when he reached wordlessly for his stack of CDs and thrust them at me.

"Put me out of my misery," he begged. "Please." And then, as though he trusted me eminently, he said flat out, "Dad announced he was getting remarried over spring break. Merry Christmas, right?"

"Ouch."

"To the barista."

I winced. "Double ouch."

"Tell me about it."

Whether it was our discussion or being in a truck with an actual working heater, I was starting to sweat. So I stripped off my mittens, unzipped my jacket. "How's Trevor taking it?"

"He's too young to get it. Mom, on the other hand . . ."

"How's she doing?"

"Doing what she does best."

"Which is?"

"Denial." Then, as he parked in front of the bakery, he said, "Your turn. So just how good was your Christmas?"

I was going to say, "Fine," but we had pledged honesty. Jacob glanced at the GPS, fiddled with one of the buttons. I got the sense that he would wait as long as it took me to tell him.

I sighed. "You really want to know?"

He didn't say a thing, just nodded.

So as the dawn colored the sky first pink and then blue and the lights at the Snagtooth Coffee bakery switched on, I told Jacob about how Dad decided Elisa wasn't good enough for Merc and how he went after her. And how Merc left an entire week early. And how Claudius hurt his hand and how I had never noticed that he injured himself any time a fight escalated. I was on a roll, and this was my chance to tell him about Erik and how he had given me lingerie, a present that made me want to cry because what did it say about me? What did it say about my relationship with Erik? But something kept me from revealing that to Jacob. Maybe it was because in Jacob's presence, I didn't feel a few degrees off from the girl Erik wanted me to be: the sexy one, the mouthy one, the available-when-it-was-convenient-for-him one. And maybe it was because I was afraid of what Jacob would think of me.

Talked out, I stopped, sighed, and expected Jacob to say something pat, commiserate with a "God, can you believe parents?" or "Are you sure your dad wasn't just trying to be funny?" But he stayed completely quiet as though he were listening to my silence, processing what I was saying without words. And finally, he said, "Even geniuses can be Class A assholes."

I stared at him, not believing I heard him correctly. That he would dare to use those words to describe my dad.

I thought about how Dad rushed Claudius to the hospital. "He's always there when we need him. He pays for everything."

"Do you hear what you're saying?"

I did. I sounded like Mom, making excuses for Dad's bad temper, rationalizing that his pointed comments were simply the truth, blaming herself when he lashed out.

Jacob was right. Even a genius like Dad could be an asshole.

"Exactly," I said, surprised, and then emphatically. "Exactly."

Somehow, admitting that to Jacob was freeing the same way it must have been for an alcoholic to admit he had a drinking problem. Or a battered woman to acknowledge that she was not to blame for her beatings.

"This one's on me," I insisted as we approached the coffee-stained counter.

"Coffee, black, for here," Jacob ordered, and then turned to me. "Lucky for you, I'm a cheap date."

That was a good thing, considering the shelves were empty of a typical coffee shop's usual arsenal of blueberry scones, buttery croissants, chewy bagels, and doorstopper-sized muffins. With Snagtooth Coffee, all you could count on was the door being open and coffee served mouth-burning hot.

Still, I made a point of looking over my shoulder at his Range Rover, sleekly expensive and virtually in mint condition, except for the dent I had left on the back bumper. "I don't think so."

"Don't judge a man by his vehicle."

"So how do you judge a boy?"

"Ouch. Hasn't anyone told you about how delicate a man's ego is?"

"Maybe men, but boys are all bravado."

"I can't catch a break from you, can I?" he asked gruffly, but I could see the amusement glinting in his dark eyes.

Laughing, I turned to order and recognized the girl behind the espresso machine: Alicia, my first bully and former prima ballerina from Miss Elizabeth's. She had long abandoned mocking me, just as she had wearing tutus and the color pink, except for her naturally pink lips that were hanging open.

I couldn't tell what surprised Alicia more: to see me out in public without makeup or to see me with a Goth in full makeup. Even with hiking boots and a jacket crafted for climbers, Jacob didn't fit into this Western joint any more than a cactus in Mom's cutting garden. I decided I didn't really care what Alicia thought of either him or me, and smiled brilliantly at her. "Hey, Alicia. Caramel macchiato, tall, non-fat, please."

"Did you just order what I think you did?" asked Jacob.

"So?"

He looked altogether too pleased with himself. So much so that I started to regret my caffeine-deprived impulse. Out of habit, I headed to the table set flush against the store windows. As soon as I sat, I regretted it. Even though it was too early for the usual parade of winter tourists — the buff couples wearing his-and-hers cross-country ski outfits, the out-of-shapers who for inexplicable reasons chose to vacation in the athlete-packed Methow — the town was small. Someone other than Alicia was bound to see us. No doubt, by this afternoon, Erik would be calling, wondering why I was hanging out with a Goth guy at Snagtooth Coffee.

Jacob swung around on the chair, leaning against the window and stretching his crossed legs out in front of him. With any other guy, sitting cross-legged might have looked somewhat effeminate, but not Jacob. He looked like a coiled snake, ready to bite me. I wouldn't have minded.

"Just so you know, speed isn't a priority here," I warned him.

He glanced at Alicia, who was still watching us like we were some traveling zoo exhibit, freakishly odd yet eminently fascinating. "I wouldn't expect it." He nodded at her. So he had noticed her staring, too. Nonplussed, Alicia suddenly busied herself with our order. "A friend of yours?"

"Former tormentor."

"Damned barista."

I laughed so hard, I snorted. That's when Alicia called my name. I jolted, having forgotten that we were waiting for our coffee.

"I'll get it." Jacob pushed back his chair.

"No, I'll get it."

As I strode over to retrieve our drinks, I could feel Jacob's gaze on me, speculative. Whether by design or sheer accident, Alicia screwed up our order, turning my caramel macchiato into a soy latte.

"My mistake. I'll make you another one." Alicia cast a wistful gaze over at Jacob as though she wished she were with a boy who could make her laugh uncontrollably, too. Before I could return to Jacob, she leaned over the counter and said conspiratorially, "So . . . you guys are having fun."

"Yeah." I smiled broadly. "We are."

I spun around, spotted a familiar gleam of blond hair outside the door before a blast of cold air preceded Karin's entrance.

"Terra, it's you, thank God!" she cried, leading her family inside the coffee shop. Parked behind Jacob's truck was their mud-splattered RV, no doubt holding her dad's latest haul of artificial decapitated heads and miscellaneous body parts from a special effects studio in Los Angeles. The next time I went over to her house, her dad would no doubt be eager to show me his newest ghoulish treasures, inventoried in his database and ready for display come Halloween.

All of the Mannions looked bleary-eyed and travel-worn, except for Karin, who was gorgeous and chic in her new outfit: skirt, boots, jacket. I caught her brief look of relief after she scanned my face before she launched into her update. "So you know how Dad's college roommate used to be the executive producer for Entertainment Tonight?"

She may have rambled on with her news, but I was still stuck on her relieved, self-satisfied expression. It was almost as if she had looked deep into the magic mirror of my face, assured that she was still the prettiest of them all. Unconsciously, I touched my cheek, aware of it now in a way I wasn't when Alicia had openly stared at me.

"Isn't that great?" Karin asked, beaming, my assent a foregone conclusion.

"No. I mean, yes."

She didn't notice my ambivalence, her attention having turned to her parents, who were still dithering in front of the chalkboard menu as if Snagtooth Coffee had actually changed its offerings once over the last five years. "God, that's how they've been this entire trip," she whispered, exasperated. Then, her practiced journalist gaze, searching for news in the making, rested on Jacob. "Oh my God, Terra. Look, your soul mate from Halloween."

I knew all too well who she was talking about. So, apparently, did Alicia. She handed me two replacement coffees, so I was double-fisting it. "Your caramel macchiato for you, and a fresh black coffee."

"Alicia, I ordered a latte." Karin looked annoyed.

"It's for my friend," I said softly. "I'm going to get back to him now, okay?"

As I started for Jacob, I could hear Karin spluttering behind me. My insecurities reared their ugly, multiple heads. What was I doing with him? Karin, not me, looked like his type. But from across the room, my Goth guy smiled at me as if there was no one he wanted at his table more. I couldn't contain the lurch in my heart.

I took my seat across from Jacob, slid his coffee to him.

"She another barista?" he asked softly.

"No, a friend."

"Could have fooled me."

As Karin stalked toward us, paparazzi chasing down secrets, I could have been fooled, too. She didn't bother to wait for an introduction, not while she slipped into full reporter mode. "And who are you?"

"Terra's friend," said Jacob bluntly.

"Well, Terra's friend," said Karin, dragging out the chair beside Jacob, "that makes two of us."

No answer.

Unaffected, Karin plunged into her interview. "So how did you guys meet?"

I started to run down the pertinent details — how I nearly crashed into him in Leavenworth — when Jacob reached over for my mug and drank deeply. That stopped Karin's inquisition more effectively than any longwinded explanation of our meeting. Her eyes widened comically, unintentionally, and then she angled me a look: *how long have you known this guy?* Jacob set the mug back down. His diagnosis: "Too much caramel."

"Geez," I said. "What happened to sipping and smelling?"

"Smelling and sipping," he corrected me, and then smirked. "Sometimes, a guy just has to have it."

"God!" I leaned over to slug him in the shoulder.

I didn't like that pinched, judgmental expression on Karin's face, as if she disapproved of me hanging out with any guy other than Erik. Jacob didn't look like he wanted to have a conversation with Karin any more than I did. He picked up a sugar packet and began tapping it on the table. Lucky for him, he got a reprieve. His cell phone rang, a sprig of classical music.

"Classical?" I asked him, lifting my eyebrows.

Neither Karin nor I missed his squeeze of my shoulder when he left to take the call outside. The door had barely swung shut when Karin demanded, "So what's going on with you two?"

"Nothing."

"That was not nothing."

"Come on, I just met him."

"I didn't figure him to be your type." Her mouth pursed so sanctimoniously I almost forgot that she managed a stable of guys who were forever fawning over her.

"We're just hanging out." True, Jacob and I hadn't done anything other than talk. And talk. And talk. But Erik — I hadn't even mentioned him to Jacob yet. Or vice versa. Still, something about Karin's implication bugged me. And then I pinpointed it. "And what exactly is my type?"

"Not him," she said, jerking her head toward Jacob, who was pacing outside, talking on the phone.

"Why not him?"

"Because . . ."

"He doesn't care about my face."

She blanched guiltily, but recovered fast. "Well, yeah, because he's got that" — she touched the smooth skin between her lip and her nose — "thing there."

"It's a scar."

I looked longingly at the front door, wanting so badly to leave. But as I sat there under Karin's gaze that judged and weighed and found me lacking, I realized I could. There was no reason to stay, no more to say. Or explain. I didn't need to be the one who always remained at home, waited for Karin's return, charted her progress in the land of opportunity. So I left the dregs of my coffee, left Karin at the table. I waved goodbye to her parents and slipped out of Snagtooth Coffee into a gust of fresh air and a posse of tourists. For once, I couldn't care less that these strangers took the scenic route of my face — glissading from my temple to chin with long, lingering looks. There was Jacob, and he was waiting for me.

"Our moms have beckoned," he said, folding his phone in half before slipping it into his pocket.

"Now what are they up to?" I asked.

"Candle-Making 101."

"You're kidding."

"Unfortunately, no. Mom's making up for lost time, learning all the crafts she's always wanted to do."

"My mom didn't mention this to me."

"They've been conspiring. We're supposed to pick up my mom now. Ready?"

From behind me, I could feel Karin staring at us through the window, confused and irritated, trying to determine if I had completely lost my mind. Maybe. But I found something else instead.

"Ready," I said and opened the door to his truck. My seat was still warm.

"You could make a killing on these in Seattle," Norah said, examining the candles Mom had set out earlier on the kitchen island as examples. Those, Mom had made months ago in preparation for Merc's homecoming. Vanilla scented the air thick as a bakery while the candles burned.

"On these?" Mom shook her head skeptically. "Oh, I don't think so."

"With the right packaging, boutiques would snatch them up. Trust me, you could price these at forty dollars apiece and they'd sell out."

"Forty each?" Mom squeaked.

"Maybe even fifty."

As if this were a lab class, Mom had divided the kitchen into different work stations: the display area for finished and cooling candles at the island. The microwave — which I was manning — to melt batches of soy wax. At the kitchen table, Jacob and Trevor had been put to work spooning wax flakes into Pyrex measuring cups. Originally, Norah had been in charge of pouring the melted wax into glass votives, but she hadn't mastered the art of straightening the wicks. So Mom had reassigned her to cutting the wicks into equal seven-inch lengths.

Now, I twisted away from the microwave and saw for myself what Norah meant by the candles. They were beautiful, but naked. With the right labels, the perfect packaging, the candles could be stunning, not to mention more valuable. How come I never thought of designing professional labels for Mom? How hard would that have been?

Over at the kitchen table, Jacob encouraged Trevor, "Right on, little man" as Trevor spooned flakes messily into a glass measuring cup. They may not have looked like brothers, but you could feel their bond every time Trevor looked up at Jacob for praise. Something tightened inside me, the familiar ache for my own brothers. Maybe Mom and I should brave China. There, I could make amends with Merc.

"I don't know," Mom said again. Dad's skepticism had worn away her confidence as surely as running water to rock, eroding it layer by layer until there was nothing left but sandy insecurity. She chuckled now, sounding eerily like Dad when he was denigrating an idea. "Could you even turn a profit on these?"

"It's all about sourcing the right raw materials at the best price, no different from coffee beans," said Norah authoritatively. She picked up one of the unlit candles, held it up to the light. "Maybe in China or India."

The microwave beeped just as Mom cried, "China!" She tempered her voice to a confiding tone, "That's so weird. My son wants me and Terra to visit him there."

"Really? I love China," said Norah enthusiastically. She set the candle down and picked up her scissors to clip a few more wicks. I noticed that the uniform seven-inch lengths Mom had specified were getting progressively shorter. "Where?"

"Well, he lives in Shanghai."

"Shanghai is one of my favorite cities. You'll love it. When are you going?"

"Oh, I don't know. . . ." Mom brushed her hair nervously behind her ears.

Norah snipped a piece of string decisively. "I'll take you."

"What?" asked Mom.

I echoed her sentiment, almost dropping the hot Pyrex measuring cup that I was removing from the microwave. "I've been meaning to bring Jacob back there," said Norah, "visit his orphanage, try to track down his birth mother."

Hastily, I set it on a hot pad and then swiveled to face Norah. As I did, I found myself searching Jacob's grim expression.

Oblivious to Jacob's look of horror and annoyance, Norah continued, "It'll be fun. I'm sure I could figure out where you could buy all the materials you needed for these candles or whatever else you wanted. And then we could hit the fabric markets, have some clothes made."

"Really?" Mom lit up, incandescent as the burning candles around us now that someone other than me would guide her. I couldn't blame her for not trusting me. Dad was right; I spun around three times and lost all sense of direction. How could I navigate China?

"Mom," Jacob cut in, his tone sharper than I'd ever heard him, "this isn't even logical. It's against the law to abandon a kid in China. So there aren't any records at the orphanage. Zero. Zilch."

I slanted a gaze at him. The look he returned was so forbidding, it was clear he didn't want the trip to happen, didn't want Mom and me to be part of any expedition to his orphanage. I didn't blame him. A trip like that should be a private odyssey.

Obstinately, Norah asked, "When were you thinking of going?"

Neither Mom nor I had seriously considered traveling to China, but

Mom now said as with the firm conviction of someone committed to an itinerary, "Spring break. That's when Merc booked the tickets."

"What about Dad's wedding?" Jacob asked, his tone goading.

Norah's face shuttered. "What about it?"

"It's the first weekend of April, too."

Norah glanced to see if Trevor was paying attention. But he was busy mounding mountains of wax flakes and running them over with his backhoe toy, complete with beeping sound effects. More quietly now, she told Jacob, "You can go to your father's wedding. Really, it would be perfectly fine with me. In fact, I want you to go. We can always visit your orphanage at another time."

Jacob stood up, shaking his head. He raked his hand through his hair. "I don't want to go."

Did he mean his dad's wedding? China? Or both? It didn't matter. Trevor glanced at him, concerned. Jacob managed a tight smile for him, ruffled Trevor's hair, before heading toward the front door. "I'll be back."

Part of me wanted to go after Jacob, especially when I heard his truck start with a disgruntled roar, but if anyone needed alone time, it was him. Besides, there was my mom to contain. We couldn't go with the Fremonts; it was that simple.

"Maybe this isn't a good idea," Mom said, uncertain now.

I echoed her doubt. "Yeah —"

"Lois," Norah interrupted, her voice low, urgent. "I don't want to be in town" — she angled a furtive look at Trevor, censored herself just in case — "then. You'd be doing *me* a favor by going with me."

Mom returned to the soy wax cooling in the Pyrex cup. Slowly, she poured the wax into the waiting glass vessels, their wicks already superglued to the bottoms like the long pond-bound roots of lotus plants.

Norah watched her, but I wasn't sure how much she was paying attention. Her breathing was fast, uneven, the labored breath of the unwittingly trapped.

I knew exactly what was driving Norah. Frenzied activity as a matter of survival was my modus operandi, too. People may have thought I was padding my résumé, but really, wasn't I juggling a job, doubling up on coursework, not to mention signing up for virtually any extracurricular all to keep from spending any more time at home than I had to? This trip wasn't about taking Mom to China or even bringing Jacob to his orphanage. It was all about escaping her ex-husband's wedding.

In her shoes, I would have done the same.

By going to China, I knew I'd be overstepping some invisible boundary between me and Jacob. Maybe he hadn't planned on us talking to each other once he went home to Seattle. Maybe he was no different from that tourist last summer who had picked up Karin, promised to call, and never did.

That didn't matter, couldn't matter. Mom's eyes sparkled, alive. I hadn't seen her this excited about anything since before Aunt Susannah died — not even Christmas with Claudius and Merc compared to her blossoming enthusiasm.

So when Mom nodded and told Norah, "Let's go, then," I didn't protest.

"I'll clean up, Dad," I assured him as soon as he stalked into the kitchen, his lips tightening imperceptibly at the untidy pile of cut wicks, the boxes of glass jars for the candles, Trevor's snowdrift of wax flakes powdering the table and the floor.

"That's okay," he said amiably, playing the good-natured father for his audience. Norah, thankfully, was still here. He wouldn't dare display his temper before her, not this powerful coffee buyer for a major company.

"So it looks like I'm taking your wife and daughter to China," said Norah brightly, almost too sweetly. I heard the challenge in her words, wondered how much Mom had divulged about our family to her when I wasn't listening. Or was off with Jacob. She continued, "You're more than welcome to come with us."

Dad was stuck; I could see it in the set line of his jaw. He couldn't order Mom not to go, not with Norah around. And he would never consent to visiting China himself, not the source of his humiliation. Still, without a word from Dad, without a shift in his expression, Mom clasped her hands worriedly. I could see our China plans wasting away in the tide of Dad's unspoken disapproval. I clamped my lips together, swallowing any antagonizing outburst I wanted to make, forced myself to straighten a line of finished candles. In the hallway hung Dad's prized collection of antique maps. All matter of monsters on these maps of Europe, Africa, and the Americas were called upon to scare off would-be travelers. But those monsters, beastly warnings, never really roamed our lands, not the two-headed flesh-eating creatures, not the gryphons, not the sharp-toothed dragons.

I turned my back on those cautionary maps now to face Mom and reminded her softly, "You always wanted to travel."

Mom licked her lips, parched of confidence. Dad made an impatient sound. So I told him firmly, "I'll plan everything with Norah," glad that Jacob's mom nodded her assent back at me. The expression on her face stayed resolutely unfathomable, completely unobjectionable so Dad had nothing to pick apart. I continued, "And we'll be able to see where Merc lives and where he works." With a meaningful look at Dad, I added, "Wouldn't it be great to see how he's really doing?"

"Yes," he admitted reluctantly.

I returned to the candles, sharing a private smile with Norah and aiming a reassuring one at Mom. Like world describers before me, those mapmakers in the seventeenth century, I had laid down my first faintly drawn border. With that one tentative mark, my world expanded by a few freeing degrees.

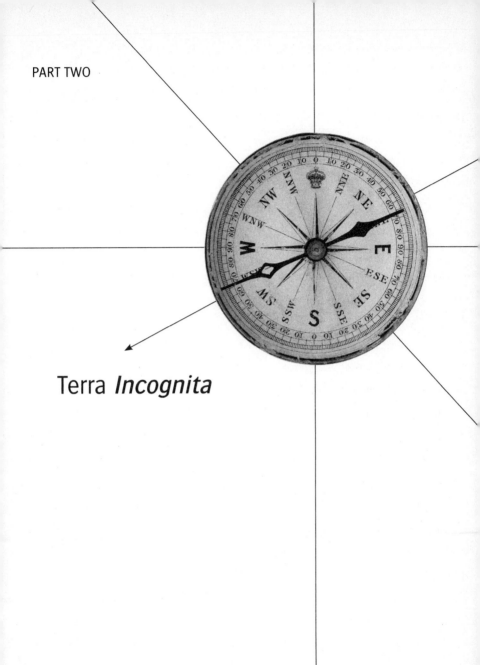

PART TWO

Terra *Incognita*

chapter eighteen

Hot Maps

THE LAST TEN WEEKS PASSED on hourglass time, each minute slipping grudgingly through the tight bottleneck of Dad's mounting aggravation. It rankled Dad, every detail of our trip to China. So after his initial consent in front of Norah, he had become Scherezade, spinning out daily anecdotes about China, one more frightening than the next. Take the story about his acquaintance who caught some weird staph infection and almost had to have his leg lopped off. Or the kid who broke his two front teeth falling down on the Great Wall, and instead of fixing them, the dentist had yanked them out. It was no wonder that Mom's enthusiasm for China waned the moment he knew we were going. Keeping her onboard was itself a full-time job, as I shored up the holes in her commitment made by Dad's battering ram of grim cautionary tales.

But here I was, on the way to the airport, hemmed in by Mom's anxiety, Dad's guilt treatment, and my own concern: how was it going to be between me and Jacob? I made the mistake of glancing into the rearview mirror. Rather than Dad's cold glare — I knew he blamed me for taking Mom away — I caught a glimpse of myself. Back in full camouflage, my face looked as heavy as it felt with all my layers of makeup on. My birthmark, despite Mom's protests otherwise, hadn't lightened. I wondered what Jacob would make of me covered. Whatever he thought, it couldn't be worse than him seeing me without any makeup.

We hadn't talked much when he first left Colville, mostly our moms corresponding with each other, and then me working out the details of our China trip with Norah. But as soon as I made it clear that Mom and I weren't interested in visiting his orphanage, Jacob began warming to the idea of us touring China together and actually started to offer ideas about what we could do in Shanghai first, then Beijing. The plan was to split up for the last part of the trip, the Fremonts splintering off to Huangzhou to locate Jacob's orphanage while Mom, Merc, and I went by ourselves to Xi'an to see the terracotta warriors and the starting point of the Silk Road. Then we'd fly home together from Shanghai.

"I labeled all your lunches and dinners in the freezer for you," Mom murmured from the front seat. "All you have to do is remember to take them out to defrost them."

"I just hope they won't get freezer burn." Dad hacked again, the slight cough that started (conveniently) two days ago had metastasized into volcanic eruptions of his lungs. What Dad needed was a good pounding, not coddling. Clearly, Mom's nursing gene had skipped me.

Mom cast him yet another worried look. "Are you doing okay?"

"How do I sound" — cough! — "Lois?"

"Maybe you should have another cough drop?" She had already retrieved and proffered the soothing drop before Dad could muster another dramatic death rattle. To his credit, those shoulder shuddering coughs were quite impressive.

I choked down a snicker. Dad overheard. He glowered at me in the rearview mirror, never mind it was Merc who had given us our passage to freedom. I looked resolutely out the window to the Cascade Scenic

Highway, newly reopened just two weeks ago. Enough snow had finally melted.

"The steering doesn't work the way it used to," Dad grumbled. Another accusatory cough. Another accusatory look.

It was really too bad I couldn't enjoy the drive, considering that my personal college savings paid for the car's repair.

Dad went back to sniping at Mom: "Why didn't you pack the cherry Ricola? You know I hate lemon." It was as if he finally realized that there was only so much nagging and criticizing you could do from halfway around the planet. So he was making up for it in the here and now.

"Oh, Grant," Mom sighed, and I willed her to remain silent, not to relent and tell Dad she had reconsidered the trip and would stay at home instead, nurse him back to health.

The upper reaches of the mountains were still thick with snow and the sides of the road were crowded with boulders, evidence of the winter's crop of avalanches. This early in the morning, there were only a few cars cruising the wending path, mostly obese RVs chugging past us in the opposite direction of the two-lane highway, heading toward our Valley. I wondered briefly if we were making a mistake, Mom and I, taking this trip.

Now Dad was telling Mom, "I just hope you don't get lost."

Mom had Dad's doubt shadowing her. I had Karin's.

"Is it that Goth guy again?" Karin had demanded a couple of nights ago while we were studying for midterms and my cell phone rang. Jacob was always "that Goth guy" to her — as if her brain, which had instant and accurate recall of every potential Hollywood contact she made, couldn't retain his name. "God, what is this? The second time you guys talked today?"

"We're just friends," I told her, even though my heart sped when I recognized his number. I would have taken the call outside, but it was raining hard. So despite her watchful, disapproving stare, I answered the phone. "Hey."

"So help me out here," Jacob said by way of hello. Once he started calling me regularly, our conversations had fallen into a routine; we dispensed with identifying ourselves and opened with a question. Today, his was: "What are you supposed to give your own dad for his wedding present?"

"You got me on that one."

"I should have commissioned you to make the happy couple a collage."

"What? Out of a broken dollhouse framed in coffee grounds?"

He chuckled, and I pressed the phone to my ear, wishing I could see him, the way his eyes crinkled at the edges and his entire body bounced when he got laughing hard enough.

Karin or no Karin, I laughed, too.

"God, Trouble Magnet, you're terrible," he said, teasing, approving.

"Me? I'm never terrible."

But the way Karin stared at me from her bed, I was. I turned my body totally away from her.

"As if we're not going to have Chinese food for the next week and a half," he said, "Mom's friends are taking us for a bon voyage meal at a Chinese restaurant tonight."

"Sounds like fun."

"Nah. Afterward, Mom will have a page-long list of complaints about how Americanized the food was and all that. Don't let her blond hair fool you. She prides herself on being more Chinese than the Chinese. Just wait until we get to China."

"I can't wait." From the corner of my eye, I caught Karin's frown. Disgruntled, she abandoned the math book to check her teeth compulsively in the mirror. She had been white stripping them on and off since Christmas. "Everyone had gleaming white smiles in LA!" I was surprised she had any enamel left.

"So," said Jacob, "what're you doing tonight — other than unpacking and repacking?"

"I knew I shouldn't have told you that!" I protested, but I was smiling. That is, I was until Erik honked from the driveway. I could lie, ply myself with excuses why there never was the perfect opportunity to tell Jacob about Erik. But here it was; a chance that couldn't have been better scripted. Even Karin sensed the moment, narrowing her eyes at me meaningfully then, instead of at her reflection.

Tell him, I thought to myself. *Tell Jacob that I have a boyfriend. That Erik is leaving for Montana with his family tomorrow morning to get an early start on spring break and we are saying goodbye to each other tonight.*

But I didn't. The truth was hard to admit: I hadn't broken up with Erik because I was afraid that no one else could possibly want me. If Erik was my "stretch" boyfriend — the one Karin and everyone thought was a stretch for me — then Jacob was well beyond my reach, residing as he was in the realm of impossibility. He was urbane, jet-setting, wealthy (for God's sake, he stayed at the River Rock Lodge for a week and a half!). What would he want with me? In all of our conversations, he had never once stepped over the line to hint at even being attracted to me.

Another honk outside; I could read Erik's impatience in it. "Look," I said hastily, "I've got to go. I'll call you later."

As soon as I hung up, Karin was shaking her head while leading the way downstairs. "Erik is here. Right here. That Goth guy" — she spun around on the landing to point accusingly at my cell phone as if it was the culprit himself — "was a tourist. He's in Seattle. Five hours away."

"I know that."

"Five hours," she repeated, as though I didn't know. As though I wouldn't ever be worth a minute of anyone's commute. "Okay, so forget Erik for a second. Why would you start something now with a guy who's still going to be in high school when you're off in college? It doesn't make any sense. And how can you be going all the way to China with him? You don't even know him."

The small details of Jacob's life — who his friends were, what his favorite movie was — those may have been unknown to me still. But they were topographical features I could fill in later. We knew each other — or at least, he knew me — in all the ways that truly mattered, the shape of my fears, the contours of my dreams. Everything, I thought guiltily, except for one thing: I had a boyfriend who was waiting for me in the driveway.

As usual, Erik didn't notice me until I was inside his truck, his loud music crowding me to the door. Our regular routine. I wanted to jump out of my skin, I felt so stifled. Between the music that I didn't even like to all of my false assurances — "I'll break up with Erik tomorrow" — and all the lame excuses for why today wasn't the day to end our relationship, I was suffocating. And shocked that he was still my boyfriend just as Mom was stunned that she hasn't lost an ounce since Christmas and Karin that she hasn't toned her thighs. Inertia is so easy — don't fix what's not broken. Leave well enough alone. So we end up accepting what *is* broken, mistaking complaining for action, procrastinating for deliberation.

*   *   *

So what if Karin was right? What if distance had only made my heart grow fonder? I now stared unseeing at the long line of cars stretched in front of us on the highway while Dad barked out his coughs, each one making Mom flinch in the front seat. Maybe my conversations with Jacob were nothing but spiderwebs, sparkling with the fresh dew of newness, stringing us together, but gaping with holes? Karin had a point. Five hours away was still five hours away. We hadn't seen each other once since Christmas. And he still had a year left in high school; I was heading to college.

I didn't have to wonder for much longer how it would be when Jacob and I were finally together again.

We arrived at the SeaTac airport.

Dad maneuvered cautiously across three lanes, so slowly he lost our place at the curb, not once but twice. Through the gap between his seat and Mom's, I could see how he gripped the steering wheel, the sinews of his hands ridge lines of impotent furor. That's how his temper worked. It pushed out of him like newly formed mountains.

"It's okay, Grant. We've got plenty of time," soothed Mom.

Dad made an impatient, silent gesture at her to shush. Berating Mom should have been second nature, but apparently thinking up all those precisely aimed insults commanded more brain power than I had assumed. He had lost his cough, too, I noticed.

Once parked, Dad shot out of the car. I followed him more slowly to the trunk, where he was efficiently hauling out Mom's tote bag and my backpack, our two other pieces of wheeled luggage, and throwing them like so much garbage onto the ground. Dad didn't breathe hard from the effort of ejecting us.

I lugged the bags to the curb, feeling every ounce of our jackets, extra medication, and back-up shoes. Norah had cautioned us to pack light. But how do you do that when you need to be prepared for all the emergencies and tragedies Dad had so generously shared with us?

"All right, everyone, move on!" the traffic cop shouted, blowing his whistle. He pointed at us. Dad waved *I know* at him before hissing at Mom, who was checking her purse: "Hurry up, Lois."

What she was looking for, I don't know. I myself had triple-checked that both of us had our passports, tickets, and boarding passes.

"People are waiting." Dad aimed a sycophantic smile at the traffic cop, who was now glaring at us.

"Oh! Sorry!" Mom apologized automatically. Her forehead and nose glistened with sweat and oil.

"Wipe your face." Dad mimed the motion roughly. She could have been a toddler, incapable of focusing on a simple set of verbal directions.

Mom pulled out a Kleenex, dabbed her face as she was told. Still, she made no move to vacate the car, a panic attack away from calling this trip off, I could tell. I abandoned the luggage at the curb and held out my hand to Mom, waited for her to take it. For a moment, she hesitated. Then, relieved, I felt her smooth palm, her soft fingers that were too wide for her wedding ring, slip into mine. I eased her out to me.

As soon as I shut the passenger door, Dad ducked his head so I couldn't read his face.

"You have everything," he said, not quite command, not quite question.

"Everything that we need," said Mom.

The cop's whistle blew again. Dad jogged to the driver's side, but not before I saw an odd shifting in his face. Under his shellacked irritation was something else. Not quite regret. More like loneliness. I hadn't seen that expression before. Or maybe, I thought as Dad gazed out the window at Mom for one brief moment, it was just that I had never allowed myself to notice it.

The car engine started with a burst of burnt smoke. The way Dad drove off, you would have thought he was making a quick getaway with a couple of hot maps, newly stolen, in the backseat.

Mom stared after Dad's car like she had misplaced something.

"He's not good at goodbyes," she explained to me softly.

"I know," I chimed in the wake of Mom's excuse. I was just as guilty of burnishing our family's outward perfection as she was. "Ready?"

She crossed her arms, chilled more from Dad's abrupt departure than the pleasant spring breeze. I swung my backpack onto my shoulders and rolled the two suitcases behind me, one in each hand. That left Mom with the lightest tote bag and her purse. As we were swept into the airport filled with people who knew where they were going, I kept close to Mom, my hot map that I refused to lose.

chapter nineteen

Orienteering for Girls

ONCE THROUGH THE SECURITY LINE, I bent down to retie my sneakers, making a note to travel in slip-on shoes the next time. Next time? Swaddled in my thick sweatshirt and wool socks (Lydia had warned me that airplanes were always cold), I was sweating. Profusely. Focused on collecting all our bits, I couldn't have cared less if my makeup was streaking. Travel was so overrated.

Naturally, our gate had to be the farthest possible point from where we stood. I waited for Mom, who had plopped herself down on a bench, legs splayed, to put on her shoes. Almost without realizing it, I scanned the crowd for a Goth guy and his mom, even though we had agreed to meet at the gate. When Mom straightened, she was huffing, proving that traveling was heavy exertion. Up ahead, an upscale food court gleamed, an oasis after the security detail. Grayish light filtered in through the windowed wall, spanning three stories of sheer glass.

"Maybe I'll get us a little something," Mom said, gazing appraisingly at the Starbucks kiosk. She glanced sideways at me. "Remember how Merc says they never feed you on the airplanes anymore."

I swiftly calculated the time we had before boarding. Over two hours. "Sure."

Intent on finding us an empty table, I nearly barreled into a guy who stepped in my path. What the hell? Considering the momentum from the weight I was carrying on my shoulders, both my thirty-two pound backpack (I had weighed it at home) and Mom's bag, I barely stopped in midstride.

"Excuse me," I muttered, not bothering to make eye contact with the dolt until he spoke.

The one voice that could make my heart whip in circles like a compass gone awry now said, "I knew you missed me, but I didn't know how much."

I looked up, grinning, and then did a double take. Gone was my Goth guy with dark eyes outlined in kohl and lips painted in black. In his place stood a fresh-faced skater dude, wearing a faded T-shirt, long baggy shorts and — no way . . .

"Flip-flops?" I asked, incredulous.

His answering smile was long, lopsided, familiar in that unfamiliar face. "Yeah."

"Don't you know those are the worst shoes to wear on an airplane? All the books say you're supposed to have your feet covered so your toes don't get smashed during an emergency. . . ."

Without warning, Jacob folded me in his arms. That, too, felt familiar somehow. Into my hair, he whispered, "I'll tell you what. If our plane goes down, I'll still let you save me."

And then he released me.

I breathed out, annoyed by his words, even more annoyed that I wanted to stay in his arms. Just like that, my fear that we might be awkward around each other — or more accurately, that I would be too self-conscious to talk to him — vanished.

"You bet I'd have to save you." I pointed at his bruised toenail. "I cite evidence A. Cover your feet."

Just as I lowered my backpack to the empty chair at my side, Jacob hefted it up, testing its weight, and then quirked an eyebrow at me. "So, Control Freak, let me guess. Three guidebooks, a month's worth of PowerBars, and your own portable medicine cabinet."

I flushed and decided now was not the time to correct him: that would be four guidebooks. A half dozen granola bars. An entire drugstore's inventory of hand wipes and antibacterial goop. And a medical supply worthy of a doctor's respect — Benadryl, Tylenol, Metamucil (you never knew). Really, it was a miracle Mom and I hadn't been mistaken for drug mules.

"You know, I liked us better on the phone," I told him, swatting his hand off my backpack.

"I don't." Jacob flushed red and busied himself with adjusting the straps on his backpack that had fit him just fine a moment ago.

"I don't either."

"So," he said, his voice gruff, "you walked right past me."

"I didn't recognize you." I waved at his new look, glad that one thing hadn't changed: his hair. That was still spiked up, but no longer orange-tipped. "Why'd you change?"

"Why did you?"

For the first time, I felt his stare on my cheek, spackled with thick makeup. I flinched, glanced away, unable to answer. Thankfully, Mom approached us, loaded with four coffees and a huge paper bag, no doubt filled with enough provisions to last our entire flight. "Jacob!" she cried. "It's good to see you again. Where's your mom?"

"Waiting for you at the gate." He easily slung my backpack over one shoulder and Mom's carry-on bag over his other. When I protested — "I can do it" — he said, "Just let me, okay?"

It was hard to let someone help me, though, when I was conditioned to believe that help was for the weak. What was even harder was watching Mom with Norah, their heads bowed together as they chortled over something or another in the waiting area. They couldn't have looked more different, Mom in her matching pale pink sweatpants and sweatshirt and bright white tennis shoes, and Norah, the picture of the world traveler, poured into brown suede pants. A camel-colored pashmina shawl was draped casually around her thin shoulders. She had lost weight since we last saw her, and I remembered that a week from now, her ex — Jacob's dad — was getting remarried. Trevor had decided he wanted to wear a tux and be the ring bearer in the wedding.

"You sure you don't want to be at the wedding, too?" I asked Jacob now.

"I wouldn't go if he was giving free tickets to . . ." He waved with the last of his cinnamon twist.

"The Galapagos."

"Exactly." Again, the grin that I had missed so much. He took the final bite of his donut and still looked voracious. So I gave him the rest of mine. "Thanks. So Mom's quitting her job."

"You're kidding. But it was everything she worked for," I said, thinking wistfully of the company jet she flew in, the countries she traveled to, the Range Rover she drove . . . all the security money could buy except for stability at home. I leaned toward Norah and Mom, wondering what they were talking about two seats down from us. My efforts to eavesdrop didn't go unnoticed.

"They're doing fine," Jacob assured me both then and again a half hour after take-off when he switched seats with Mom so she and Norah could keep each other company.

For the fifth time since she left our row, I leaned across the empty aisle seat to make sure Mom was okay up in the roomier business class section where Norah, as a frequent flier, had been upgraded. She didn't return my look, too busy chattering with Norah.

"Do you want to switch seats?" Jacob asked. "Look out the window for a while?"

"No, thanks." The window seat made me feel trapped, confined. I didn't like losing my ability to jump up and out if I needed to, whether to help Mom or escape if the plane went down.

"Just so you know, they're ordering wine."

"They are?" I craned into the aisle again. Sure enough, the flight attendant was handing them two small bottles of wine. And then came Mom's unmistakable snort, which meant she was really laughing, a belly laugh that was rare as an endangered species at home.

Jacob stretched his legs out in front of him. "I know it's a foreign concept to you, but just kick back."

"I can relax."

"Yeah." Again with the teasing grin. "So what's up with the yoga poses?" He mimicked me maneuvering in my seat to spy on Mom.

I laughed so hard, the balding man in front of us turned around to shush me.

Chagrined, I sobered. But Jacob nudged my shoulder. "So Trouble Magnet, I bet that's never happened to you at school. You've always been the ideal student. The good girl."

"Well . . . ," I hedged.

"It's going to be a hell of a lot of fun corrupting you."

"I'd be more scared if you were in your Goth getup."

Now, he started on the scone Mom had bought for him, licked the sugar crystals off his fingers. "It's all costume." He plucked at his polo shirt. "This is, that was."

"So why Goth and not . . . ?"

"Prep? Soccer guy?"

I nodded.

"Because . . ." He rapped his fingers on the tray as if he was uncomfortable. If we were on the phone, distance making intimacy safe, he'd answer me straight up. I thought he'd drop it now, use the flight attendant who was asking us if we wanted water to deflect this conversation. But as soon as she pushed the beverage cart on, he answered, "Because people stared at me whenever I went out with my parents. I mean, you might expect little Chinese girls to be adopted, but not boys."

I hated to admit it, but I had done the same. I confessed: "I'm one of the lame ones. Sorry."

He waved aside my apology. "So I figured if people were going to stare at me anyway, then I would choose the terms of their staring. I can dictate what they see."

"So what's with the surfer look now?"

"People aren't going to be staring at me in China; they'll be staring at Mom." He smirked. "And you."

"Oh, right." I toyed with my cup of water, overly iced, but I had been too polite to protest when the flight attendant handed it to me. I admitted, "I had never thought of dress as costume." Just makeup as mask. "So what's next? Geek chic?"

When Jacob spluttered in good-natured offense, I didn't even mind that the guy ahead of us turned around to scowl at us again. As Jacob and I cackled about that quietly to ourselves, all I have to say is that being corrupted felt oh so good.

chapter twenty

Large-Scale Maps

TWENTY-FOUR HOURS INTO THE TRIP, I'd pretty much determined that traveling was all about waiting. Waiting for the trip to start. Waiting to load onto the airplane. Waiting to unload. Waiting to have our passports inspected and stamped by grim-faced administrators.

"You doing okay?" asked Jacob.

To tell the truth, I was woozy from waiting around, partly because I had only dozed for a few hours on the plane — Jacob and I had spent most of the time talking — and mostly because of the crowds, waiting with us to have their passports checked. An old man in a modern Mao suit jostled past me and barked something at Jacob. He shrugged, replying defensively, "I don't speak Chinese."

It was Norah who answered in Mandarin, surprising me and the old man, who nodded brusquely and moved to another line after casting a final disparaging look at Jacob. He flinched, looked down at his feet. Norah missed that silent exchange, too busy telling Mom, "Jacob stopped speaking Mandarin almost as soon as we brought him home. I even went to Chinese school with him, but he refused to say a word. I have no idea why. So I just stuck with it."

From Jacob's reticent expression, I had an inkling why he had clung exclusively and stubbornly to English. As obvious as my birthmark was, at least I could cover it up. How could Jacob hide that he was adopted whenever he stepped out with his blond mom? And it wasn't as if Norah wasn't forthright about his adoption herself. I mean, she openly explained to us — veritable strangers — in Leavenworth that little boys were abandoned in China, too, not just unwanted girls. Maybe using English was one way Jacob blended in.

Ahead of us, Norah was confiding to Mom, "Being a foreigner now is no big deal, but two decades ago when I first started coming to China, I'd never been that stared at before."

In this airport thronging with almost entirely Asian people, I was acutely aware that I was the minority, and not just because of my birthmark, but because of my entire appearance — my hair, my skin color, even my height. I couldn't have felt more different, more obvious, than if I were dressed as a Goth in Colville. I leaned over to tell Jacob that, but caught him peering warily, almost disdainfully, at these people whose ethnicity he shared.

I let out my breath fast, a gasp of recognition. For as long as I could remember, I scanned crowds, too, looking for anyone with a port-wine stain, not to befriend them, but to keep my distance. I wasn't one of Them and I didn't want to be mistaken as one of Them. If I had more guts, I would take Jacob's hand, hold it in solidarity, a declaration that he was With Me. That he wasn't one of Them. All I could think to do was touch Jacob's arm to get his attention and whisper, "I didn't know your mom even spoke Chinese."

He smiled faintly at me. "Like I told you, she's more Chinese than the Chinese."

I had to leave Jacob's side to approach the passport check with Mom. The official at the desk scowled at her passport, then mine. Even though we hadn't done anything wrong, I was worried. Dad had warned us about people who had been detained and then deported. At last, the official waved us through so curtly, I felt like I really was guilty of something. And then, that's right, we waited for our luggage at the carousel along with half of Shanghai. Mom sighed wearily.

"Go sit, Mom," I told her. "I'll take care of this."

Mom tottered to a bench, slumped down, not noticing — or pretending not to notice — the people staring at her, laughing. She was easily three times the size of the other women milling in the baggage claim area. Offended, I wanted to tell them to shut up, to throw a blanket around Mom so she wouldn't be so noticeable. This was a mistake, bringing Mom here.

"Your mom's ignoring them. You should, too," Norah murmured to me, but she collected Mom and stood next to her as we went through customs. One last line. One more set of doors. A waiting crowd, held back by ropes, stood outside the doors. The medley of their conversations sounded harsh to my ears, words I couldn't make sense of. A few people held signs, some in Chinese, others lettered with Anglo names — Bodmer, Anderson, Knight. None had ours.

"Didn't Merc say he was going to meet us here?" Mom asked as if I hadn't prepared a ten-page itinerary for her, complete with logistics and important numbers in case we ever got separated.

"He'll be here," I said more confidently than I felt. Like Mom said, Merc inhabited his own time zone — an hour later than everyone else's — and he perpetually underestimated how long it would take to get ready. I had hoped today would be different. That he would suspect we'd be anxious; that he'd be early, eager to make us feel at home.

Mom worried her lip. "How are we going to get to his apartment? Do you know how to get there?"

"Mom —"

"Why don't we wait over there?" interrupted Norah, already herding us to an empty spot away from the main fray of reuniting families and couples. "Terra, why don't you check to see if he's waiting outside?"

While I headed for the doors with a last backward glance at Mom, checking compulsively to make sure she was still with Norah, I found Jacob at my side. He grimaced apologetically. "God, my mom can be the ultimate delegater. You just have to ignore her."

"At least she knows what she's doing. You don't have to come outside with me."

"I want to."

The night air was cool enough that I wished I had grabbed my jacket out of my backpack. I wrapped my arms around myself, smelled the exhaust from the idling cars. I inspected the sidewalk, every passing car. No Merc, just Jacob. He was still with me.

According to our plans, Merc was supposed to pick all of us up, drop the Fremonts off at the Jinmao Tower, where they were staying in one of the best hotels in the city with the added benefit of being in the same building as his office, and then drive Mom and me to his apartment. I checked my watch. Merc was forty minutes late. Sighing, I told Jacob, "Maybe you guys should go on to your hotel. You don't have to wait with us."

"Yeah, and God knows what kind of accident is waiting for you if we left you, Trouble Magnet."

"Gee, thanks." I was too tired to formulate a witty comeback and would have forgotten it anyway when Jacob nestled me close to his side, tucking me into the warmth of his body. It felt so good to be held by him, I decided it wouldn't be disastrous to wait all night for Merc. But I heard my name being called. At the curb, Merc hopped out of a minivan from the passenger side, and waved at me. He said something in Mandarin to his driver, who got out, too, and opened the trunk. I was reminded of Elisa. She had stopped e-mailing me about a month ago after we had exchanged a couple of messages; I chalked it up to her being busy, figuring out her life though I suspected it had to do with more than that. And now I wondered whether I'd see her at all.

Merc approached us, his expression assessing, making me aware of how close Jacob and I stood next to each other, how easily his arm rested around my shoulders. I quickly pulled away from Jacob as though we had been doing something wrong.

No welcoming hug from Merc, just: "Hey, you made it."

You did, too. "Yeah, miraculously." I wondered what Jacob made of us, our stilted welcome. "I can't believe you have a driver."

"My company requires it," he said defensively. "Liability. Don't want the expats getting into accidents and getting sued."

After I introduced Merc to Jacob, I said, "Mom's inside."

Instead of apologizing for keeping us waiting, Merc now barraged Mom with a million questions about the trip, how she was feeling. That's what living with Dad had made us good at: deflecting. Rerouting. Diverting. We were the air traffic controllers of conversations. Merc threw himself into becoming our one-man porter, carrying our heavy luggage over my protests.

It was strange how commanding and self-assured Merc was here amidst unfamiliar words and people, makes of cars I'd never seen before. While Merc and his driver wrangled the luggage into the minivan, I felt my world expand far beyond Dad's gridlines, far beyond Colville. The weariness of travel sloughed off me. Only then did I allow myself to admit that I had made it. Me, the girl who had dreamed of traveling but hadn't left Washington State except for once. I was standing in China.

I was in China.

I breathed in, chain-smoking the acrid fumes of the passing cars. In those fumes, I smelled my freedom.

It was completely dark by the time we reached the Jinmao Tower. I only woke when the minivan stopped abruptly. How could I have fallen asleep and missed the Shanghai skyline, famous for its futuristic, fantastical buildings?

"Don't worry." Jacob had guessed the reason behind my sigh when I followed everyone out of the minivan only to have the tower's overhang block the view. "You've got plenty of time to see everything."

Still, I wanted to rush around the city now, a giant geocache, find everything I had read about in the books I had borrowed from our tiny library. I wanted to taste the food, listen to the people. Energized, I set for the tower's gleaming gold doors, needing to get to wherever we were going fast.

"Someone's awake now," said Norah, yawning. Her shawl was askew and her makeup worn off. As well-traveled as she was, the trip had taken its toll on her, too.

Before dropping Jacob and his mom off at the hotel reception desk on the fifty-third floor, we all stopped at Merc's law firm on the forty-second. The most personal object in his office was an antique map, handsomely framed, a high school graduation present from Mom and Dad. Other than that, there was nothing personal in this corner office designed to impress with its sleek desk and aerodynamic chair.

"The view's better up on the observation deck," Merc said. "Eighty-eighth floor."

"This is high enough," said Mom nervously. She stood, hand on his door, as far from the windows as possible.

Not me. Nose to glass, I relished Shanghai's whimsical skyline. It was as if the city's architects had thrown away everything people assumed about what buildings were supposed to look like, and tried new forms: orbs! Triangles! Even Jinmao was a reimagined pagoda, hard-angled as it strained upward to reach a steel-and-concrete heaven. If Karin's dad saw this nighttime spectacle of rainbow-hued lights, he would have felt shamed, his 60,000-watt homage to Halloween a faint shadow of this citywide lightscape.

"Mom, look," I said, beckoning to her. "It's beautiful."

She shook her head slightly, too scared of heights to move from her comfortable corner. So I walked over to her, took her hand in mine, and guided her to within a foot of the window, holding on tightly.

"Can you believe you're in China, Mom?" I asked.

"No." Mom shook her head as she peered tentatively down at the cars, the people, the bustle on the streets far, far below us, swallowing at the vaguely dangerous sight. This city didn't just dwarf Colville; it eclipsed Seattle.

Mom made a choking sound. I squeezed her hand comfortingly, glanced over at Norah, who hadn't said a word since we came in here. She was staring bleakly out the window, looking at absolutely nothing. I bet I knew where she was — half a world away in Seattle, with Trevor. And with her ex who was days away from remarrying and starting a new life without her.

Then Merc, too, noticed Norah, and ambled over to her, pointing something out in the horizon. Both of them looked hungrily into the yawning night, these two titans of the business world who had everything at their disposal. It was as if they were searching for something. Or someone. I'd never seen two more lost people.

"We could check out the observation deck tomorrow," Jacob said, now at my side.

Tomorrow. I grinned at him.

"You kids can do that. Lois and I have plans," said Norah with a conspiratorial wink at Mom.

"We do?" Mom asked, too taken aback to notice that though I was still standing close to her, I had let go. She turned to Norah, hesitating like she had no idea what she wanted. And then, she said, "Well, sure. But what are we doing?"

"It's a surprise."

It was Mom's face that betrayed surprise when she realized she wasn't holding her usual safety net, me. Before she could panic, I grasped her arm and led her out of Merc's office. "See? That wasn't so bad, was it?"

From behind me, I felt Jacob, his breath kissing the back of my neck, making me shiver as though his lips had been pressed in that same exact spot.

Not bad. Not bad at all.

chapter twenty-one

Keys

YOU WOULD THINK I'D FALL asleep as soon as I collapsed into bed. Mom had. Through the walls, I could hear her light snoring next door in Merc's bedroom, sighs mixed with breathy rumbles, sounding sad even in her dreams. I was buzzing. The gleaming highway lights from Jinmao to Merc's neighborhood in the Jing An district could have been running in my veins, powering the replay of the last twenty-four hours in my head: my marathon conversation with Jacob on the plane, Norah and Merc staring out at Shanghai like the two loneliest people on the planet, Mom and me here at last in China.

My thoughts turned to tomorrow. Despite my best intentions to remain Zen about traveling, I fretted about us veering off our itinerary. Days ago, I had memorized the activity-by-activity matrix I had mapped out of all the things we would do and see while we were here. Along with the route we'd take to get from one place to another, I had created a list of things to pack according to day and activity — notebook and coloring pencils for sketching at Yu Gardens, the photocopied map I had found of every building on the Bund, my laminated synopsis of Shanghainese history. But now that we were stopping at Jacob's hotel in the morning for Norah's "surprise," my schedule was obsolete before we'd even started. God only knew what that surprise would be.

After twelve hours on the airplane, my mouth felt sucked dry, so I went in search of water. For some acoustical reason I didn't understand, I could barely make out Mom's snoring in the hall. I peeked into the living room, saw no one, continued to the tiny kitchen. It was almost two in the morning. Merc must have slipped out while I was showering off the traces of travel, but where?

My hand was on the faucet before I thought better of drinking water from the tap — yup, you got it: Dad had told us about a guy who picked up some stomach-eating bacteria from tap water. So I used the purified water from the cooler in the corner. As I automatically wiped up the few drops of water that had leaked from the cooler onto the floor, I noticed how antiseptically clean the kitchen was, devoid of any scent. I doubted Merc ever cooked in it. Even the vents behind the cooktop gleamed shiny new.

Sipping my glass of water, I paused in the living room, surprised at how adult it looked. Merc's apartment was bigger than I thought it would be, furnished more tastefully than he could have pulled together by himself. Elisa was stamped all over the décor, from the tailored sofa accessorized just so with orange and green throw pillows to the elaborately carved curio cabinet. As if my brother knew what curios were, much less bothered to collect and display them. But there they were, knickknacks: a carved chop in his Chinese zodiac sign, the horse. An oxblood red vase. Some kind of bronze combination lock with Chinese characters etched on its five wheels. Proof that Elisa was important to him.

A key jiggled in the front door, and Merc shuffled in, his necktie loosened, his briefcase slung over his shoulder. He was so haggard he was gray.

"Hey," said Merc softly, surprised I was still up. He dropped his keys on the hallway table carved with dragons before lowering his briefcase quietly to the floor. "Can't sleep?"

"I'm too wired," I admitted. "Where were you?"

"I had some stuff I had to finish at work."

"At two?"

He shrugged, shook out of his jacket. Hanging above the dragon table was the collage I had made for him a year ago, the same piece Elisa had mentioned at Christmas. That's when it occurred to me; I hadn't seen a single photograph of Elisa. Or anyone else, for that matter.

"So when do we get to see Elisa?"

My abrupt question startled Merc so much that he forgot he was hanging up his jacket. He mumbled something or another while closing the closet door, jacket still on his arm. And then he grabbed an inch-thick document from his briefcase and flung himself into a chair in his living room. The motion was so practiced, this had to be his regular routine: work at work, then work at home.

"What'd you say?" I asked.

"We're not together anymore."

"Why not?"

"It's complicated." He opened his document, and immediately deflected, "Is Mom asleep?"

"Yeah. She was worn out."

"It was a huge trip for her."

I nodded.

"She wouldn't have come without you," he said, and I knew that was as close to him ever saying "thank you for bringing her" as I was ever going to get.

Even if he couldn't say the words, I would: "Hey, thanks for sending us the tickets."

He nodded brusquely, almost embarrassed.

I should have apologized to Merc for my abrasive e-mail — what better chance would I get? — but sitting across from him with his jaw so set, his hand poised to continue working, I let the opportunity die. Our lack of intimacy had never bothered me much. I'd always been a lot closer to Claudius, which Mom attributed to our being just three years apart, but the distance between me and Merc had to do with a lot more than the twelve years spanning us. He was a floe of ice unto himself, remote. That's why I liked Elisa, really liked her. I had hoped that she would have been my guide to the real Merc, the one she had thawed.

I stifled a yawn and sat on the couch across from his chair, despite knowing that Merc wanted privacy to finish correcting his legal brief. The careless pile of pillows, sheets, and comforter that he would use later crowded me to one end of the couch. So I shoved them to the middle, and settled against the colorful throw pillows.

"What?" he asked, his question sounding like: *what are you still doing here?*

If I were Mom, I would have left the room — complete with a profuse apology, accepting that her very presence was a nuisance. Instead, I asked conversationally, "So what are you working on?"

With his red pen poised for future corrections, Merc answered me, as professorial as Dad ever was: "A Chinese company is about to go public on the NASDAQ. So I've got to review all the initial public offering documentation." He said something else, but I lost him at NASDAQ, his legalese a foreign language to me.

"Uh-huh." I suppose a truly interested person would have probed more deeply and a good conversationalist would have asked more scintillating questions, but my traveled-out brain couldn't even form the simple words: *what are you talking about?* Right then and there, I lost Merc to his work again; he was back to poring through his document.

My outreach to Merc stalled, I was about to give up, call it a night, when I noticed the two six-foot-long maps hanging above the mantelpiece, mounted and framed without glass. The topmost map was of China, the bottom, a map of the world; both were covered with pushpins. Now, I could ask him about the fragment of the China map I had brought with me. Now, I could ask him how it had gotten onto our property, whether he had anything to do with it.

Instead, I asked, "You've been to all those places?"

"What?" Merc blinked, waking from the mind-numbing effects of dense legalese.

I pointed to the maps. Merc glanced at them like he'd never seen them before. "Oh. Just the orange pins. The green ones were the places on our — my — tick list before I leave."

I asked, "When's that, exactly?"

"I don't know. Another two years?"

"But you said two years, max, in China."

He shrugged. "Plans change, Terra."

No, I wanted to say. Plans don't change for no apparent reason, especially changes to my master plan. See, according to *my* plans, Merc was supposed to move back to Boston — which, compared to China, wasn't too far from Williams. According to *my* plans, I'd be able to see him a hell of a lot more than we had seen each other these last two years. But then again, I wasn't going to Williams anymore. And he wasn't moving back to his practice in Boston. Plans did change. What was the point of being an adult if you couldn't control your master plan?

I twisted my hands around my glass of water, no longer cold but lukewarm. "So you love it here?"

"Love?" The word sounded so unfamiliar, so distasteful, in Merc's mouth, he couldn't bring himself to say it without making the idea suspect, something contagious. "China's trying to figure out what it wants to be. And that's tough to do, especially if you've never had any choices before. So, no, I don't love it here. But it's an exciting time to be here."

God, I wanted to shake him. He sounded so buttoned up, like he was being interviewed, giving intelligent, pat answers devoid of any feeling, any passion.

He raked his hand through his short curls, rumpling them. Gruffly, he said, "You must be tired."

I was now the bone-liquefying kind of fatigued, unsure whether my own legs could support me. But I nodded, said goodnight. As I passed the front door and my collage, I thought about the piece I had made for Elisa, carefully swaddled inside my backpack. Merc was no longer correcting his document, but staring at the map of the world as though trying to recall a route once taken.

I could have continued to my bedroom now, but I said softly, "I made something for Elisa. Can you give it to her?"

He whipped around to face me, startled. A forensic scientist didn't need to tell me that this wasn't the clean and easy breakup he professed it to be. Their relationship hadn't died its natural death, two people changing out of sync so they no longer fit together. Anyone but Merc could tell that he was still pining for Elisa. Now he tapped his pen on the document, an impatient rhythm. "She moved to Beijing."

"Beijing?"

"Yeah, I'll tell you what. I'll give you her address. You and Mom could visit her in a couple of days when we're there. You'll love her boutique. Sleep well, okay?"

Dismissed, I slipped back into the guestroom, my limbs curling together against the cold sheets in bed. As I listened to the song of Mom's sighs, it occurred to me that I had inadvertently stumbled on the key to my own map. I had always followed Merc's path blindly: power through high school, get into college, then work for my financial independence. Maybe that master plan had been flawed. His fancy degree from Harvard, his lavish apartment, his sizable bank account made Merc no happier than Norah, these two people who had everything money could buy but the one thing that could be given freely: love.

Mom and I overslept. I could hardly believe it when she rapped on my door, murmuring it was already eight thirty. For a brief moment, showered and dressed, Mom looked refreshed. Her relaxed humming stopped when she strolled into the living room and found the sheets folded neatly at one end of the sofa. Merc had already left for work, leaving us to fend for ourselves. The familiar worry line creased her brow, instantly aging her.

"How are we going to get to the hotel?" she asked, clinging to the sofa back like the railing on a lurching ship. "Do you know the way?"

I didn't, but I didn't want to admit that and worry Mom more. Still, a faint wisp of irritation wound around my stomach. "I've got a map," I said, resenting the pressure of always needing to know the way. Just once, I'd love to see Mom take action, make a plan, figure it out on her own.

The cell phone on the kitchen counter rang, and Mom recoiled as if she had never heard one before. Her eyes widened at me, all but asking, *What should we do?*

Sighing, I answered it. "Hello?"

"Good, you guys are up," said Merc quickly, sounding busy. A picture of him checking e-mail and reviewing a stack of documents while he was talking to me formed in my head. "I left the phone for you guys to use. Peter, my driver, should be waiting outside. So whenever you're ready, just tell him where you want to go."

"Cool. Thanks. That's so —"

He interrupted, "There isn't much in the fridge, so just grab something at the coffee shop in Jinmao before heading up to Norah's room."

"That's okay, I brought stuff," I said.

No answer. Then, his muted murmurs as he addressed someone in his office. I waited, imagining how his girlfriends must have felt. On hold, waiting for him to return. Always second in life, after Work.

Mom sidled up to me. "What's he saying? Is he coming back for us? When?"

I sighed, shrugged, wished I could shrug off Mom. And then immediately, I felt guilty. So I whispered, "He's talking to someone else."

Finally, Merc came back on the line, no apology, and continued, "Remember to take the phone in case you need me."

But would you show up if I called? Probably like all of his former girlfriends, I said, "Sure," but he had already hung up.

"Just don't look over the edge," I advised Mom as we stepped onto the seventy-fifth floor in search of the Fremonts' hotel room.

"Trust me, I won't," Mom said, her face pale.

This hotel was a nightmare for people afraid of heights. Rooms and halls made up the perimeter of the hotel while a thirty-three-story open-air atrium ran its entire vertical height. Lean over, and you could see straight down to the café with its grand piano. It would be a very long way to fall.

I knew better than to ask Mom for Jacob's room number, so I checked my notebook, where I had jotted down their contact information last night. As soon as I knocked, Jacob wrenched the door open so fast he could have been watching out the peephole for us. He was tousled and antsy, bouncing in his Vans.

"Save me," he pled.

From inside the suite came raucous laughter, then a spate of Chinese. If I hadn't known better, I would have said it sounded like a party.

"What's going on?" I asked.

"Shopping, Mom-style. You better go in, Mrs. Cooper. They've been waiting for you," said Jacob ominously as he widened the door, allowing us through.

Norah was standing with her arms spread, a scarecrow whose waist was being measured by a woman kneeling on the floor. Fabric swatches were spread like a cloth rainbow across the table along with a small stack of file folders.

"You made it!" cried Norah, smiling broadly. She waved Mom over to the empty spot at the table. "We'll measure Terra next and then you. That way, the kids can get on their way."

"Sounds like fun, doesn't it?" asked Jacob.

Mom looked uncomfortable, and I knew why. Buying clothes for herself had become a loathsome chore since she started gaining weight. I couldn't remember the last time she bought anything, much less tried something on in front of me. Getting measured in front of Norah would be her idea of hell.

"This is Mrs. Liu," said Norah, introducing the slight woman who was now writing down measurements in her dog-eared notebook. "One of my best friends uses her every time she comes here. She is the best tailor in Shanghai." Quickly, Norah translated for Mrs. Liu, who nodded pleasantly at Mom. "She'll take our measurements, go over the designs with us, and then we'll head over to the fabric market. I've been collecting ideas for the last month."

"Two months," corrected Jacob.

Mom stood frozen: frozen smile, frozen stance. I considered her faded purple pants and T-shirt embroidered with a sprig of tiny pansies. She was dressed for gardening, not a day of sightseeing and shopping in the chicest city in China outside of Hong Kong. Even worse, she looked a decade older than her forty-nine years. Norah, who must have been around the same age, could pass for a woman in her early thirties.

"Come on, Mom," I said with an encouraging smile. I took her arm and led her to the table. "This could be fun."

Jacob snorted from behind us.

On the table was a file folder, marked with Mom's name. Since Mom looked at the folder as though it were radioactive, I opened it to a stack of pages, neatly clipped out of fashion magazines and clothing catalogs. Various pieces — shirts, skirts, pants — had been marked with stars, Mom's name labeled next to them.

Mom looked lost, a foreigner in this fashion land. I could see her calculating the cost of these ensembles, trying to picture herself in these clothes for a life she didn't have. I cleared my throat, because, really, how uncomfortable is it to mention money when we were in the company of people who seemed regularly surrounded by it? Take this hotel room tricked out with an enviable sound system and high-tech automatic blinds that Jacob was maneuvering with a push of a button. Shanghai kowtowed at our feet from our lofty position in the sky.

"We're on a pretty strict budget for this trip," I said, picking my words carefully.

"Don't worry, Mom's the ultimate bargain hunter," said Jacob.

Just as though she were negotiating to purchase coffee beans from a farmer, Norah told Mom flat out what the pieces would cost: a fraction of the best end-of-season sale prices. Mom's face cleared; I breathed in relief. Nascent interest glimmered in her eyes.

"Terra, you should have some things made, too," Mom said.

"No, that's okay, I've got plenty," I countered politely. The last thing I wanted to do was shop, not when I was finally here in China. I looked impatiently at the door, ready to leave.

"Really," insisted Mom.

So I found myself holding my arms out, getting my chest measured in front of Jacob. The tailor said something to Norah; they twittered. And when Norah didn't choose to translate, I could only imagine what they were saying about my chest. Compared to Norah, I was voluptuous. Not one of my finest moments.

As soon as the tape measure dropped from my inseam, measuring from my crotch down to my ankles (trust me, mortifying), Norah clapped her hands. "Why don't you kids look around town? I've got a long list of shops we have to visit."

"Do you think this is a good idea?" Mom looked worriedly at me, the idea of us splitting up petrifying her.

Even though the same concern troubled me, I bristled. I could take care of myself. And Mom would be with Norah. That was exactly what Norah said.

"We'll all be fine." She checked her watch. "We'll see you for an early dinner." To Mom, she said, "The place we're going to tonight has the world's best dumplings. Really, I dream about them."

"Come on," said Jacob, nodding toward the door. "Before they change their minds."

Half of me wanted to stay, make sure Mom wouldn't be embarrassed or treated badly, but she was already studying the fashion portfolio Norah had assembled for her, inspecting each picture like it held a key to a new route she'd never considered taking.

Jacob was waiting at the threshold, doorman to my own possibilities. "Ready?" he asked.

"Yeah," I said softly. And then, with more force, "Definitely."

The seventy-four-floor descent to the lobby was such a stomach-dropping plunge, I thought for sure my feet would lift off the floor. Around the thirty-second floor, my stomach returned where it belonged. Able to talk again, I quoted my plan for the day from memory: "The Yu Garden opened at eight thirty. We could walk the Bund after and then hit the museum in the afternoon. Although Mom may want to go to the museum, so we could shift that to tomorrow. Do you think that's what your mom would want to do, too?"

"This is very cruise director of you."

I glanced swiftly at Jacob to see if he was mocking me. Not mocking, but his lips were curved into a gentle, teasing smile.

"I'll tell you what," he said, leaning against the elevator wall.

"What?"

"Are you always this suspicious first thing in the morning?"

The problem was, I tended to be suspicious all the time, expecting people to tease me. I shrugged noncommittally. "Go on," I said.

"You choose one thing for us to do in the morning, and I'll choose something for the afternoon."

"But —"

As if he timed it to interrupt my protests, the elevator reached the ground floor just then, doors gliding open. Immediately, men and women surged on, a wall of suits preventing us from leaving. Jacob grabbed my hand, forced his way through, tugging me along with him until we were free of the crowd. Only when we were outside on the sidewalk did he release my hand, but I could still feel the warmth of his touch on my palm.

"So," he said. He pressed his hands together as though my touch lingered with him, too.

"So," I repeated.

A loud clang from the building being constructed next to the Jinmao Tower interrupted whatever Jacob was going to say. I craned my neck to see what was going on, but couldn't. The building was too tall, its pinnacle out of my sightline.

"You're looking at what's going to be the tallest building in the world," said Jacob.

"Poor Jinmao." It was about to fall even further from its former claim to fame. As it was, the tower could only brag that it was the fifth tallest in the world. Who knew that remaining the best at anything is hard, even for a building?

"Aren't people afraid it's going to topple or something?" I asked.

"You've got to have faith that some people know what they're doing." His eyes crinkled from his smile.

"Implying that you do?"

His grin widened in answer. "So sound good, garden first?"

"And you're going to pick what we do after?"

He nodded.

"What *are* we going to do after, exactly?"

"We'll wing it," Jacob said. Again, the maddening half smile.

But I didn't wing things — not tests, not artwork, not my exercise route. That would mean trusting in the risky unknown outside the Methow Valley. No, it was safer to have the trip mapped out, destinations picked beforehand, routes to and from plotted well in advance. So I unzipped my messenger bag to pull out the typed itinerary. (I had read somewhere that nothing makes Americans stand out as tourists more than their backpacks and sneakers. Hence, my black messenger bag and athletic Mary Janes.) My research was the advance team, blazing the trail before I made a single move.

"Do you know where the word 'itinerary' comes from?" Jacob asked as I scanned my perfectly formatted document of opening times and tips on how to bypass long lines and which routes to take during prime drive times.

"What does this have to do with anything?" I countered.

"Everything. It's from Latin, for 'journeys.' So trust me. You'll have fun."

Two corporate types exited a taxi just then, both of them lost in conversations they were having, not with each other but on their separate cell phones. The man and woman might have been traveling together. They might have been doing business together, but they were not having fun together. I thought of Merc living the jet-setting life I had dreamed about, but there was nothing glamorous about a life centered on paper and deals, meetings and conference calls.

Safe, I decided, didn't leave much room for fun.

I nodded. And with that, I left the end of the wagon line to join the advance team in the front.

chapter twenty-two

Bearings

SHANGHAI'S MOST FAMOUS GARDEN HAD been open for two hours before Jacob and I even made it to the Old City, a fact that irked me. All the guidebooks I'd studied had advised to be there, in line, for the garden's daily opening to avoid the crowds. For good reason, too. The Yu Garden had been first commissioned back in 1559 to be a place of tranquility, but peace and calm seemed to be the last thing found here today. On both sides of the narrow footbridge Jacob and I walked upon, other tourists staked their right to meander. Apparently, they thought that included the right to meander right over me and Jacob.

"I can't breathe in here," I said.

"Do you want to leave?" asked Jacob a mite too eagerly. All I had to do was say the word, and he'd lead me out of here. After all my research, though, I was determined to check this site, its opera house and museum off my tick list.

"No," I answered grimly and continued through a curved moongate that framed a tiny picturesque courtyard. There was no point in removing my camera from my messenger bag, not with this constant flow of people.

No one looked particularly moved by the ancient rock gardens or stone bridges that gleamed bone-white in the sun. I supposed that when you were busy making sure you weren't nudged into the pond by accident — and then mauled by the creepily hungry carp lurking in the polluted depths — it somewhat diminished your enjoyment of the garden. Still, as many people as there were inside the garden walls, it was an oasis compared to the bazaar outside, thronging with tourists bargaining for slippers embroidered with fantastical flowers, bundles of chopsticks, thick-handled art brushes, and the odd mandolin to slice vegetables into long curling strips.

"What are all these people doing out on a Monday morning?" I couldn't help grousing when an old man literally pushed me to the side so he could get up the stone steps first, and then scowled at me for inconveniencing him.

"Tourists, like us," said Jacob.

"I want to be a traveler, not a tourist." I stepped quickly to the end of another bridge when I heard the impatient clacking of heels behind us, two women walking determinedly, more than ready to run us off.

"What's the difference?"

"Huge. A tourist looks; a traveler participates."

"You will. That is, if you slow down and actually enjoy where you're going."

"We're going to end up in the water if we aren't careful," I said, looking pointedly at the crowds around us. "Anyway, you walked this fast when we were geocaching."

"Are we geocaching?"

"Well, no . . ."

"And we're not snowshoeing."

"No . . ."

"Then slow down. We've got all day."

"I would have thought you'd want us to speed through this."

"What would have been the point of coming then?" He guided us to a covered walkway set atop pillars of craggy rock over the pond. Miraculously, no one lingered here. It could have had something to do with the lack of seating aside from the railing. If only a while, we could claim this space our own. Jacob dug in his pocket and pulled out his ticket to the garden, handing it to me. "Before I forget."

Automatically, I accepted the slender strip of paper, feeling burdened the way I do with Mom, me always managing the minutiae, the keeper of the details: passports, emergency contact information, extra U.S. dollars in case the market failed and we needed our way out. It was exhausting to be paranoid and prepared. I asked, "Do they spot check tickets here?"

His brows furrowed. "No, I thought you might want it for a collage."

"Oh." I shook my head at my own misgivings and tucked his ticket with mine in the manila envelope I had packed specifically to hold whatever materials I encountered that would be perfect for a future collage. Now I took out my camera, and when Jacob wasn't looking, I snapped his photograph. At the last second, he turned to me, a half smile forming on his lips like he was about to tell me something salacious, something he knew would make me laugh uproariously and then be chagrined. I would know that smile anywhere. I lowered my camera, tucked it back into my messenger bag, wishing I could tuck away my painful thought just as easily: if you had asked me at that moment to close my eyes and conjure Erik, I couldn't have.

"What are you thinking about?" Jacob asked, straddling the railing like he was riding a horse, resting one foot on the bridge, the other on its ledge.

"Nothing," I said hastily, and perched on the railing myself, both feet on the ground. "Why?"

"You were someplace else for a second."

"Nope," I said, breathed in. The air here wasn't fume-choked, possibly because the garden and surrounding marketplace were pedestrian-only. Instead, I caught a whiff of earthy bamboo, the ripe odor of pond water, and the heavy scent of my guilt. "Just thinking this is exactly where I want to be."

I looked away from Jacob's inquiring stare, wishing I could tell him about Erik but not knowing how to explain that I had a boyfriend, especially after we'd had so many conversations. How would I bring it up now — *oh, by the way, I've been seeing this guy at home?* How could I explain that the routine of staying together with Erik was easier than the drama of breaking up? I could barely admit to myself, much less out loud, that I hadn't broken up with Erik because of the real risk that no one else would want me.

I swallowed, gestured around the garden. "Can you imagine what this would be like without all the people?"

"Nah, you need people for a garden to feel real, otherwise it's just a lab, some kind of social experiment with plants." Jacob leaned against the carved column, looking at me. "Me, though? I prefer Mother Nature, weeds and forest fires and bugs and all."

"But isn't this perfect?"

"It's manmade," he said slowly, considering his words. He pointed to the carefully placed waterfall tucked in the far corner, the garden's focal point. "I think there've been a lot of misguided attempts to change what's already perfect."

"Nothing's perfect."

"Maybe we don't have the same definition about what's beautiful. So define it. Define true beauty."

I watched a sinuous rivulet of water pour into the pond, thinking that I'd only had this type of conversation with the Twisted Sisters. It was as if we spoke a common language: art. The few times I had tried to express myself on this very topic — on why I was compelled to try to interpret and reflect beauty in my work — to Karin, to Erik, even to Claudius, they all had stared back at me, eyes glazed with boredom or indifference.

Without looking at Jacob, I said slowly, "Well, it seeps into you. It doesn't make you forget yourself, but totally the opposite." I chanced a glance at him. He was watching me intently. No glaze in his eyes. So I continued more bravely: "It connects you with everything and fills you with awe that you share the same space with something that glorious. Like a sunrise or a clear blue day or the most extraordinary piece of glass. And then suddenly" — my hands escaped their tight grip in my lap, and now my fingers splayed wide like fireworks in the air — "you have this epiphany that there's more to the world than just you and what you want or even who you are."

I stopped, embarrassed I had gone too far. I dug my nails into the railing at my hips, berating myself. Now, he'd think I was strange. Or worse, cerebral.

Jacob didn't say, *I know what you mean,* the way Erik might have even if he had no inkling what I was trying to say. Jacob didn't try to one-up me in a Dad-esque way to illustrate how uninformed and sophomoric my ideas were. Instead, he simply said, "That's exactly why nature always trumps gardens. Gardens are just reality pruned of chaos. What doesn't work, you rip out."

I thought now about Mom's garden, the one she labored over, planting vegetables and trees that had to be encircled in mesh to protect against deer. "Heaven forbid there's a dying patch of grass."

"Exactly."

"You've thought about this a lot."

"My dad's a landscape architect, you know." Jacob, for once, sounded bitter. "His job is to orchestrate beauty."

"I remember you telling me that." Gently, I asked, "You okay?"

"The wedding's in five days."

I nodded. I remembered that, too.

He sighed, clasped his arms around himself. "God, he's as clichéd as the gardens he designs."

I waited. I was good at waiting, and while I did, I listened to his breathing and the tinkling of the waterfall that drowned out everything but him and me.

"You know," he finally continued without meeting my eyes, "Mom put him through school, supported him while he was making a name for himself, and now that he's the go-to guy for people who've got money to burn and know zip about plants or design, he leaves her for a bimbette."

"At least your mom has her own career," I pointed out.

"Had."

"Had," I conceded. "But she isn't a cliché. That's a woman who never had a job, who became a stay-at-home mom and is stuck in a terrible relationship and can't leave because she doesn't think she can make it on her own." I didn't realize how angry I was at my mom until those words blew out of me, a micro squall in this garden. "Your mom can get a job tomorrow if she wanted. She doesn't need your dad."

"Maybe that was the problem," Jacob said softly. "Don't we all need to feel needed? That we'd be missed if we were gone?"

Three enormous carp swam to us, their heads emerging from the water, mouths craning wide in hope of a free meal. They looked a little too rapacious to be trusted. Still, as scary as their gaping mouths were, I felt bad. I had nothing to give.

Jacob stood abruptly. "Which way do you want to go?"

The pavilion had two entry points, one leading back to where we had come from, the other to places we had yet to see. North and south, east and west, regardless of the direction we could take, there were people, more and more people. This wasn't the China I had come to see.

"Out of here," I said.

His hand settled comfortably on the small of my back. And with an unerring and enviable sense of direction, Jacob found our way out of the walled garden.

The Shanghai Jacob showed me couldn't have been farther removed from the gleaming, futuristic skyline we had left this morning, or the populous garden we had just vacated. Instead, the narrow alley we were exploring was cramped, dark, filled with fetid smells. Where the markets surrounding the garden had featured beautiful architecture — those soaring, upturned rooflines that looked poised to take wing at any moment — I couldn't believe that people lived crammed in here amid molding wooden pallets, upturned buckets of uncertain origin. Parked outside a few doors were rounded pots. I didn't have the guts to peer inside.

"Please tell me those aren't what I think they are," I said. I kept my messenger bag clutched at my side.

"Well, they don't have toilets, if that's what you're asking."

My toes curled inside my shoes. I decided it would be wise to watch where I stepped while keeping a sharp eye overhead.

"A different world, isn't it?" Jacob asked.

"Definitely." I sidestepped a suspicious-looking puddle.

"Places like these won't last much longer."

Thank God, I thought.

He said, "Isn't it weird to think that this neighborhood has survived here for centuries, but the next time we're here, all of this will probably be razed for another skyscraper?"

"Progress is hard on history."

He glanced at me, a small jerky nod of approval. I breathed in, wished I hadn't. The pond in Yu Garden smelled like paradise compared to this rancid odor. But because I didn't want Jacob to think I was someone I was not, I admitted, "It'll be sad for this to disappear. But I have to tell you, I couldn't live here. I like indoor plumbing too much."

"Nothing wrong with modern conveniences. But just think: this is nothing compared to the rural villages."

We came to another intersection, headed right. I hoped Jacob knew where we were going since I was too disoriented.

"So what is" — I made quote marks — "'real Chinese culture'? Is it this? Or your hotel?"

"It's anything to do with money."

"Jacob!"

"I'm not kidding. Everything in China is tied to making a buck."

I wondered about what he said, whether it was just a deliberate comment to distance himself from his heritage, declare that he was wholly American, not somewhat Chinese. We passed a house with a cancerous mass of exposed wires. A round red lantern lay on the ground next to a battered stool. I stopped, riveted. Above us hung laundry, so gray Mom would never have deigned to use them even as rags back home. Who wouldn't be consumed with money if they lived in such squalor, if they had to worry about their next meal — and whether they would have a home because of the threat of progress.

I lifted my camera, photographed the laundry that fluttered languidly, tattered flags of surrender.

The funny thing was, after that, the longer we walked, the less revolted I felt. I slowed down, appreciating the unexpected vignettes as they revealed themselves to me: a tiny overgrown courtyard glimpsed through an open door. A bird serenading itself inside a bamboo cage. Three sun-faded lanterns hanging gaily in a row, like old women who still loved to dress up.

As I lifted my camera to a peeling door, Jacob marveled, "You could see beauty anywhere."

That's what I wished he could see, too, in China: that even within its ugliness, there lay a surprising beauty, breathtaking because it was so unexpected.

On our phone calls leading up to this trip, I'd relate some new fact about China I had dug up to Jacob. For all that time and all those conversations, there was one thing we never discussed: his orphanage.

"Can I ask you something?" I asked now from behind the comfort of my camera, unable to resist my urge to snap his picture against the weather-worn door.

"Shoot."

"Do you remember anything from when you lived here?"

Jacob thrust both hands in his pockets, his shoulders hunching. He quickened his pace, passed an open door, uncharacteristically didn't peer within, curious about what it hid. He was so silent, I thought he might ignore my question. God, me and my big mouth.

Then, suddenly, Jacob said, "I remember a few things, but I wonder how much of it I remember because of the pictures Mom took. Like at the orphanage. Do I remember the nursery or is it the picture of all those cribs?"

"I didn't think they allowed people to take pictures?" I asked quietly, remembering what I had read about China's orphanages. I kept my eyes on the ground now, not to look where I was going but so I could focus on Jacob's words, undistracted by anything else around me.

"They don't now — and they stopped letting people right after Mom adopted me. Some stupid BBC program about Chinese orphanages shut down adoptions for almost a year. They claimed that there were dying rooms for certain kids."

I could imagine those kids. The ones with birth defects or diseases, cerebral palsy, club feet, cleft palates. Port-wine stains.

"There was no real proof of them," Jacob said. "Anyway, Mom slid right on in before that lockdown."

"How old were you?"

"About three."

"Three."

"Some of the kids stay at the orphanages until they're eighteen." He shrugged, matter-of-factly. "That's where I probably would have been still. I mean, who would have wanted a boy with a cleft lip when they could have tried for a normal kid?"

"But your mom saw you."

"She was thirty and had given up on finding her soul mate. So she decided to adopt. And then a couple years after that, she met Dad. She should have held out."

"I know what you mean."

Jacob stopped, drew in a breath, and then looked meaningfully at me. "But then we wouldn't be here."

"True." I never thought I'd be grateful to my dad for anything. But standing here with Jacob in this dirty alley within sight of at least two chamber pots, I was. Without my father, I wouldn't be here.

"And what about your dad?"

Again, Jacob went quiet, and this time, instead of assuming that he was blowing me off, I knew he was just thinking before he chose his words carefully. He stopped before a door that had been painted cinnabar red once, the color now a faint streak over bare wood.

While I waited for him to answer, I zoomed into the rusty brass handle. I lowered the camera to find his intense gaze on me. "He's such a hypocrite. For all his talk about naturally occurring beauty, he left Mom for a younger woman. God, I think Bimbette even has fake boobs."

"Would your mom have been happier if they stayed together?"

"Happier?" He cocked his head to the side, ran his fingers along the warped door. "I think she just wanted to have the choice."

"Your mom doesn't seem like the kind of woman who'd stay with a man who didn't want her."

"Would you?"

It was a rhetorical question, not a personal one directed at me. Still, I couldn't look at Jacob when all I could picture was Erik's face at Christmas, ashamed that his cousin had seen me after my surgery. And here I was, still officially together with him.

We were at the end of the alley now, back near the bazaar. Above the roofline of these decrepit buildings was Shanghai, gleaming, modern, and new. The narrow streets were packed with even more shoppers now. Jacob checked his cell phone for the time. "We can do one more thing before lunch. Unless you're hungry."

"I need a little something," I admitted. And then, more suspiciously, "One more what?"

"Oh, ye of little faith" was all he would say.

"Just like home," Jacob said, smiling wryly as we wandered back in the direction of the Yu Garden, toward a circular sign with a familiar green mermaid. He was right; we could have been in Seattle except this Star-bucks sign hung off the corner of an upturned roof just like the ones in the garden.

"No, remember?" I said. "Colville's too small to have a Starbucks. This is nothing like my home."

It usually took a day before I got tired of Seattle's sprawl and busy-ness, its steep hills that were hard for me to drive, its maddening one-way streets. Just three hours away from Merc's quiet apartment and I was overwhelmed by Shanghai and the sheer number of people walk-ing, driving, and biking. Scores of bicyclists pedaled past us, their no-frill bikes nothing like the tricked-out roadsters the tourists in the Methow rode in their flashy spandex and special shoes.

"You'll get used to all the people," he assured me as we crossed the street to Starbucks.

"Okay, hang on," I said, holding my hand to my chest in mock hor-ror. "You're actually stepping foot in a bastion of American consumer-ism over a homegrown place? Geez, I need my camera."

"Take a look inside. This is China."

True, there were more tourists in the teahouse across the street than in the Starbucks. Chic women tottered inside on impossibly high heels, a man in a tailored suit had not one but two cell phones at his ear. This was modern Shanghai.

Jacob opened the door to the familiar scent of dark coffee. "Adven-ture in life is good; consistency in coffee even better."

"Spoken like a true coffee snob."

"That would be aficionado. Anyway, we need caffeine; you're crash-ing." He grinned at me, flourishing me inside.

"Sorry, I have to document this." But as soon as I removed my cam-era from my bag, the barista snapped something sharp at Jacob, glaring at him. He shrugged, shook his head: *I don't speak Chinese.*

The barista raised her eyebrows at him, obviously concluding he was an imbecile before she tapped emphatically on a sign at the counter: NO PHOTOGRAPHY. Chagrined, dumb tourist me, I dropped the camera back in my bag, but not before I whispered to Jacob, "Damned barista."

Jacob chortled, hugged me to him. "You got that right."

chapter twenty-three

Cartouche

THE NEXT MORNING, I ROSE early, around four. I couldn't fall back asleep. Mom must not have, either; she was rustling around in her bedroom. So I grabbed my journal from the bedside table and tiptoed to her room, careful not to wake Merc in the living room.

"Jet-lagged, too?" she whispered when I opened her door. I nodded. Her packages from yesterday's shopping excursion were laid out on the bed in a semicircle around her. She could have been Scrooge, counting her gold, just as gleeful, but much more generous. Mom turned down the sage green coverlet and scooted over to make room for me, giving me the warm spot.

"Are you having fun?" I asked Mom, careful when I crawled in beside her not to jostle her few purchases: the three bundles of raw silk, all in muted beiges. A few brocade frogs, like the ones used for clasping traditional Chinese clothes. And four small gold tassels.

She nodded, her eyes glowing. "I just can't believe I'm here. Susannah would have been so proud."

I kept quiet, afraid to make a noise for fear of scaring off this unexpected conversation. Mom rarely mentioned her big sister.

"You know, I was supposed to come here with her, oh, about twelve years ago," she said, dreamily. She pleated the soft green sheet that draped over her stomach. I didn't have to ask what stopped her: three letters, begins with D, rhymes with "cad." "We're following the itinerary almost exactly, too — a couple of days in Shanghai, then Beijing, then Xi'an, then back home." Her lips pursed unconsciously at that unintended reminder: home.

I didn't want to think about home any more than she did. So I asked, "What did you buy yesterday?"

"Oh, some things for your bedroom. You know how I've wanted to redo your room for the longest time. I thought I could make you curtains with this," she said, fingering the silk. "It'll go with everything."

Beige was no color I would have picked out for myself, not when there were verdant greens like the ones on Merc's bed. A flash of irritation tugged at me. Why had she wasted her money? I was going to college, damn it. I wouldn't be in that room much longer.

"Mom," I said mildly, "you should keep this for yourself, especially if you like it."

"I'm having a few things made."

"Not much. One skirt." Norah had regaled us at dinner with the story of their expedition to the fabric market, how Mom couldn't believe that stall after stall sold materials and buttons and zippers. "All of, what, seven dollars?"

"Five. I don't need anything more," she said simply.

She meant, she didn't deserve anything more.

My stomach growled. We had eaten an early dinner with Jacob and Norah, Merc too busy to join us at five. Before I could stop her, Mom heaved out of bed and bent down to her luggage, withdrawing an unopened bag of trail mix.

"Here, honey," she said, tearing the bag open for me. She looked sadly at the plastic bag, and I knew she was wishing she could pour the contents into a hand-painted ceramic bowl. Food, she always contended, tasted better beautifully presented.

Immediately, I felt guilty for being so irritated with her. Her first thought was always about me, my comfort, my pleasure. "Do you want some?"

Automatically, Mom reached for the bag, but as her fingers dipped inside, she withdrew them, empty-handed. "Actually, I'm not really hungry."

I must have looked surprised. God knew, I was. But Mom shrugged. "The tailor told me I was too fat."

"Mom!" I forgot to modulate my voice, I was that outraged. Mom shushed me, casting a wary glance at the door as though she expected Dad, the joy police, to barge in. But there was only Merc outside in the living room, sleeping. No, probably working. We hadn't seen him come in last night. The image of the tailor laughing at Mom, making fun of her, got to me. I knew I should have stayed with Mom yesterday. My voice I could quiet, but my words refused to remain silent: "That's awful. Why didn't you tell me yesterday? Why didn't you call me? I would have come."

But then Mom did the oddest thing; she laughed. "You know, she was just telling me the truth. I am too fat."

Mom, you are not. The denial was so ready on my lips, but I swallowed the false words when I saw the relaxed expression on Mom's face. She had closed her eyes, a little smile playing on her lips like she was remembering something fondly.

I demanded, "So what did Norah do? Did she say anything?"

"Oh, she said quite a lot. Until I stopped her." Mom turned her head toward me, eyes still closed, like a stuporous cat basking in the sun. "You know what, though? I appreciate the candor in this country."

We were quiet then. I wrote in my journal, catching up where I had left off last night, too tired to write. I probably should have stopped sooner yesterday; over the course of a page, my handwriting had gone from perfectly architected letters to illegible scrawl. Mom sighed contentedly beside me, and I thought she might have fallen back asleep until my stomach gurgled especially loudly.

"Go ahead and eat, honey," she said.

"Do you think Merc will mind though? Me eating in his bed?" I whispered like I was doing something wrong. The concept of breakfast in bed was unheard of at home; Dad would have lectured us about all the millions of germs a single bite of food invited into bed.

"Oh, who cares?" Mom said blithely, still not opening her eyes. "They're just crumbs. No big deal."

So I took one peanut, popped it into my mouth, chewed. Mom nodded, satisfied that she had fulfilled her maternal duty of keeping me well fed.

"So, honey," she said, only now opening her eyes, "what . . ." Her voice trailed off. I could feel Mom wanting to say more, her silence so pregnant with thoughts she was unable to express.

"What, Mom?"

"Oh, noth —" She stopped abruptly and sighed. Then, "Just be fair to him."

I flushed guiltily, knowing instantly what she was getting at. In a rush, she continued, "Be fair to Jacob. And Erik." She sidled an uncertain look at me, afraid she had overstepped her bounds. "Jacob's already been abandoned once, and now his dad's left. . . . Just be fair. Okay?"

"Mom, I am," I said, shaking my head adamantly as if I wasn't doing anything wrong. "We're just friends."

"Are you so sure about that?"

No, I wasn't. But I couldn't admit to Mom any more than I could admit to myself in my journal that in the most screwed-up way, it was beginning to feel like I was cheating on Jacob whenever I thought about Erik. Not the other way around.

That morning, we were supposed to catch a ride with Merc to Jinmao Tower, eat breakfast with him, and then reconnoiter with Jacob and Norah in their hotel lobby to go to the Shanghai Museum together. What happened instead was this: Merc received an emergency call at six in the morning (apparently, business happened round the clock in Shanghai), decided he didn't have time to eat breakfast with us after all. So to save money, Mom and I hitched a ride with him to work, where we planned to forage a cheap pastry of some kind. But then in the lobby, Mom said, "Let's call the Fremonts, see if they want to join us."

So I called. Mom looked relieved when Norah agreed to find a café with us as though a foray by ourselves would have been doomed to failure.

By seven thirty, we were done with our coffee and buns filled with barbecued pork. Norah checked her watch, asked, "What time does the museum open again?"

"Nine," I answered. I chose to ignore Jacob's snort as I bussed our table of the cups and plates. Yes, I was the walking, talking itinerary.

"What should we do now?" asked Mom. I noticed she had left a bite of her Chinese pastry on her plate.

"Let's head over anyway. We can poke around a park," said Jacob, playing with a packet of sugar. He glanced at me, grinned wickedly. What was he up to now?

I couldn't wait to find out.

As early as we were, the park Jacob picked for us to visit was already bustling with activity. We walked past a man who was doing some kind of calisthenics on a bench, balanced on his head, legs splayed open in a feat of astonishing male flexibility.

"Hey, can you do that?" I teased Jacob.

He grimaced. "Ouch."

We left our mothers before a group of old men and women practicing tai chi, their graceful, balletic movements belying their age. Dressed in loose tops and roomy pants, they followed the same routine like a choreographed dance. There was no instructor, no one calling out the ancient moves. How many times had they practiced this? A lump formed in my throat, their fluid motions were so beautiful. Jacob had already started up the path, and I was about to follow him when, without any embarrassment, Norah started miming their slow swinging of an arm, the meeting of the hands in the middle.

"Wait," I called to him softly.

Jacob turned back around, groaned. "Oh God, Mom. Just wait, she'll have your mom out there in a second."

"I doubt that."

Mom stood uncomfortably beside Norah, the two of them adjacent to the group. I didn't want to leave her, an outsider when all the other kids had been chosen for a team, when the game had already started without her. But Norah beckoned her silently. Slowly, slowly, Mom raised an arm. She stood there, immobilized, while the others flowed to the next position.

Oh Mom.

And then, Mom kicked out a foot, slow, graceful. She swooped low, a diving swan.

"She looks good," said Jacob, surprised.

She did. And as she spun slowly, her arms winding, I remembered when I was a little girl, Mom would turn on music to clean the house before Dad came home. I loved the way she had twirled me, admired the way her hips swiveled effortlessly one way and then another.

"She used to dance," I said and wondered when she had stopped. And why.

"She is again," Jacob said.

I could have stayed there all morning, forgotten the museum, just to watch Mom. But she noticed me there a ways up the path, stopped, and tucked her hair behind her ear self-consciously.

I knew Mom wouldn't continue while I stood there. The last thing I wanted was for my presence to rob her of this moment. "Let's go," I told Jacob, swallowing hard. Quickly, I yanked around, hurried along the path, not daring to look back.

Jacob caught up to me and said softly, "It's not you. Sometimes you can be more yourself with people you hardly know."

"But I want her to be herself with me," I whispered.

"It takes two." He held out his hand, not to hold mine, but to give me his GPS.

"What are you doing?"

"We," he corrected. "We are going geocaching."

I held the device away from me as though it were a poisonous snake and grimaced. Even though I had tried geocaching on my own, I couldn't make sense of the coordinates, somehow ending up north when I meant to go east. I admitted reluctantly, "You know I can't read these things."

"It's easy once you get the hang of it." Standing behind me, Jacob wrapped his hand around mine so that both of us held the device. If we could geocache all day like this, then sign me up. I could feel the heat of his body against mine. God, how easy it would be to lean back into him, forget the stupid cache. I wanted his arms around me, and I had to close my eyes against the strumming of my body.

One problem: Jacob didn't seem to notice me at all. He nudged me forward as though I were a marionette. "Watch the northern coordinates." According to the GPS, the last few digits on the latitudinal coordinates were growing smaller. "So if north and south run this way" — he pointed — "which way do we go?"

"This is a math problem," I accused him.

"You're good at math. Which way?"

I took a tentative step forward, then another, and this time, he slid his warm hand in my free one that wasn't holding the GPS. We continued hiking through another patch of grass, stepping over flower beds and squeezing through shrubs. So absorbed in feeling his hand in mine, wondering exactly what he thought about me, I completely forgot why we were foraging through a park until Jacob pulled his hand away. He reached for the GPS and said, "Bingo."

I blinked at him.

"We've reached the exact southern coordinates," he explained, and gave me back the GPS. Forget the device, I wanted his hand. "Now the eastern coordinates. Which way?"

"You're testing me again."

"No, proving to you that you're less directionally challenged than you think. So which way?"

Sighing, I turned to my right, walked a few steps. The last digits of the longitudinal coordinates increased, instead of decreased. So I backtracked, went the opposite direction, holding the GPS out like a divining rod.

"Okay, try not to look so obvious," he remarked from behind.

I spun around. "Hello? Let the driver drive, please."

We tromped across the grass, straying from the paved path. We passed countless flower beds, scarred park benches, old men playing chess. We circled around a lotus pond, all platter-sized leaves, no blooms. It was too early in the season for flowers. And through all of that, I kept thinking about why Jacob had held my hand . . . and why he wasn't holding it now.

"Okay, cruise director, we must be getting pretty close," said Jacob, ambling along so close to my side now that our arms brushed against each other. I have to admit, I was navigating by instinct as well as by GPS device. Before us was a tiny enclave made up of a park bench positioned some ways from a statue. The site looked promising, so I stopped, checked the coordinates. Astonished, I said, "I think we're here."

"You think or you know?"

"We're here." I held up the GPS. "Look for yourself."

He didn't. He had already dropped to his knees, scouring around the bronze statue when a man in jeans and a goatee walked past, eyed us suspiciously before moving on. He cast another accusatory look over his shoulder before dialing a number in his cell phone.

"So do you think he's calling the police?" Jacob asked me.

"Hurry, find that stupid cache!"

Jacob laughed. "Most people would abandon this about now."

"I'm not most people."

When Jacob started shaking the shrubs, I snickered and called out, "Okay, try not to look so obvious, will you?"

All the caches I had found with Jacob were hidden in sneaky, clever places: tucked inside a log, welded to a bolt, lodged inside a fake electrical box nailed to a tree. So I stood there, in a wedge of sunlight, and got my bearings, studying the surroundings. Jacob had moved to the bench, now peering underneath it, behind it. And then I saw it — or saw what looked like the ideal hiding spot for a crafty geocacher. The cache wasn't on the bench, but behind it. I hurried to the conspicuous clump of dead leaves under the spiky shrubs, used my shoe to brush away the debris, and there it was: a small metal green box.

"Found it!" I cried, proud of myself. But the treasure I most cherished was Jacob's answering grin.

Something must happen to women's plumbing when they reach a certain age, because both mothers needed to use a bathroom when we returned to collect them. This, after they'd just visited the facilities at breakfast. And no, they couldn't wait for the museum to open in just fifteen minutes. Luckily, Jacob remembered seeing a bathroom while we were geocaching. I could have located it by its odor alone. The reek was even worse inside: no toilet, just two holes. In the ground. With nary a sheet of toilet paper in sight.

"You know, the toilet in the Venice train station is even worse," said Norah conversationally as she dropped her pants.

On so many levels this was wrong. First, forget the toilets-around-the-world retrospective. This facility was bad enough; I didn't want to imagine worse. And second, I really didn't need to see Jacob's mother or my own — oh God, she was sliding down her elasticized pants, too — doing their business. Me, I needed to pee now, too, but was afraid to use the holes. This was not a good traveler moment. Or even a good tourist one. I had become the epitome of stupid American visitor, the one I vowed not to be, the one who was squeamish and judgmental of local customs.

"I don't suppose you have any tissue left?" Mom asked Norah.

"No, I used it all yesterday."

"Oh." Both women stared at each other, stumped. Then, Mom: "My legs are shaking; I don't think I can hold this position for much longer." They started cackling. Then came the snorts when Norah bounced a couple of times, to dry off, I suppose.

And me, the girl who thought she had prepared for every contingency, was caught without my Kleenex. I had left it in my backpack when I changed to the more chic messenger bag.

I knew who had a cache of napkins. So I told the moms to wait a moment, which elicited some groaning. Why they had already squatted and used the toilet without fully sussing out the situation, I don't know. Quickly, I flew out, breathing in big gulps of fresh air. Jacob was waiting outside.

"What's with all the laughing?" he asked.

I shook my head, grudgingly asking him, "Could I have a napkin? Better make that three."

He grinned, removed a handful from his pocket. "Thought you'd never ask."

"Trust me, I never thought I would," I said, and all but sprinted back to the bathroom.

Let's just say there's a reason why Chinese women have such svelte figures. It takes awesome thigh muscles to squat.

When I came out of the bathroom, I squirted half my antibacterial cleanser into my palm, rubbed vigorously. And then I pushed the tiny bottle on Mom and Norah, who were standing next to Jacob, watching an old man holding a calligraphy brush three feet long. He dipped the brush in a bucket of water, and with one hand behind his back like a fencer, he began writing on the pavement, his movements every bit as graceful as the tai chi practitioners, deft, assured, meditative.

I approached the man slowly, not wanting to interrupt his flow, glad that the mothers had quieted, too, as if they knew whatever this man was doing was special. I don't think the calligrapher would have noticed me anyway, so lost in that moment. Not lost, I corrected myself. Found. I had never seen a person more present than this man, writing that vertical drop of characters over and over.

"What's he writing?" Mom whispered to Norah, trying but failing to be quiet.

Norah stepped closer to the words, the watery characters already fading, deciphering them in silence. I was drawn to those words myself, traversing the length of the sidewalk. But I wanted those dancing characters to remain a mystery, draw what meaning I wanted from those unknown glyphs before they vanished like poems recited into the wind.

"His name," Norah said. "Wisdom. Gentle wisdom."

His name. I was surprised. What had I thought he'd be writing? Some Buddhist koan? An ancient Tang poem? With one last downward stroke, a subtle flick of his wrist, he finished the final character — was it gentle? Or wisdom? Then he dipped the brush in water and held it out to me.

I smiled, shook my head, embarrassed. Me?

Again, without a word, he urged the brush on me.

I glanced at Mom, feeling foolish, about to step away from this old calligrapher, his face the wrinkled bark of an ancient tree. On the path, Mom shifted, her movement reminding me of her practicing tai-chi, the first time I could remember her trying something new. Even without Dad here, my presence had censored her. Made her self-conscious.

I didn't wait for the calligrapher to offer his brush to me for the third time. I inclined my head respectfully and took the brush from him, its weight unfamiliar in my hand.

What to write? What to write? As beautiful as the calligrapher's name was, it was fast evaporating in the sun. In another fifteen minutes, those watery marks would be gone, almost as if they had never been there.

Memento mori.

I had yet to sign a single piece of my work, had never thought myself worthy of a cartouche, never claiming my creations. Or that I was the creator.

I held that long brush, and I wrote my name on this forgiving canvas. My first attempt was clumsy, one thick line, no swoops, all blurs. But it, like the master's beautifully formed name, started to fade.

So I tried again. *Terra,* I wrote. Better.

Terra.

I forgot about Mom watching me. I forgot about Norah. And even Jacob. This moment was mine. And it would last until it merged fluidly with the next beautiful moment and the next. What was there but this moment, this brush, the sidewalk as my scroll, and my name?

Terra

Terra

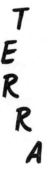

chapter twenty-four

Wanderlust

HALFWAY DOWN THE NARROW COBBLESTONED street, flanked on either side with long flags naming the expensive boutiques and trendy restaurants within the old buildings, I could hear Mom and Norah cackling. And then Mom's voice, incredulous, brayed loud above all the other dinner conversations: "There's a naked spa? In Lynnwood? Really?"

"You'd think they were in college," Jacob said as though he were divining my thoughts.

"Where'd they get their energy?"

"Shopping high. They must have found some bargains."

Clearly, Jacob understood women — or at least our mothers.

Was I the only one flagging, my head fogging with weariness? After spending the entire morning in the Museum and then sharing a lunch of dumplings, the moms had split off to — what else? — hit the Pearl Market while Jacob and I found another geocache, this time on the Bund, Shanghai's waterfront.

Mere feet away from their patio table, our mothers still hadn't noticed us, too engrossed in talking about Norah's monthly trips to some Korean spa outside of Seattle. A half-empty bottle of yellow rice wine sat on the table between them. Jacob held the restaurant door open for me. Like the rest of the Xintiandi neighborhood, this restaurant was located inside a refurbished stone gatehouse, the kind the majority of Shanghainese lived in up until the Second World War.

Inside was the most exquisite restaurant I had ever seen, a world apart from the rustic brew pub in Colville with its sticky scarred tables and rifles mounted on the walls. These walls were painted a soft brown, and the far wall a deep eggplant purple. Votive candles nestled in thick glass vessels, orange as a sunset, flickering on the modern wood tables around the dining room. Carved screens hung from the walls and created intimate alcoves for couples whose heads were bent close together. Slabs of smooth stone, worn from time and use, lined the floor. I wondered if they had been salvaged from ancient villages.

"So much for third-world country," I whispered to Jacob.

"Welcome to the new China," he said as a hostess glided to us, a young woman dressed in the restaurant colors, her tailored dress of brown edged with purple clung to her tiny figure. "For better or worse."

"Better or worse?" Was he ogling the hostess? Was she the better? Her waist was so tiny, I could have encircled it with my hands. With her hair pulled on top of her head, she looked every bit the city sophisticate, and I felt country gauche in my dark jeans, Pumas, and black T-shirt. I wished now that we had made time to go back to Merc's so that I could have changed into the one dress I had packed. It may have been shapeless, but it didn't wrinkle and it was black.

The hostess quickly sized us up and asked Jacob something in Mandarin, her tone as snooty as anything I'd heard at school or in the movies. Clearly, she had written us off as poor backpackers who couldn't afford a single strand of noodle.

Jacob sighed before answering equally emphatically in English: "I'm American." This was at least the third time today when someone assumed based on his features that Jacob was a native speaker. As innocent as that assumption was, it wore on Jacob — just as it did on me when people expected me to be the poster child for the port-wine-stained, patiently explaining the what and whys of my birthmark.

"I don't speak Chinese," he continued.

Deftly, the hostess switched to English, unflustered. Amazing, she was bilingual in condescension, now eyeing him as though it were some mental defect that prevented Jacob from speaking Mandarin: "How may I help you?"

"Our mothers are outside." Jacob murmured into my ear, his warm breath against my neck making me shiver, "Worse, you asked? Attitude, for one."

Ignoring the hostess, we walked to the patio door. If any of the cosmopolitan diners lifted their heads, branded me a tourist, as we passed them, I didn't notice. I was so focused on the heat and the pressure of Jacob's hand through the thin cotton of my shirt.

As beautiful as the restaurant had been, I was relieved to be out in the night air. Although more casual, the patio was still lovely, lit by the same votives, decorated in the same rich brown-and-purple hues. But the conversations were convivial, looser, with Mom's and Norah's intermittent laughter punctuating the evening. It wasn't until we were nearly upon our mothers that they noticed us, both placing their glasses on the table at the same time. I could smell the sweetish scent of their wine when Mom broke into a few latent giggles, unable to contain herself.

"Terra, you won't believe what Norah just told me. There's a spa just for women near Seattle" — her voice rose in delighted scandal as I took my seat beside her — "where you walk around completely stark naked."

Norah topped off Mom's wineglass. "It's a traditional Korean bathhouse where they scrub you until you're almost raw."

"Sounds like fun," said Jacob doubtfully.

Mom's eyebrows quirked. She was agreeing.

"You two have to try it sometime," Norah urged as I unfolded the heavy napkin and placed it in my lap. "I tell you, it's transformative."

Mom nodded. What Norah took as assent was merely Mom being polite. Going naked in front of other women? She'd never submit to that willingly. Nor, come to think of it, would I. I had missed my normal workout, my five hundred stomach crunches, for the last three days. Tonight, I promised myself. Tonight.

The candle sputtered, laughing along with the mothers, until it burned bright and steady again. In its light, and with laughter lingering on her face, Mom lost a full decade. Instead of this morning's fat-woman uniform — another oversized shirt worn unbuttoned over an embroidered T-shirt — Mom had changed into a vivid orange blouse, a color I had never seen on her. In fact, I couldn't remember her wearing anything more vibrant than pale purple since her weight gain, certainly not since Dad had likened her extra-large clothes to a circus tent. As subtly as I could, I pulled out my camera, its click drowning out Dad's remembered *chuckle, chuckle*.

Mom's hand flew to her double chin self-consciously, belatedly hiding it. "Why did you have to do that?" she asked.

"Mom," I said as I put away my camera, "you look beautiful." Ignoring her denial, I tested the silk of her new shirt, soft yet thick. "This is a gorgeous color on you."

"To tell you the truth, it was a miracle I found anything that fit," Mom said simply, not defeatist or with shame. "You like it?"

I nodded.

"Good, I got you one, too."

"I can't wear this."

"Why not?" A frown creased Mom's forehead, a cloud over her happiness.

I don't wear bright colors, I was going to answer. I never wore colors that either called attention to or clashed with my birthmark, which basically resigned me to drab. How was I any different from Mom, dressing dowdily as though our roles were to recede in the background, never pop to the foreground? Norah must have understood my internal battle, because she flipped open the menu decisively and said, "Just say thank you, Terra. Anyway, you better get used to saying that with all the clothes we ordered for you."

"What clothes?"

She and Mom smiled conspiratorially, and it was Mom who said, "For college."

I fell back against my chair. It was the first time Mom had ever acknowledged my leaving for college. Little earthquakes were constantly shifting earth's plates beneath our feet; I knew I had just experienced one of them.

Norah pulled out her BlackBerry, called up her favorite shopping haunts. "We have one more shopping day ahead of us tomorrow. Everything we're having made should be ready when we meet back here next week."

"Everything?" Jacob asked now, nodding his head in thanks when the waiter poured some bottled water in his glass. "Should I have packed another three empty suitcases?"

"Yes, my Sherpa, and that's not even counting the silk market in Beijing," said Norah seriously. And then to me: "Your mom has more stamina than anyone I've ever shopped with."

Mom held her glass up to Norah's and they clinked them together.

"Which is saying a lot," muttered Jacob good-naturedly.

Eagerly, Mom dragged one of her packages to the table, unmindful of the landmines of wineglasses and water cups. She pulled out a set of bed linens, bright red peonies scattered on an expanse of green, a cutting garden of fabric for the bedroom.

"That's so . . . bright," I said, thinking of Dad and his muted earth tone mandate for our house. There was no way he'd ever allow anything this alive in the master bedroom.

"I fell in love with them," Mom said, shrugging helplessly. The way she laughed, I was glad she felt so happy and carefree. And safe — safe enough to purchase what she loved, not what was practical.

Here, sitting in Shanghai, a million light-years from Colville and my father, I got a glimpse of what my mom would have been like had she never met a certain cartographer. This was mom, unbounded, uncharted. A land that was still a little wild, a lot unknown, and painfully beautiful.

We were halfway through the second basket of dumplings filled with hot broth, pork, and crab — the first basket so delicious we needed another — when Merc finally collapsed into the empty seat at our table.

Not that this was helpful or useful, but I told him, "God, you're the one who looks jet-lagged."

"Tell me about it," he said, and barked out an order for beer. "Rough day. My deal is falling apart. So what did you do today?"

Our short recap didn't hold Merc's attention. Even as I told him about our bathroom escapade, Merc pulled out his BlackBerry, checked a message, and then admitted, "I haven't made it to that park yet." He sighed, waved his BlackBerry as though it made an acceptable excuse. "Mom, I won't be able to take you guys to Beijing. My client's IPO is imploding."

"It's okay," Mom said, instantly absolving him of any guilt. It was as if she had become so accustomed to disappointment, so inured to people reneging on their promises that she expected setbacks, heartbreak. Couldn't Merc see the panic in her eyes? Couldn't he see how she focused on me, expecting me to figure everything out?

More combative than I intended, I asked, "Why not?"

His lips thinned, reminiscent of Dad and his quiet, fomenting rages. How many of Merc's girlfriends had seen those thinning lips? How many of them decided they didn't want a lifetime of those thinning lips?

Mom intervened. "Really, it's okay."

Jacob and his mom exchanged a look I couldn't quite interpret, her silent ask and Jacob's answer. Then, he nodded. Norah placed her chopsticks on the table, rested her chin on her folded hands, and asked, "Why don't you two come to Hangzhou with us instead of Xi'an? I have one meeting in Beijing, and then you could fly with us there. Or, it's just a two-hour drive from here. You could cancel Beijing altogether, and just meet us there in two days. Your pick."

I was stunned. All through planning the trip, Jacob had made it clear that after a day together in Beijing, he and his mom would fly alone to Hangzhou, where they'd make the pilgrimage to the village that housed his orphanage. I understood that: that journey was personal, concerning him, his mother, and his birth mother, no one else.

"Oh, no," I said at the same time Mom declared, "I would love that."

I blinked at Mom, the woman who had never voiced her opinions about anything, who viewed change of plans as anathema.

"You'd be welcome," Jacob said, his gaze holding mine steadily, warmly across the table. I knew what this meant, this offer to share in his past.

"We can skip Beijing and Xi'an, can't we, Terra?" Mom asked.

Merc missed the undercurrents of the invitation, not entirely surprising when he was more focused on reading between the lines of an e-mail and answering in a flurry of thumb-typing.

Jacob and our mothers turned to me as if I was the decision-maker. The least risky route would be to follow Jacob and Norah — let them continue to be our tour guides. But as I glanced over at Mom, fingering her wedding ring on its chain around her neck, I didn't want to always be married to the safe route, especially if it meant giving up what we wanted. As much as I welcomed spending more time with Jacob, I also yearned to see the Great Wall, the Forbidden City, the Summer Palace. The Great Wall was all Mom could talk about — her sister's favorite place in all of China.

"How about if we do Beijing on our own for two days and then meet you in Hangzhou for the last two?" I asked. That would give the Fremonts time to visit the orphanage on their own. "We can save Xi'an for another trip."

"But how would we get to Hangzhou by ourselves?" Mom asked, panic swelling in her eyes at the thought of us traveling alone. As though we were totally defenseless.

"We'll figure it out, Mom," I said.

Norah said soothingly, "It's an easy two-hour flight from Beijing." And then, "Merc, why don't you have your assistant make the flight arrangements for them?"

"What?" For a moment he looked flustered, and then said, "Yeah, my assistant can change the airplane tickets, if it's really what you guys want."

No doubt his assistant had altered his travel arrangements a million times, trips with girlfriends canceled last minute. Trips back home never booked. Work always took precedence over fun and family. That laid-back, affectionate guy at Christmas was simply a disposable costume, tried on and discarded. Too bad; I had really liked that guy.

Across the table, Jacob smiled at me a little crookedly, a little uncertainly, as if dumbfounded by this step he had taken, inviting me to Huangzhou. Even so, his eyes were so warm, they made fondue of my thoughts until I saw Merc sidle a glance from Jacob to me, wistfully.

Maybe Merc had been afraid of the guy he became when he was with Elisa — looser, freer, like intimate chats on a patio compared to staid dining room small talk. I knew how hard it was to reveal myself, each admission of my secrets and dreams making me vulnerable because they could become weapons to scoff at me. To echo the doubts so stubbornly lodged in my head. As I suspected, Merc returned to his BlackBerry once more, his face setting like hardening cement into its normal, dispassionate business mask. Work was as good a shield as any to protect against intimacy that could scrub someone raw.

The last thing I wanted to do now was return to Merc's apartment and listen to him clacking away on his computer late into the night. Mom must have felt the same way, because after dinner she said, "Could we walk a little?"

"You just want to window-shop," teased Norah.

"That — and I'm so full," said Mom.

I glanced swiftly at Mom, surprised by this admission. But she had already strolled ahead with Norah, Merc trailing slightly behind them — now on a phone call. I could hear Norah's voice piercing the night air with her excited plans: "Just wait until you see the silk market in Beijing. I'll make sure you and Terra have all the details."

Back home, Main Street pretty much shut down at ten with the one exception of the pub. That closed at the late hour of eleven. But here with midnight on the horizon, people were still thronging the Xintiandi neighborhood, filling it with a vitality I had never felt in my town. A line of the fashionably black-garbed, not much older than me and Jacob, snaked down the narrow pedestrian street. Every so often, the door to the nightclub opened, and a few measures of loud music escaped before being shut behind the door again. It was weird to think that this would be my life in college, just five months away: hitting the town with friends, going clubbing. I couldn't help but think of Karin's exasperation now: *Forget Erik. Why would you start something now with a Goth guy who's going to be in high school for another year?*

She was right; it didn't make sense, but I loved being with Jacob. As if he knew, he smiled at me and then nodded to the bouncer, a sumo wrestler of a man whose hair was pulled into a slick ponytail. The man motioned to me.

"What does he want?" I asked Jacob nervously.

"You to be one of the beautiful people inside."

I laughed, not believing him. But the bouncer gestured more emphatically and started to unhook the red velvet stanchion barring the door. For me. I shook my head, *no thanks,* conscious now of the swing of my blond hair. As strange as it was to be a foreigner, so obviously different from everyone else in this land, it was also strangely freeing. Back home, everyone knew about my port-wine stain. Here, I was a blond, blank slate.

Jacob and I had fallen behind the rest of our group, silent now as we passed a handbag store, then a shoe store where dainty sandals were displayed like sculptures atop pedestals.

"This is beautiful," I said, ignoring the shop windows to trace the gleaming stone walls fronting another boutique.

"You know what's funny?" Jacob asked. He didn't wait for my answer. "You can see beauty in everything, except for yourself."

Deflect, deflect. Heat rose to my face. "Oh, you mean that bouncer back there?" I gave a self-deprecating shrug, bunched my hair in my fist and laid it over my right shoulder. "That had to do with me being different, that's all."

"Exactly." Gently, he brushed a strand of hair off my cheek.

I swallowed hard. Erik thought my body was beautiful, Karin that it was enviable. At random times, people had noted that my hands were beautiful, or my hair. The Twisted Sisters had called my art beautiful. Mom had the best intentions and always told me before and after my laser surgeries that I *would* be beautiful. But no one had ever said that *I* was beautiful, all my parts taken together, not just my bits and pieces.

Jacob had stopped a few steps back, but I hadn't noticed, just forging fast ahead, until I sensed that our comfortable silence had become merely silence. I found him behind me in the middle of the alley, his arms spread wide.

"So how is this any different from that neighborhood yesterday?" he asked, meeting me halfway as I starting walking toward him.

I knew what he was talking about: that warren of dirty streets outside the Yu Garden, the ones filled with chamber pots and random debris. This neighborhood must not have been all too different once. It wasn't hard to imagine this alley, filled with trash, smelling of urine and grease.

"Someone saw its potential," I said. "That there was beauty in the old."

"Isn't that weird? Someone noticing is all that saved this neighborhood from being neglected like the other one?"

"But what happened to all the people who lived here?" I looked across the alley to a boutique, filled with couture clothes I could never afford. How could most of the people who lived here in China?

"That's the Chinese way. You raze the old to raise the new."

"So they were kicked out?"

"Presumably relocated."

I felt guilty for standing here, belly full, preparing to take Mom to the silk market for another mini-spending spree in Beijing. Guilty for the packages Mom was toting far, far ahead of us now. "Isn't there a middle ground? Like making the living conditions better without booting out the people?"

"Take what you have and just make it the best it could be?" he asked.

I nodded; my reflection — that distorted copy of myself, blurred from both the shopwindow and my thick makeup — did the same.

"That" — Jacob took my hand in his and squeezed — "that would be ideal."

He didn't let go. Neither did I.

chapter twenty-five

Prime Meridian

IF THERE WAS ONE THING I refused to be, it was an insignificant footnote in some boy's history. For one frightening moment, it seemed as though I was going to be an insignificant footnote in Beijing's 3,000-year history. As Jacob, our mothers, and I crossed the busy intersection, separating modern Beijing from its old city, we narrowly missed getting flattened by a fleet of speeding bicyclists. It was one thing for them to have a death wish, pedaling around without helmets, and another for them to kill us. Instinctively, I yanked Mom onto the sidewalk, looked back. Jacob was at the rear — he literally had our backs — so he'd be the one hit, not us. He met my eyes over our mothers' heads. "You okay?"

I nodded.

Norah yelled at the bicyclists in Mandarin. They ignored her. Still, she glared righteously at them. At least she had the satisfaction of shouting insults. Meanwhile, Mom trembled at my side, she was so scared. I didn't blame her.

"God, Mom," groaned Jacob, tugging his vitriolic mother over to the safety of the sidewalk. "I can't take you anywhere."

A slight man had stopped at the corner with us, dressed like one of the jock-tourists in the Methow with shorts that showed off his muscular legs and a long-sleeved shirt so he wouldn't burn. "Very impressive," he said in English, and then switched to Mandarin. For a moment, Norah was all coquettish smiles, laughter, modest shakes of her head. Death had borne down on us a scant two minutes ago and she was flirting.

Jacob stood close to me, as though he were still trying to keep me safe. On my other side, Mom was chuckling as the man finally left, alone. I thought it was a latent response to our near-accident, a precursor to a meltdown. So did Norah. She asked, concerned, "Are you okay, Lois?"

"We almost get killed, and you get picked up?" said Mom. "Some women have all the luck."

At that, Norah looked surprised, then bemused, her expression finally settling on relief. "I can still work it, can't I?" Her eyes crinkled as she smiled broadly. "Not bad for a menopausal fifty-year-old."

Mom nodded. "You can say that again."

"You can, too, Lois," said Norah before she went back to leading our way.

Mom looked thoughtful as we strode past a corner crowded with canopy-covered rickshaws. I caught her skimming her hands along her hips, almost like she was trying to reconnect with the athletic body she used to have.

Before the Fremonts had to leave for the airport in a few hours, we had decided to tour the *hutongs* together, the ancient, labyrinthine neighborhoods of Beijing. Like the old neighborhoods in Shanghai, these were also threatened by China's national bird, the crane with its wrecking ball of a beak. A group of rickshaw drivers, all men, stopped their conversation to stare at me. I glanced away uncomfortably, but not before Jacob stationed himself at my side, buffering me from the men, claiming me as his territory. I probably should have been annoyed, but I have to admit, his protectiveness was flattering.

"We can just walk in the *hutongs*," Norah said, dismissing the rickshaws as rolling tourist traps. Past the long row of pedicabs lining each end of the street like anxious wallflowers at a dance, jostling to be the chosen one. We headed toward the alleys, too narrow for cars. I checked to make sure Mom was with me. She wasn't. Panicking, I stopped, scanning the crowds of tourists being waylaid by the rickshaw drivers. At last, I spotted her half a block down, lingering by the pedicabs, lost in thought.

"Mom, you scared me," I said after backtracking to her. I placed my hand on her soft forearm. "I thought I lost you."

"Oh, I'm sorry." Mom shook her head, freeing herself of her trance. She turned her back on the rickshaws.

Holding her arm, I rose on tiptoe to search for Jacob and his mom, spotting his blond mother among the mostly Asian crowd. I had forgotten to let them know I was going back for Mom, kicked myself for that oversight. "We should catch up, Mom," I told her urgently, tugging on her arm gently. Once we lost the Fremonts, we wouldn't be able to find them, especially not in these unnamed alleys.

"I'm sorry."

That easy compliance, those automatic apologies, made me stop, ask myself what I was doing. I dropped my hold of Mom's arm, scalded by the realization that I was no different from Dad, rushing her just when she wanted to poke around. He was forever hovering, ordering her to hurry up, get going, don't look, don't touch. What did it hurt, really, if we slowed down? So as Mom started toward the Fremonts, I touched her hand gently. "What were you thinking about?"

"Oh." She laughed self-consciously, waved her hand in the air to bat away her dreams. "Never mind. It was nothing."

Before, I might have accepted that. I would have rushed to catch up to Jacob. But I waited, giving Mom space to continue. And in that space was my invitation: *go on, tell me.*

"Well, if you really want to know . . ."

"I do."

"I was just remembering how my dad took me to New York when I was thirteen. He took each of us there when we turned thirteen, all by ourselves. Susannah first, then Jonathan. And then, finally, it was my turn." She stared at one of the blue rickshaws, the fringe on its canopy swaying hypnotically in the light breeze. "Dad hired a pedicab to tour us around Central Park, and it dropped us off for dinner at the Tavern on the Green. I felt like Alice in Wonderland."

This Alice looked like she was regretting climbing out of the hole, leaving Wonderland. "Mom," I urged, "go on a ride."

"Oh, no." She shook her head instantly. "It's too expensive."

Hiring a rickshaw was expensive, for us at least. Merc, out of guilt, had tried to push some money on us, but Mom had her pride. I did, too. We declined his cash. Even though we were on a strict budget, I wasn't going to let money get in the way of making another memory for Mom. We'd scrimp on a couple of meals, no big deal. "We'll only be here once."

She hesitated then and looked down at herself as though remembering now that she wasn't the skinny girl of her youth, or the toned woman who'd ride horses and hike the Cascades for miles just three years ago. "I'm too fat."

One of the rickshaw drivers must have sensed a tourist getting away, because he waved her urgently to his pedicab. Her weight clearly wasn't an issue.

Again, Mom demurred. "We should catch up."

I took a deep breath and approached the driver, an underfed man who was all corded muscles in his arms, his calves. Between Norah's language, Jacob's sense of directions, and Merc's English-speaking driver, I hadn't had to navigate on my own or try out my meager vocabulary.

"*Duibuqi,*" I said, feeling silly to be using the few phrases I had mastered from the Mandarin language tapes I'd checked out of the library. For all I knew, my tones were off. But, surprise, the driver smiled and responded in a spate of fast Mandarin.

I blinked at him: *Huh?*

He repeated himself, slower now.

I shrugged helplessly.

He tried again, louder, hoping volume would help me understand. Now what? I looked helplessly at Mom, embarrassed and frustrated, ready to give up. It would have been so much easier to walk away, but Mom smiled in encouragement. So taking a deep breath, I turned back to the driver. What I couldn't express in words, I could try with a combination of hand signals and charm. I smiled, pointed to his rickshaw.

He quoted me a price slowly now. I knew because I heard *yuan* — but clearly, I should have studied numbers more. I had no idea how much yuan he had asked for.

Flummoxed, I rubbed my neck nervously. And then I remembered my notebook in my heavy messenger bag, which I handed to him now. The price he wrote was more than I remembered reading about in my DK tour book. So I shook my head, countered on paper. At the end, he smiled. I smiled back at him, even though I was certain I had overpaid.

"Nice, Master Negotiator," I heard Jacob saying behind me. I spun around, my face hot. He and Norah had listened to my lame negotiations? Were they groaning that Mom and I had succumbed to a touristy experience? Then, I decided that I didn't care. I had done my best, I secured a rickshaw, and Mom was finally doing something she really wanted.

"Aren't you coming, too?" Mom asked me nervously.

"Oh, no," I said, even though it did look fun. I just didn't want to admit that she was too big for us to share a rickshaw, and we couldn't afford two of them.

If only she didn't look at me with such pleading now. So I reassured her. "Mom, it's totally safe; all the guidebooks say so. And it's just an hour."

"Why don't we all go with your mom? You kids can share a rickshaw," offered Norah, already pulling out her wallet. "I'll be the grand pasha of my own."

I shook my head, not wanting to accept any charity, however generously offered.

Norah protested vehemently at that, and with much more efficiency than my negotiations, Norah sealed a deal for the rickshaws. Just as I suspected when she whipped out some cash, I had overpaid and felt at once inadequate and cheated. Norah caught my look and said, "Think of it as the dumb tourist tax. Any time you travel, you just figure that you'll be overcharged at least once. It's part of traveling."

I caught Jacob glancing at the drivers — some of whom looked like they could use a good couple of hours in a dentist's chair and then a week's pass to an all-you-can-eat buffet — before jerking around, purportedly to study a sign.

"You know what, Mom? I want to walk around," Jacob said firmly. In his pause, I heard his unspoken *by myself* and then saw his second swift look at the drivers. A lot of the drivers weren't all that much older than the two of us. In another life, would Jacob have been one of them? In Jacob's place, I decided I wouldn't have wanted to ask one of these guys to haul me around so I could gawk at ancient dwellings either.

I nudged Norah as I climbed into a rickshaw with a teasing, "After traveling with three women, he's probably sick of our chitchatting."

Jacob nodded slightly at me, relieved, and I knew I had guessed right: he needed some head time, especially before hopping on a flight that would bring him one step closer to his orphanage and his past.

Norah agreed slowly, "We'll see you here in an hour."

With a grunt, the first rickshaw driver pushed off, pedaling Mom away. I heard her abrupt bark of laughter, couldn't decipher if it was fear-driven, but they disappeared around the bend. Even with us following, it was as if Mom's driver had ridden off with my heart.

"She'll be fine," said Norah, and she swept her hand in the direction where Mom had vanished.

"I know," I said, softly. I had to let Mom go on her own just as she would have to let me go in a few months. I glanced at Norah's anxious face. "He'll be fine, too."

Norah nodded, her body stiff beside mine, practically restraining herself from returning to Jacob. And then as if she were blessing his journey, she repeated, "He'll be fine. He'll be fine."

Getting ready for the trip and waiting for it to start had seemed interminably long, yet already we were saying goodbye to Jacob and Norah.

"It's just for a couple of days," I overheard Norah assuring Mom from across the table where we were finishing lunch. Plates with the barest remnants of fish, eggplant, fried tofu covered our table, Norah going a little gourmand on us, ordering five dishes to sample. I had tried not to worry about the cost of this five-star restaurant that Norah had been eager to visit based on one of her foodie friend's recommendation. Now that I was stuffed, I couldn't muster enough care to worry about our budget. I didn't want to see Jacob and Norah leave any more than Mom did, any more than Jacob wanted to go. He couldn't have looked more morose than if he were back in his Goth getup.

"Here," said Norah, pulling out her pen, "let me write down all the names of the silk market stores you *have* to visit tomorrow."

The promise of shopping buoyed Mom's spirit at least. As they bent their heads down to confer, Jacob pushed away from the table. "Do you want to walk outside for a bit?"

Mom glanced up and nodded her permission at me, though she watched us leave with a slight frown. What was that about? I started to wonder, but then I remembered. *Be fair to Jacob,* she had told me. Even as I chose to ignore her perturbed expression, I could feel her concern as palpably as I could the memory of her smooth hand on my forehead whenever I was sick, measuring my temperature with her mysteriously accurate mother sensor. "A hundred and one," she'd pronounce, Dad insisting that she check with a thermometer. Her intuition was always right.

As it was now to be concerned . . . because Jacob held the restaurant door open for me, waited for me to walk before him through the restaurant's small bamboo grove, as solicitous as any boyfriend. More solicitous than mine who was back home.

Be fair to Jacob.

I assured myself that it was only natural for me to accept Jacob's hand over the last bumpy step on the stone bridge, sided by pock-marked rocks. But Jacob kept my hand in his even when we reached the busy lane fronting the lake. Nor did we let go when we joined the other couples meandering the shoreline. I could no more release Jacob's hand now than I could have canceled this trip, despite Dad's best intentions to scare us into staying put.

Alleys radiated around the twinned lakes of Hou Hai and Qian Hai, surrounded by the last holdouts of ancient courtyard houses, some seven hundred years old. There was very little concept of street appeal here; mostly the houses presented flat blank walls since they faced inward into their namesake private courtyards.

"Is this what you expected?" Jacob asked me.

At first, I thought he meant us — that we would fall into this very familiarity. But he was looking out at Beihai and at the green-striped paddle boats in the middle of the lake.

Reading about this city and this country — and talking to the Twisted Sisters, who had all traveled here one time or another — had been one thing; being here a vastly different experience. It was like describing color to someone born blind. Even at their best, words were only a feeble approximation for the real thing.

"I didn't know that the world could be so mind-blowingly beautiful," I admitted.

Jacob turned his gaze from the lake to me. "Neither did I."

Discomfited, I finally released his hand and started for another arching stone bridge. Its reflection turned the bridge into a full circle, half submerged in the calm lake. Off to the left, an old man sat on a bench, legs crossed, his back hunched in the same angle as his long curving bamboo fishing rod. He didn't move, and I had a feeling that if we watched him for the next hour, the next decade, he would be right there, fixed in place like a painting.

Jacob turned away first and said, "I have something for you." He reached into his pocket, pulled out the GPS, handing it to me. "So you don't get lost, Control Freak."

Touched — even though I had my doubts about the device ever helping me to find my way — I smiled at Jacob. As I was about to put away the GPS, a tiny paper stuck to its back scratched me. Curiously, I flipped the GPS over; two coordinates were written precisely on hotel stationery.

"For the Great Wall," he explained. And then added more bashfully, "It's my favorite geocache in the world. My dad took me there when I was ten."

I knew what it was like to share something I loved, a collage I had labored over, a book that changed my view. So I assured him, "I bet I'll love it."

"You will." And then his lips curved into the mischievous smile I so loved. "I have one more thing for you." From the depths of his pockets, he withdrew a pile of napkins neatly enclosed in a clean plastic bag. "Your own stash, Trouble Magnet."

I laughed so hard I snorted. I couldn't help it, but the napkins were so silly, so perfect. The bathroom inside the restaurant hadn't had either toilet or toilet paper, and I suspected there would be a few more of those primitive latrines in my future. I was still laughing when I tucked both the napkins and the GPS safely inside my messenger bag, and when I looked up, Jacob was staring at me as if he wanted to tuck me away safely, keep me with him.

There must be a few times in life when you stand at a precipice of a decision. When you know there will forever be a Before and an After. Mom's life was twice marked: Before Dad, After Dad. Before her sister's death and After. I knew there would be no turning back if I designated this moment as my own Prime Meridian from which everything else would be measured. Mom's urging to be fair to Jacob, Karin's warning about losing the security of a miracle boyfriend, the image of Erik's easygoing grin itself — all those conspired now, convincing me to stay in the Before.

And then there was Jacob, who stepped closer to me and then

waited, letting me decide whether I would take that next step. Balanced there in indecision, it was as if the Twisted Sisters were before me, shaking their pom-poms, asking: *But what is fair about staying with a guy who is ashamed to be seen with you?* What was so miraculous about a relationship that was based more on my gratitude than mutual respect?

I wanted more. I wanted better. I wanted Jacob.

Even knowing that what I was doing was wrong, I jumped off my Before and reached for my After.

I traveled that short, short distance separating Jacob from me and stepped into his waiting arms. My face tilted up, my lips parted, so ready for Jacob's kiss. Unexpectedly, he let go of me, and my breath caught, painfully, deep in my chest. Had I so misread this map leading me to him?

Then slowly, so slowly, Jacob cupped my face in his hands, his thumbs brushing gently across my cheeks, the good side and the bad.

"You know, I don't even see your birthmark anymore," he said to me, tracing the ragged edges of my port-wine stain beneath my makeup with the tip of his finger. I shivered. "Which makes me sad," he continued, "because it looks like Bhutan. That's the one place in the world I've really wanted to see." His lips replaced his finger, equally soft as it explored the contour of my cheek, down to the corner of my lips. I had never been so aware of my mouth before. My lips were buzzing. *Just kiss me, damn it.* I parted them and heard the answering intake of his breath.

Jacob's gaze, inexpressibly warm, bored into mine, saw past my prickly outer surface. I closed my eyes, then decided I didn't want to hide anymore. So I opened them. Only then did he lower his lips onto mine. That first kiss was so gentle, a fleeting touch, barely there. It was a kiss meant to tease, to leave me wanting more. More. His mouth hovered above mine, for one breath, then two. My lips swelled from wanting him. Just as I pulled urgently on his shoulders, his lips came down hard on mine.

Mine, I thought. And I swear, in his kiss, I heard his echo: *Mine.*

chapter twenty-six

Mappery

FROM THE VERY CORNER OF the street where we had nearly experienced our own Pamplona of stampeding bicycles, Mom and I now waved at the Fremonts as they got into their cab, bound for the airport. Jacob didn't exactly smile, but his last look at me from inside the cab was nothing short of smoldering. My lips tingled in response, as if it was his soft mouth, not his eyes, that had just raked me.

The cab pulled away from the curb. Mom sighed. I would have sighed, too, except I didn't want to be one of those pathetic girls who pined for their boyfriends . . . even though I was pining. And worrying. And feeling guiltier than ever. I wished I could go back to all those opportunities I had to tell Jacob about Erik. Or better yet, go back and actually break up with Erik.

I tore my eyes away from the receding cab. Boisterous as a camp counselor, I told Mom, "Okay, onwards to the Forbidden City."

Mom sighed again. "Onwards."

"We'll be okay."

She squeezed my hand. "I know we will."

I just wished she'd sound more sure of us. I wished I were more sure of us, too. Swells of familiar worry that I'd get us lost, or worse, get us lost and in trouble tumbled over me even as I started to cross the street. The traffic gods were with us this time. We made it to the other side with not even a close call. Already, I spotted the tall walls separating the former home of two dynasties from the masses. How hard could it be to navigate to the most massive palace in the world?

Obviously harder than I thought it would be. According to my research, most tourists entered the Forbidden City through the south via the Meridian Gate, but the lines were shorter from the opposite end in the North. The problem was, I didn't know which way to turn.

We don't need the Fremonts to be our pathfinders, I reminded myself. And had to keep reminding myself of that when Mom echoed the question in my head: "So which way do we go?" Her helplessness was as burdensome as my second-guessing, which was plentiful enough as it was. I wondered about her chicken-and-egg relationship with Dad. Which came first? Her helplessness or his controlling?

If Mom wasn't going to take charge, I would. I couldn't wait on this corner forever. I studied the map, couldn't make any sense of it. A woman passed us, an Asian version of Norah in a bright red suit, carrying a briefcase. Here was a woman in control of her destiny.

So for the second time that day, I tried out my rudimentary *Excuse me*. For a moment, the woman's plucked eyebrows furrowed, not understanding me. I covered how shy and stupid I felt with a smile. Let me just say this. Anyone who transplants from their homeland to another country, trading in their culture and language for a different one — that is a person of courage. Grudgingly, I had to admit, that included Merc. I could feel Mom pressing in on me, wondering what I was doing, but not doing anything herself.

Imagine my surprise when Mom grabbed the map out of my hands and tapped on the North gate.

The woman nodded in understanding and pointed wordlessly in the direction we should take.

"*Xiexie,*" Mom said. I straightened in surprise. I had yet to hear her speak a single word of Chinese — not a single "thank you," not one "delicious" after a meal. For all I knew, she could have been practicing in private all along.

The woman smiled back at us. "*Bu yong xie.*"

Maybe getting around in life was nothing but map-reading. A skill that required practice. A key to unlock where you wanted to go. A legend to show where you were.

"Mom, you kicked butt," I told her as we went to the North Gate.

"*Xiexie.*"

True to Fodor's word, there was barely a line in the back entrance, just a few people and one tour group, led by a woman lofting a yellow umbrella over her head. As much as it would be nice to have a tour guide paving the way for us, I was glad to be alone with Mom.

"Ready to walk among the emperors?" she asked me now, while I held both of our tickets and she put away the change.

"Definitely." I straightened my shoulders like a woman warrior, and before the tour group had gathered around their guide, Mom and I were already striding toward the Gate of the Divine Prowess.

Visiting the Forbidden City backward was like stepping inside a huge three-dimensional collage — seeing the most intimate layers first, the Inner Palace, where only the emperor and his family were allowed to live. The deeper we went into the Imperial Gardens — past the enormous planters, trees that looked as old as the Forbidden City itself — the harder it was to remember that modern-day Beijing in all its pollution and population existed just outside the gate.

By silent agreement, both of us halted before a red-painted door, decorated with bulbous knob-shaped nails too big to fit my palm. Set in rows of nine by nine, I had read they symbolized luck.

"Rub one, Mom," I encouraged her, camera to my eye. "Make a wish while you do." She looked up at me in surprise, unable to fathom making a wish for herself. I grinned at her from behind my camera.

"What would you wish for? A house like this?" Then I told her about the sheer magnitude of the Forbidden City, an astonishing eight hundred buildings, and ten times as many rooms.

"I wouldn't have wanted to be the maid," Mom said, stepping away from the door hastily.

"I'm not sure I would have wanted to live here, period. There was too much court intrigue, everyone plotting against everyone else. Living in a city-sized palace definitely has its downside."

"Living in a log cabin in a small town has its fair share, too," Mom said.

I lowered my camera, waited for Mom to say more, but she motioned me to the door, telling me, "I'll take your picture, and you make a wish."

Wishes were dangerous. You only had to pick out any of the fantasy books in Claudius's bedroom to know how many misadventures started with one bad wish, haphazardly worded, impetuously made. I inspected these bronze knobs, and finally settled on one, the highest I could reach, that didn't look too worn: just enough power to grant a wish, not enough to distort it. Wouldn't you know it? As I wished for us to be safe on this trip, I thought of the fragment of the China map I had carried with me in my messenger bag. Merc had denied any knowledge of the Kryptonite geocache on our property when I had asked him about it on our last night in Shanghai.

That left Mom. I took out the notes I had made of the Forbidden City, and now I pointed out the animal statuettes on each of the building's roofs, the more animals the more important the building. You can imagine how many animals there were on the emperor's private bedchambers.

I shot Mom a look and said casually, "The world would have been a different place if China had kept on exploring. Just think — what if Dad was right and China really had discovered America first? Everything would have been different. Our houses, our clothes. We'd probably be speaking Mandarin right now."

Mom looked startled; I wasn't surprised. We never talked about Dad's shame, his fall from cartographic grace that made him exile himself — and us — to Colville, the hinterlands of Seattle.

"But they didn't," she said finally, her lips pursing. This was not a topic she wished to revisit.

So I continued our tour, kept to the script, pointing out the Hall of Preserving Harmony and the palace's most precious stone carving, an enormous ramp of two hundred tons of marble, etched with dragons. Even if Mom didn't want to discuss it, I couldn't help but think about that pivotal moment in China's history. Instead of exploring and sending out more intrepid adventurers like Zheng He, China had turned inward. This great civilization wheeled backward the way Europe had in its Dark Ages. Advancements made over a thousand years before the western world — like its invention of the movable type printing press, compass, paper — all that great technological lead had disappeared. Other countries rose in power and knowledge, and China went to sleep.

The dragon was waking now.

Mom was making motions like she was ready to move on to the next building, shifting her weight from foot to foot. Still, I stared at those dragons, their sinuous snakelike bodies, their claws. I'm sure they were protecting the emperor — everything in this city was designed to protect the emperor — but to me, the dragons looked like they were circling each other, preparing to battle for supremacy.

The one person I could remember standing up for Mom when Dad berated her was Aunt Susannah. The last time Susannah came to visit had been five years ago, two years before her untimely death. That, as far as I knew, was the last time Mom saw her — any of us saw her.

On that last visit, Dad began his incessant nitpicking at Mom's cooking — the eggshell she purportedly had left in his brownie.

"It's an eggshell, no big deal," Susannah had said softly, but I could feel the tension in her toned body as she rested her hip against the kitchen island, ready to pounce and gouge and protect her little sister if necessary.

Dad smirked in response. From where I stood at the sink, washing the dinner dishes, I hoped that, for once, he would let this questioning of his authority pass. It was a sister's prerogative to stick up for her sibling, especially her little sister. And Aunt Susannah was a guest.

But, no, Dad had to correct her in that calm patronizing voice of his: "It's a big deal to me."

Instead of being cowed, Susannah pulled herself to her full five feet. I knew that because I had just turned eleven and Susannah herself had made a point of measuring us against each other, back to back. We shared the same height, the same shoe size, but not much else. She had courage to spare; I had barely enough.

"Then let me make this perfectly clear," she said, every bit as calm as Dad. "Don't disrespect my sister."

Mom fluttered around like a helpless bird caught away from her nest.

"Or what?" Dad asked, resting his newspaper on the table.

Susannah merely stared at him. "Lois, pack your things. You're coming with me."

"Lois." That's all Dad had to say, her name, and Mom stopped moving. She would have stopped breathing if she could. I did, even as my hands continued to wash and dry, wash and dry.

"You deserve better than this," Susannah continued relentlessly, not shifting her eyes off Dad as though he were a rabid dog, unpredictable and out of his mind.

Five years ago, Merc was long out of the house, finishing up law school at Yale.

Five years ago, Claudius was out with his friends, getting high again. He wasn't there to get into an accident to distract Dad.

But I was.

I remember staring at the reflection of my face in the window above the kitchen sink, hating my face. Hating that underneath the port-wine stain, I could see Dad and his blue-green eyes and his aristocratic nose. I remember taking the stain remover from under the kitchen sink, rubbing the cleanser on my face as if it were one of the fancy toners Mom bought to beautify my skin, not abrade it. The reaction was instantaneous. My skin bubbled, hiding the purple stain and my father within my face.

It worked. Mom gasped, "Terra!"

She stayed, Susannah left, and Dad fumed impotently. Another crisis diverted.

But how many more times would we hurt ourselves to diffuse Dad?

The miracle was, Dad wasn't here. He wasn't anywhere close to here. China was the last place he would go, this country of his shame. No wonder Merc had moved to this very country. Here, he was safe.

Here, Mom and I were both safe.

For all that I'd studied about China, reading at least eight different guidebooks, poring over expat discussion boards about Beijing and Shanghai, borrowing Mandarin tapes from the library. As much as I read *Wild Swans* and Amy Tan and Lisa See, reread Da Chen and *The Red Scarf Girl*, nothing prepared me when I turned around to face the Hall of Supreme Harmony — that iconic building in the Outer Court. Nothing prepared me for the sad opulence, this tragic grandeur that once had been the bastion of both royalty and their eunuchs and concubines — all battling for survival.

"Even emperors toppled," I whispered. Empires are overthrown. Emperors lose power, die. The last emperor of China had been forced to serve as a farmer for seven ignoble years.

No power was total, no power permanent, no power absolute.

Not even Dad's.

There is a time to study a map passionately, obsessively. To see where you've gone, where others have gone before you. To commit to memory every obstacle, every danger. Shakespeare had a term for this obsession: mappery. But there is a time, too, when you say, *come dragons. I challenge you to find me.*

I shivered, thinking about how life would have been so different had Mom kept on her path instead of stepping onto Dad's. Had she enrolled in college, gotten her degree, could she have been like Norah, mistress of coffee beans, ruler of profit-and-loss statements? Could she have been fearless like her own sister and ventured to countries whose names I couldn't pronounce, much less place on a map?

What would life have been like for me without my port-wine stain?

I opened my lips, then closed them. "Mom," I said. Again, my lips parted and then pursed. I lifted my finger to them, not shushing my questions, not locking them in, just indecisive.

"What, honey?"

Oh, nothing. These words poised for their normal swan's dive, that headlong plummet that would end any intimate sharing. I cleared my throat.

"Would you look at that," said Mom, laughing in wonderment. "A Starbucks right here in the Forbidden City."

"What?"

I looked where Mom was pointing. There was no telltale sign, no emblematic mermaid to lure the thirsty and caffeine-deprived inside. That is, there was no sign of the Starbucks until a man stumbled out the nondescript door, clutching his coffee in one hand, a wad of napkins in the other. If ever I needed a nudge telling me I was on the right path, there it was.

"Mom," I began afresh, "what should I do about Erik?"

"You mean, what should you do about Jacob? Or why you're still together with Erik?" she asked, surprising me. She was striding fast now, faster than I had ever seen her walk in the last few years. I don't think she saw any of the buildings we were passing, not the Hall of Supreme Harmony or the Hongyi Pavilion. Finally, she slowed, panting a bit, sweating a lot. "Why are you?"

"Because . . ."

"Because you slept with him?"

"Mom!" And then grimacing, I looked away, mumbled, "How did you know?"

"I just did." She waved impatiently. "And I don't agree with what you did. But that's not a good enough reason to stay together with a boy."

I'm not sure what I expected Mom to say, but her commentary on my sex life wasn't it. After all, she had always warned me that relationships were hard work. That divorce wasn't an option. I had so needed to know that I had someone, it didn't matter that that someone wasn't right for me.

She chewed on her lip, wanting to say something more.

"What?" I asked. *Jump the moat, Mom.*

"You didn't get pregnant the way I did. You don't have to be stuck."

I swallowed. "You don't have to stay stuck, Mom."

She just shook her head as if it was too late for her. "Be careful with Jacob. That boy has been through enough."

"I know," I said sharply. And then softened my voice. "I know that. I should have broken up with Erik before coming. I just wasn't sure of Jacob."

"Are you now?" she asked quietly, but her eyes never left mine.

With no hesitation, I nodded. Jacob was the kind of guy who never said anything unless he meant it. He was the kind of guy who would break up with a girl if his heart wasn't into the relationship. He was also the kind of guy who would never date someone who already had a boyfriend.

"I'll break up with Erik as soon as we're back home," I said out loud, more for myself than for Mom.

Mom nodded. "That sounds like a good idea."

Without needing a map, I knew what lay before us: the Meridian Gate, the central entrance to the Forbidden City that was once the exclusive domain of the emperor. He alone strode through this entrance. Directly outside lay Tiananman Square, the site of protests and repression. But even quashed rebellions leave us different. Because freedom may be a forbidden fruit in tyrannies, but once tasted, it is unforgettable. No matter how desperately Dad tried to contain us, we were all spinning out of his control. My brothers had orbited away from home. I took my untreatable face to the dermatologist against his wishes. The one person he had corralled with any effectiveness was Mom — and here she was, thousands of miles away from him. We had all mounted our own private rebellions successfully.

Unexpectedly, Mom asked, "Honey, did you know that the empress was allowed to go through this gate only one day in her life?"

"Yeah, her wedding day. How did you know?"

"Norah told me."

Probably during one of their talks about marriages . . . and her ex-husband's remarriage. I looked at Mom, knowing the same idea was already forming in her head from the way she narrowed her eyes at that gate, daring it in a game of chicken. And I said, "Well, it's time to change history, don't you think?"

I took her hand in mine, not the way I used to hold hers as a child, but with our fingers woven together. And we strode through the archway of emperors and into the open — hand in hand, my mother and I.

chapter twenty-seven

New World

THE NEXT MORNING, AFTER AN early start, Mom and I sat aboard a cable car, sailing us up the lush green mountainside to the highest point on the Great Wall in Mutianyu, a remote section of the Wall off the beaten tourist track.

"You might not want to look down," I advised Mom. While I wasn't scared of heights, I did wonder about the safety of the cable car, swaying as it was on the thin overhead cord of wavering steel.

Even though her face was white and her hands gripped the edge of her seat, Mom kept her eyes open, fixed ahead. When we disembarked and started past a group practicing tai chi on the Wall, Mom actually dared to peek over the ledge. While she gasped — it was a long way to the ground — she didn't back away. Instead, she motioned me to her side, and both of us studied the expansive vista of hunchbacked mountains and the Great Wall itself undulating in front of us, the spine of the dragon, some call it. I could see why. It was as if the mountains themselves had been peeled back, laying open the skeletal wall. Mom squeezed my arm. "It's beautiful, absolutely beautiful."

What was beautiful, I wanted to tell Mom, was both of us on this wall, designed to keep invaders out, but failed. The nomads still sacked China. When it came down to it, there was no way every section of this 3,000-kilometer wall could be kept intact and protected, not when someone was determined to break in. Like us.

I approached a man, asked him to take a picture of us by way of lifting up my camera, pointing at Mom and me, and then smiling. Jacob was right; smiles were disarming.

Later, Mom and I began to walk the length of the Wall, which had so many more stairs than I thought it would. For some reason, I had pictured the Wall as one continuous flat; it was more like a gentle roller-coaster with hills and valleys.

"Oh, I think this might be as far as I go," Mom said, gazing uneasily at the fifth steep flight of uneven stone steps rising before us.

"Here, Mom." I held her arm to help her up. "Just a little ways more." And then to distract her: "Can you believe we're here? On the Great Wall?"

"No." She was breathing hard, her face flushed from exertion. I started to worry that I was pushing her too much. She might have a heart attack; she hadn't exercised like this in years.

"Have a seat, Mom." I wiped off a block of rock for her and crouched next to her. "So was this worth it?"

She threw her head back and laughed openmouthed in a way I had never seen her at home, a deep-throated chortle that started from the very depths of her soul. "I had a moment when we were touring the . . . what was it called?"

"The Forbidden City?"

"No, that old neighborhood."

"Hutong."

"Right." She clapped her hands. "The hutong. And my rickshaw almost crashed into another. Then I wasn't so sure."

"I didn't see that."

"No?" Mom smiled secretly, proud of her own adventure. "I had no idea. . . ."

"No idea what?"

"That there was so much to see in the world."

We both looked over the Wall to the west, where I could imagine the thundering of horses' hooves as nomadic warriors approached the Wall, intent on breaching it. To the west, the rest of the Silk Road lay with its promise of sand dunes and camels and caravans. And beyond that Europe.

"There *is* so much to see," I repeated. And then, "It's too bad Merc didn't come with us. You know, he hasn't seen anything in China." *He hasn't seen anything of us. Of me.*

Mom looked thoughtful, brushing grit that I had missed off her seat of stone. Then she said, "It's his loss. All we can do is tell him what he missed, and hope that next time, he'll make a better choice."

I snorted. As if telling him that would convince him to put down his BlackBerry.

"You know, honey" — Mom wound a loose thread from the bottom of her sweatshirt around her finger, pulled, and tore it off — "one day he'll realize what he's sacrificed."

I guessed from her wistful expression as she blew the thread into the air, watched it fly and disappear over the Wall, that she was thinking of all the trips she hadn't taken with her sister. I was shocked when she admitted ruminatively, "I was supposed to go with Susannah to Guatemala. I had promised her."

"I didn't know that. I'm glad you didn't go!" If she had, Mom wouldn't be sitting here next to me. She would have been on the bus that had plunged over the cliff, killing the passengers, including Susannah. "Why didn't you?"

"There was that conference in Seattle for port-wine stains, do you remember?"

I reared back so hard that I lost my balance, the truth bowling me over. I stood up now and rubbed my tailbone. I had always assumed that it was Dad who prevented Mom from going, from living her life, from traveling with her sister. "You didn't go because of me?"

"Susannah didn't understand that. She was so angry with me." Mom puffed out her cheeks and then blew, remembering what must have been a nasty conversation with Susannah. "I should have been on that trip with her —"

"Mom, don't say that."

"— and there were so many others that I should have gone on with her." Mom nodded emphatically, fell silent, and I knew that was all she was going to say. Her breathing, I was glad, had evened out. And then suddenly, Mom grabbed my hand. "Merc and Claudius are your only brothers."

"I know, Mom."

"No," she said fiercely. "They're the only ones you'll ever have."

I heard what she was telling me: *don't do or say anything that will push them away forever.* But did they realize that I was their only sister?

I stretched up on the balls of my feet, feeling antsy. I needed to move, needed to get away from this conversation. "Shall we?" I asked.

"You know, I'm going to rest a bit and turn back. You go on, though. I'll meet you at the bottom of the cable car."

I looked at the Wall, undulating in front of me into the horizon. Jacob had left me with the GPS and coordinates for a geocache not far from here. And then there was a toboggan ride at the end of this section of the Great Wall that I was dying to try. I mean, tobogganing down the Great Wall! Mom would never get on one of those sleds. But this was all moot; I remembered how much she had struggled on the steps to get this far. "I'm not leaving you here by yourself."

"Then I'll just sit here and look out. You can come back for me, then. Really," she said firmly, "it's what I want."

Without another word, Mom took out the journal I gave her on her birthday a couple weeks before the trip. I had yet to see her using it. But then again, it could have been because she never had privacy; I wanted to give her that now, space to think with no one intruding or eavesdropping or demanding something from her. So I said, "I'll be back in half an hour."

"Take your time, honey," she answered without looking up from the journal. "We're only here once."

There still weren't many people on the Wall, which freed me to go at my own pace. The wind had picked up, and while it didn't feel strong enough to blow me off the Wall, I shivered and threw on the sweatshirt that I had tied around my waist just in case.

As I approached the first watchtower, I checked the coordinates on the GPS. Still too far south. So I climbed the steep steps but didn't linger at the top of the tower, not wanting to be away from Mom for long. I jogged down the stairs and the next section of the Wall. A couple looked at me strangely as I ran past them, but I didn't care. I had missed my morning runs, missed the way my legs stretched in front of me until I felt like a gazelle, missed the fresh air after Beijing's smog. The uneven stones reminded me of running on the trails behind my home, and I slowed enough to watch my footing.

Another watchtower lay directly ahead. The coordinates on the GPS started matching up with the waypoints Jacob had left with me. This was it, I thought excitedly. This was where the cache was hidden. Thirty feet, twenty feet. Knowing how crafty geocachers could be at hiding their treasures, I started poking around the Wall, looking for the cache as soon as I scaled the steps to the watchtower.

Not being a purist, I had peeked at the clues Jacob included for the microcache. I knew it was in a tiny film canister, and then there was this: "where those without wings could fly."

Whatever that meant.

I kept probing the small crevices along the wall, found graffiti written and carved on the stone, counted a couple of pieces of chewed bubble gum. No cache.

I must have tramped the full circuit around that watchtower twelve times, first on tiptoe, then crouched low. I seriously considered crawling until I remembered how much spitting I had seen in Beijing. No crawling.

My back hurt from bending over. So I stood and looked at the view, really looked at it. I wished Mom were here with me, because who knew? Who knew that the world itself was one giant cache, stashed with hidden places of infinite beauty like this for people to find? I was about to give up and finally thought to check the time. A full hour? Mom must have thought that I had peeled off the wall, my body broken on the rocks below.

As if wishes could come true, I saw a familiar pink sweatsuit: my mother picking her way to the watchtower. She was so focused on the uneven path, she didn't see me watching her slow progress.

And sure enough, here in the places where those who can't fly do, I raced down the stairs as quickly as it was safe, and rushed to Mom. She was panting, her face flushed. But her eyes? They sparkled with pride.

"What are you doing?" I asked. "I was just about to come back to you."

"I know. But I decided I didn't want to miss out on anything."

"We can head back now."

Her brow furrowed. "It can't be much longer to the other cable car from here."

"It's not. Maybe another twenty minutes."

"Then let's go. I didn't come all this way to turn back," she said, already setting up the stairs I had just descended. Slowly, we climbed, and I wondered how Mom had made it all this way by herself. Slowly, I thought. One deliberate step at a time.

"Look, Mom," I whispered once we reached the vantage point where the serpentine Wall disappeared into the horizon. "Forever is thataway."

She stood beside me, panting. Her hand rested near an arrow hole, the arrow hole where the ancient guards of China could let loose their weaponry against the Mongol invaders, let their arrows fly.

"No way," I muttered. I bent down and peered through the arrow hole, searching for the hidden canister. Not there. I tried another arrow hole just a few feet away.

"What are you doing, honey?" Mom asked, bending down herself, ready to help me find whatever I had lost.

As I patted around, I found a tiny crevice to the east. My fingers slipped in, touched smooth plastic.

"We found it!" I announced, triumphant, pulling out the black canister carefully.

"Found what?"

In answer, I handed Mom the cache. She read the note taped around the canister's outside, explaining in both Chinese and English that this was an official geocache site. Those not geocaching were respectfully asked to replace the cache where they found it.

"A geocache," Mom said, opening the lid and shaking out its

contents into her cupped hand. Just paper, tightly rolled into a minia-ture scroll, and a pencil stub. "Susannah used to geocache."

"She *did*? Wait, you know about geocaching?"

"Sure, she was so goal-oriented, she couldn't just hike like me."

And then it occurred to me where those fragments of China map came from, how the cache had gotten placed on our property. I dropped my backpack to the ground, chancing generations of dried spittle, and dug inside for the envelope where I had been stashing tickets and other ephemera as collage material. I lifted the piece of the China map, still sealed in its plastic bag, and held it out to Mom. "This was Aunt Susannah, wasn't it?"

Her eyes widened when she saw what it was. "Where did you find this?"

"At home. There's a geocache at our home. A pile of these were in it."

"No, but how?" Mom shook her head, and then her mouth opened to a wide O. Embarrassed, she said, "I sent Susannah those pieces one day when I was mad at your dad."

"Do you think she started the cache when she came to visit?" I asked.

Mom shook her head, bewildered, still staring at that tiny piece of the China map.

I continued. "And maybe she scattered them in geocaches around the world. But why would she . . ."

I had my answer when Mom propped her hands on the wall, ducked her head like she was woozy, and breathed deeply. It was Susannah's quiet rebellion, mounted against Dad all these years. A warning to in-trepid travelers not to trust in maps blindly.

Here be dragons.

"Sign your name," I told Mom, handing the logbook to her. The list was short, just about thirty geocachers, including MM — Memento Mori: Jacob and his dad — dated almost exactly seven years ago. It was strange, holding this paper, knowing that Jacob had held it before me. And knowing how different his life was now from what it had been seven years ago. How different Mom's was five years ago when Susannah was still alive. And Dad's twelve years ago before the China map was deemed a fraud.

"But I didn't find the cache," protested Mom.

"I couldn't have found it without you," I pointed out.

So reluctantly, she took the stub of a pencil, thought for a second before carefully lettering a geocaching nickname: *Crafty Mama.* Nothing — nothing — made me more proud than to see Mom signing that name in the log. I may have been the pathfinder. But she was an explorer, too.

"Here," she said, pressing the log onto me.

As I signed my name under hers, I knew what to do with that frayed piece of map that I had carried from one continent to another. I looked at Mom; she nodded in approval. So I rolled the log around that piece of map, not a shroud so much as a cocoon, an adventure preparing to take flight.

More than walking the Great Wall had worn Mom out. She looked wilted by the time we reached the end of the Mutianyu section, and I suspected it had to do with the potent memory of her sister. So when Mom encouraged me to ride the toboggan instead of the cable car down — "If it's something you want to do, then do it, honey" — I took her up on it. I knew better than to ask her to join me.

Apparently, the toboggan wasn't as popular as I thought it would be. There was only one couple in line with me, and they were from Germany, backpacking across China. We all laughed at the enormous warning sign, listing every potential hazard of the ride and illustrating them with a stick figure. Seated in my cart, waiting for my turn, I wasn't laughing anymore, certainly not when the woman blasted down the upturned steel track ahead of me, screaming. It wasn't a happy euphoric scream either. Her husband followed at a more cautious pace.

The ride operator nodded at me. As nervous as I was, I knew that if I bailed now, I'd regret it. So I breathed deeply, released my brake, and started coasting down the metal chute. There was no roof over the track. Pick up too much speed and I'd be the stick figure flying clear off the rail. But — oh, God — tobogganing was so much better than running on the Great Wall. I rounded a bend, speeding along so that my hair whipped behind me, a victorious knight's banner. A young man leaped out of the trees on the hill, waving a sign at me: SLOW DOWN! I braked. Really, I did, but I must have still been racing too fast, because another man jumped out, yelling at me this time.

Their glares and warnings didn't faze me, not one bit. What were they but mere stings compared to Dad's menacing glowers. I careened to a stop at the bottom, laughing out loud, where Mom was waiting for me, just the way I knew she would be.

No sooner did we return to our hotel room than Mom flopped onto the bed, not even removing the coverlet, which was probably crawling with all kinds of germs I didn't even want to think about. (I had seen an undercover news report on the sanitation levels at hotels around the world, and it's almost enough to pack your own sleeping bag.)

"I'm done for the day, honey," she said, and flung her arm over her eyes to block out the light.

Funnily, I was still exuberant from my toboggan ride three hours earlier. "Do you mind if I run out?" I asked Mom, standing over her single bed. "I'll bring back dinner."

Her voice was muffled. "Sounds good."

By the time I had collected my things, Mom's breathing had evened out and she was asleep.

"Sweet dreams, Mom." I turned off the light, and very gently, I closed the door.

Supposedly, the 798 Art District was to Beijing what SoHo was to New York. I couldn't say for sure how accurate that analogy was since I'd never been to Manhattan, and my entire frame of reference for artist communities was Nest & Egg. My saving grace for actually finding the boutique Elisa shared with two other designers was that the art district was fairly small, spanning a few blocks of studios, stores, and restaurants. That, and I had the receptionist at my hotel write down the name of Elisa's store in Chinese characters for me to give to the taxi driver.

I stood outside her boutique uncertainly. Now that I was here, I wondered why I had come. Through the window, the tiny shop could have been an aviary, but instead of exotic birds, unapologetically bright dresses hung off branches, stripped of leaves and arranged around the jewelry box–sized store. Only the self-assured could pull these dresses off, women who enjoyed attracting attention. Like the three women Elisa was waiting on when I finally forced myself to enter the boutique.

The oldest must have been Mom's age, slender and chic, her hair twisted into an elaborate updo. She frowned at herself critically in the mirror, shook her head, no.

"Terra!" Elisa called when the door set off tingly chimes announcing my entry. She sounded surprised, but pleasantly so. To my astonishment, she excused herself from her customers to stride over to me, her dress swinging loosely around her body. She threw her arms around me, pulling me in for a tight hug. She had lost weight since Christmas, her once plump body now bony, almost frail. The break-up had marked her, too. "You found me." She squeezed my hands. "So is China everything you expected it to be?"

"More, a lot more."

"I know what you mean."

"You broke up with Merc," I said. Even though we had exchanged a couple of e-mails, I never felt comfortable enough with her to ask about Merc. So now I flinched at the overt accusation in my unintended words more than she did. "I mean, it was my fault you broke up. I'm sorry."

Immediately, Elisa glanced over her shoulder at the dressing room door, so old it must have been salvaged from an ancient courtyard house. She squeezed my shoulder apologetically. "We'll talk in a few minutes, okay? Have a look around." Then she grabbed another dress off a branch — silvery purple, the exact shade of Mom's Russian sage.

Had this not been Elisa's store, I would have been intimidated by its very poshness, its aggressive hipness. It would have been the kind of place where I felt like I had to apologize for my presence, the kind I would have left two seconds after I'd entered. Even as I inspected one dress after another — each with a slight Asian flair — I surreptitiously observed her customers, the oldest again cocking her head to the side, frowning at herself in the mirror. Geez, what did she have to be dissatisfied about? From head to toe, she looked enviably gorgeous, but her hands kept smoothing the jersey dress over her nonexistent hips. The girl, my age in showstopping orange, must have agreed with me.

"Mom," she said decisively, "you look brilliant."

"No, Syrah, you look brilliant," countered her mother. "That is a yes."

The third woman, taller than the other two, stifled a smile unsuccessfully. "All I know is Age's eyes will pop out when he sees you next week."

"Really?" Syrah angled herself in front of the mirror, met my eyes as if asking my opinion. I nodded, *oh yeah.* She grinned. "Then this is definitely a yes."

What would it be like to look in the mirror and actually accept what you saw? Not loathe the reflection, or despise it, or be resigned to it? But to like it?

As soon as the women fluttered out of the shop, purchases in their hands, Elisa turned to me.

"Don't be an idiot," she said, as though we were in the middle of our conversation. "It wasn't your fault at all. God, how could you even begin to think that?" Her eyes bore into mine, challenging me to say otherwise.

"If we hadn't talked about my collages at Christmas —," I began.

"This had nothing to do with that. . . ." She turned away abruptly, fussed with the dresses on one of the branches, arranging them so they had precisely an inch between them. Room to breathe. And then with her back still turned to me, she said, "No, I'll be honest. Christmas opened up issues between me and your brother that I hadn't wanted to deal with."

"Like what?" I asked.

She shook her head, now placing a sage green dress next to a teal one.

But I had to know. "What? Dad?"

"Not per se."

"Then what?" I followed Elisa to the dressing room, where she picked up the rejected fuchsia dress from the tiny leather chair, slipped it back onto the hanger. "I'd never seen Merc . . . so easy . . . with any of his other girlfriends."

"I know," she said. "I know that."

As unrelenting as Jacob had been when he was pursuing the truth, I knew I was being worse. And I knew how uncomfortable that had made me. But I couldn't back off now.

"He brought you home," I said.

She held the dress to her middle, unconsciously shielding herself. "He did, Terra. And he's a great guy. I just can't be with a man who doesn't stand up for his mother." Her free hand reached for me in for-giveness. "Or his little sister."

I swallowed hard, this lump of bitter truth.

Her eyes darkened, curiosity tinged with challenge. "Is he here?"

I shook my head, unable to speak.

She sighed, impatient, disappointed. "One of my girlfriends is a counselor, and she says that couples get unhappy when they start ex-pecting things of each other. But I disagree." Elisa hung up the dress she was holding and then swapped its position with another. "I'm not talking about expecting a diamond necklace and getting a box of choc-olates instead. But support and loyalty? You should be able to expect that much from your partner."

I had never admitted to myself how I always felt like Merc had abandoned me. Never calling or e-mailing me on his ubiquitous Black-Berry to see how Mom and I were faring at home, and now dumping us in China when neither Mom nor I had ever been overseas. Or spoke the language. Or knew where we were going.

"We made it just fine," I assured her.

"I knew you would, but that isn't the point."

I slipped another dress on a hanger, handed it to Elisa without a word. All along, I had attributed their breakup to a history of dates he had cancelled on her, their vacations he had postponed. To their unsatisfying time together, which had probably been long bouts of him on his BlackBerry interspersed with a few minutes of conversation. But it was more than that. The same elements missing in my relationship with Erik, and Mom's with Dad, were the ones absent in Elisa's with Merc: tenderness, attention, and the assurance that we had their unconditional support.

I stood before Merc's ex-girlfriend now, watching her hang the dress back in its proper place. I expected her to dismiss me now, return to her busy day and to her business.

"I have something for you," I told her. From my backpack, I withdrew the collage she had asked for back at Christmas.

"It's a beautiful piece of art," she pronounced, laying her hand on the collage, a benediction.

I don't know why her simple statement of faith made me tear up. But it did.

"You really have so much talent. *Jolie laide*," she said.

"What?"

"It's a French term."

I blushed, remembered how Dad had flung it at me. "I know. 'Pretty ugly.'"

"I suppose in the strictest translation that's what it means." She set the collage on a chair, upholstered in a leopard print, then took a few steps away and cocked her head. Finally, she explained, "This isn't actually beautiful; it says too many hard things for it be beautiful in the traditional sense." She took a step closer. "And yet it draws you to it. And when I close my eyes" — she did so now — "I can still see the image, as if it has bored into me here" — she pointed to her heart — "and here" — she touched her head. And then opening her eyes, she turned to me. "That is *jolie laide.*"

Unexpectedly, she picked up the summer version of the dress she had worn at my home, the one I had admired, but instead of wool, it was silk jersey.

"Try this on," she urged, holding the dress out to me.

"I can't."

"It's my welcome gift to China."

It was more than that. We both knew that. It was her goodbye gift.

"Trust me on this," she said. "It'll be perfect on you. Try it on."

So I did.

"That is so you," she said when I stepped out of the dressing room.

Like the customers before me, I gazed at my reflection, surprised that I liked what I saw. "That's what I was thinking, too."

In another time, I would have lingered in this neighborhood, an artists' community I could envision myself living in, working in — despite being thousands of miles from my comfort zone. On Elisa's block alone I counted five galleries. I hated every step I took that led me out of this pedestrians' enclave, led me away from Elisa, who I had hoped would be the sister I never had. I hated this drifting away feeling.

But Mom was waiting at the hotel, and I didn't have time to poke around. Still, I couldn't help but slow down and then stop altogether in front of the last gallery on the street. With its sleek white shelves and chrome fixtures, edited of every frivolous angle, the showroom was the antithesis of my homey Nest & Egg Gallery. Displayed in the front window on a plinth was a sculptural ball, wound with long strips of tie-dyed bandages. On one side of it was a marble, a miniaturized green and blue Earth seen from above. On the other side, its identical twin, smashed, like the glass globe Claudius had crushed in his hands. One large shard of glass lay on top of granules, fine as sand.

If art made you think, then this was Art. Staring at the ball, made of layers and layers of cloth, I wondered about the glass marble at its heart. What if you wanted to reach that marble? Make sure it was still whole?

You'd have to remove the layers. You'd have to risk breaking the ball for a chance at freeing it. Fear, knowledge, certainty — you'd have to be willing to let them all go.

chapter twenty-eight

Pathfinder

AS MUCH AS I ACHED to see Jacob again, wanted to know what he thought of his orphanage, leaving Beijing upset me more than I thought it would. Neither Mom nor I minded when a woman jostled us with her overstuffed luggage as we waited in yet another line to check in for our flight to Hangzhou. Which I took to mean that we had acclimatized to crowds pressing in on us all the time. For all Beijing's pollution and people, it was the first place where Mom and I had been a team, not us against the world. But us with the world.

Mom must have felt the same way, because she sighed. "Where does time go? Half the trip is over."

"But we still have half to go," I reminded her.

"True."

"Where else would you want to go?"

That made her first bark with laughter, then hoot loudly, ending with a horsey snort. She was a symphony of animal noises. A few people turned to stare at her, but Mom didn't mind. She wiped the tears from the corners of her eyes.

"What?" I demanded.

Mom snorted once more, pushed her luggage forward, bulging with a few more purchases from yesterday's foray into the silk market. "It just seems so ridiculous to be planning our next trip while we're still on this one."

"True." I shifted my messenger bag to my other side and grinned at her. "But it took us two years to work up the guts to visit Merc."

"And he's not even here."

I sidled a glance at her and told her the truth: "You know what? I'm sort of glad."

She paused, her mouth turning into an "O" of surprise, and then admitted without a trace of guilt, "Me, too."

Thank goodness for the emergency cards I had made back at home, those business card–sized papers laminated with our hotel and flight information, Merc's phone numbers, and the contact info for the U.S. embassies. Back in Beijing, I had asked the concierge to update mine and Mom's with the hotel's address outside of Hangzhou, which the Fremonts had booked for us. Our meager phrases — excuse me, hello, thank you — wouldn't have gotten us far with the taxi driver in this city. (His English was even worse than our Chinese.) So at least I was able to hand him one of the cards.

Jacob's orphanage was located in a village an hour's drive from the city, and a harrowing hour's drive it was. If there were traffic laws in China, our taxi driver didn't obey them. He sped through red lights, made a U-turn straight into oncoming traffic, and blasted the horn at anything that moved slower than him. Which, as far as I could tell, included every truck, motorcycle, and car, except for other taxis. Not a second too soon, he dropped us off at the right hotel, looking proud of himself.

Mom was ashen. Sweat matted her bangs to her forehead, and she whispered, "I think I lost another five pounds."

I threw open the door, glad for the fresh, fragrant air infused with tea. From what I had read about Hangzhou, the city and its surrounding towns and villages made up some of the primest tea-growing areas in China. But if we had passed any plantations on the way, they had slipped by in one big green blur.

Norah and Jacob were waiting outside the hotel, instead of inside the way they had said they would. Neither had noticed us yet from the bench. Jacob's arm was thrown consolingly around his mother. She nodded in resignation, not agreement, to something he said.

Beside me, I heard Mom's tiny, pitying "oh, no."

Perhaps it was all the bargaining at Chinese markets where only the shy overpaid, but Mom didn't insinuate her way into their conversation. She crashed it.

"Norah, what happened?" Mom barked as soon as she sidled out of the taxi, the drive immediately forgotten. Still, I noticed the big splotch of sweat on her back, had no doubt mine sported the identical belying mark of my nerves.

Her flat statement startled Jacob and Norah. They both stood. Where Norah smiled feebly, Jacob broke into a grin.

"Terra," he said.

Norah brushed her hair out of her eyes and blurted, "That damned orphanage turned us away again. Second time in two days."

"Mom, it's just a screw-up," said Jacob, resting a hand on her shoulder to calm her.

"I did everything right. I called the agency, I filled out the paperwork. They assured me we'd be able to visit," Norah ranted. I had never seen her this angry, this out of control. "And of course, our caseworker back in Seattle has to be on spring break. They all are!"

"Mom, it's really okay."

Norah pulled herself together, literally straightened so she reached her full height, which was just shy of Jacob's chin. I was always surprised at how petite Norah was; she carried herself tall. As though she had never made an emotional outburst, she peered at Mom and asked her solicitously now, "How was your trip?"

"Fine, fine," said Mom, blasé as a seasoned traveler. "I want to hear about you inside." She wheeled her suitcase through the hotel door. And this time it was Norah who followed, which left me outside with Jacob.

"How are you doing?" I asked him.

He shrugged, scuffed the toe of his Converse sneakers on the pavement, and then took my luggage.

"I can do that," I said.

"Let me feel helpful."

So I let go of the handle, knowing how immobilizing helplessness was. Instead, I simply held the hotel door open for him.

"The worst part," said Jacob as he headed past the dining room filled with a few roughhewn tables and benches, and then lugged my suitcase up a flight of stairs, "is that Mom has been using this trip to distract herself from the whole divorce-remarriage mess."

All along, Jacob had claimed that visiting the orphanage was his mom's mission, not his. Still, I had to believe that when he was turned away at the orphanage, a patched-up part of his heart must have flaked off, exposing the abandoned boy he once was. I remembered the photos Norah had shared with us earlier, the ones of her collecting Jacob from China. The snapshot was unfocused, grainy, a younger Norah with frizzy hair wearing a blouse with enormous shoulder pads, holding a toddler-sized Jacob on her hip. What came through the most clearly was Jacob's untreated cleft lip, and I could imagine him burying his head in Norah's shoulder to hide his face the instant after the shutter clicked. As it was, trapped on film, Jacob faced the camera, unsmiling and wary as though he was used to being stared at, ridiculed.

Mom and I had arrived too early to check in. So we hung out in the plain room Jacob and his mom were sharing. It was nothing like their luxurious high-tech room in the Jinmao Tower, perched high above Shanghai with its marble bathroom and expensive surround-sound stereo. Here, there were two single beds topped with quilts of questionable taste and uncertain cleanliness. In the corner squatted an intimidating-looking air conditioner, plastered with operating instructions translated into incomprehensible English. The bathroom, which I had to use, had no tub, just a spigot overhead with no shower curtain, which meant that the sink and the toilet must get soaked every time the shower was turned on. But at least there was a toilet. While their hotel room was clean, it was also stifling, too small for four people, especially with disappointment crowding in with us.

"This is nice," Mom said, back to her forced cheeriness, but I was glad for it. The pall around Norah was so heavy, I could almost see a black aura around her.

Usually so get-up-and-go, Norah sagged wearily against the pillow. Half of me wanted to yank her up — and not just because millions of germs were infesting the bedcovers. But because it was against the natural law of order for her to be this depressed, this depleted.

"I would like to see this orphanage for myself," announced Mom.

"Go right ahead." Norah waved listlessly at the door.

"You're giving up? Just like this?"

"Just like this." Norah said curtly. "It's over."

Living with Dad's comments, which were tufted with verbal poison, inured us to Norah's sharpness. Mom got off of Jacob's bed to sit next to Norah. The bed dipped dangerously low to the ground. She asked Norah, "What's this really about?"

"Fourteen years ago, I came here to pick up Jacob. And then I met Dave. He adopted Jacob, and I believed that we would be forever. But it's over. It's really over, isn't it?"

Mom and I exchanged a look. Her ex-husband's wedding was tomorrow, which made her failure to access the orphanage doubly acute. Who wouldn't have a meltdown, particularly Norah, who hadn't sought a divorce in the first place?

Had this been home, we would have redirected the conversation. Changed the subject, wondered out loud, "So what's for dinner?" But here in this hotel room, I watched Jacob do the exact opposite, the bravest thing I could imagine. He sat at his mom's other side and cradled her in his arms.

"Mom," he said, "you still have me."

More than feeling useless, I felt like I was intruding on them, standing there with my arms hanging at my side. But then Jacob lifted his hand for me, pulled me next to him so we were all piled on the bed like refugees on a tiny raft.

"This is pathetic," said Norah finally, authoritatively. "Totally pathetic."

Even as I was relieved to hear her back to her decisive self, I got an inkling of how Norah must have approached the orphanage: barreling her way in. Calling the shots. That open aggressiveness might have been effective in Corporate America, but after a few days in China I suspected that a different negotiating tactic might work better.

"Okay, let's go have an early dinner." Norah stood as if everyone had agreed.

"No," said Mom firmly.

I stared at her; we all did.

"Well, what do you want to do instead?" asked Norah.

"I would like to go to the orphanage."

Nobody could have been more surprised than I was. Jacob shrugged at me as if it to say, *Why bother?*

A pathfinder's job is hard enough — blazing trails where there are none, guided by nothing but hearsay and gut. While you're hacking your way through bracken, worrying about lurking beasts, all you can do is hope you had chosen the right direction.

I wanted to help find the way, wherever it took us. So I held out my hand to my mother: "I'm in."

"Mom, enough already with the pictures," Jacob protested futilely for the fifth time since we loaded into the cab half an hour ago. He, Norah, and I were crammed in the backseat, Mom up front.

Forget the pictures; enough already with the taxi ride. Thankfully, out in the desolate village there were fewer cars, but that didn't mean that we were safe on the dirt road. This taxi driver accelerated at turns, and demonstrated zero ability with the brake. It was as if he was road racing, but racing against whom? The three bicyclists we nearly ran over? The water buffalo and its baby who were ambling on the side of the road?

I barely heard a peep from Mom, who was probably white-knuckling it, clenching her seat as if that would prevent her from catapulting through the windshield in the event of a collision.

"Mom, you doing okay?" I asked.

We took a curve especially hard, and I swear, the car listed so much on its side, two wheels caught air. Jacob slid into me so that I could smell his scent of fresh laundry. How did he manage to smell so good when we'd been on the road for six days? My clothes were rumpled, and I was already sick of what I had brought. So I breathed him in, wanting so badly to feel his lips on mine again.

Finally, Mom answered, releasing her grip on the strap above her door, "This could possibly be the best diet I've been on. I've officially lost my appetite indefinitely."

We all laughed; even Mom managed a feeble giggle. As soon as we were back on a straightaway, she handed me a photocopy of a note in Chinese, slightly damp from her sweaty grip. Underneath the Chinese characters was its translation into English: *Please take care of my son, Yi-Guan. He is a good boy.* And then at the very bottom, in parentheses, was one last sentence: *Jacob was found beneath a tree, wrapped inside a blanket with this note and a few coins.*

"I can't wait to see your baby pictures," said Jacob low in my ear. His breath tickled my neck. I wondered what his mouth could do to me on that very spot. Drawn to his lips, I stared at them now. Mine tingled in answer, the ghost of his kiss still lingering on them.

"I'd love to show them to you!" said Mom, all of a sudden finding her inner rodeo queen.

"Mom . . . ," I groaned.

"There's an especially adorable one. She and her brother, Claudius, are standing naked in front of the bathtub. Oh, she loved taking baths. Their chubby little legs . . ."

"I bet you were so cute," said Jacob.

There should be a law against mothers reminiscing about their children's babyhood. The stories are always beyond humiliating, as I could personally attest when Mom segued to the time when I spit up into her mouth (what was she doing holding me above her face?) and then the one where I had a major blow-out — "I had no *idea* poop could come in that color and consistency!" — at the Pacific Science Center.

The only redeeming thing about having a reckless driver intent on leaving Earth was that he had no intention of spending any more time than he needed in the temporal world. We stopped abruptly in front of a plain building, a picture of neatness and organization. A sign had been painted in bright blue over the door, words in Chinese characters, which Norah translated for us: Child Welfare Institute.

"When I first came to collect Jacob, the taxi drivers had no idea there was even an orphanage here," said Norah, scooting forward to pay the driver. "None of the kids were allowed outside back then, you see. So no one knew."

As Mom opened the front seat door, she stopped to study us over her shoulder. "Now, people know."

Following was obviously a genetic trait Norah was missing, because even though she may have been the most reluctant of our group to be back on these doorsteps — with Jacob coming a close second — she couldn't help but knock on the door herself. As we waited for someone to answer, I inspected the orphanage. For all its cleanliness — not a weed in sight — the place was bankrupt of anything beautiful. But it wasn't just the orphanage. All the surrounding buildings were dismal gray, as though beauty were a frivolity of the rich. What Mom could have done with a simple planter and a few colorful flowers.

"You doing okay?" I whispered to Jacob.

He nodded, looked like he was going to say something, but the door opened. A young woman, hair cropped short, stood before us in ill-fitting baggy pants and a dingy T-shirt. Her face was coarse and round like a koala's, so it surprised me to see it harden when she spied Norah. She shook her head emphatically — the international sign for "What part of 'no' don't you understand?"

With that, Mom pushed her way to the front, partially obscuring Norah. In her tentative way that always made me cringe — whether it was here or at a store — Mom started with an uncertain but friendly *"Ni hao."* I hated that obsequious tone, because it sounded like she was begging for charity instead of asking for help, as if she didn't have the right to be where she was. To my surprise, Mom turned to Norah and said, "Why don't you ask her for her name?"

Norah's forehead furrowed. "What?"

"Ask her for her name." And then after a beat, Mom continued softly, "And you could try it with a smile."

Norah sighed. But she did what Mom had asked. While the conversational question may have taken some of the edge off the orphanage worker's face, no longer so self-righteous, she still looked impatient. Both eyebrows were cocked up, poised to shutter at any time.

No wonder Mom was so silent in the taxi. She must have been strategizing on the drive over, practicing in her head for this moment, because she murmured something more to Norah, words I didn't catch, but I wasn't the intended listener. Whatever Norah now said disarmed the young woman, who glanced briefly at Jacob and nodded while she answered rapidly — too many words that weren't part of any language tapes I had studied. I was starting to hope that we'd be let in, but instead, the young woman closed the door, gently but firmly.

"What did she say?" I asked Norah. And then, "What did *you* say?"

"That this place saved Jacob's life and that all he wanted was to thank his caregiver." Norah considered the closed door and then briskly, she said, "Well, that was an excellent attempt. Let's go."

"No, let's wait," countered Mom, holding her spot, "just for a little bit longer."

And magically, the door opened, this time framing a middle-aged woman. Her friendly eyes inspected us from behind round-rimmed glasses. She looked like she was playing dress-up in her oversized shirt worn over a long, ankle-length skirt. On her feet were flats, the kind that always brought out Karin's inner fashion critic. Old lady shoes, she derided them. The woman didn't waste time looking at any of us, just Jacob. And then she nodded as if in answer to a question. The door widened in invitation, and Mom motioned for Jacob and Norah to enter first, but Norah stayed back, whispering to Mom, "But I told her almost the same thing earlier — that Jacob wanted to meet his *amah*." She was clearly confused.

Mom smiled at her and then murmured, "Who knows? Timing? Or the way you asked?"

We trailed behind Norah, who was back to her confident, verging on peppy, stride. Trust me, nothing was going to derail Norah now that Mom had gotten us inside the orphanage. I thought about Mom as she huffed at my side, trying so hard to keep up. How many times had I wanted to cringe when she begged Dad for every little thing: extra money for Christmas groceries so the boys could have their favorite meal — filet mignon for Claudius, rack of lamb for Merc. The car to bring me to the dermatologist. She never asked for anything for herself, yet without any hesitation, she'd humble herself for us.

"Mom." I stopped in the hall and turned to look at her, to really look at her. I swear, for the first time, I saw past the body she inhabited now, the one that humiliated Dad whenever he was seen with her in public — the one that embarrassed me, too, the few times she showed up at a school function. I saw Mom the way she had been and could have been and was becoming in these days free of Dad. "You're amazing."

"I was wrong," said Jacob, overhearing us. Or maybe he had been listening for me. He waited now for us to catch up.

"How?" I asked.

"Your mother is more Chinese than the Chinese. She takes humility to an entirely new degree."

Mom — my mother with her brown curly hair and green eyes —

glowed at those words, unused to compliments, orphaned as she was from Love and Security. And this time, when she demurred, "No, no, not really," I wasn't irritated at all. She was just being more Chinese than the Chinese.

"We're supposed to wait right here," said Norah, arms crossed, as we were first shown and then left in what must have been the director's office. The Spartan room was as unlike Merc's high-tech office as our modest home was to a mansion. The office was just large enough for the four of us to squeeze in snugly before the metal desk. An ancient boxy computer claimed most of the real estate on that desk. Filing cabinets, one after the other, lined the back wall like guards, ramrod straight in their matching uniforms. I wondered if Jacob's file was in there somewhere; Norah must have wondered, too, since she was staring at the cabinets as though she was prepared to pilfer them.

Four girls my age marched past the office, sidling curious glances at us. They gawked at me, whispering. Not that I blamed them. Just how often had they seen a tall, blond girl — someone who they could have been, but for the happenstance of birth? Then — I swear to God — their jaws dropped at Jacob like he was a rock star, boy manna from heaven dropped down for their delectation. I would have been jealous, but I was too busy reeling at my own ignorance.

Call me stupid, but I had expected these orphanages to be populated with babies, maybe a handful of toddlers. I wasn't prepared for these teenagers, girls who could have fit in at Any Town, USA's high school — even mine. They looked perfectly normal — no birthmark, no physical defects — and perfectly pretty. And still, no one had taken them home.

The girls continued down the hall, now chattering and laughing. I should have studied my Chinese harder; I wanted to know what they were saying. I was going to ask Norah, give Jacob a hard time, but as the girls opened the door, the cry of babies pierced the air. And through that open door, I made out a woman diapering an infant in her crib, the director standing just behind her, talking to her.

Jacob stood up. It didn't matter that we were told to stay in that office. It wouldn't have mattered if we had been threatened with expulsion for not obeying that one simple command. He sprinted down the hall, heading for that closing door.

"Jacob?" called Norah, following him now. We all were.

Jacob didn't listen. His hand was on the knob. He pushed the door open. I saw the director's look of surprise darken into annoyance, then disapproval. But her reaction didn't matter. The extra three feet and hundred pounds that Jacob had gained since leaving the orphanage as a toddler didn't matter either. All that mattered was the nursery worker who Jacob was staring at. Her own eyes widened in disbelief. She would have recognized him even in his Goth incognito outfit. With her tiny hand at her mouth, the woman ran flatfooted to Jacob, calling him by his first name: *"Yi-Guan, Yi-Guan."*

He towered over her, but she patted him on the back as though he were still a baby who needed soothing. I could picture Jacob's adoption story so vividly now, the one Norah had told us on the harrowing ride to the orphanage. How this woman, his amah, only reluctantly handed Jacob over to her those fourteen years ago, how she had cried like a piece of her was dying when Norah had left with Jacob. How she visited their hotel the next morning with a bag full of his favorite sweets. That was her week's salary, Norah had said.

My eyes misted now, and I had to look away.

"Hao kan, hao kan," his amah kept saying.

Like me and Mom, Norah hung back, unwilling to intrude. But Jacob's initial impulsive excitement had faded to awkwardness, unsure now. I don't think he was prepared for this onslaught of affection. Or for the reality that he could no longer communicate with the woman who had cared for him as if he were her own. And it was to his mother where he looked for help.

"Mom?"

Norah didn't smile, but her eyes glimmered. She was needed. At last, she stood next to him, murmuring now in translation. "Good-looking," Norah explained softly, knowing this moment was so fragile, so tenuous, a loud noise could destroy it. "She's calling you handsome."

Word by word, his face softened and he was reeling back in time, remembering, too. As though he were dehydrated and hadn't known it, I could see fine lines filling in, his cracks and crevices healing. The amah gestured to Jacob now, trying to make sense of his height, shaking her head in amazement. No translation was necessary: Where had time gone? She could have been my own mother, mourning the end of every developmental stage.

Then Norah looked surprised at something his amah was saying.

"What?" Jacob asked.

"She said that the woman who found you still comes by every year to see if there's been any news." Jacob blinked hard at that, and I could see the tears glistening in his eyes.

Norah blanched. "I wish I had known. I would have sent photos. A present at the very least."

It was Mom who said the words Jacob needed: "You were so loved, Jacob."

He couldn't have stopped those tears now if he tried. As if in agreement, Mom and I stepped back, cooed at some babies in their cribs. All these unwanted children who had been abandoned.

Years of being self-conscious trained me to notice when someone was staring at me. Like now. I looked over my shoulder and found a little girl by herself in the corner. As soon as she saw me notice her, she dropped her head, her bob sweeping down like a curtain over the curve of her cheek. Where others might have mistaken that for shyness, I knew it for what it was: shame. As if she knew when she was being stared at, too, the girl spun around to the wall, but she moved too fast. Her hair swung up and away from her face for an instant. But that was all it took to unmask the bright red birthmark splashed from the left side of her forehead down to her nose and cheek. It was as if she had swabbed her left hand with red paint and forgotten that as she held her head in deep thought. There was absolutely no doubt why her birth mother had broken the law and abandoned her — whether it was at a police station, on hospital steps, or beneath a tree. It was all because of a goddamned red mark, a permanent slap on this girl's face.

"What's wrong?" Mom asked, putting her hand on my arm.

Too slowly, I shifted my eyes back to her. Mom had followed my gaze like a mama bear protecting her young and she frowned at the little girl. "What's she doing in the nursery?"

I knew why: because babies couldn't talk, couldn't tease. There was safety and solace in silence.

"I need a bathroom," I told Mom, my voice tight.

Her eyebrows furrowed as if she knew I, too, was hiding something. "We passed one on the way in."

I nodded, couldn't choke out any more words, not even the ones that would diffuse Mom's concern.

As quickly as I could, I left the nursery, glad to escape, glad that Jacob was too busy getting reacquainted with his first family — that was what his amah was, after all — to notice my flight from a little girl who could have been me.

chapter twenty-nine

Cartographic Lies

RULE FOR THE WISE: WHEN you're trying to escape yourself, don't look in the mirror. Which, of course, is what I did in that dingy orphanage bathroom. There were no doors separating the stalls, just holes in the ground. But the need to see myself outweighed any discomfort to my nose. So I rested my pelvis against the grayish vanity, and leaned so close to the mirror, my breath fogged the lower half of my face. The safe, blemish-free half of my face. I stared back into my faded blue eyes that Karin thought I should make a jewel-like amethyst courtesy of a pair of tinted contacts. Fake, I had scoffed at her. I didn't want to be fake.

And finally, finally, I looked at my cheek, shrouded as usual in makeup. How was this any different from fake eyes? Or a fake personality, warm in public, cutting in private?

And how the hell was I any different from that little girl, both of us ashamed of our faces? Even if she wanted to cover her mark, how was she going to find makeup or afford it? Her very clothes looked too small for her.

I leaned my forehead against the mirror, feeling the cold, sleek surface against my skin. This close to the mirror, I couldn't make myself out. I was just one big blur. Was that what I was going to do for the rest of my life? Hide forever behind my mask of makeup? Veil myself like I was too hideous for public viewing?

I hated all those layers of makeup then, the weight of the foundation and powder and moisturizer. I was breathing harder than if I had gone snowshoeing for two, three hours. My hands gripped the sink, the edge cutting into my palm. My face was nothing but a cartographic lie, told to placate my father, who could stand nothing less than perfection. A lie to assure my mother that I had every chance for the happiness that she was denied.

Without pausing to think of any of the consequences, I turned on the faucet. Had the water run brown instead of clear, I still would have splashed it on my face. Over and over, I rubbed the frigid water over my cheeks, my forehead, my temple until my face was frozen and my hands went numb.

When I finished, both of my cheeks bloomed red from cold. I didn't let myself linger there in the bleak bathroom. I headed back to the little girl in the nursery. She was still crouching in the corner as if that was the only place where she belonged.

Mom gasped quietly. I could have been eleven again, wearing the evidence of stain remover that worked only on manmade materials, not man himself. "Terra! Your face!"

At that, Jacob spun around to make sure I was okay.

"Terra," Mom called again.

Without breaking my stride, I kept walking to the girl who was watching me suspiciously. I knew the exact moment when she saw my port-wine stain. Her eyes widened, her gaze shifted to my cheek, and she stared the way everyone had stared at her for her whole, short life. I didn't flinch. How could I? It was the first time I wanted someone to see my birthmark.

The little girl skittered back against the wall when I knelt beside her. I tucked my hair behind my ear and turned my cheek, not away from her, but to her. And then I had to trust in the universal language of a smile. Jacob had told me to smile at all the starers, that ultimate act of disarming. As he said, it was the reason why so many doctors gave their time to perform cleft palate and cleft lip surgeries. Smiles biologically bonded mothers to their babies, kicked in their mothering instinct. Fix the smile, save the child. So I bet on it now. I smiled.

Then, gently, I brushed her hair off her face — her perfect, perfect face. For a long moment, I cupped that round, befuddled face in my hands as if it were the most precious treasure of all — a sacred geo-cache I hadn't even known I was searching for until now. All those well-meaning comments from strangers — the ones who told me they knew people with port-wine stains — all of those I understood now. In their own haphazard, clumsy ways, they were trying to tell me that I was fine the way I was. That I wasn't alone.

I didn't have the language to communicate that to this little girl — or to communicate that beauty — real everlasting beauty — lives not on our faces, but in our attitude and our actions. It lives in what we do for ourselves and for others.

So I did the best thing I could.

For a long moment, I waited for her gaze to lift away from my birth-mark and back to my faded blue eyes. When she did, I realized I knew all the Mandarin I needed to express myself to this girl.

In my faltering Chinese, I used the same words Jacob's caretaker had when she saw him. I told her in words that I struggled to say to myself whenever I looked in a mirror.

"Hao kan," I said gently, quietly, firmly as if it was a pact between the two of us.

She blinked. I wasn't sure if she understood. Or if she believed that she was beautiful. So I pointed to her and then to me. And I repeated with utter conviction, *"Hao kan."*

Those words, my pronouncement, won me the girl's slow nod. I nodded back. And when she smiled, wide and open, I tell you, there was nothing more beautiful than that.

PART THREE

Terra *Firma*

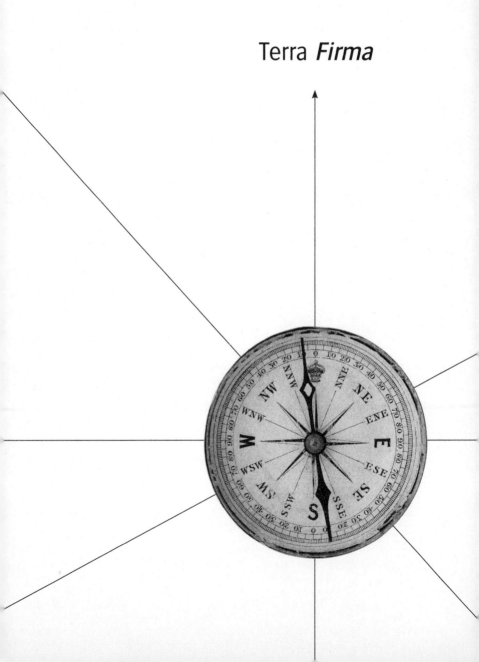

chapter thirty

Large-Scale Maps

I USED TO THINK THE tourist couples who sat companionably at Snag-tooth Coffee without talking, the ones who read the paper in silence while they were on vacation, were worse than boring. They were in re-lationship purgatory, just drifting along, waiting. Waiting for what? They had lost what little zing they must have had once. But sitting beside Jacob halfway through the flight back to Seattle, neither of us talking? There was real comfort in being quiet.

After I had changed spots with Norah, he had smiled at me, saying all of two words: "Big trip."

"Huge," I had agreed.

And then he closed his eyes, not because I was boring. But because we didn't need to talk. We didn't need to impress each other. We could just be.

With my head resting on the seatback, I reclined, not worrying about the thousands of people who had shared this very seat and left behind grease and germs. Comfort also came in knowing that countless travel-ers sat in this very spot before me, each going her separate way. Hun-dreds of different routes, thousands of different adventures started right here from this very seat.

I let myself close my eyes instead of keeping watch. A few moments later, Jacob reached over and took my hand in his. I needn't have worried. The zing was still there. He rested our hands on his chest, his hand over mine, my hand over his heart.

To dream, you need to starve doubt, feed hope. I intended to do that. So as I dozed off, I imagined myself with Jacob. As a couple, despite our differences, despite the distance. I dreamed of us being one of the success stories, a couple that worked out.

Too soon, we were disembarking from the plane and walking through the gate where our travels had first started.

"It's almost as if we hadn't even left," said Norah.

"We could turn around and go again," Jacob said, his shoulder brushing mine as we walked side-by-side. Norah was wrong. We definitely had left. And we definitely had returned. In a very un-Mom way, she had her cell phone out, now calling Dad, as we walked through customs.

No answer.

I hadn't expected one. Silence in Dad's hands was never companionable, but always a weapon. Troubled, Mom tucked the phone in her purse.

It was strange how in the company of strangers in China, I hadn't minded spending the rest of the trip bare-faced. The only person I knew had been Merc, and he was too busy working, head down, to notice a little thing like missing makeup. But now, in the company of these strangers, I felt so conscious of my face, despite my lipstick and eye shadow. I had to resist the urge to pull out my mirror, double-check my cheek.

While our mothers rode the escalators up to baggage claim, Jacob and I took the stairs, racing each other.

"No fair," I said, as we started. "You've got longer legs."

Jacob glanced over his shoulder at me, grabbed Mom's spillover purchases that I had stuffed into one of his extra carry-ons. "Take your excuses somewhere else, Trouble Magnet."

I looked past him, trying to measure how much farther I had to sprint with my heavy messenger bag banging against the side of my body. What lay ahead arrested me on that staircase.

I had been so busy blocking out the inevitable homecoming with Dad that I didn't think about the other guy I had so carefully forgotten. So carefully pretended didn't exist. Now, I crashed headlong into my Denial.

Erik was waiting at the top of the steps, holding an armful of red roses.

chapter thirty-one

The Great Trigonometrical Survey

WHEN I WAS IN SECOND grade, I did my should-be-famous person report on one Nain Singh, who surveyed over 2,000 kilometers from Nepal to China. That alone might not sound entirely worthy of a report, but consider he accomplished this in 1865 and on threat of death. Tibet wasn't so tolerant of foreigners back then, famous for beheading uninvited visitors. So Nain set out, disguised as a lama on a pilgrimage to Lhasa, to conduct the Great Trigonometrical Survey and triangulated his way across the Himalayas, using two known points for every unknown to measure the length of his country. He survived.

I wasn't so sure I'd be that lucky as I mounted the last few steps that led to my two known points: Jacob, who was standing next to Erik. They couldn't have been more different, those two. And I was the unknown in this triangulation problem.

While Jacob may not have noticed Erik, Erik was certainly making note of him. He lowered the roses to his side, their blooms hanging head down. And his face, the one I had always trusted to be placid, now wore a foreboding frown.

"What's wrong?" Jacob asked, already jogging down the steps, his hand stretched out to lighten my load if I needed it. "Hey, you okay?"

No. I was a liar. And a cheater. And a coward. No different from his barista of a stepmother and his philanderer of a father.

The hundreds of excuses I'd told myself so that I didn't have to admit to Jacob that I had a boyfriend — technically, still had one — were as untrustworthy as the antique maps Dad collected and hoarded. As beautiful as they were, painstakingly hand-painted, they were wrong.

I wanted to sprint down the stairs, but instead, I forced myself to walk with Jacob to that top floor where Erik awaited, stony-faced. How could I tell Jacob that I was going to break up with Erik as soon as I was home and that I couldn't do it over e-mail when Erik himself was standing here? He deserved better, too.

"Jacob," I said quietly but clearly so I wouldn't have to repeat myself, "this is my boyfriend, Erik."

I cringed when Jacob glanced from Erik back to me, his look of confusion fast giving way to calculation as canny as Nain Singh's, that great surveyor. Jacob narrowed his eyes at me, seeing me clearly without my two-faced mask, both sides made up — one with cosmetics, the other with lies.

"You hate roses," he said, flat and hard.

"What?"

"I bet you hate roses," Jacob continued relentlessly. "Don't you?"

"Jacob . . ."

"Don't you?"

I nodded. He was right about me again. I did. I hated roses. I hated them for being so trite, so clichéd, a default, all-purpose flower that said I love you, I'm sorry, and get well soon. Give me peonies and tulips, orchids or gardenia. Those were flowers with character.

Without another word, Jacob stepped around me, stopping only to thrust Mom's packages at Erik, a perverted changing of the guards. And then he strode away at a fast, angry clip.

"Excuse me," said a man, irritated, behind me. "Do you mind?"

Numbly, I moved out of his way, noticing my somber mother, Jacob's disappointed one, as they filed off the escalator. Ashamed, I studied the carousels, wishing I could jump on one, swirl away. I wouldn't have thought that Mom would stand by me, but she did, striding toward us. She had to stop momentarily to jockey up her sagging pants, but she was at my side soon enough.

"Erik," said Mom, "we weren't expecting you here."

"Mr. Cooper asked if I could pick you guys up." He shrugged, as if driving hours for me had been no big deal. It was more than what Dad was willing to do for Mom and me.

As if she felt the sting of Dad's neglect, too, Mom's smile wobbled, a leaf blown about in a squall. "That was very nice of you."

Erik shrugged again.

"Well," Mom said, shooting me a meaningful look, "I'll meet you over in baggage claim."

I watched Mom go, watched as a petal from those unwanted roses drifted to the ground.

"So," said Erik, not looking at me, but off at the reader board, listing all the arrivals at the airport. There was an awkwardness, an uncertainty on his face that I had never seen before; he was usually so sure.

"So," I repeated, not knowing what to say any more than he did. I couldn't have missed my usual shield of makeup more.

But Erik didn't ask about my face, almost as if he hadn't noticed or didn't care that I was barefaced. Instead, he wanted to know: "So who's the Chinese guy?"

"He's American," I shot back automatically.

He waved impatiently in the air, having forgotten that he was holding the roses. A faint trace of fragrance trailed in the air when Erik lowered the bouquet hastily, embarrassed. His real questions hovered unspoken: *are you into him? What is he to you?*

Deflect, that's what my instincts were telling me. Deflect. Reroute. Send him on a different it's-fine-everything-is-fine path, but that was an uneven, graveled route. Easy to trip yourself up on. I couldn't go back in time, couldn't change what I had done, couldn't pretend that I hadn't loved the idea of being with a popular jock. But Erik deserved to be more than my vanity plates. He deserved to be so much more than proof that someone could find me attractive.

I took a deep breath. "I'm so sorry, Erik. I should have been up-front with you."

"You should have." Then, a memory clicked. "He was the guy you were hanging out with over Christmas."

I nodded miserably.

"While you were 'sick.'"

"I'm sorry."

"Did you hook up with him then?"

"No. God, no."

"In China?"

"Does it matter?"

"It does to me," he said. Where was this dogged persistence coming from? Something had unlocked the key to Erik.

"We kissed; that's it." What did I mean, that's it? That was more than enough. I whispered, "I'm so sorry, Erik." And then, finally, I let him go. "You and me . . . we shouldn't see each other anymore."

He didn't answer, his hand tightening around the roses. Suddenly, he winced, loosened his grip. A thorn must have punctured him; blood welled in the curved archipelago below his thumb. I withdrew a napkin from my pocket, doubled it over, pressed it against his hand. Across the baggage terminal, Jacob had just lifted his mom's luggage off the carousel and as he set it down, he caught sight of me at the same time I did him. And now, he stared at me in disbelief, my hands still wrapped around Erik's. I ripped my hands away, took a step away. It was too late. The swarming crowds blocked Jacob from view. I knew he had wrenched around anyway.

Erik nodded over to the carousels that were spitting out baggage blithely, everybody's downsized lives fitting into neat packages. "Let's get your stuff."

"You don't have to drive us home."

His eyebrows furrowed, offended. "What kind of guy do you think I am?"

Apparently, more of a guy than I had given him credit for when we first hooked up. Erik walked toward the baggage carousel. I lagged behind, awkward now that we were heading to Jacob, who was flanked by Norah and my mom as if they were protecting him. From me.

"Tell me something," Erik said gruffly, waiting for me now.

I pushed back my hair and studied Erik, his full mouth that I had always thought too lushly feminine for his face. Those rough hands that had touched every bit of my body. Now those hands balled up the napkin and were tossing it along with the roses into a trash bin a few feet away from us. He made the shot. When had he ever not?

"So what's with that guy?" he asked, nodding over at Jacob, who was striding with his luggage and his mom's out the door without a backward glance at me. Norah lifted her hand for a halfhearted wave before disappearing through the sliding doors, too.

I knew what Erik was getting at: Why Jacob? Why this lanky kid who Erik could take down in a moment?

"He got me," I said simply.

chapter thirty-two

Magnetic North

IF IT WEREN'T FOR OUR luggage by the front door where we had parked them, we might never have left the house. Within minutes of Erik dropping us off (after what was quite possibly the most uncomfortable car ride in the history of girlhood), Mom was back in the kitchen. And I was back to hovering in the background, patrolling in case Dad blew.

We'd been gone for eleven days, and the first thing Dad had to say when he finally deigned to notice us from where he was sitting in the kitchen, reading his newspaper? "What are we having for dinner?"

As though Mom knew she was being set up for a crime she didn't commit, she opened the refrigerator cautiously. The three main shelves were empty. Not even Mom, the culinary miracle worker, could do much with only organic butter and homemade jams, jars of honey Dijon mustard and plum sauce for ingredients.

"He didn't go grocery shopping?" Mom muttered to herself. I don't think she was even aware she had spoken aloud. My stomach tightened, and I glanced automatically at Dad. I hoped he hadn't overheard.

Naturally, he of the big ears heard every word. "If I didn't have to go for the past week and a half, why would I have gone now?"

At least I could make tea, placate Dad while I ran to the store.

Hastily, I turned on the Instant Hot faucet. I was in such a rush that I scalded the mound of my palm in almost exactly the same spot where Claudius had cut himself over Christmas. *Slow down,* I told myself as I ran cold water over it. Calm down. Jacob had told me that the best coffee — and best tea — began with cold water gently boiled. And that is what I did. Dad could wait for his tea. More mindful of my actions, I filled the kettle from the regular faucet, set it on the stovetop, switched the heat on.

Silently, Mom opened the freezer. Every single precooked and prepackaged homemade lunch and dinner that Mom had prepared in the weeks before our trip, neatly stowing them in their own Ziploc bag complete with her precise thawing and cooking instructions — all of them were gone, eaten. She just stood there, riveted by the sight of her freezer so cleaned out.

Without moving from her spot, Mom tugged her orange silk shirt down as though it had shrunk a size in the caustic heat of Dad's presence. Or like she was finally gearing up for battle.

Not now, Mom. Dad was hungry; I was tired. These were not good battle conditions. All I craved was a quick retreat to my bedroom, forget about Dad and Erik and Jacob. Jacob and his last look of utter betrayal before he left the airport. But I couldn't leave Mom.

Dad, of course, had to notice Mom adjusting her shirt. "Are you sure that's a good color on you? It's like looking directly into the sun, isn't it?"

The kettle whistled. By accident, I had overfilled the kettle so that water leaked out and sizzled on the cooktop as it hit the hot surface.

"We're out of tea," Dad said accusingly, implying that I was the biggest idiot this side of the Cascades. "So why would you be heating up water?"

I turned off the heat and glared at Dad through the wispy steam. My tiredness disappeared. I was fully alert now. Mom was bending down to her tote bag.

Dad's pent-up criticism, stored over the last week and a half, all but spewed out like storm water in a stopped-up gutter. He slapped the newspaper on the table.

Deliberately, Mom pulled out the three expensive boxes of tea she had selected especially for Dad in Hangzhou: dragon well tea leaves, handrolled into tiny pearls. Bundles of jasmine leaves, stitched together into a pellet, which would bloom like a flower when steeped in hot water. Aromatic strands of Iron Goddess. She set them down on the island now, one after another, in a straight soldierly line.

"Which would you like?" Mom asked mildly.

Dad's lips tightened, thwarted. His eyes narrowed at Mom, at those tea packages that offered her this unexpected reprieve. "Are you sure they're safe? They didn't spike them with preservatives? Chemicals?"

Diffuse him. Since Dad didn't choose a tea, I did randomly. With surprising calm as though Dad weren't in the room with us, I sliced the package open, shook out a heaping tablespoon into the waiting teapot, and poured the boiling water slowly over the dried leaves.

Mom murmured so softly I could barely make out her words, "If you don't want them, I can find someone else who would." And then, as though shocked, as though she heard the echo of those words, the implications reverberated inside herself. She could find someone else.

Mom looked at Dad then, scrutinized him.

She could find someone else.

The same look of dazed surprise that she wore after her rickshaw ride and again when she talked our way into the orphanage now emboldened her eye. It was as if it finally occurred to her that she had been navigating Dad's ever-shifting mercurial moods, always changing her course to accommodate him. Every time he lashed out and ha-rangued and criticized and demeaned, Mom apologized and rational-ized and accepted the blame, a tango that kept her off-balance.

He glowered, then repeated his question — "What are we having for dinner, Lois?" — more slowly, like Mom had lost her language skills in China. I maneuvered myself closer to Mom so that I stood between the refrigerator and the kitchen table, ready to defend her if it came to that.

Mom frowned at me. "I'm not hungry. Are you, Terra?"

I shook my head.

"Then I think we both better go to bed. I'll do the grocery shopping tomorrow." As clearly as Dad did upstairs in his office, creating his maps, Mom drew a line now, firm, unmovable.

She didn't so much as glance uneasily at him when she collected her bags from the front door. Instead of going upstairs, Mom rolled her suitcase to Claudius's bedroom, retreating there, fully conscious of her decision. Her statement. I thought she might close the door now, but instead she said so firmly, "Come on, Terra, it's time for bed," I could have been a little girl, the one who needed protecting.

The tea had steeped for too long in the hot water. No doubt, it'd be a bitter brew, but I poured Dad his mug of tea, placed it on the table. Only then did I see the box I had opened blindly. Iron Goddess.

"What are you doing, Lois?" demanded Dad, ignoring the tea to stalk toward Claudius's bedroom.

Mom didn't answer, waiting calmly for me to find safety in my bed-room. When I was at my door, she nodded. "Good night, Grant." And only then did she close the door. *Do not cross this line.*

"What? Why should I have gone grocery shopping?" Dad demanded. "You were the ones gallivanting off on vacation. I had to do all the work around here."

Even from my bedroom, I heard the click as Mom locked the door. Her answer was all too clear: I don't trust you.

And then I did the same.

At first, I waited for Dad to pound on her door, threaten to break mine down. Certainly, we must have had the key to these bedrooms lying around somewhere.

Nothing.

I slumped against the door, listening, remembering every story I had ever read about fathers snapping and killing their families.

Still nothing.

And then it occurred to me that maybe Mom didn't need my protection as much as I thought she did. She couldn't have drawn her line more clearly. Her line that said, *From here you do not cross. From here I will not budge.*

She'll be fine, Norah had assured me in China. For the first time, I allowed myself to truly believe that my mother just might be fine. And I was free to breathe.

chapter thirty-three

True North

ACCORDING TO KARIN'S WEEKLY PODCAST, *Love and Hate in High School,* thou shalt not call a boy more than once a day, preferably every other day if one must. Broke that rule by nine that night. Not that it mattered. I kept ringing directly into Jacob's voicemail. It was probably for the best; how many ways can you say you're sorry? How many times can you try to explain yourself before your excuses sounded more and more like guilt-ridden rationalization?

At the very least, I would have thought that jet lag would knock me out. But between Mom's snores rumbling from Claudius's bedroom and my habituated listening for Dad, I couldn't sleep. I flipped over, covered my head with my pillow, and finally flung it to the floor. The clock read two. I sighed and decided I might as well be productive. As I powered on my computer, I could almost hear Jacob teasing me about it: *are you always this compulsive?*

Well, yes. You know that . . . just as you knew I hated roses.

Impatient at myself for pining like the pathetic boy-centric girl I vowed I would never be, I grabbed my camera from my backpack and downloaded all five hundred and twenty-two of my China photos. If anything, reviewing the pictures made the trip seem even more distant than it really was. We had said *zaijian* to China less than twenty-four hours ago.

There was Mom and me at Sea-Tac Airport, the one Norah had taken of us at the gate, waiting to board. We looked way more nervous than I remembered, with the same half smiles, the same pocket of worry creasing the middle of our foreheads. Then came the shot of Mom and Norah on the airplane, giggling as they clandestinely swigged their mini-bottles of wine. They hadn't seen me sneaking up on them. And then at dinner after their first day of shopping in Shanghai, Mom wearing the same bright silk shirt she had worn today.

I cropped the picture down to Mom's face. This wasn't the pale vestige of the beauty queen Mom had once been, but the queen herself. Her head was cocked to the side and she was smiling mysteriously, transported by a great story. Ink was so expensive, I saved it for the really good pictures. This was one of them.

As the printer worked its magic, I studied the next photo, a group shot at that same dinner. It wasn't Jacob or Mom that held my attention, but Merc who was — surprise, surprise — checking his BlackBerry, frowning, completely unaware that he was sitting before a feast. I flipped through a sequence that Mom must have taken, one of me sleeping in Merc's apartment, mouth open. I almost deleted the three of them, but then, that was the trip through Mom's eyes.

I skipped ahead to the orphanage, wishing I had been able to take more. But it was a miracle I had been able to snag even the few shots I did before I got chastised by one of the nervous staff members. Photographs within the orphanage walls still weren't allowed. But there was one of me and Peony — I finally teased the girl's name out of her before we left the orphanage — cheek to cheek, birthmark to birthmark. Another picture worthy of my printer ink.

But it was the last photograph, the one I had asked Mom to take of me and Jacob on the doorstep outside the orphanage that made me lean forward. Something about our expressions was different. I zoomed in. More than relieved, we looked whole. Triumphant. Only then did I notice Jacob's scar, that faded rainbow over his upper lip. When had I stopped seeing it when I was with him?

You know, I don't even see your birthmark, he had said to me at the lake's edge in Beijing. *Which makes me sad.*

I understood that now: how nothing looked more beautiful than that scar of his, that borderline that separated what Jacob could have been had he stayed in that orphanage from who he was.

While the printer whirred for yet one more ink-worthy photograph, I knew better than to check my cell phone, turned to its highest volume and placed by my bed so I wouldn't miss his call. But I did. No messages. What had I expected? It was compulsive and control freakish, but I wanted to clean up this mess I had made between us, make things right. I could have listened to one of Karin's podcasts. But I didn't need her relationship advice; I needed a map that would tell me where to go, which way to proceed. I lifted my eyes to the wall, papered with Merc's maps. Those weren't going to help. Merc was more lost than I was, mistaking exhaustion for enlightenment.

Anger that I never allowed myself to feel expanded inside me now. I could feel it strumming in my stomach, my head, my fingertips. I had been there, in Merc's adopted country, in his apartment, and we had spent a total of six hours together. Jumping to my feet, I ripped down the maps: the free road maps from AAA. The cheap topographical ones inserted into *National Geographic.* The world map pinholed with the places Merc wanted to visit, and the places he had already seen. The pins scattered on the floor, making even tiptoeing dangerous. But I excelled at that. After all, didn't I walk on pins whenever Dad lurked nearby?

Spent, I fell into bed, closed my eyes, and dreamt of torn maps falling on me like fresh snow.

The next morning, just as I was finishing my e-mail to Merc, I heard a light rap on my bedroom door. Mom called softly, "Terra? Are you awake?"

I pushed away from my desk, scampered across the floor swept clean of last night's rain of pushpins, and unlocked the door. Mom was back in her pink sweats and sneakers. But she had makeup on, lipstick, eye shadow, the works.

"I'm going grocery shopping. Is there anything you want?" she asked. She noticed the maps strewn on my floor, raised an eyebrow at me. "What's going on?"

"I'm redecorating."

"Is that all?"

"And e-mailing Merc."

Her eyebrows rose even further.

When I awoke this morning, I realized had I been straight with Erik and Jacob and myself, I wouldn't be in this mess. Just be honest. So I told her, "I want Merc to know that it hurt that he didn't want to spend more time with me in China." I bit my lip. It was hard to be that vulnerable, to make my feelings known. "It's good to let him know how I feel, isn't it?"

For the longest time, Mom stared at the overlapping maps that created a great collage on my floor. Then she nodded. "That's brave of you."

"Give me fifteen minutes and I'll go with you to the store," I told Mom now, suddenly.

"You have school." But then she looked at my baggage, still

unpacked in the corner, the photographs laid out on my desk. She walked over to them now, inspecting them silently one by one. Then she murmured, stunned, "These are beautiful." Mom picked up the picture I had worked on last night, the cropped one of her at the restaurant. I thought she'd put herself down, comment about how fat she looked, how many double chins she had. Instead, she set the photograph carefully back on the desk. "I don't suppose missing one more day will hurt. Can you be ready in five minutes?"

"Twelve," I countered, like we were bargaining in one of the markets she had dragged me to in Beijing.

Mom laughed. "Ten."

After I threw on some clothes and brushed my teeth, I went back to my computer, ready to hit send, but hesitated. Before I sent the e-mail to Merc, I wanted to review my words one last time, make sure I said what I wanted to say without antagonizing him or accusing him. The wrong words could damage our relationship; that's not what I wanted. So I clicked on save instead.

Control freak that I am, it was one thing to have my clothes still neatly folded inside my suitcase, and another for the maps to be strewn like a great, messy collage on the ground.

A collage.

When the creative impulse sweeps over you, grab it. That's what Lydia always advised. You grab it and honor it and use it, because momentum is a rare gift. So when I had the impulse to roll up the maps and scrounge under my bed for my Beauty Box, I followed it. A layer of dust had settled on the box's lid since the last time I had added to its contents. I grabbed the pile of China map travel bugs I had removed from the cache outside and kept in the bottom drawer of my desk, under a box of old papers. I now swept them into the Beauty Box. Then I stowed box and all inside my backpack. I was about to leave my bedroom when — don't ask why — I darted into my bathroom and plucked my vials of makeup off the counter — the thick Covermark made especially for port-wine stains, all my concealers in descending shades of beige from tanned brown to ashen white, my powders, both the cakey ones and the shimmery sheers.

Only then was I ready for Mom.

Like always, I headed to the mudroom to take the car keys off the rack so I could drive. But as I passed Claudius's bedroom, I stopped. Mom had covered the bed with her new duvet, the one she had bought in China. So cheerful and bright and wholly feminine, it should have looked out of place with Claudius's fantasy books and posters. But like all of Mom's creations, this mysterious alchemy of design worked somehow.

Mom was waiting for me outside, facing the valley spotted with cabins and homes among acres of rolling green from the few remaining farmlands. As expansive as the view was, my hometown had shrunk without anything changing but my perspective. This, my home, was an anthill compared to even the smallest towns in China, which numbered at a million people.

We headed silently to the garage. Dad's keys had been missing in the mudroom. And so was his car. It wasn't like him to leave the house this early.

"Where's Dad?" I asked Mom, worried. What was he up to now?

Mom shrugged — she didn't know. Or maybe she didn't care. "Shall we?"

"So," I said casually, as I opened the trunk to stow my backpack, "I saw your sheets in Claudius's room."

Mom nodded, fussed with the zipper on her sweatshirt, yanking it up, pulling it down. "I thought I'd stay there for the time being."

I wondered what Dad thought of that, Mom moving out of their bedroom, and closed the trunk firmly.

"Hey, Mom," I said, "do you want to see the geocache that Aunt Susannah left here?"

For the longest time, Mom didn't answer, her hand turning white as she gripped the passenger door. "Okay," she said finally. Before she could change her mind, I grabbed my backpack out of the trunk and led Mom toward the cache, letting her set the pace.

The geocache was exactly where Jacob and I had left it last winter, seemingly undisturbed through back-to-back seasons of snow and snow melt. I was surprised to find two new entries in the logbook that Susannah had started and was about to read them to Mom. But she hadn't even glanced inside the box. She was staring at the box itself, lettered boldly with the name of the cache: *KRYPTONITE.*

"What, Mom?" I asked her gently. "What is it?"

She swallowed, tracing the letters on the top of the box. "That was Susannah's nickname for me growing up. Kryptonite."

"I don't get it."

"Lois. Lois Lane."

I followed her. "Fell in love with Superman . . ." Then I got it. Kryptonite. It was the only thing in the universe that crippled his powers.

"I used to be quite popular with the boys," Mom said, smiling feebly. She sat on the log with a shaky sigh. "Susannah always said that I was Kryptonite to them. Made them fall to their knees."

From my Beauty Box, I pulled out the handful of travel bugs Susannah had made of these ragged, fading fragments of the China map, and held them out to Mom. I'd let her decide what to do with them. Susannah's intention with these travel bugs wasn't the noblest — cast Dad's humiliation around the world. I was no better. Left to me, I'd disperse them myself at every geocache I encountered.

But Mom? She just cupped the bagged scraps of her past in her palms. Through her tears, Mom smiled at me. "Susannah just wanted to remind me of who I am."

I sat beside Mom on that tree trunk that must have fallen in some past windstorm when no one had noticed. The air swam with the thick piney scent of the living trees around us in this small copse. Neither of us said anything as the sun rose higher, warming the air. A hummingbird — an early migrator — buzzed by, coming back to hover near Mom. It inspected her pastel sweatshirt as through expecting her to spout nectar freely. Disappointed when she didn't, it darted away.

Out of nowhere, Mom blurted, "If you want to go to Williams, you can."

"What do you mean?"

"Susannah left me some money. Our brother has been holding it in trust for me. And I'll get a job."

"Mom," I said softly, "that would be great if you got a job for yourself. But I'll find my own way." As I said those words, I knew it was true. It was funny, but everyone had found their own path to escape Dad — Merc moved around the world, Claudius bulked up, even Mom had reclaimed herself. I'd find my own path, one that led me from Dad but that I'd keep clear for Mom to follow, if she ever wanted.

"You were wrong, Mom," I said.

She looked startled and I thought she'd apologize, her instant reaction. Instead, she asked, "About what?"

"Susannah didn't need to remind you of who you were. You remembered all on your own."

She nodded proudly, pointing at herself and then at me. "We both did."

And she was right.

Later, as we trudged back home, out of habit I pulled the keys from my pocket before we even reached the driveway just to have them ready in my hand. They jangled, a ringing of freedom as clear as any bell peal.

I held the keys out to Mom. "Do you want to drive?" I asked her and gestured down to the greening valley below. We didn't have to go all the way to China to see beauty. Or to have an adventure. They were both right here, literally in our backyard. "The snow's melted."

At first, she looked scared at the thought, then just thoughtful.

"Maybe I will." And she took the keys from me.

No sooner did Mom ease the car into the Red Apple grocery store's parking lot than she slammed on the brakes. Luckily, no one was behind us. And we were only going about five miles per hour so there was no risk of whiplash.

"I don't believe it," she whispered.

There, coming out of the store was Dad, toting one small grocery bag against his shoulder as if it were a child. It was as incongruous seeing him here as it would be seeing Mom at the Naked Spa Norah had been raving about — or finding her now in the driver's seat. He spotted us at the same time I did him, stopping so suddenly that plumes of dust flew around his feet. His look of shock and disbelief mirrored Mom's before his changed to embarrassment. Brusquely, Dad nodded at us and without any further acknowledgment, he slid into his truck as though he were in some kind of witness protection program for husbands whose wives finally had their say.

I stated the obvious: "He went grocery shopping." Well, sort of. Mom's idea of grocery shopping was filling the trunk, the more bags the better; I could only imagine what was in Dad's lonely-looking bag, perhaps a grapefruit, a couple of bagels, and a frozen chicken. But he had gone.

Dad exited from the opposite side of the parking lot, while Mom and I idled near the entrance. As he drove past us on the street, Mom unclenched the steering wheel and finally parked the car at an awkward angle, sprawling into two spots, but I didn't point that out. Everyone else could find a space around us.

"I don't think I'll go grocery shopping after all," Mom said.

"Where do you want to go instead?"

She adjusted the rearview mirror belatedly — and I could only hope that she had been able to see her blind spots on her drive here. "I think I'll just walk around for a little while."

I was going to offer, *I'll come with you.* But she had a lot to think about, and only she could figure out what she wanted to do with this olive branch Dad was extending to her, whether she'd snap it like a twig or accept it and hope it'd flourish.

When she dropped me off at the gallery, I was grateful that no one else was there — no one to distract me with conversation about my trip to China or ask me about my college plans. Just blissful solitude. I hurried up to my studio, dropped the maps on the ground, and salvaged my Beauty Box from my backpack. Then I placed the photographs from China on my desk under the bright light. Everything was unpacked, laid out. A blank board waited. But all my ideas, my inspiration had fled.

I was lost.

I wiggled in my chair, waiting for an idea — any idea — to overtake me.

Nothing.

I rearranged the pictures on my desk, browsed through the baskets of raw material.

Nothing.

I could almost hear Jacob, telling me that being lost was just another way of saying you were exploring. That the most direct route to a geocache might not be the right one. Like the path I had been following: hurrying through high school to get to college only to become a mini-Merc, married to my BlackBerry. I didn't want that future anymore.

I swung my leg impatiently. My foot knocked over a canvas beneath my work table. I leaned down to pull it out. My Beauty Map. The one I had kicked under my table, hoping that Jacob wouldn't see it that first time he visited my studio. I had forgotten all about it, hidden there, never hanging it up. Now, studying my work, the map didn't look finished so much as empty, all the blank white space of undiscovered territory surrounding those images of plasticized beauty.

God, had I been following the wrong set of coordinates my entire life, my eyes set on Beauty instead of True Beauty?

I opened my Beauty Box and dumped out the contents: the dermatological brochures of all the latest and greatest treatments that I used to collect, the fashion magazine articles I clipped, those before-and-after shots of women undergoing the knife and accepting poison to change themselves — the lines on their faces repaved like old roads, their bulbous noses whittled into aristocratic ridges.

All of those images, I ripped up now. I didn't slice them with a brand-new razor to create clean, sharp edges. I tore them. Messy strips, tiny confetti — all of them, mismatched pieces of a puzzle that were never meant to be put together.

Done.

But where did I go from here?

I squared the collage on my worktable. The model with the fake violet eyes stared back at me from the center of my Beauty Map. That was my focal point? My North Star that I had been following so futilely? If I tried to strip her off of the board, it would ruin the collage.

Ruin . . . or make real?

I scraped at a corner of the glued image until a tiny edge lifted from the board. I pulled. A sliver of paper ripped off unevenly, leaving the surface mottled like peeling paint on an old building. It scared me, how ugly the effect was. But I didn't allow myself to doubt. Over and over, I tore until the model was zebra-striped, her beautiful epidermis interspersed with frayed dermis.

I had always felt a foreigner in this made-up Land of Beautiful, and it was a relief to see Extreme Beauty for what it really was: fake, make-believe, insubstantial.

I would build on top of it, use its history as my foundation.

My foundation. I smirked, working even more quickly now.

From the basket on the floor, I grabbed my white paint, poured a little into an old salsa container. And then I shook out a few drops of my makeup into the paint, stirred, marbleizing beige into the white paint. But the foundation disappeared, the paint remaining resolutely white. So I dumped a healthy teaspoon. Still not enough. Then, like a mad scientist — or Mom getting good and ready to create a wholly new recipe — I just dumped the whole darn bottle in. It felt deliciously decadent and wasteful, yet so right when I slathered my concoction on one side of the model's face. The other, I left alone.

Which one looked more real? Which side more beautiful?

Then still working fast, I layered all the scraps from my Beauty Box around her head, building on top of that outline with those fragmented words promising miraculous change. Photoshopped eyes, noses, mouths. Surgically enhanced breasts. I stepped back to get perspective. The Land of Beautiful was missing something.

Since Mom didn't have an opinion what to do with the pieces of China map, I placed them all back into the geocache, the way Aunt Susannah had wanted, save one piece. That, I had held onto, intending to put it into a geocache some day; I hadn't been sure where, only that I would know when I found it. I found my cache, right here, taking shape before me. I stuck that torn map fragment now over the model's mouth.

I frowned at my collage map. Something was still missing, but what?

There had to be inspiration in all the bits of the world I collected in the baskets above my desk. With my eyes closed, I reached inside, letting my fingers roam, touch, discard until I felt a tiny stub of metal. I pulled it out. The crumpled piece of my car, the warped piece I had salvaged after crashing into Jacob's Range Rover.

That, I placed on top of the Land of Beautiful. I made a note to myself to call Magnus, that cantankerous artist who worked in metal, and ask him for a lesson. What was the worst he could do?

Make me feel dumb? Inadequate?

Dad had done his damnedest to do that, to steer me to Terra Nullis, that godforsaken empty land where one might survive but never flourish. To keep me in Terra Incognita and remain a girl as undiscovered as Unknown Land itself.

He had failed.

I crossed my arms and took another step back to see how my creation was shaping up. It was literally shaping up. I was surprised. The layers were building, one on top of another, not a flap map, but a topographical one, complex and multidimensional.

Note to self: keep my dorm room locked next year.

Without so much as a warning rap, the door to my studio flung open and Karin's voice blared: "There you are. I bumped into your mom — she was walking! — and she told me you were here. How was your trip? Where were you at school? God, I've been dying to talk to you."

I sighed softly, hating to be interrupted while I sketched the last of the cartouches. There were five different styles of mapmakers' marks in all, each one of them flourished around my name. I hadn't been able to decide which I liked best. Perfect, I could ask Karin for her opinion now.

Still, it irritated me how she strode into my studio without my invitation and without apologizing for interrupting. Her dainty bronze sandals, dulled from its covering of fine Methow dust, nearly spiked the maps on my floor.

"Hey, watch where you're going," I said, frowning at the trail she was haphazardly bushwhacking to me. I leaped out of my chair to stash the maps safely under my desk.

"God," she said, "what happened in here? Looks like you had a tantrum."

"I'm making art." I had waited a long time to say those words, and I thought it would be hard to use them, that the claim would be too big for me. Surprisingly, it wasn't. I had grown into the words.

"Not that I would blame you if you threw a conniption fit."

"Why would I throw one?"

"You know, if you called Erik. . . ."

I set down my pencil. "How do you know about it already?"

"Well, there was a party last night." She peered at me through her thick fringe of lashes. Now, she perched on the edge of my desk, oblivious to my collage drying behind her or of the cartouches I had been doodling on paper. "He was hanging out with Alicia."

I think we were both waiting for my jealousy to rear its ugly head. But it didn't even bother lifting its cheek off the floor.

"Good," I said, meaning it. "I'm glad for him."

"Call him now, and he'd give you another chance."

"What if I don't want another chance? What if I've moved on?"

"I don't get you. How could you let the best thing that's happened to you go just like that?"

"He was a good thing, Karin. A great thing. But not the best thing."

"And what? That Goth guy is?"

I glanced at the picture of Jacob near her hand. "His name is Jacob."

Karin shrugged, dismissing anything I could have possibly said in Jacob's favor — that he had an uncanny ability to find beauty in the most unlikely places: our arid Valley with its cash crop of rock and dirt. A squalid neighborhood in Shanghai still using chamber pots for toilets. And my birthmark.

As much as I hated the grid that Dad had tried to box me in, I chafed at this invisible fence that Karin had erected around me. What may have started as protective — she had designated herself as my champion in ballet, after all — had become suffocating. I unshackled the collar I didn't even realize I was wearing and told her firmly, "Karin, I don't want to be with Erik, and I'm cool with that."

"Why not?" She began her litany of reasons: "He's pretty cute, he's a stud —"

"And I don't love him."

"It's that Goth guy, isn't it?"

"No. It's me." I paused, and then drew my line harder into the rocky soil of our friendship. "When you keep pushing me to stay with Erik, when you talk about him as the best thing that's ever happened to me, it makes me feel like I'm so ugly I should be grateful to have him as a boyfriend."

"I never said that." Offended, Karin frowned, her face scrunching up. God, I had to tell Jacob: physical beauty was temporary. A vessel without soul. I didn't want to be her vessel anymore, filled with only what she thought was best for me.

I didn't back down. This was my line, fortified by my will, declared with my voice. "I don't want to be with a guy who doesn't notice me half the time."

No answer.

I shrugged, said what I had to, decided I didn't need to explain myself any further. I was about to wave at my work, my *art* work, tell her that I was busy when Karin surprised me. She leaned over my sketches of cartouches. Before she had barged in, I was about to select the best of them and scan it into the computer so I could touch it up.

Karin asked softly as if she had never noticed my art before either, "What are you working on?"

"My cartouche. It's kind of like a mapmaker's logo. Which do you like the best?" I asked her now, moving my sketches closer to her so she could see them better.

She passed a cursory look at them, her face losing its pinched expression. "They all kind of look the same to me."

"They're not. They're all different. You just have to look closely."

I wasn't sure if Karin would, but she leaned down, drawn to my cartouches. Three were set within scrolls, and the other two inside heraldic shields. I had embellished one with cherubs, another with curled ribbon. And one with a sea dragon that I knew wasn't for me at all.

"This one," said Karin, pointing to the simplest one, flourished into the shape of a heart. "This feels like you."

"I think so, too."

"You know, these are amazing." Her eyes gleamed now as if her idea factory had switched on, mind whirring, while she transformed the idea of a cartouche into something new. "Can you make one for me? For my podcast show, since it's basically about mapping new relationships? Maybe my name could be in an iPod screen instead, or —"

I interrupted firmly, "After I finish mine." And then I laughed, because her brainstorm was only now starting. Within an hour, she'd have iterated the original idea at least fifteen times. I pointed to my work-in-progress and said, "I really want to finish this now. I'll call you later, okay?"

Thankfully, Karin took being dismissed well. In fact, she nodded like she was actually respecting my space and left quietly, even muffling the usual sharp staccato of her footfalls. I put a last downstroke on my favorite cartouche, added a few fantastical curls. As I glued the cartouche to the bottom right of my collage map, I finally pinpointed what was missing.

I picked up the photographs from China now. I had never defined myself as beautiful. But studying these images — with me, Mom, and Jacob — I saw it. I'd never be classically beautiful, never be modelesque. But I could see what the people who loved me saw.

I lavished the back of the photograph of me with Peony, the little girl from the orphanage, with a covering of medium, and set us down firmly far to the north of Beautiful. In that grim nursery, I had told Peony we were both handsome. But a better term would have been *jolie laide.*

Back in Shanghai's overcrowded Yu Garden, I had told Jacob that True Beauty connected me with everything. In its presence, something cleansed me like a wash of warm water so that even afterwards, I could appreciate every color and shape, every vista and vignette before me. It had just taken me until this moment, until I created this collage, to realize that the magazine world's vision of beauty had the exact opposite effect on me, shriveling me so that I only paid attention to my own imperfections.

Enough with that.

Physical beauty wasn't the same as True Beauty, any more than pretty ugly meant truly ugly or Magnetic North meant True North. I preferred my brand of beauty where Norah was more beautiful than any bimbette, and Mom was beautiful whether sized extra-small or extra-large. Where Peony could look at herself in the mirror and murmur, Wow, look at me. Just look at me.

Now I propped my collage against the wall behind my desk, and I backed up all the way until I stood at the opposite wall and looked, simply looked.

I nodded once, satisfied.

Let the glossy spreads have their heart-stopping, head-turning kind of beauty. Give me the heart-filling beauty instead. Jolie laide, that's what I would choose. Flawed, we're truly interesting, truly memorable, and yes, truly beautiful.

chapter thirty-four

Theatrum Orbis Terrarum

IT'S A PRETTY TOUGH AND lonely road, marching to your own drummer. Especially when your father stops you with a horrified "You aren't going to school like that, are you?"

"Like what?" I asked, playing dumb. I knew all too well what he was getting at: my naked face poised for its official debut at Kennedy High, thirty-five minutes and counting.

Bypassing breakfast altogether so I wouldn't have to stay in the same room with Dad was tempting. But hunger won out. With Mom walking mornings now, she rarely cooked a hot breakfast anymore, not that I was complaining. Mom doing things for herself was the best souvenir we could have brought back from China. I poured cereal into a plastic container that I could eat dry on the way to school. A blah-bland breakfast was a small price to pay for peace.

"Easy on those carbs," he said, sipping his antioxidant green tea. "You don't want to pack on your freshman fifteen before you even start at Western Washington, right?" *Chuckle, chuckle.*

Just to spite him, I shook more cereal into my Tupperware, too vigorously as it turned out. Cereal bounced from the container, carbohydrates cascading plentifully onto the floor. I bent to scoop the bits up, and as I straightened, my head whammed into the sharp kitchen island ledge. How many times had any of us hurt ourselves on account of Dad? Even overeating — like Mom — wasn't that a rebellion that in the end only hurt us?

What Dad did next, though, made me forget my throbbing head. He waved a white postcard, a matador's cape of paper. My first thought — and hope — was that it had something to do with Williams College again, maybe asking me to reconsider my decision: please come to our school; we need you.

"Your appointment card for your next treatment," said Dad, eyeing my face in that same accusatory way I've seen my entire life. As if I had begged in vitro for a birthmark, this personal affront to his sanitized, temperature-controlled world. "Not that any of it's done much good."

It's my face, I almost automatically retorted. *I'll do what I want with it.*

But as I took the postcard from him, I smelled the aromatic scent of the tea he was drinking. Iron Goddess.

I thought about the Iron Goddesses I knew: Mom, who had figured out our way into the orphanage. Norah, who had traveled the most dangerous parts of the world in search of the perfect coffee beans, Susannah in search of adventure. Even Karin for all her flaws was absolutely fearless in chasing her dreams. Not one of them clung obstinately to a map, static and out-of-date, when a new, interesting opportunity emerged. Sometimes, they simply let their instincts and intuition guide them.

"People are going to laugh at you," Dad warned me flatly.

There it was, the mapmaker's warning, an apocalyptical prediction. Sail too far and you'll drop off the edge of the Earth. Venture into the Unknown and an untold Beast will have you for dinner. But in the end, Dad's warnings were as false as any fabrication cartographers put forth before him. I thought about Peony, the little girl at the orphanage, who inspected my naked cheek in disbelief, awed that someone like her would dare hold my head up high. How I proclaimed her beautiful. And she me.

If Jacob was right and clothes were costumes and makeup a mask, then our attitudes and habits must be our shields. Isn't that what compulsive eating was for Mom? And round-the-clock work for Merc? And Dad's meanness, his sniping, his criticism — wasn't that just a front to cover his shame? His humiliation?

"You know something?" I asked, dumbfounded at that thought. I set down the postcard reminder of my next laser treatment, this invitation to continue spiting my father by hurting myself. And now, I told Dad earnestly, "No one knows about the China map." He blanched before he shook his finger violently in my face, shushing me, his face growing alarmingly red. I plowed on. "I bet the Chinese don't even know about the China map, Dad. And if they did, they wouldn't care. So that leaves, who? Five experts in the entire world who remember? Who care? Do they really matter?"

Deflect, that was my family's defense mechanism, and that was what Dad did now. As if I had said nothing at all, he snapped, "Your face will never change. You've got to know that, correct?"

There were far worse things than wearing a map of Bhutan on my face for my entire life. Then again, maybe that map was just a temporary fixture, a henna tattoo that would wear off in time, because who knew? In another sixteen years, some genius might invent a new technology that would obliterate my port-wine stain with one (truly unpainful) zap. And then maybe I'd revisit my decision. But for now, I didn't want blind defiance to define me. Not anymore.

Throughout history, wars were won and lost based on maps — who had the best maps, who had the inaccurate ones, who owned the boundary lines, who knew the terrain. And I knew the terrain of my family intimately, our private fears, our embarrassing weaknesses, our cached secrets. This time, I knew what to say to my father.

"But Dad" — finally, I looked at him face full-on — "Dad, I have nothing to hide."

I won't lie by saying that it was easy to leave the house with Dad sputtering behind me, singing his siren's song of doubt. But that was a cinch compared to getting out of my car to brave even the school parking lot, much less the school itself. Without my protective covering of makeup, I felt exposed and displayed in a way I hadn't in China. There, no one knew me. And I was fairly positive I'd never see any of them again. But this was school. And these were kids I'd known since preschool. I couldn't help but stare at myself in the rearview mirror, turning my face from side to side, wondering what people were going to say when they saw me.

Before I left the house, I had pulled my hair off my face into a high ponytail. A small salvo at Dad to show him that I really couldn't care less if people laughed at me; what can I say? But now, I slipped the brown ponytail holder off, shook my hair free so that it could veil me if I needed it. As I twisted around to stuff the elastic into the front pocket of my backpack, I saw my collage-map in the backseat.

I had made an appointment with Magnus for an after-school art lesson in metal today so I could weld the crumpled remains of my car accident to my collage. Funnily, he wasn't nearly as scary as his crotchety reputation made him out to be. "Anything for an honorary Twisted Sister," he had said when I called yesterday. And then more ominously, "Just bring your work."

So there was Peony again, looking out at me from our photograph with her cautious, wondering eyes. I hated picturing her cowering in the nursery — and maybe in a car someday in the future — because she was scared of what people in the Land of Beautiful might say or think about her face. *Let them say what they want.* That's what I would have told her. *Leave Terra Bella to the shallow, and claim the world for your own.*

The entire world, that's what I wanted. I wanted to travel it, experience it, revel in it. Abraham Ortelius made history in 1570 with his *Theatrum Orbis Terrarum,* the Theatre of the World, the first modern atlas of Earth as was known and catalogued at that moment.

It was time to update that atlas, and what better place to start than with my own collection of collages. What were those but maps that charted women's journeys as they traversed the rocky terrain separating girl from woman? Wasn't that what I created for Lydia? For my mother? And finally, for me? Our maps, our histories, our reminders of how we found our truest selves?

I settled back in the driver's seat and nodded at my reflection. If there was one thing I learned from Lydia and the rest of the Twisted Sisters, it was that artists do not cower. They live to make statements. So I forced myself out of my isolated cocoon of a car and headed for the toughest audience in town: Theatrum Prisonus Terrarum, my high school.

"So she's really got a honking thing on her face?"

I looked up from my locker to find Erik and his group of wrestler buddies strutting by in that thick-limbed way of theirs, arms too muscular to tuck into their sides. The guys stopped to stare at me, the local recruit in a traveling circus. I waited for that knife-edged moment when Erik distanced himself, first flushing with embarrassment and then studying his beat-up work boots as if he'd never seen them on his feet.

Six weeks, I told myself. That's all there was left to high school. Six weeks and I would be out of here.

"No wonder you broke up with her," said one of the guys, chuckling.

It wasn't Dad's malicious *chuckle, chuckle* exactly, but close enough to make me flush angrily.

"Actually —" I started to say.

But Erik interrupted, "She broke up with me."

In that moment, I liked Erik so much more than I ever had.

"But you should have broken up with me." I grinned at him, probably my most real smile that I'd given him since Halloween. To his credit, he gulped. Hard. I heard him. Never before had he made me feel more beautiful.

And there, shimmering between us, was a moment when one of us could have made a move. A step, a sorry, a let's try again, and we could have slipped back into the past, into each other. I didn't want that. And I didn't need anyone — even this good guy of a jock — to assure me of my beauty. The moment disappeared as surely as sea monsters vanished from maps once explorers ventured into the Unknown and made the world Known. Erik went his way to gym, and I went mine to Advanced Biology.

A week later, I received a call as I headed out of the house earlier than usual. (I was craving a caramel macchiato, what can I say?) Hoping it was Jacob, I foraged for my phone in my backpack on the passenger seat next to me. Not Jacob, but Lydia, who rarely used her cell phone. So now she shouted in my ear: "Is that you, Terra?"

God, at her age, maybe she fell, hurt herself. Why else would she call at seven fifteen?

"What's wrong?" I demanded, equally loudly.

"I thought I'd get your voicemail," she said, stymied now to be speaking with me.

"Are you okay?"

"Oh, I'm just fine. The question is, will you be after you hear the news?"

Clearly, building up my anticipation was part of Lydia's grand announcement plan. So I played along. I had about an hour before I had to brave school. Let's just say, I'd become a connoisseur of stares — although my classmates to their credit were starting to get accustomed to my face. Slowly. "Tell me, I'm dying here."

"So you met Magnus," said Lydia.

Yeah, I had met Magnus. He had frowned so fiercely when I first showed him my almost-final collage, complete with my cartouche in the lower-right corner, I thought he was going to deride my "good first effort." Instead, he had given me a new term to describe the heavy layers that I had built in the Land of Beauty, one on top of the other: *pentimenti.* "It's from the Latin," he had said in that growly voice of his. "To repent. And correct."

Lydia continued in her drama-filled voice, "Magnus said you showed *real* promise."

"Meaning that I've got a long way to go."

"Meaning he actually bought one of your pieces. I just picked up the messages from yesterday!"

"No way."

"The one you made for me. But the real news is that he wants you to work with him as his apprentice, once a week," cried Lydia, so breathless, she panted. "He never mentors anyone."

"You're kidding."

"It'll be free, of course. And he's a real piece of work, so you'll hate working for him. But that's art for you."

It takes a lot to make me cry. Years of living with Dad had something to do with that; he inured me of tears. I rested my head on the steering wheel and wept. After working alone in my studio, wondering whether I was wasting my time, wondering whether anyone would respond to my work, this hard-won affirmation undid me.

"Terra?" Lydia said, not worried. She knew what this was: a release. "Your last piece was beautiful."

"Thank you," I said, taking a shaky breath. I knew it was, too.

My personal map was layered with experience — my trip to China with Mom, my cheating on Erik, the phone call I received from Merc the other night, apologizing for how he acted in China. How there'd be a ticket waiting for me and Claudius the next time he accumulated enough frequent flier miles, which wouldn't be long, I knew. Together, we'd see Xi'an and the terracotta warriors. Even Dad added to my collage, adding one hard layer after another. And then, there was my old focal point, my port-wine stain. They were all just parts of my whole, pieces of my collaged life. It was time to explore a new subject. I wasn't sure what, exactly, but I was ready to venture out. And in the meantime, there was Mom's collage. God knew it needed updating and would again, depending on whether she was going to stay with Dad or leave him. Either way, the decision was Mom's; she was comfortably in charge.

"Lydia, if you all were still interested, I'd love to be in the show," I said.

"Good," she responded tartly. "We sent out the invitations yesterday." With that, she hung up.

I stared at my phone, then pocketed it with a bemused smile. As I backed out of the garage, I saw Mom's fresh footprints in the dirt heading toward the new running path I had forged earlier this morning. I rolled down the window, breathed in the clean Methow air, pungent with evergreens and newly flowering sage. And then I drove.

At the crossroads, my usual route lay to the left. Since junior high, I never strayed from the path that took me to school five days a week: left onto Main Street, right onto Grover Street. Today, I hit the gas pedal and plowed out of the Valley. Independence, straight ahead.

chapter thirty-five

Geographia

OTHER THAN MY RECENT TRIP to the airport, I literally could not remember the last time I had driven to Seattle for any reason other than my face. I didn't stop to question my intentional ditching of school for the second time ever — and both in a single week. I didn't worry about what my parents would do or say when they found out. I'd deal with those repercussions later. For now, I just drove.

The passage out of the valley is always exquisite, but especially so at the start of spring. Then, the two-lane highway bisecting the Cascade Mountains passes jubilant waterfalls fed by fresh snowmelt and exposed rock faces so sheer they make you dizzy just looking at them.

I turned off the radio, the one station that broadcast from Colville having gone fuzzy. Before me now rose Liberty Bell, that massive bell-shaped shaft of granite, its face some 1,200 feet high. I took my foot off the gas pedal and rolled down the window to inhale the sharp scent of liberation at the foot of this mountain.

*   *   *

Forty-five minutes before reaching Seattle, I saw signs I'd never noticed before for Lynnwood. The city sounded vaguely familiar —
Lynnwood, Lynnwood — and then I remembered. That was the location
of the spa Norah had told Mom about, the one that had Mom almost
crying from laughter because she couldn't even fathom a place where
women went around in the nude willingly.

Why not? I thought. Why the hell not?

I took an exit, looked for a place where I could pull over safely to
call for directions, and found the Convention Center with its large expanse of asphalt parking lot that I could smell even with my windows
rolled up.

"What listing?" asked the prerecorded, teleprompted operator in her
droning voice.

"Ummm . . . Naked Spa?"

A live operator came on. "What are you looking for?"

I explained as best I could: "There's supposed to be a Korean spa in
Lynnwood, women only. You go naked there."

"Naked."

I blushed, glad she couldn't see me.

If there is such a thing as fate and things happening for a reason and
things that are meant to be, then I was meant to go to the Naked Spa.
Miracles, the operator located the spa for me, official name the Olym-
pic Spa. Not only that, but it was right in front of me — as in I could
walk across the parking lot to its front door. As fated as this appeared
to be, that's not to say I didn't have doubts about it. I did. Located in a
strip mall, the "spa" looked like a refurbished bowling alley, down to
the ugly seventies stripe of terracotta across the front of the building. I
was highly skeptical, Norah or not. Even the most shopping savvy have
their off-moments.

But inside, the spa was an oasis, from its soothing earth tones to the tinkling of a tiny water fountain. Two friendly receptionists manned the front desk, which held an odd assortment of plastic barrettes and random Hello Kitty paraphernalia. The professional decorator must have finished the job, never checking back in to see how the misguided spa owners accessorized the place.

Having never been to a spa, I had no idea what I was supposed to do and looked blankly at the menu of services. I almost turned around right then, almost sprinted to the door; everything was so expensive. But then again, I had just sold my first piece of art, and I wanted to celebrate.

"Have a body scrub," one of the young women recommended.

Which sounded promising until they handed me a thin cotton robe, two towels, and a little pink cap. Norah did not mention any little pink cap. The benefit of the little pink cap, however, became instantly clear. I was too busy feeling stupid in my little pink cap to worry about being nude. Plus, Norah had overstated the whole naked business — the only section where nudity was mandatory was in the Jacuzzi room where I was supposed to marinate myself for an hour in four hot tubs, each hotter than the last.

While the spa wasn't thronging with women, the ones here were a chocolate box's assortment of shapes and sizes: grossly obese women who made Mom look svelte, emaciated ones who could have packed on fifteen pounds and still look gaunt. Women the age of the Twisted Sisters; a wedding party of women in their twenties.

That's when it struck me: how gorgeous we all were, even with cellulite (saw a lot of that) and stretch marks, scars and tattoos. Let me just say this, not a single body was perfect, not even the fittest of women there. (She was a triathlete; she told me so after we dared to use the glacial plunge pool.)

The long treatment room had a full five stations, with nothing separating the vinyl tables from each other. I will admit: I panicked as I lay there on my stomach, naked before everyone in this tiny microcosm of the world. But the moment the middle-aged woman, bulging out of her black camisole and shorts, began scrubbing me with her hands enveloped in yellow mittens, I forgot to be embarrassed or scared. Norah was right. My heels, elbows, chest, stomach, upper thighs — every part of me was scrubbed clean, even my face. Twice. And then three times. And in between each round, the woman doused me with hot water infused with mugwort.

Little eraser dander of skin clung to the white table when I sat up for my final, cleansing rinse. I seriously had no idea how much dead skin one body — one live body — could produce. I swear, my entire epidermis had been sloughed off. She probably even skimmed a little from my underlying dermis. What was left of my skin felt smooth and baby soft.

After the service, I had to use the bathroom, and as I was washing my hands, I caught a glimpse of myself.

I glowed.

It was almost a shame to put on my clothes.

"So did you enjoy yourself?" the receptionist asked when I was ready to check out, but not ready to leave. I could linger in the serene quiet here for hours. But there was someone I had to find.

"Definitely." And then I paid the spa the highest compliment I could: "I'm going to bring my mother here."

Even with my unplanned pit stop at the spa, I still had almost two hours before I could intercept Jacob at school. Because he was, I had to admit, the real reason for my trip.

So I drove now to the University of Washington, asking myself, How hard could it possibly be to find a campus that was some twenty-two million square feet? Hard, as it turned out. Unintentionally, I found the University Village shopping mall. Which was definitely worth a drive-by look. But I turned around on 45th Avenue, and finally arrived on the campus.

The cherry trees in the main quad were at the end of their bloom, a few blossoms, pink and white, were left, interspersed with bright green leaves. Students milled around, some of the girls so dressed up they looked ready to go clubbing. The funny thing was, standing there in this university that I had written off as too monolithic, too overwhelming, I felt completely at home. After China, how could any place feel too large or too hard to navigate? I had walked through squalid alleys, negotiated the Forbidden City, and didn't just figure out a way to get to the Great Wall — I geocached and tobogganed there. I did all of that with just a handful of Chinese words and one big smile.

There was no reason why I had to go to Western Washington.

I could handle UW. Take classes in its fine arts program. And major in business school, if I wanted.

This university wasn't on Dad's sanctioned list, but its tuition? That, I could afford on my own. And I had gotten in, after all.

I almost laughed out loud when I drove up to Jacob's private school, Viewridge Prep with all its ivy-covered brick buildings (buildings!) and lush green soccer fields (soccer fields!). My school was a squat, two-story building, shared between the middle schoolers and high schoolers. We had Astroturf, because nothing save sagebrush and weeds grew in happy neglect in the Valley.

But it wasn't our differences that I wanted to focus on. So I parked in one of the visitors' spots and pulled out the GPS I had taken to carrying in my backpack when I went running. I switched it on so I could pinpoint my coordinates, the longitude and latitude that placed me here and nowhere else in the world. The problem was, inside the car, the device couldn't locate the satellites, so I unrolled the window, stuck my hand out and held the device to the sun. As soon as it calibrated, I grabbed my notebook from my backpack, ripped out a random page, and wrote my position on the paper. As I folded the sheet in half, I caught sight of my meager notes from the lecture about Fate Maps all those months ago.

Genetics might be our first map, imprinted within us from the moment the right sperm meets the right egg. But who knew that all those DNA particles are merely reference points in our own adventures, not dictating our fate but guiding our future? Take Jacob's cleft lip. If his upper lip had been fused together the way it was supposed to be inside his mother's belly, he'd probably be living in a village in China right now. Then there was me with my port-wine stain. I lifted my eyes to the rearview mirror, wondering what I would have been like had I never been born with it. My fingers traced the birthmark landlocked on my face, its boundary lines sharing the same shape as Bhutan, the country neighboring Tibetans call the Land of the Dragon. I liked that; the dragons Dad had always cautioned me about had lived on my face all this time. Here be dragons, indeed.

I leaned back in my seat now, closing my eyes, relishing the feel of the sun warming my face. No, I wouldn't trade a single experience — not my dad or my birthmark — to be anyone but me, right here, right now.

At last, at 3:10, I open my door. I don't know how I'll find Jacob, only that I will. A familiar loping stride ambles out of the library. Not a Goth guy, not a prepster, just Jacob decked in a shirt as unabashedly orange as anything in Elisa's Beijing boutique. This he wore buttoned to the neck and untucked over jeans, sleeves rolled up to reveal tanned arms. For the first time, I see his aggressively modern glasses, deathly black and rectangular. His hair is the one constant: it's spiked as usual.

What swells inside me is a love so boundless, I am the sunrise and sunset. I am Liberty Bell in the Cascades. I am Beihai Lake. I am every beautiful, truly beautiful, thing I've ever seen, captured in my personal Geographia, the atlas of myself.

"Jacob!" I call, not minding when my voice echoes off the library building, so loud he and his friends turn to me.

For once, Jacob doesn't look sure what he wants to do, whether he wants to stop or keep going. But I do. I know. I shut the car door behind me and venture into the Unknown. His walls are up, fortified by days and days of silence. To my relief, while his face is carefully blank, he doesn't turn away when I near.

I feel his friends, both guys and girls, watching me. And I realize this might be a colossal mistake, a public humiliation. Maybe Jacob is seeing someone else now. Maybe he'll never forgive me. His friends draw behind him like bodyguards.

I have no words, just myself and this piece of used paper, which I hold out to him.

Jacob takes my note silently and reads the two coordinates. "What's this?" he asks gruffly.

This is what I want, I tell myself. He, of all people, is worth this risk of being transparent, of letting him know how I feel, what I want. So despite his friends who are watching, I straighten, throw my hair over my shoulder, and stand before him, utterly vulnerable.

"A geocache," I say.

"A geocache."

"If you've got the guts to find it."

For the first time, his eyes glint with something like amusement, something like curiosity. "Well," he drawls, "that depends on the cache."

I shrug and shake my head. "It's a new one. No one has ever found it."

"So tell me more."

"It'd take . . . oh, gosh, an entire day at least to tell you all about it."

"I've got time," he says easily. "Give me a clue."

"You?" I ask in mock horror. "You, an expert geocacher, are asking for a clue?"

"For especially gnarly caches, I make exceptions."

"Gnarly?" I frown.

"Complicated," he amends. The beginning of his crooked smile begins to form, and the murky Unknown solidifies into familiar terrain. "So what's the cache called?"

That, I hadn't prepped for. So I improvise: "I'm a Moron and I'm So Sorry. But then really good geocachers know it by its nickname: I've Missed You So Much." A breeze tangles my hair, and when Jacob reaches out to brush a strand off my cheek, the tension releases in me. "But the truly brilliant geocachers?"

"Yeah?" he says. "What about us?"

"They know it by its real name. Terra Firma."

"Terra Firma," he repeats. At last, he slips his backpack off his shoulder. I know what he's looking for.

I take a breath. "You don't need your GPS for this cache."

His eyes don't move off mine; he's watching me so carefully. "You don't, huh?"

"Nope," I say.

Some things are meant to be kept — what you learn from experiences good or bad, smiles from an orphaned girl, a boy who is your compass pointing to your True North. So I look Jacob full in the face with nothing obscuring him. Or me. And then I step closer to him. And closer. And closer yet.

"Here I am," I tell him. "Here I am."

ACKNOWLEDGMENTS

My thanks to all the wind deities who blew this novel in the right direction: Dr. Julie Francis and Janice Hendrickson for answering my every last question about port-wine stains; Lillian Thogerson and Lynn Gibson for their passionate commitment to complete families with children from around the world and for sharing their stories about orphanages in China; Francine Shore, for opening my eyes to the pentimenti of life and art; the artists at the Confluence Gallery for showcasing beauty in all its forms; and Bob Larson for giving me a masterful overview of the mapping industry. (Please note that while the China map written about in the novel is fictitious, I've taken care to ensure that the rest of the cartographic information and historical references are factual.)

A special shout-out to Mary Williams, the former coffee buyer at Starbucks and the reason why people worldwide experience truly exceptional coffee. She not only taught me to cup coffee properly (and to warn me never to rest my purse on the ground in a cupping room where people *spit*) but is a role model for living fearlessly. Any mistakes in the novel on any of these topics are mine alone.

I wish all writers had someone like Steve Malk to steer them with such unwavering faith, canny guidance, and a bolstering cup of green tea (no offense, Mary). I'm talking pep talks and well-placed jokes on weekends, holidays, and midnight. Lindsay Davis, you are a true and sparkly star.

Thanks to my Little, Brown constellation of goodness: Megan Tingley, Andrew Smith, Gail Doobinin, Rachel Wasdyke, Lisa Laginestra, Christine Cuccio, and Saho Fujii. And most especially, my heartfelt gratitude goes to Alvina Ling and Connie Hsu, whose incisive and sensitive editorial direction turned Terra Nullis into Terra Firma. You are the priceless maps I read carefully and follow closely and keep nestled in my heart.

Like all authors, I owe a litany of thanks to the best matchmakers on the planet — the passionate librarians, booksellers, and bloggers who get my books and so many others into the hands of the readers who need them most. In particular I would like to thank Nancy Pearl, the entire Chicago Public Library and Teen Volume gang, Chauni Haslet, and Kathleen March. As well, the masterful writers Meg Cabot, Lisa Yee, Julie Anne Peters, Deb Caletti, K. L. Going, and Carolyn Mackler have been exceedingly good to me.

To my beloved Iron Goddesses of friends Janet Wong, Nicole Ueland, Shelli Cheng — and readergirlz Janet Lee Carey, Dia Calhoun, Lorie Ann Grover, Allie Costa, Jen Robinson, Jackie Parker, Miss Alexia, and Miss Erin — thank you for seeing the beautiful in me and my work, especially when I've been the most profoundly blind. Lydia Golston as well as Duaine and Vieno Lindstrom, you keep much more than our keys. Jessica and Fiona Saunders, Reid and Cameron Chen, Matthew and Christopher Headley: embrace the dragons and author your own adventures.

And finally to the best geocaching buddies on the planet — Robert, Tyler, and Sofia — you are my treasure, my True North, my Bhutan.